Lynda Page was born and brought up in Leicester. The eldest of four daughters, she left home at seventeen and has had a wide variety of office jobs. She lives in a village near Leicester with her two teenage daughters. Her previous novels, *Evie*, *Annie*, *Josie* and *Peggie*, are also available from Headline.

And One For Luck

Lynda Page

HEADLINE

First published in 1995
by HEADLINE BOOK PUBLISHING

First published in paperback in 1996
by HEADLINE BOOK PUBLISHING

10 9 8 7 6

ISBN 0 7472 4855 9

Printed and bound in Great Britain by
Clays Ltd, St Ives plc

HEADLINE BOOK PUBLISHING
A division of Hodder Headline PLC
338 Euston Road
London NW1 3BH

In memory of those I have loved and lost.

Love is a precious commodity, not bestowed lightly, but when imparted how easily the lucky recipient can take its gift for granted. It is not until it is lost, for whatever reasons, that we appreciate how fragile are the threads of life.

Despite the pain of loss, we will always have our own special memories.

Those are ours to treasure forever.

Lynda Page 1995

ACKNOWLEDGEMENTS

Thanks to Maggie and Tony Bailey and Frank and Hilda Wright for their wonderful childhood memories. Phil and Karen, not forgetting Terry, of the Black Cat Bookshop and Market stalls, Leicester and Hinckley, for their great contribution towards promoting my books. Jean Cooper and Nina Turner for being such devoted and enthusiastic fans and helping to spread the good word. I don't pay 'em, 'onest!

Thanks to my daughters, Lynsey and Laura, for growing up sufficiently to appreciate now that their mother is only human after all.

With extra special thanks, once again, to Darley Anderson. Was it fate or just old-fashioned luck the day I picked your name at random and plucked up the courage to call? Regardless the luck albeit was on my side. I have no doubt whatsoever that without your help, guidance and faith in my abilities, I would not be doing what I so enjoy doing today.

Chapter One

'Bloody ironic, ain't it?' Bessie Rudney complained loudly to herself as she struggled to ease her comely body out of the passenger seat of her husband's boss's flat-back lorry, her huge black handbag bulging to bursting with insurance policies, rent book, birth, marriage and death certificates, school reports, receipts for purchases made years previously and all manner of other items. 'First time in years we manage a proper 'oliday and that 'Itler decides 'e wants a war.'

Standing on the cracked pavement outside her dilapidated back-to-back terrace, one in a row stretching as far as the eye could see, she adjusted her Sunday best floral dress and raised her fleshy face towards the hot September sun, still relentlessly beating down with not a breath of wind to cool it.

All around a flurry of activity was in progress. Harassed women collected clean washing from ropes stretched across yards; some taking a well-earned breather leaned on doorframes or squatted on steps, nattering to neighbours; barefooted children played noisy games, mouths stained by blackberry jam, liquorice sticks and aniseed balls; young men lounged on street corners eyeing the girls who giggled as they sidled past; men, grudgingly anticipating the coming of a hard week's graft, strode to the pub for a welcome pint of beer, their wives' warning for them not to be long or get drunk mostly ignored.

1

Despite the serious nature of the announcement on the wireless only that morning, one that would have catastrophic consequences in the years to come, the declaration of war did not seem to have changed these streets. Life carried on as normal. The only people seemingly affected were the Rudneys with their enforced return from holiday.

Bessie wiped the sweat from her brow, turned and addressed her brood, still perched on the pile of belongings stacked in the back of the lorry which her husband had pleaded with his employer to let them borrow for their trip. 'Inconsiderate, if yer ask me. 'E could have waited. What difference would another week 'a so 'ave made?' She wagged a podgy finger. 'Warra you lot waiting for – a bus? Get down and start unloading. And, you, Polly, find the kettle and put it on. I'm parched!' She let out a loud guffaw of amusement. 'Eh, that's good, innit? "Polly, put the kettle on".'

Polly, a skinny twelve year old who had been blessed with a fine mane of hair the colour of platinum, almost translucent flawless skin and wide light blue eyes, scowled deeply, transforming her usually angelic face. 'I don't think it were funny, Mam. And I wish you'd stop calling me Polly. Me name's Pauline!' She jumped down and joined her mother, a blackened battered kettle in one hand and a straw bag full of odds and ends in her other.

Bessie slapped her fat hands gently on the side of her daughter's face and rubbed the pale cheeks vigorously. 'Pauline's too plain for a pretty thing like you. You can blame yer father for that. Watched too many Perils of Pauline at the tuppenny rush, he did. 'Sides, I can call you warra like. I gave birth to yer. I can still feel the pain.' She grimaced playfully, then grinned broadly. 'Now put the kettle on, there's a love. I'd better organise this lot or we'll be 'ere all blinkin' night unloading.'

She paused for a moment and quickly glanced around,

adjusting her plastic-fruit-adorned black felt hat more comfortably on her head. 'And where's yer dad disappeared to? Don't tell me – the pub! I'll give him bloody pub when he comes back!' She tutted loudly as she waddled towards the back of the lorry, her large backside wobbling, reminiscent of two footballs bouncing inside her knickers, just as a wail of protest hit the air. Her face softened at the sight of fat tears rolling down the face of her youngest son, Robert, leaving white tracks as they washed his grubby cheeks. She reached up, scooped him into her flabby arms and pulled him to her bosom. 'There, there now, me darlin', stop yer bawling. I know yer 'ungry and as soon as we get the lorry unloaded, I'll get yer summat ter eat.'

Bobbie's howls grew louder. 'Sand,' he wailed.

Bessie nodded sorrowfully. 'Ah, you wannid to play in the sand, din't yer? Well, so did I, me duck, and have a paddle. I wa' looking forward to me paddle.' She gazed at him sadly, then her hazel eyes twinkled. 'Play in the sand, eh? Well, me darlin', play in the sand yer will.' She raised her head and addressed a miniature replica of herself struggling to pull a battered brown suitcase held together with a thick piece of tow rope off the lorry. 'Maureen, stop that fer a minute. Take our Willy and go and get a couple of those sand bags stacked by Vinny's shop.'

Nine-year-old Maureen stopped what she was doing and stared at her mother through large troubled green eyes. 'Mam, them sand bags are for when the bombs drop. Us kids have been warned not to go near 'em. Mr Wilkins sez . . .'

'Mr Wilkins?' Bessie erupted. '*I'm* yer mother, not Mr Wilkins. Thinks he owns this street does Mr Wilkins. Now get those sand bags and hurry up about it. Eh, and mek sure no one sees yer,' she added as she turned and made towards the house. She stopped as she saw her neighbour from next door but one, Grace Wilkins, emerge from her own front door, smiling, and nodding a greeting to her. 'Some 'oliday, eh, Mrs Wilkins? Soon as we get there, we're ordered to come back. Never even got to see the bloody sea. It ain't fair, yer know. We've been lookin' forward to this 'oliday for months. The kids are right upset.'

Grace joined Bessie and smiled fondly at Bobbie, patting her slender hand affectionately on his tousled fair head. 'No, it doesn't seem fair,' she agreed. 'I thought about you this morning when we heard the news on the radio. But maybe this is a false alarm, like the last time? Mr Wilkins is convinced it is. He reckons it's all talk to keep us on our toes.'

Bessie grimaced. 'And 'e would know. He seems to know everything, does your husband,' she said before she could stop herself, and smiled remorsefully. 'I'm sorry, Mrs Wilkins, I didn't mean . . .'

Grace gave a tight smile. 'I know exactly what you mean. And don't worry, I didn't take offence.'

She gazed longingly for a moment at Bobbie, wistfully thinking of the children she would have given anything to have had as well as her daughter Charlotte, and not for the first time wishing she could swap places with Bessie.

Although complete opposites in nature and looks, each woman fought hard to make ends meet, doing the best she could with what little money she had. But unlike Bessie, Grace's life wasn't filled with love and laughter; unlike Bessie she didn't look forward to her husband coming home from work of a night; and unlike Bessie, her husband hadn't done his best to try and take his wife and youngest members of the family away to the seaside for a few days to savour the fresh air, away from the hustle and bustle, dirt and grime of the city. Bernard Wilkins thought holidays a waste of good money, same as he did any nicety that bought just a little ray of sunshine into an otherwise monotonous existence.

Her thoughts were interrupted by the sight of Maureen

and Willy struggling across the cobbled road with two heavy sand bags, one leaking its contents behind them from a split in the seam. She raised her eyebrows.

Bessie, noticing Grace's quizzical stare, quickly told her what she intended doing with them. 'In any case,' she finished, 'a few sand bags ain't gonna save us from the bombs. All we'll get is sand blasted!'

Grace laughed. 'You're right on that score. The government must think we're all stupid. The bags we've been allocated wouldn't go round all the street anyway, so who's going to miss a couple?'

'Your 'usband?' Bessie asked tentatively.

Grace smiled reassuringly. 'I don't think he personally stands and counts them all. And I certainly won't be telling him what happened to the two missing ones. Anyway, I think your idea is grand. At least it might help make up for the young 'uns' disappointment.' She paused for a moment, then her light blue eyes sparkled merrily. 'I've an old basin in the coal shed. You could use that for some water, then Bobbie'll have a bit of sea to go with his sand. I'll go and dig it out now.'

Bessie beamed. 'Oh, ta, Mrs Wilkins. I'm much obliged.' She looked at her son, nestling in her arms. 'D'yer 'ear that, Bobbie? You're gonna have a paddle. In fact, I think I'll join yer.' The idea of soaking her swollen feet in a basin of cold water after the day she'd had suddenly seemed very inviting.

The long hot journey to Mablethorpe in the uncomfortable lorry with wails from the back of 'Are we there yet?' which had started ten minutes into the journey, then cries of protest all the way back, had strained her nerves to breaking point. But that she had coped with; what she couldn't was the thought of war and all it entailed. She had two strapping sons over the age of sixteen who she knew would insist on doing their duty.

She quickly shut her mind to impending worries and

watched Grace disappear inside her own house. Bessie shook her head and again asked herself the question she had many times over the ten years she had lived in this street. How could so lovely a woman as Grace Wilkins have saddled herself with such a humourless, domineering specimen of a man? The woman must have had a brain storm the day she agreed to be his wife.

To Bessie the likes of Bernard Wilkins should have been strangled at birth, or better still not been conceived at all. His archaic Victorian attitude suffocated the life out of his wife and their daughter Charlotte, and she knew instinctively he took great delight in giving vent to it.

She sniffed disdainfully as she hitched Bobbie further up in her arms. To her mind it was a miracle that Charlie had ever come about in the first place. She just could not imagine Bernard participating in any activity that involved showing anything remotely like affection.

Grace Wilkins now, she was different. She cried out for love. She should have married a kindly man, one who appreciated her worth, had a horde of children clinging to her skirts, living in a house filled to bursting with laughter and happiness instead of the austere confines she had now.

Not that Bessie had any idea of what the inside of the Wilkins' house looked like. So far as she was aware none of the neighbours, including herself, had ever so much as stepped across the doorstep. And neither had she ever been on much more than nodding terms with Grace. But Bessie's instincts told her that was not Grace's doing, but her overbearing oaf of a husband's. He acted above himself in every way and his wife could not take an extra breath without his wanting to know the reason why. Neighbours heard things and talked, he must realise that. They all knew what he was about and how he treated his own family.

The corner of Bessie's mouth twitched. One day Bernard

Wilkins would come a cropper. People like him always did in the end.

She pulled a now dozing Bobbie tighter against her vast bosom and not for the first time counted her own blessings. Was she not the luckiest woman alive? The day she had met her Tom outside the Picture Palace on the Uppingham Road as they had all queued for the Saturday morning showing, armed with their oranges and two pennies, had been the best day of her life. Not that she had realised that at the time. Tom, intent on showing leadership to his gang of mates, had pinched the grubby yellow ribbons securing her straggling plaits and given them to his sister. It wasn't until later, when he had caught her on his own as she had struggled home with the shopping from the Co-op as she always did for her mother on a Friday night, that he awkwardly asked her out.

Out! That was a laugh. They had sat on a low factory wall at the bottom of the street, hardly saying a word to each other, and had ended the night with a tuppenny bag of scratchings from the chip shop and a pickled onion to share between them. But from that beginning they had become a couple and at the age of seventeen and sixteen respectively, married and settled for the interim with her parents in an already overcrowded, damp, bug-infested terrace in Leamington Street, off the Braunstone Gate situated in the West End of Leicester.

Twenty years, six children and many rented homes later, she and Tom were still together and neither would have had it any other way. They bumbled along, neither worrying too deeply on what the day would bring but accepting what came about in their own haphazard manner. Bessie knew most of the neighbours thought her slapdash and her children unruly, but she didn't care. She was happy with her brood and her big loving husband and, given the chance, would change nothing.

She sniffed loudly and peered down at her son, now sleeping soundly. She wished she could follow suit, but it would be a long time before she saw the old patched sheets on her bed and loitering here in the hope it would all be done by the time she ventured indoors was just wishful thinking.

She made towards the house just as her handsome husband strode around the corner of the street. She fixed her eyes on him and scowled deeply. 'Chucked yer outta the pub, did they?' she bellowed. 'Well, if yer think yer've got outta 'elping to sort the 'oliday stuff, then yer wrong.'

'I haven't been ter the pub,' he said defensively as he joined her.

'Don't gimme that.' She raised her head and sniffed. 'I can smell it on yer.'

'Well, if yer can, Bessie, yer nose wants seeing to, 'cos I ain't bin near the pub. I've been to the chippy. Thought I'd save you the bother of cooking after the day we've had.'

Sheepishly she eyed the large newspaper parcel tucked under his arm, something that normally wouldn't have escaped her notice. She grinned. 'That were nice of yer, Tom.'

She linked her free arm through his just as the younger members of the family gathered on the doorstep.

'What yer got, Dad?' Willy shouted, leaping forward, the others close behind.

'N'ote that you'd like, lad. Just some cod and chips. Oh, and a few pickled onions,' his father chuckled.

A whoop of delight rent the air.

'Can we eat it outta the newspaper? Can we, Mam?' Maureen demanded, skipping happily across the path.

'It's the only way, and don't we always?' Bessie answered. Her eyes sought out Polly. 'A' yer mashed that ruddy tea yet? I could drink the pot dry.'

Chapter Two

Grace carefully opened the back gate and tiptoed towards the coal shed. Deftly lifting the latch she let herself inside and rummaged around for the chipped enamel basin she knew was in here somewhere. Coal shed it may be named, but there was hardly room for the small pile of coal between the odd assortment of items that had been discarded over the years. She poked behind the mangle and dolly tub she used each Monday to do the laundry, moved aside rusty old paint tins and broken wooden boxes, and finally found the basin covered in a thick layer of dust and spiders' webs.

Finding an old piece of net curtaining, yellow with age, she wiped it over, smiling as she visualised the youngest member of the Rudney family paddling his feet in the water it would soon hold. A movement from behind startled her and she swung round, her hand clutching her chest.

'Oh, it's you, Bernard. My, but you did give me a fright!'

He fixed humourless hard grey eyes on the enamel basin. 'What a' you doing with that?'

She stared down at the basin. 'This? Oh, I . . . er . . . promised to borrow it to Mrs Rudney for the children to paddle in.' She smiled tentatively. 'They were ordered to return from their holiday. It's a shame, isn't it? The children are really upset.'

'Shame?' he spat. 'The shame is that people like that can

afford a holiday in the first place when hard-working types like myself can't even think on such luxuries!' He snatched the basin from her. 'If they want to paddle, they can use their own basin. They must have one somewhere in all that junk they harbour.'

'But, Bernard, I promised . . .'

'Well, you can unpromise. And I don't take kindly to you giving away my stuff without consulting me first.'

Grace's face fell and her shoulders sagged. 'But it's only an old basin. I didn't think you'd mind.'

'Mind!' he erupted. 'Well, I do. Besides, that basin isn't yours to give away. And it would have been given away. I wouldn't have seen it again once the Rudneys got hold of it.' He leaned forward, his eyes wide, his lips tight. 'But more to the point, you defied me, Grace.'

'Defied?'

'Defied,' he repeated harshly. 'I've told you never to associate with the likes of them, and here you are not only associating but having the nerve to give them my belongings. What do you think this makes me look like, eh? I have standing in this community – respect. My family has lived here for decades. Highfields used to be the place to live. Monied folk resided in these parts.' He waved his fist in the air. 'Look at it now! Look what it's come to now people like that have moved in. And what do you think the decent people that are left are going to think when they see my wife associating with scum like that, eh?' He jabbed his finger into her shoulder. 'They live like pigs, Grace Wilkins. Decent folks would've had the sense to put the money to good use instead of squandering it on a holiday. The children are threadbare. I've seen better clothes on a Guy Fawkes. And as for the state of the house – well, it'd take an army of WVS women a month of Sundays of elbow grease to make it anywhere near decent.'

His face distorted in anger and he threw the basin behind the mangle. He filled his lungs with air and hooked his thumbs inside his braces. 'It's bad enough that I have to work with two of them Rudneys. If I had my way they'd have been got rid of long ago. Wasters, the pair of them. Never done a decent day's work since they started their apprenticeship. And now here's you, hob nobbing with their parents. Well, I'll not have it, Grace, d'you hear? I'll not have my good name jeopardised just because you feel the need to be charitable.'

She lowered her head as her husband's face drained white with temper. His condemnation of the Rudney family was totally unfounded and unwarranted. Tom Rudney held down a decent job. He might have to work all hours and his wages were poor but he provided for his family nevertheless, and Bessie kept her house and the children as clean as she could. The rope in her back yard was always filled with washing.

Children like the Rudneys, who were allowed and encouraged to explore and develop inquisitive minds, were bound to get dirty and tear their clothes. Keeping them dressed and shod was a continual uphill battle and one that was more than likely lost in the list of priorities when money was eked out.

To hear Bernard talk, the Rudneys let their children run wild; Tom had never done a day's work in his life and daily drank the pub dry; the house was disgusting – when in reality the opposite was the truth.

But she knew, should she dare express any opinion that did not mirror her husband's, she and Charlotte would suffer his wrath for days, possibly weeks, as he allowed the insignificant incident to fester and grow out of all proportion, giving him the ammunition he continually sought to assert his authority over them both, secretly enjoying the discomfort and pain he caused. She had learned long ago and the hard way to keep her own counsel.

Hesitantly she raised her head and looked into the eyes of the man she had once loved – a feeling she had held for him so far in the distant past, she hardly remembered what it felt like. 'I didn't think,' she said softly. 'I'm sorry, Bernard. It won't happen again.'

He tightened his mouth, annoyed that her submissive apology closed the matter. Still, at this moment other worrying matters filled his thoughts, and ones that needed his undivided attention. 'I should think so,' he said harshly, turning from her and stepping into the yard where he paused and turned back. 'Never forget, Grace, that it's my hard earned money that supports this family. You haven't brought in a penny piece since the day I married you.'

How could I, she thought, a flood of anger spreading through her, when you never let up from telling me that fact? And how am I supposed to bring in any money when the mere mention of my going out to work sends you into a blinding rage? You hold that a wife's place is in the kitchen. She should be seen and not heard, have no opinions of her own; from the moment she signs that piece of paper her whole purpose is to serve her husband. No better than a slave.

If only I had known, she thought, anger suddenly replaced by sadness. If only I'd had the ability to see into the future.

She caught him staring at her and shivered, wondering for an instant whether he knew what was going through her mind.

'I thought you were on the way to see my mother?' he snapped. 'You'd better go before she thinks we've abandoned her. Oh, and don't bother going past the Rudneys. You can go the other way in future. That'll put a stop to any temptation, won't it?'

She opened her mouth to protest, but quickly noticed the steely glint in his eye. He was willing her to resist his instructions. Well, she wouldn't give him the satisfaction.

'Yes, Bernard,' she said lightly. 'The walk will do me good.'

'Huh!' was his response, as he turned and stalked back into the house.

She stared after him blankly, her eyes coming to rest on the crumbling red-brick wall that divided the small yards at the back of the houses. A ginger tom reclining on top eyed her lazily as he basked in the evening warmth. She sighed heavily. Why her husband thought himself better than their neighbours defied her reasoning. Like herself, he had been born and raised in this area, the people here were their kin and, to her mind, better people she could not wish to live amongst. Especially people like the Rudneys who brought new blood to the area and kept it continually thriving.

Their children attended the schools and Sunday schools and brought life to the streets with their games and caperings; the adults worked in the numerous factories dotted around and spent their hard-earned money in the abundance of local shops that between them supplied goods needed. Grace shook her head. This community would have died long ago if new inhabitants hadn't moved in. Did Bernard realise, she wondered, that the pawnbroker Sammy Joseph's main source of income was from the monied folk who had fallen on hard times? He probably did know, but would never admit it.

He was right in one respect: Highfields had at one time been very affluent. Once only people who could employ servants and a cook could afford to live in the grand Victorian three-storey properties. But all that had been many years ago before a tiny area of two up, two down terraced houses that had been built originally to accommodate the workers for the London Road main Leicester railway station had expanded and grown, and many of the monied people had moved into the adjacent area of Stoneygate. But that would have happened anyway. It was called progress.

She sighed deeply. Oh, Bernard, she thought sadly. Why

can't you just live and let live? Why can't you be content with your own life instead of ridiculing everyone else's? But she knew he would never change. If nothing else, the last twenty years of marriage had taught her that Bernard was narrow-minded in the extreme, and if he lived to be a hundred would never change his outlook.

If only . . . she thought again. But then, life was filled with 'if onlys'. One crucial mistake made when she was barely old enough to know her own mind – the simple one of agreeing to marry Bernard – had sealed her fate, and there was nothing she could do but shoulder that responsibility and get on with it. But thoughts of the years stretching ahead were not pleasant.

Straightening her back, she plunged her hands into her skirt pockets, one of only two skirts she possessed, and headed down the yard, through the entry that divided the houses. Turning right she hurried down the street, hoping that none of the Rudney family was outside to notice her departure and enquire after the basin. She did have one idea that might salvage the situation and give the promised paddle to the children without upsetting her husband . . .

Arriving at her first destination, she tapped lightly on the back door and let herself in. The gloomy interior quickly enveloped her and settled in oppressively. She squinted to focus her eyes.

'Mrs Wilkins,' she called. 'Cooee, Mrs Wilkins. It's me, Grace.'

Hearing no response, as she'd known she wouldn't, she ventured further. She found Bernard's mother sitting bolt upright in the worn fireside chair, the fire itself laid with the minimum amount of coal needed to keep it alight. The rest of the room was sparsely furnished. Everything – the furniture and the walls – was brown.

An unpleasant odour reminiscent of overcooked cabbage

permeated the stale air. As usual, a bowl of senna pods stood on the wooden draining board, ready for the old lady to drink the juice before she slept. The sight of them made Grace nauseous. They looked disgusting.

She longed to part the half-drawn dingy dark brown curtains and throw up the sash windows. Fresh air and sunlight would dramatically improve the atmosphere, but she knew any such suggestion would be forcefully squashed by the evil-tongued woman whose sharp grey eyes, identical to her son's, were shrewdly watching her every move.

Ida Wilkins scowled deeply. 'Yer late.'

Grace forced a smile as she gathered together the dirty crockery from the meal she had brought around earlier. 'Am I? Well, never mind, I'm here now.' She placed the dishes in the sink ready to wash. 'Now, would you like anything before I get you ready and tucked into bed?'

'No,' Ida barked. 'And stop speakin' ter me as though I'm an idiot. Tuck me into bed, indeed! D'yer think I enjoy bein' an invalid? D'yer, eh?'

Yes, you do, Grace thought, though invalid you're not. She knew without doubt that her mother-in-law's medical problems amounted to no more than old age and bone idleness, but to challenge her would have caused more trouble than it was worth.

Ignoring Ida's question, she went across to the sink and filled a basin with warm water from the kettle, picked up the coarse yellow soap and piece of towelling. She placed them on the small table to the side of Ida's chair and mentally prepared herself for the nightly ritual.

'Right then, let's get you undressed and washed.'

'I can do it meself. And I had a wash last night.'

'You need to wash every night, Mrs Wilkins. Cleanliness is next to Godliness, so they say.'

'There's n'ote in the bible that sez anythin' like that and I

15

should know. My father, God rest his soul, made us study the bible daily.'

Yes, the drunken sot! thought Grace ruefully. And you in turn did the same to Bernard, and look what it did to him. And although you might not be a drunk, you're certainly a hypocrite. She fought to hold her tongue, knowing that everything she did and said got back to Bernard. His mother had a perfect knack of twisting the truth.

'I'll have a tidy round whilst you get on with it then,' she said matter-of-factly, wishing she would hurry up or she wouldn't have time to visit her own parents before returning home. Bernard clock-watched, and if she took longer than he thought necessary, she was cross-examined. He wanted to know exactly where she was and exactly what she was doing every minute of the day. But question him back – that was a mortal sin.

As she busied herself she silently fumed at the tell-tale evidence proving that Ida was far removed from the helpless cripple she professed to be. A chair had been hurriedly pushed back against the table and the net curtains hanging at the front window were askew – curtains Grace herself had straightened that very lunchtime when she had brought round the old woman's dinner. Ida had been participating in her favourite pastime, nose twitching behind a chink in the curtains as she watched the comings and goings in the street, storing every minute detail for future use.

Ida meanwhile grudgingly ran the soap between her gnarled palms and dashed water over her face, watching Grace out of the corner of her eye.

How she hated the younger woman. Had Bernard heeded her warning and not married her, they would have been in the money by now, not living hand to mouth like the rest of the scum that had moved into these parts. But 'she' had put paid to that. Grace Turner, as she always referred to her daughter-in-law, had a lot to answer for.

Cecily Janson had had prospects, being the only daughter of the factory owner where Bernard worked. Cecily had spotted Ida's handsome son's talents; seen his potential, and gone after him. Ida had no doubt that by now Bernard could have been running the show. They'd both have been living in luxurious surroundings, as his position would have warranted. Money no object. But Grace had arrived on the scene, Ida didn't know how, and had seduced him into marrying her. Bernard, her handsome, gullible son, had fallen for the oldest trick in the book – a woman's cunning ways – and in so doing had sealed both their fates.

'Damned harlot!' she hissed loudly, purposely dropping the towel in the bowl of water.

Grace turned. 'Did you say something, Mrs Wilkins?'

'You heard me,' she spat. 'Damned harlot, I said.'

Grace sighed loudly. 'Mrs Wilkins, do we have to go through this every night? I didn't force your son to marry me. You know that as well as I do. Bernard asked me and I accepted.'

'Liar! You tricked him. I don't know how, but yer did. You'll pay, you will, when the time comes.' She grimaced hard, her icy eyes narrowing to two thin slits. 'The devil knows his own.'

Grace straightened a chair by the table. 'Well, me and you'll be good company for each other then, won't we, Mrs Wilkins? When we're both roasting in hell.' She walked over and picked up the bowl, ignoring the sopping towel. 'Right then, if you're finished, I'll get you into bed and make you a nice cuppa tea.'

'Don't patronise me, woman. I don't want any tea.'

'Don't you? All right.' Two could play at that game, thought Grace. Ida was always ready for a cup of tea, never refused. She was just being awkward as usual. Besides, the woman was quite capable of making her own cup of tea should she want one, and no doubt would as soon as Grace left.

She breathed deeply, wanting to be away from Bernard's mother and her dismal decaying house before she said something she regretted. The old woman's spiteful tongue was enough to try the most patient of people and after years of her jibes and unfounded accusations, Grace had about had a barrowful.

As if her twice-daily visits weren't enough, Ida was hinting strongly that she should give up her own house and move in with them. She would never come straight out and ask. That was not her way. She would chip away until it was impossible to refuse. But living with Bernard was hard enough; his mother as well would prove more than a saint would bear. At least whilst he was out working, Grace had time to herself. If his mother moved in . . . dear God, it didn't bear thinking about!

Her mind suddenly flew back to the day it had all begun. A day just like any other, but a day that would change her life forever. The day she had met Bernard Wilkins.

It had been a typical Leicester November morning, dreary and damp, the gas fire in the dark office in Janson's Tool Makers giving out little heat. But the weather and the oppressive atmosphere was of little consequence to Grace or her colleagues – the Great War was over.

The last three dreadful years had stretched endlessly for the young Grace as she had striven with her mother to cope with the hardship war inflicted, together with continual worry over the safety of her father, friends and neighbours who were somewhere in France up to their armpits in mud, fighting disease, shortage of food, no home comforts, continually bombarded by the enemy, constantly aware that this dawn could be their last.

Now that was all over, her father was back safely, the country and its people putting themselves back together again. The discomfort in the office was of little consequence to what they had all just come through.

A noise from across the room cut through the silence, causing her to lift her eyes from the ledger she was working on. The sight of Bernard Wilkins striding towards her, eyes ablaze with temper, made her catch her breath. Oh, but he was handsome, his thatch of bright auburn hair plastered down with Brylcreme, a splattering of freckles across his angular nose. Even in his grubby factory overall, he cut a swathe.

She had seen him before, of course; had often spotted Bernard Wilkins around the factory as they had each gone about their business, he usually chatting to workmates or standing in a doorway enjoying a crafty cigarette. Grace never envisaged for a moment that the likes of him would know of her existence. She of course had heard the rumours about him and the boss's daughter, but one thing that Grace did not do was listen to gossip.

The next moment he was standing in front of her. Embarrassed, she had felt herself reddening. The momentary pause before he spoke seemed like an eternity. She was fully aware of Mr Dumble her supervisor glowering at her and lowered her head, returning to her work. Mr Dumble was not a man to cross. He saw everything through his thick bottle-top glasses. He even knew what his staff were doing when he wasn't in the room. She could well believe he had eyes in the back of his head.

'It's Jean, ain't it?' were the first words Bernard ever spoke to her. She should have heeded the warning then. But at sixteen, and as innocent as a babe in arms, all she felt was a thrill that he had actually spoken to her. Bernard Wilkins, the man the girls all giggled and gossiped over, the factory

Casanova, was standing before her desk addressing her, even if he had got her name wrong.

She had lifted her head, swallowing hard. 'It's Grace, actually.'

Bernard half-turned and looked towards the door he had just stormed out of. He stared at her. 'Well, what you doing tonight, Jean?' he asked loudly.

She was struck silent by his unexpected question, and also very conscious of the interest being shown by her other colleagues and the fact that Mr Dumble had risen from his desk and was making his way over.

'I'll meet you at seven then,' Bernard said, sauntering off down the office. 'Outside the Picture Palace.'

Grace was aware of Mr Dumble peering at her sternly as he leaned heavily on her desk. 'Finished your entering, Miss Turner? You must have if you've time to gossip.'

'Er . . . not quite, Mr Dumble.'

'Well, get back to it then. I've plenty more work waiting. There ain't room in my office for slackers.'

For once, Mr Dumble's words were lost on Grace. Her mind was too occupied with thoughts of Bernard. She had been asked out on a date! Not that she, with her thick mane of chestnut hair, nicely developing figure and the best pair of legs in the street, was short of admirers, but Bernard Wilkins was different from the usual teenage male who requested her company. He was a grown man and, to her mind, a very attractive one.

Fearing her parents would not approve because of the five-year age gap, she kept him a secret, and before she knew it, was in love – so much so she was besotted. Bernard filled her every thought, waking or sleeping, and the gossip, rumours and warnings from well-wishers to steer clear fell on deaf ears. They did not know him like she did. They did not see how caring and considerate he was. It was all jealousy because they secretly wanted him for themselves.

When she did pluck up the courage to introduce him to her parents, they, like she, were enchanted, thinking what a nice man he was, just the kind they would be happy to see their only daughter settle with.

But none of them suspected what Bernard in his cleverness hid. They only saw the side of him he wanted them to see.

One lunchtime, several months after their first date, when the sun had broken through the heavy grey clouds, heralding the first signs of spring, when people's spirits were lifting at the thought of casting off their drab winter clothes, Mr Janson called her into the office.

'Have you got a minute, please, Miss Turner?' he asked, beckoning her over.

Heart sinking rapidly, thinking the worst, she hesitantly entered the inner sanctum, a part of the office she had never been allowed in before.

She had often, as she had beavered away over her books, envisaged this room, but on entering was quite shocked. Instead of the luxury she had expected, the office was not much better furnished than the one she had just left.

He indicated an upright chair in front of his dark oak desk. She sat down, hands clenched tightly in her lap, suddenly not so worried about her worn down shoes or the hole in one of her thick stockings where she had caught it earlier on the corner of her desk.

He smiled at her. 'Miss Turner.' He hesitated. 'I . . . er . . . cannot help noticing your growing attachment to young Bernard Wilkins.'

Grace, not expecting conversation in this vein, frowned quizzically.

'Just be careful, my dear. He's quite a charmer is Mr Wilkins, and I wouldn't like to see you taken advantage of.'

As he spoke Grace stared at him. To her, Mr Janson had

always appeared an unapproachable man whose only concern was the profit figure on the bottom of the yearly balance sheets. This kindly man – old to Grace's young eyes but, despite his approaching fortieth birthday, still very handsome – did not match that picture at all. Then it struck her. The picture created had been Mr Dumble's doing. The staff under his wing were always being threatened with 'a visit to the boss' if their work wasn't up to scratch. With that threat constantly hanging over them, Grace and the rest of her colleagues always kept their heads down, and especially when Mr Janson was around.

She looked straight into his hazel eyes, and for all her young years and inexperience could not help noticing the sadness that lay behind them. For a fleeting moment she wondered what that sadness was. She knew he was prosperous, living in a sprawling gabled house in Knighton Fields, with servants and two gardeners; had a glamorous wife, albeit one whose allure was down to her twice-weekly visits to the beauty parlour and the fine clothes her husband bought her. According to rumour she was quite a forceful lady. Was she the cause? she wondered.

Maybe it was his daughter Cecily. A striking young woman of around Grace's own age, of medium height, with short blonde hair cut into the latest bob, she possessed a charming nature and was never short of admirers. Whenever Cecily visited her father, she always smiled and greeted the workers as she passed through the office.

No, it couldn't be Cecily. And as Grace couldn't think of anything else that could trouble such a man as Philip Janson, she put it down to her own imagination.

'I know it doesn't appear so,' he was saying, 'but I do take an interest in my staff. Mr Dumble speaks very highly of you, my dear. In fact we were discussing you only the other day.'

'Oh?' she said enquiringly.

'Nothing detrimental, I can assure you.' He cleared his throat and ran his fingers through his greying hair. 'We are thinking of training you in book keeping. You show a lot of aptitude in that direction. I feel you have the potential to go further, my dear, and so does Mr Dumble.' He leaned forward and fixed his eyes on hers, choosing his words carefully. 'You could jeopardise everything by getting entangled with the likes of Wilkins. You do realise that?'

Grace grimaced hard. Mr Janson was wrong. Bernard Wilkins, her Bernard, was a good kind man, a pleasure to be with. But just what did he mean by 'that kind of man'? 'I don't understand, Mr Janson. Bernard is a good man. And kind. And . . . and . . . I love him,' she added in a whisper.

Mr Janson sighed heavily and shook his head. The poor girl seated before him was in far deeper than he had realised. How did he tell her that Bernard Wilkins, the man she said she loved, was nothing more than a waster, and a liar to boot, and that if he could have had his way, Bernard would have been sacked long ago.

Bernard Wilkins only did the minimum amount of work required to keep him in employment and at every given opportunity stirred up mutinous feelings in others without their realising it. Then he would sit back and watch the results with satisfaction. Three men had lost their jobs several weeks ago after making excessive demands that he could not possibly meet, and which, more importantly, they were not entitled to. Philip Janson knew without doubt they had been put up to it by Wilkins.

But Janson couldn't sack him because he hadn't enough evidence against him. Besides, for some unfathomable reason Wilkins was well favoured on the factory floor, especially by the younger set, and a seeming misdemeanour on the part of the management could cause havoc amongst the workers.

No, however much he wanted rid, he could not for fear of losing the capacity to meet his order book. Not only would he suffer, but more importantly in his eyes, his faithful workers would also.

As if Wilkins's bad attitude and laziness were not enough, Philip Janson had discovered to his disgust that the man had his eye on Cecily, the one pride and joy of his own life, and was blatantly bragging of his supposed conquest to anyone who would listen before it had even taken place.

One thing Philip Janson could not do was sit back and listen to filthy rumours and unfounded gossip, especially not about someone so close to his own heart. He'd had to put a stop to it.

Wilkins did not take kindly to his summons or the choice words that Janson used. The young man had sneered, denied all knowledge of wrongdoing and made a threat to sue for slander, warning that if Janson dared to take matters any further he would have the whole factory out.

Philip Janson was cornered. He had no evidence against Wilkins, only gossip which he knew wouldn't stand up in any court in the land. Much to Janson's anger, the man had sauntered out of his office and made straight for Grace. This poor girl seated before him was on a downward spiral to nowhere if she stuck with Wilkins, and Philip Janson felt it was all his fault. He had to try and do something. The girl showed such promise. She was pretty and intelligent, and although her family scratted for every penny, it was obviously a loving one. The fact shone from every trusting look she gave him.

Janson again sighed heavily. 'What I'm trying to say, Miss Turner, is that, well, judging from your work you have prospects in this company but they could be hindered by any association with Wilkins.' He softened his voice. 'My dear, the company doesn't encourage employees' liaisons. They're

24

not good for business. Too much time wasted chatting.' He lied and hoped she didn't realise it. Several generations of the same families worked for the company. As far as he was concerned the continuity provided stability. The company supported whole families, and without the company those families would suffer. Regardless, he hoped he had worded his feelings strongly enough at least to make her sit up and take notice.

Grace lowered her gaze, settling her eyes on the large black telephone sitting on the side of the desk. It was a shame, their not encouraging work associations. She liked the sound of studying book keeping and the possibility of further advancement. She enjoyed her job and the people she worked with. But it was no use. Her association with Bernard was something she did not want to put a stop to. They were in love and she knew it was only a matter of time before he asked her to marry him.

She raised her head, clasped her hands and took a deep breath. 'I'll not give him up, Mr Janson. I love him, you see. I've heard the rumours and spiteful things people say, but they're all lies. He's a good man is Bernard.'

For the third time, Philip Janson sighed heavily, much deeper this time. 'I see,' he said slowly. 'Well, all I can do is wish you the best, my dear. I do hope you'll be happy and not live to regret . . .'

Regret, regret. The word echoed in Grace's ears. She could hear it now as if it had been said yesterday and not nearly twenty years ago. But regret her marriage she did, almost instantaneously. The ink had hardly dried on the marriage certificate when Bernard's attitude towards her changed. The caring, considerate man she had courted became unrecognisable and very soon she dreaded time spent in his company. And as if Bernard was not enough, she now had the added burden of his mother, Ida.

Grace had never had any illusions about Ida. From the outset, she was left in no doubt of the older woman's bitter feelings towards her, but Grace in her young years thought her mother-in-law would change her attitude once they got to know each other better. This was not to be. If anything, Ida grew worse. Grace had married her son; had taken away the only chance she herself had of getting out of the squalor in which she lived. That was unforgivable and Grace must suffer for it.

And suffer she had, at every opportunity.

She learned very quickly that whatever tactic she tried was wasted; the only way to cope, especially with Bernard, was to appear to agree with everything and be submissive. It was not her choice to act this way, but she had no other recourse. Nine months to the day from their wedding, Charlotte Constance Wilkins had screamed her way into the world, after a long and difficult pregnancy, ending any chance Grace might have had to escape from her miserable life. Charlotte's birth bound her to Bernard forever.

Regardless, Charlie as she was to become known was Grace's salvation. From the moment they set eyes on each other, a bond so deep it hurt bound them together. As time went by and no more pregnancies appeared, Charlie became even more precious to her. All the love that would have been lavished equally on her husband and whatever other children she might have had, was given in its entirety to Charlie. Not even Bernard's harsh attitude or Ida's spite could alter that.

Thinking of Charlie now, Grace smiled. Her baby was a woman approaching her twentieth birthday, and a very beautiful one at that. Although strong of character, she also possessed a caring nature and was well respected by those who knew her. All Grace's sacrifices had been more than worth it. If she had to live her life again, she would go the same path for the sake of Charlie.

Ida's grumbles brought Grace back to the present and she took a deep breath. The last twenty years had been hard, but she had made her choice in marrying Bernard so the blame for her mundane existence lay entirely with herself.

'A' you listening ter me?'

'Pardon?'

'A said, a' you gonna stand there all night like a vacant idiot? Yer can put some more coal on me fire 'fore yer go.'

'Oh, right. Yes, okay.'

Grace absently reached for the coal bucket, so rusty and full of holes it was a wonder anything stayed inside it. She shook a few lumps into the grate. All this thinking of the past had depressed her. She needed to get out of this house and go and visit her parents. Restore sanity before she returned home.

Finally she closed the door behind her, her duty towards her husband's mother over for that day at least.

Relaxing her shoulders, she turned and hurried down several streets until she came to her parents' home, a tiny decaying one-bedroom cottage in the middle of a courtyard of six, tucked amongst surrounding terraces. As always she felt warmth rush through her at the thought of seeing them. She hoped her father would still be at home and not already gone to his job as a night watchman at a factory on St Saviour's Road. At nearly seventy years of age she felt he was too old for work, but although her parents never admitted it, she knew they needed the money. Without it they would be destitute. Respect for them both stopped her voicing her suspicions, and to ease their pride she helped with whatever she could, whenever she could – always discreetly because of Bernard's prying eyes.

Her father's job was no pleasure. The hours were long, the pay a pittance, conditions appalling. It consisted of patrolling the archaic Victorian building several times during the long night with a torch that gave out little light. His patrolling done, he would then spend his remaining solitary hours in a chilly wooden hut no bigger than their outside privy. These warm nights weren't so bad, but the winters were hell. He would come home frozen to the marrow, the chilblains on his hands and feet bigger than walnuts, and by the time he thawed out it was time to go back. His job would be the death of him one day. Grace had lost count of the times she'd wished she could do more to ease their burden, but with Bernard handling every last farthing of the household budget, she had no hope.

She tapped on the door and let herself in.

'Mam!' she called.

'That you, our Grace? Come away in, gel.'

She hurried down the tiny passageway and poked her head around the door which opened into an all-purpose room. Her mother and father were sitting either side of the range in ancient identical leather armchairs. The chairs had originally been given to Grace's grandmother on her marriage by an employer. They had been due to be thrown out. It was a family joke that if the ceremony had been any later she would have ended up with the usual pair of linen sheets. As luck would have it they got the chairs and these had been cherished ever since.

At their feet was a large peg rug, including material from the whole of Grace's childhood. Every item she had ever worn had had several pieces cut from it before it had been discarded, and hooked into the sacking backing. Her mother always maintained that way Grace was always with them. Because they had only ever been blessed with one child, she was even more precious to them. Just like herself and Charlie. One child in the family seemed to have become the pattern.

On her father's lap sat a tin tray filled with pieces of wood. He was holding a small piece in his hand and fashioning it into a child's toy boat with a pen knife. These he sold at Christmas to people not much better off than himself, helping to eke out his meagre income.

From his ears protruded small ear phones attached to his crystal radio set, his one pride and joy. Arthur Turner looked up as his daughter entered, gave a broad smile and pulled the earphones from his ears.

'Hello, Grace love.' He patted the stool to the side of his chair. 'Come and park yer body for a minute. We're only listening in case there's any more news.'

'And is there?'

Her father shook his head. 'N'ote definite. But now war's bin declared it's only a matter of time.' He shook his fist. 'Just let Gerry come over here. I'll give 'em what for! Pity I'm too old to do my bit.'

Connie Turner tutted and laid down her knitting, rising stiffly. 'Fight 'em single-handed, won't yer, Arthur? Well, let me tell yer, you did enough the last time round. Let the young 'uns do their bit now.' Making her way over to the old gas stove, she picked up the kettle and shook it. 'Time for a cuppa?' she asked her daughter.

Grace shook her head. 'It's only a quick call, Mum. I've come to ask if I can borrow your old tin basin?'

''Course yer can, me duck. Where is it, Arthur?'

'Where's what?'

'The tin basin. If I remember right, you had it last.'

Arthur frowned in thought, then his eyes lit up. 'Yes, yer right I did. Let me see . . . it must have bin the summer of '23. I filled it wi' water for young Charlie to play in. Yes, that's right. Then she screamed her little head off when it were time to go 'ome so we told you to tek it with yer. It's in your coal shed, behind the mangle. Or it was the last time I had a poke round in there. Why d'yer need it? Is yours 'ad it or summat?'

She shook her head. 'No, Dad. It's for the Rudney kids to paddle in. They had to come back from holiday this morning 'cos of the announcement and they'd only just got there.'

'Ah, what a shame,' said Connie. 'Ain't that a shame, Arthur?'

'Yeah, it is. Poor little tykes. They can 'ave the basin gladly, Grace love.'

She smiled in pleasure. 'Thanks, Dad.'

Her father beamed and patted the stool at the side of him. 'Now come and tek the weight off yer legs for a minute, gel. Surely you've time for a natter with yer old mam and dad?'

Grace smiled warmly. 'All right, just for a minute.' She eyed her father affectionately. 'You haven't been round to see us lately.' She looked across at her mother. 'In fact, neither of you have. Why don't you come for your tea next Sunday? I'll make a jelly.'

Arthur and Connie looked at each other. The look spoke volumes and was not lost on Grace. She stared at them both quizzically.

'Is there something wrong?' she asked worriedly.

'No, no, why should there be?' Connie said just a little too quickly, which made Grace even more worried. There was definitely something amiss.

'There is, Mam, I can tell.'

Connie made a ploy of busying herself with the making of the tea. Just how did she tell her daughter what had transpired the last time they had visited? How could they explain their guilt ever since?

It had been a Saturday afternoon two weeks before. A glorious day, one that made you feel glad to be alive. They had both, she and Arthur, felt like that as they had made their way towards their daughter's home, delighting in the thought of a pleasant afternoon with the family ahead.

As usual Grace had made sandwiches with leftover meat

from a joint of mutton, and a fruit cake. Connie had taken along some bottled beetroot and a packet of arrowroot biscuits as their contribution, and had been warmly scolded for doing so. Grace and she had chatted, putting the world to rights, swapping cookery hints and discussing Charlie, whilst Arthur had pottered around in the back yard, hammer and nails at the ready to fix anything that needed repair. Bernard had returned from his visit to the allotment and Grace had given them some of the produce he had brought home. Then Charlie had come in from her visit to her friend and they had eaten tea.

It had been a very pleasant afternoon. Although, as usual, Bernard's remarks had slightly blighted the proceedings.

Connie had seen him scowl at the amount of potatoes Grace had put in the bag for her parents to take home; grimace at the sandwiches, asking for mustard piccalilli when he knew Grace had none, saying he could not eat mutton without it. Then he proceeded to pronounce the fruit cake dry and said Grace should ask his mother for a decent recipe. But Bernard's conversation was always in that tone, and she and Arthur accepted it as the norm after all these years. Although it was never mentioned out of respect for Grace, she wondered how hurt her daughter was by his remarks.

Just before they were due to leave, Bernard invited Arthur out into the yard to ask his advice about digging up the slabs in the yard in order to put in an Anderson shelter. Did Arthur think it big enough? He had been surprised. Never before had Bernard asked his father-in-law's advice on anything.

'With the prospect of war looming, I have to think ahead for Grace and Charlie's sake,' Bernard had said.

Arthur nodded and smiled as Connie came out to join them.

'Bernard and meself are just discussing Anderson shelters.'

'Oh,' said Connie, surveying the small slabbed yard. 'I

think one of them's a bit on the big side to go in here. Mrs Wallace who I used to clean for has got one. She's had earth put over the top and planted flowers. Looks really pretty. Why don't you go and have a look before you decide? I bet she won't mind. You can judge for yourself then.'

'Hmm,' Bernard mused. 'I might just do that. Mind you,' he said, breathing deeply and wiping sweat from his brow, 'if we have to buy our own shelter, I doubt I'd be able to afford one being's money's so tight. We're having a job to make ends meet as it is.'

'Are yer?' Arthur asked, concerned. 'I thought the pay weren't too bad at Janson's?'

'Who told you that?' Bernard replied flatly. 'Janson's a tight old stick. He'd have us working for nothing if he could get away with it. Whoever told you that has their facts wrong, and I should know. I've worked for the bloke for the last thirty years. No, we barely manage on my wages as it is. We've no spare for luxuries. Take these teas, for instance. Grace has to cut back all week so we can provide the sandwiches and fruit for the cake.' He stopped abruptly, face ashened. 'I'm sorry, I shouldn't have told you that. You know how much we enjoy your visits. We don't mind going without. Forget I said anything.'

'No, no,' Connie said remorsefully, placing her hand on his arm. 'Are yer that badly off? I never realised. Grace's never said a word.' She turned to her husband. 'Oh, Arthur, I feel so terrible, puttin' a strain on the children's finances like that.' She turned back to Bernard. 'Why didn't you say summat before?'

He smiled wanly. 'I didn't want you worrying, Mrs Turner. Nor does Grace. You know what she's like for putting on a brave face. Always the martyr, is Grace.' He scratched his chin. 'She mustn't know I told you about our burdens. She'd be distraught if she knew.' He sighed forlornly. 'Just come as normal, that's the best thing. We'll manage, don't worry.'

Connie and Arthur looked at each other.

'We can't, lad.' Arthur said. 'Not now we know. I couldn't enjoy eating the food knowing you were starving yerselves for the rest of the week.'

'No, Arthur's right, we couldn't,' his wife agreed. 'We'll just have to put a stop to our fortnightly visits, that's all. We'll think of somethin' to tell Grace. I can't have me daughter goin' wi'out like that just to feed us. Shame,' she muttered. 'I love me visits, and so do you, don't yer, Arthur?'

'Yes, I do. But just 'cos we won't stop for our tea in future, don't mean I still can't come and do me fixing for yer.'

Bernard bit his bottom lip anxiously. 'Well, that's it, you see.'

'What?' asked Arthur.

Bernard sighed heavily. 'Well, I suppose I'd better tell you. I don't like to. But while we're having this chat, I suppose I'd better.'

'Out with it, lad. Say what's on yer mind,' Arthur prompted.

'Well, it's about your hammering and fixing. It'll have to stop. Not that I ain't been grateful for what you've done. I have. But it's the landlord, you see. He reckons things have been bodged?'

'Bodged!' Arthur erupted. 'I've never bodged anything in my life.'

Bernard's face set gravely. 'That's not what Mr Janson reckoned when he came round to inspect the place. Said it'd cost a fortune to put the wrongs right. And you know I daren't cross him. That's the worry when you live in a house owned by your boss.'

'And I always thought he was such a nice man,' Connie said softly. 'He thought so much of our Grace when she worked for him.'

'I've a good mind to go and see him,' Arthur said, his face reddening indignantly. 'Let him tell me to my face I bodge!'

'Now, Arthur,' his wife said sharply. 'Don't take on so. It'd only make matters worse for Bernard. Think what would happen if he lost his job.'

'Hmm, yes. I suppose.' Reluctantly he relented. His face was sad. 'I shall miss doing my little jobs for you. I enjoyed meself.'

'Yes, made him feel useful, it did,' Connie said. 'Never mind, Arthur, you've plenty to do in our house.'

'That's the spirit,' Bernard said, his face brightening. 'Let old Janson pay for the repairs in future. If you ask me, I think he should be grateful for what you've done instead of complaining, but you know what these monied folks are like.'

'Yes, all heart,' muttered Connie. 'I never thought Philip Janson was like that. He's shocked me he has.'

'Who's shocked about what?' Grace asked as she joined them.

'Oh, er . . . We were just saying that we'd probably get a shock . . . er . . . about the price of Anderson shelters,' her father said, his mind racing for a plausible answer that wouldn't arouse his daughter's suspicions to their real conversation. 'Bernard's thinking of putting one in.'

Grace looked at her husband in surprise. 'Were you? Oh!' It was a shock to her to hear that her husband was considering anything that would benefit herself and Charlie. Besides she understood that these shelters were free issue so why was he worried about the cost?

She suddenly realised that his gesture was purely for the sake of her parents. The shelter, like anything else, would never come to fruition. She hooked her arm through her mother's, deciding that any further words on the subject would be a waste of breath. 'I've packed the rest of the sandwiches for Dad's pack up.' She winked at her father.

'And I've put in a bit of cake. Don't say I never spoil you.'

Connie breathed sharply. 'There's no need, Grace love. I could easily whip up yer dad's sandwiches when we get 'ome.' She patted her arm. 'You keep 'em, love. Yer might get 'ungry yerself later on.'

Grace stared at her mother quizzically. 'What's got into you, Mam? I always give Dad the leftover sandwiches. In fact, I make extra for that reason.'

'She's right, Grace love. You shouldn't bother about sandwiches for me. In fact, I don't bother now, do I, Connie? I have a bite before I leave and that lasts me 'til breakfast.'

'Now I know there's something funny. The day my dad goes to work without a pack up! What's wrong, Dad? You're not sickening for anything, are you?'

Bernard cast a warning glance at Connie and Arthur.

Arthur coughed loudly. 'N'ote's wrong, gel. Just didn't like to put you to the bother, that's all.'

'Bother! It's no bother and never has been.' Grace unhooked her arm, leaned over and planted a kiss on her father's aged face. 'Now you'd better get going or you'll be late. Eh, and don't forget the food. It's in the kitchen.'

The sandwiches had stuck in Arthur's throat that night as he sat in his lonely hut, forcing them down. All he could think of was how Grace and her family went without to provide them and had done for years. The thought pained him deeply and in the end he had gone hungry. The sandwiches, minus the two bites that had stuck in his throat, were fed to the birds.

Now Connie picked up the mugs of tea and walked across to Grace, sitting staring at her, waiting for her answer.

She asked the question again. 'Mam, there's something wrong, I know there is. What is it? Is it something I've done?'

Connie handed over the mugs and sat down. 'No, no, love. Nothin's wrong.' She looked quickly at her husband, then settled her eyes on the cheap tea leaves floating on top of the pale-looking liquid in the mug. She silently prayed that the Lord would forgive her for the lies she was about to tell, and sighed heavily. 'It's just that me and yer dad are getting a bit old to traipse round to yours every other Sunday and . . .' She lifted her head, glanced quickly again at her husband, then across at Grace. 'To be honest, it's very tiring, for yer dad especially. He has to go to work afterwards. We're not as young as we used ter be.'

Arthur awkwardly rose from his seat, his touch of rheumatics suddenly giving him gip. Like his wife he hated telling lies to his daughter, even if they were to save her pride. He grabbed his cap off the hook on the door and turned to face her. 'Yer mam's right, Grace love. We enjoy coming round, but it's all a bit too much for us now.' He pulled on his threadbare cap over his sparse grey hair. 'Now I'd better be off else I'll be late, and we can't have that, can we? Me wages'll be docked.'

Connie rose to join him and kissed him affectionately on his cheek.

'Be careful,' she said fondly, handing him a packet of sandwiches, which he put in his pocket.

Grace stared at them both saying their goodbyes. She suddenly saw how old they both looked, how fragile, and it struck her that she might not have them both for much longer. Time was running out for them and the knowledge that she had been so thoughtless in her lack of regard for their welfare shamed her deeply.

She jumped up and ran over, embracing them both affectionately.

'I'm so sorry for being so thoughtless. Please forgive me.' She pulled back and eyed them both as a thought struck. 'But we don't have to stop our Sundays. We'll just bring the food round and have it here. There you go, that's the answer to that one.'

She looked so pleased with herself, Arthur and Connie didn't have the heart to say anything that would spoil her pleasure.

Arthur cleared his throat. 'If that's what yer want. Only . . . er . . . don't make so much food, eh, Grace? You make far too much and you know me and yer mam can't stand to see anything wasted.'

She laughed. 'You know nothing's ever wasted, Dad. I don't know how you can say such a thing! But that's settled then. In future we'll come to you and save you the walk. Next Sunday then, all right?'

Connie and Arthur looked at each other. Connie smiled and patted Grace's arm affectionately. 'All right. Bless you, me duck. We'll look forward to it.'

After kissing her mother, Grace walked with her father to the end of the street. They said their goodbyes and each went their separate way, both secretly dreading their destination, but each having to go for different reasons: Arthur because he desperately needed the money; Grace because her husband was waiting, ready to question her for her overlong absence.

As she approached the house, the usual heaviness settled in her heart. She tried to shrug it off, but to no avail. Her home had not felt like a sanctuary for as long as she could remember.

Lifting the latch, she quietly stole through the gate and tiptoed across to the coal shed. Once inside, and breathing as shallowly as she could, praying that her husband would not hear her, she gently moved things aside and retrieved the tin basin Bernard had thrown there earlier.

She reached the street without detection and breathed more freely. She saw Maureen sitting in the gutter, knees tucked under her chin, sucking a stick of liquorice, and beckoned the girl over.

'Give this to your mother for me, please. Tell her I'm sorry

I took so long about it but I got waylaid.'

Maureen's black lips parted into a smile, revealing stained black teeth and an even blacker tongue. Her red-spotted dress had come undone at the hem and was trailing past her calves. It was grubby and ripped under the arms. One half of the sash that was supposed to be tied to make a bow at the back was missing, the other trailed past the hem. The black plimsolls she wore had more holes than material and revealed her sockless grimy toes. Grace hid a smile. Even though she knew the Rudney children were scrubbed near skinless every night, this child looked as though she hadn't been near soap and water for at least a month.

'Ta, Mrs Wilkins,' Maureen said appreciatively, grabbing the basin.

Grace smiled back. 'It's my pleasure.'

She watched as Maureen skipped happily away, the basin held aloft, and it pleased her greatly to think that the children would after all get their promised paddle. And, if Bernard did happen to miss it, which she gravely doubted – after all it had lain, gathering dust in the shed for the past eighteen or so years – then she would tell the truth. The basin had been her parents' and it was they who had given permission for its use.

Chapter Three

Meanwhile, slumped in his armchair, Bernard fixed angry eyes on the clock on the mantel and grimaced hard. Where was that damned woman? She had been gone over an hour and a half. For God's sake, how long did it take to settle his mother down for the night? He was desperate for a cup of tea but was damned if he was going to make it himself. That was woman's work, and as such Grace should be here now to see to it. He went to work and earned the money that kept her, didn't he? The least she could do was be here when he needed her. Well, he'd give her what for when she finally condescended to come home.

He leaned over and twiddled with the knobs on the wireless. He had been listening to a lively concert of popular music, but didn't see why Grace should have that pleasure when she came home. Rights like that were reserved just for himself. He switched it off and settled back.

The years had not been kind to Bernard. His once smooth face was now deeply lined and heavy jowls had formed, hurried on by years of scowling. The deep furrows across his forehead and around his eyes were not from laughter. The vivid redness of his hair, that had once attracted many a woman, was now a dull lifeless grey, and it had thinned to leave him practically bald. His body had thickened, from greediness and lack of exercise, and a paunch hung over his waistband. Bernard had grown into an unattractive man, the kind who went unnoticed in a crowd.

He was of the type who, had he been given every chance and encouragement – money, tools, know-how, and had had it all laid out before him – would still never have amounted to anything. He was lazy, he found almost everything too much bother, and at every opportunity, if he could get somebody else to do it, he would.

He couldn't believe his luck the day he happened upon Grace. Women had always fallen for his looks, but once the surface was scratched and they realised what lay beneath, they soon beat a hasty retreat, congratulating themselves on their lucky escape. With Grace it was different. Her youth and inexperience went against her and he never gave her time to draw breath. Cleverly, he swept her off her feet, and before she knew it, she was trapped by marriage.

If Bernard had been as clever as he thought he was, then he would have seen in Grace his passport to prosperity. But instead of nurturing her, listening to her ideas and opinions, encouraging her to extend herself and develop, continuing what her parents had started, he had scoffed, ridiculed, browbeaten her into submission and never, ever given her credit for anything. He wanted a wife who would cater for his every need. He didn't want one with a brain. So he made her stop using it, unless it was for something that would benefit him.

It never entered his head to wonder what she was feeling and he never bothered to ask. She was his wife. For her that should be enough and she should be grateful.

Moving his eyes from the clock, he shook out the newspaper and glared down at it. Bold headlines leapt out. WAR. He tutted disgustedly. That was all that had been talked of for months now and he was sick of it. He was sick and tired of hearing about the whys and wherefores everywhere he went. At work, in a shop, down the pub. What business was it of theirs if Hitler had invaded Poland? Let the Poles deal with it, it was nothing to do with them. He grimaced hard. Obviously others in high places did not share his views and matters were looking pretty grim, especially after this morning's announcement by the Prime Minister.

He drummed his thick fingers on the arm of the chair. The authorities of Leicester had already held a major trial run of a total blackout, held air raid warnings and organised shelters, issued gas masks and all manner of other things in readiness. He supposed they wouldn't go to all that trouble and expense for nothing. For a long time now, war with Germany had been only a matter of waiting.

The corner of his mouth twitched. Well, war or not, one thing was for sure: he was not under any circumstances going to join up. Let other fools run round with guns and lose their lives. He had better things to do. What things he was not quite sure, but they had to be better than dressing in an ill-fitting uniform, with little more to eat than bully beef and dried biscuits, shipped off to foreign parts fighting for people who didn't even understand English.

He leaned back in his chair and raised his eyes to the ceiling, deliberately ignoring the dingy painted paper. How was he going to get out of going? There was talk of call up papers and if the war really did take off it would be only a matter of time before they got round to men of his age group. If you were able, you went. He blew out his cheeks, exasperated. It was a pity he wasn't older than his forty-four years.

What excuse could he come up with that would justify his not going, and not lose him face? He would have to think hard and quick before it was too late and the brown envelope came through his door.

He lowered his head quickly as he heard the sound of the back door. It was Grace. He recognised her footfall in the tiny kitchen.

He threw the newspaper on the floor and rose, hooking

his arm through his braces and hitching up his grey flannel trousers. He stood in the doorway and glared at her.

'Where've you been?' he demanded.

Before she answered, she grabbed the kettle, shook it and placed it on the old stove, lighting the gas, worried for a moment that he knew about the basin. Well, if somehow he did, then it was too bad. She was ready to face the consequences. It would be worth it to give that little boy a bit of pleasure. She turned to face him, squaring her shoulders.

'You know where I've been, Bernard,' she said evenly. 'I've been to settle your mother down for the night and on the way back I dropped in to see my parents. The last time I saw them my father wasn't looking too grand and I've been worried about him, so I took the opportunity to pop in.' It was a lie but she had to add the excuse, always feeling she had to justify anything she did.

Bernard snorted disgustedly. 'There's n'ote wrong with your folks, Grace. Strong as 'orses the pair of them. But it comes to something when you put them above your husband. You were only going to settle my mother for the night, you didn't say you were going galivanting. What if I'd needed anything? What was I supposed to do whilst you were enjoying yourself? You're a selfish woman, Grace Wilkins. That's what you are, selfish.'

She stared at him in astonishment. If her husband thought her selfish, then what was he? But she couldn't say what she felt. If she did he would have just the excuse he needed for a go at her. 'Oh, Bernard, please don't make an issue of this. I visit your mother twice a day. I haven't seen my own for nearly a week.' She took a deep breath. She'd better tell him about the arrangements for Sunday. Better to get it off her chest now than to leave it for him to make a meal of at a later date. 'I've . . . er . . . arranged for us to go round for our tea next Sunday. It's getting too much for them to come here so I said we'd take the food to them. I thought that would be nice, Bernard. Make a change for all of us.'

He reared back his head, temper showing by the redness creeping up his neck. Damn and blast the woman! he inwardly fumed. It had taken ingenuity on his part to put a stop to the fortnightly visits. For years the sight of her parents gobbling his food, paid for with money he had earned in that Godforsaken hole of a factory, had eaten away at him. As if her mother's prattling wasn't enough to drive the sanest man crazy, he had had her father to contend with. Him and his fixing had nearly driven Bernard insane. He could swear the man was trying to make him feel inadequate.

Well, finally, after all his years of suffering he had managed to put a stop to it once and for all. Now that silly bitch had gone and ruined it! Well, he wouldn't let her. No wife of his was telling him what to do.

'You should have consulted me first, Grace. I'll not spend my Sundays cooped up in that hen house for no one.' He sighed heavily and shook his head. 'Oh, why can't you ever act like a proper wife?'

Her mouth dropped open. 'A proper wife? Bernard, what do you mean? I have been more than a good wife to you.'

He smiled at her scornfully. 'Have you, Grace? I would question that. A proper wife would consider her husband's feelings before she made plans behind his back. Good God, woman, I work me guts out all week in that hell of a factory, then afterwards down the allotment. All I ask for is a bit of peace and quiet on a Sunday afternoon. Is that too much to ask? But then you wouldn't think about that, would you, Grace? No, off you merrily go, making plans and not even considering the one person who should come first with you.'

'Oh, Bernard, I didn't think you'd mind. I thought you enjoyed seeing my parents.'

'Well, you would, wouldn't you? Because you don't think.

43

I sometimes wonder if you have a brain in that thick skull of yours.' He looked at her and shook his head sadly. 'I often wonder what would've become of you if I hadn't took pity on you.'

She gasped. 'Pity? Bernard, did you say "pity"?'

'I did. Well, let's face it, if I hadn't married you, I doubt anyone else would've.'

Her mouth dropped in astonishment. 'Bernard, that's unkind!'

'Unkind or not, it's the truth. I could have married Cecily Janson. The girl was all over me. But no. I settled for you because I knew you needed me.'

She stared at him blankly. How many times had she heard that tale? And tale it was. She knew without doubt the likes of Cecily Janson would never have taken up with someone like him. He was fooling himself, but she could never quite bring herself to tell him. It wasn't long after they married she knew the rumours about him and Cecily were untrue and probably started and fuelled without foundation by Bernard himself. Did he really think she was so stupid as still to believe what he said? But she had only herself to blame. Mr Janson had tried his best to warn her.

She stood rigid as he stepped into the kitchen, walked over and leaned his back against the pot sink. 'Everyone felt sorry for you at Janson's. He told me himself that he was considering having to let you go.'

Grace clasped her hands to the sides of her face in shock. 'Bernard,' she cried, horrified, 'that's not true! He told me he was going to teach me book keeping.'

'Grace, Grace! Stop fooling yourself. The man was just being kind. Why won't you realise that I saved you? The best thing you ever did was to marry me. Let's face it, you're not much good at anything, are you? But do I ever complain?'

Well, yes, all the time, she thought. But before she could

say the words, he answered for her.

'No, I never do, because I know you do your best.' He looked at her pityingly. 'Where would you be without me, Grace? I'll tell you. In the gutter, that's where. I provide the roof over your head and food for the table. And you should be grateful.'

'I . . . I am, Bernard.'

'Well then, think next time, Grace. Think before you go off on a tangent and arrange things you have no business doing. You owe it to me, to consider me first. Have I made myself clear?'

She slowly exhaled and lowered her eyes to study the cracked cardinal red floor tiles. 'Yes, Bernard, very,' she said slowly.

He righted himself. 'Good. I'm glad at last something has sunk into that brain of yours. Now I'm going for a pint. You can make me a sandwich for when I come home. But don't wait up, I might be late.'

She sighed deeply. 'Yes, Bernard.' She waited until he had donned his cap and was half out of the back door. 'I'll . . . er . . . tell my mother it'll be just me and Charlie on Sunday then, will I?'

He stopped, turned slowly, raised his eyebrow and smirked at her, deliberately pausing in order to cause her discomfort. 'Grace,' he spoke patronisingly, 'you've got things wrong as usual. When I say I'm not going, that includes you as well.'

'But . . .'

'No "buts", Grace,' he erupted. 'We're not going and that's that. I've already told you my reasons and that should be enough. Besides, I'm fed up with feeding other people. It's about time these so-called tea parties stopped. Now I'll hear no more on the matter.' He turned and strode down the yard, leaving her gawping in dismay behind him.

He took a jaunty stride as he ambled down the street

towards the public house. How he had enjoyed that little exchange. It had made him feel important seeing his wife squirm. He found great enjoyment in ridiculing her. A good session of ridicule set him up for days as he savoured every last moment. Besides, his actions were all justified. Grace had to be kept in her place. It wouldn't do for her to get ideas above her station.

How clever he was. He had his wife and daughter exactly where he wanted them. There was no doubt in anyone's mind just who ruled in the Wilkins' house and that's just the way things should be. Many men would give their right arm to know my secret, he thought smugly. Pity it couldn't be bottled and sold. I'd make a fortune.

He pushed open the saloon door and walked inside as he had hundreds of times in the past. Several pairs of eyes glanced at him, alarmed, then quickly turned away. People who frequented this establishment had learned long ago that Bernard Wilkins was a boring, gutless excuse for a man. His conversation was limited and what there was was spiked with complaints against anything he felt warranted it.

Sighs of relief were expelled when Bernard, armed with his half pint of bitter, settled himself in a quiet corner. He was oblivious to any anxiety he aroused. Luckily for them he was not in the mood for company, too busy going over the conversation with Grace and too pleased with himself to notice the relieved expressions.

He sat, sipping slowly, a satisfied smile on his lips.

Defeated, Grace dragged herself wearily back inside the house. She sank down on a chair at the table and rested her arms on the top, staring blindly at the dingy wall. A tear of despair rolled down her cheek. Why was it that Bernard strove to spoil any pleasure she might have? Why did he deliberately do everything in his power to cause her misery?

He knew how much she loved her parents, how much pleasure she gained from spending time with them.

And what about the things he had said? Had he really only married her because he pitied her? She wiped away the tear with the back of her hand. As usual, he had made her feel worthless. Was that what she was – a nothing?

She lifted her head as a flood of tears threatened. What had she done to deserve this treatment? She tried hard, she really did, but nothing would please him. She couldn't remember the last time he had paid her a compliment. He had never thanked her for any meal she had cooked. His attitude was, he had eaten it, hadn't he? What more did she want? Never had he said she looked nice, even when she had made an extra special effort. He had never even so much as sent her a birthday card. That was for lovesick fools, not married couples.

She sighed heavily. Was it all worth it? Was it worth all the bother just to have him treat her like this? She wondered what would happen, how he would react if she herself stopped bothering as he had done as soon as they had married.

She heard the back door shut and her back straightened rigidly. She prayed it was not him. She could not stand another tongue lashing tonight. She turned and her heart was gladdened by the sight of her daughter entering the room.

Grace rose and filled the kettle. 'Hello, love,' she said lightly.

She took the loaf from the bread bin in the pantry, carried it through, placed it on the board on the table and cut two slices, spreading them thickly with butter. She didn't need to ask, she knew her daughter would be hungry. Charlie could eat as much as she wanted and not an ounce of fat would go on her shapely hips.

She eyed her and couldn't help but smile. Charlie looked a picture in her pretty summer cotton dress, her auburn tresses, the same colour as Grace's own, cascading gently on her shoulders. No wonder the lads all stared after her when she walked down the street. She'd be a catch for any man should they be lucky enough to capture her heart. Grace only prayed that when Charlie did make her choice she didn't make the same mistake as her mother had done. She hoped Charlie knew her man inside out before she finally agreed to spend her life with him.

Charlie plonked her gas mask on the table, thrust her hand inside and began to empty it of lipstick, powder compact, a packet of hair grips, comb and identity cards.

Grace shook her head. 'Charlie, that is not a handbag. You'll get shot if they catch you using it like that.'

Her daughter laughed. 'Oh, Mam, we all use it to put things inside. Having to lug this around is enough without carrying a handbag as well.' She threw her arm around her mother and squeezed her affectionately. 'Many of my friends don't bother to take it with them any more. At least I still do. So stop fussing,' she said smiling.

Grace tutted, resigned. 'Did you enjoy yourself at Marion's?' she asked.

'Yes, I did, Mam. Thanks. We had a good laugh. You know what a card Marion is.' She flopped back in one of the armchairs by the fireplace and pulled off her shoes. Resting her long legs on the hearth she looked across at her mother cutting slices of cheese. 'She's worried though for her boyfriend, Carl. He's told her he's gonna do his duty tomorrow and join up. He wants to be one of the first.'

Grace put the cheese between the bread and cut the sandwich in half. She handed it on a plate to Charlie. 'You don't know whether to be proud of our young boys or sad for what faces them. Still, it's a good thing he's doing, Charlie, make no mistake about that.'

'Yes,' she agreed whole-heartedly. 'It is. And I shall do my bit as well.'

Grace raised her head, worried. 'Bit? In what way, Charlie?'

She shrugged her shoulders. 'I dunno yet, Mam. But there must be something an able-bodied woman like me can do. If our men are going to be fighting for us, the least I can do is something in support.'

Grace smiled wanly. 'Let's wait and see what happens first. It's still early days. With a bit of luck the whole thing might be called off. There's still time for that Hitler to change his mind.'

'I doubt it, Mam. It's said he's a madman. Besides, you've only got to look what he's doing to other countries in Europe. He's killing people, Mam. Killing them needlessly. It's only a matter of time before he turns his attention to us.' She bit into the sandwich gratefully. Her mother had guessed right. She was starving. Charlie suddenly noticed her mother's drawn face as she sat down in the armchair opposite, nursing a mug of tea between her hands. She frowned, concerned. 'What's the matter, Mam?'

Grace inhaled sharply. 'With me? Nothing.' She took a breath and planted a smile on her face. 'I'm just a bit tired, that's all.' She lowered her voice to a whisper and leaned forward. 'My monthlies are due.'

'Huh,' Charlie responded, unconvinced. 'Since when have you been having two a month, Mam?' She wiped crumbs from her mouth and put her empty plate on the hearth. 'Has Dad been having a go at you again? He has, hasn't he? He's not happy, he's not, unless you're upset.'

'Charlie! What do you mean? Your father never has a "go", as you call it. What he says is just his way. He doesn't mean anything by it.'

'Doesn't he?' Charlie looked at her knowingly. 'Mam, my father treats you rotten and you know it. Why do you put up with it, that's what I want to know? He treats both of us like we should be beholden to him, and you worse than me if that's possible. If I ever met a nice man, how could I bring him home to face Dad? You I'd be proud to introduce, but him! The poor lad'd run a mile after one of Dad's "I know it all" sessions.'

'Charlie,' Grace retorted crossly. 'He may be your father, but he's also my husband and I would ask you not to speak about him like that.'

'Why? Why shouldn't I speak like this? He does. He's never said a good word to either of us. He treats you like a slave, Mam. You can't breathe unless he's given you permission. Oh, he's clever though is my dad. He never beats us, but what he says is worse if you ask me. D'yer know, it'd serve him right if one day you just didn't up and leave? I'd certainly give you my blessing. In fact, I'd be right by your side. I just hope to God he does do his duty and joins up. Give us both a bit of peace.'

Grace gawped. Charlie had never spoken so openly before and she was shocked at this outburst. 'What on earth has got into you? I've never heard you say such things before.'

Charlie took a deep breath and smiled sheepishly. 'Maybe I felt it was time, then. I ain't a kid any more and I do have a mind of my own. Maybe it's all this war business. Talk of loved ones going and all that. I thought about Dad, and do you know, it didn't shock me to realise I wouldn't miss him at all if he went. I just felt myself wishing he would.' She paused for breath and searched her mother's face. 'Do you love him, Mam?'

Grace blushed scarlet. 'Why, Charlie, what a question to be asking your own mother!'

'That's why I can ask it, Mam. 'Cos you are my mother, and I love you. Now, you ain't answered me. Come on, Mam. For once be honest. Do you love him? Would you miss him if he went away?'

Grace froze. 'Yes, of course I would,' she said hastily.

Charlie shook her head. 'Why is it I don't believe you?' She sighed deeply, then smiled tenderly. 'I've always been proud of you, Mam. You're the best-looking mother for miles around and you're still young enough, you know.'

'Young enough? Young enough for what?'

'To find happiness. That's all I wish for you, Mam – happiness.'

Grace jumped out of her chair, grabbed the dirty plate from the hearth and busied herself clearing the table. 'Charlie, you're speaking a load of nonsense. I *am* happy. Now I never want to hear you talk like this again. I married your father because I loved him. I promised to love, honour and obey him, and I'll do that until the day I die.'

Charlie rose and joined her, collecting several items off the table to take though to the kitchen for washing. 'Why, Mam? Because you think you've no other choice?'

Grace spun round. 'Charlie! I said, enough.'

She backed away, knowing she had gone too far. 'Okay,' she said flatly. Suddenly she felt a sharp pain in her stomach and groaned. 'Oh,' she complained. 'All this talk of monthlies has brought mine on.'

Grace, who had gone into the kitchen to deposit the dirty dishes, came back, wiping her hands on a towel. 'I knew it! I knew there was something making your mouth run away with you. The curse does that to women. It turns their thinking inside out. You'd better get to bed. I'll bring a hot water bottle up to ease the pain.'

Charlie smiled. 'Thanks, Mam.' She threw her arms around her and hugged her tightly. 'I'm sorry if I upset you. I just felt the need to say those things.'

Grace returned the hug. 'It's all right, my love. I understand. Everything is upside down at the moment.'

Charlie kissed her on the cheek, paused slightly and kissed

her again. 'And one for luck,' she said softly.

Grace beamed at her words. Ever since she could remember Charlie had always kissed her twice whenever they had parted, right from being a toddler, and the little saying had always been added. It was kept just for themselves, for their own private use, and those little words meant so much to both of them. They meant all was right between them and always would be.

An hour later Charlie was in bed asleep, hugging the hot water bottle, Bernard's sandwich was made and the house straightened. Grace sat quietly in the armchair going over her conversation with her daughter. She was still shocked. She and Charlie were as close as mother and daughter could ever be, they had respect for each other as well as love, but never had she heard her daughter speak with such intense feeling.

She had always thought Charlie to be oblivious to Bernard's ways. She herself had striven hard to hide the realities. Obviously she hadn't succeeded. Bernard was right, she was a failure. But as Charlie had said, she wasn't a little girl any more. She was a woman with eyes in her head. It hurt Grace to think Charlie knew how her life really was and she felt humiliation rise as she wondered for a moment if anyone else knew too.

She sat for an age, thinking deeply. Her daughter was right again. She did not love her husband and truthfully would not miss him at all if he went to war. She would be concerned for his welfare, worry if he was getting enough to eat and sleep, but that was about all. It was not love as she should love him. She had realised this years ago, but never before had she dared to admit it to herself.

But Charlie was wrong about one thing. She had no choice. She could not leave Bernard. She knew of women who were battered regularly; men who drank and gambled their wages away; women who in fact put up with far worse than she did. It was only Bernard's desire to be lord and master and his laziness that caused the problems. If only he would mellow just a little, life would be a lot more pleasant.

Besides, if she did ever pluck up the courage to leave, where would she go and what would she do? She had no trade to speak of besides cooking and cleaning and couldn't dump herself on her parents. They had a hard enough struggle to cope as it was without herself and Charlie adding extra burdens.

She shook her head. If her parents ever found out how her life had been since she had married Bernard they would both be distraught and, Grace knew, would demand she and her daughter move in with them. So she couldn't even hint. They were too old for such worries and upheavals. No, better to let them think, as she prayed they had always done, that her marriage was happy, that she was happy.

She gazed around the sparsely furnished room. Like the rest of the house she itched to make it more homely and comfortable but had never had the means or the encouragement. The housekeeping Bernard allotted her hardly covered the food and bills. There was nothing left over for anything else. Regardless, though, this had been her home for the past twenty years and would remain so unless something unforeseeable happened.

She pressed her fingertips to her throbbing temple. It was all right for Charlie to speak about leaving. She was young, and to the young these days everything seemed so simple, so cut and dried. Grace herself had been brought up to honour her commitments, which was the way she thought she had raised Charlie.

She sighed heavily. It was this war, it must be. The young were full of it. They thought of it as an adventure and it was turning their heads. Values were being thrown to the wind and it had hardly started. What were things going to be like when it really got going? This war's going to change everything, she thought, remembering vividly the Great War, the war to end all wars.

Suddenly, everything came flooding back. The terrible loss of life, shortage of necessities, the worry, the sheer hell of it all. She wondered how her mother, she and everybody else had coped, and now here it was starting all over again. Only this time it could be worse. The world had moved forward. Armies were much better trained and equipped and the carnage dealt out as each side fought to overcome the other could be far worse than that inflicted the last time around.

She shuddered as a cold fear gripped her. And they'd said it would never happen again! How wrong people were to listen to their so-called betters. When this war was all over, nothing would be the same, of that she had no doubt. And at times like these, individual problems took a back seat. People, including herself, Bernard and Charlie, should be thinking of sticking together. They would all need each other more than ever if they were going to get through.

Those precious words, spoken such a short time ago, came back full force. 'And one for luck.' She shook her head worriedly. They would need more than one piece of luck before it was all over. This little island of theirs would need all it could get.

Later that night Grace lay in bed and stared up at the ceiling. Her eyes held tears. She felt used, but couldn't quite understand why she should feel this way. After all, she was Bernard's wife and he had only been taking what was rightfully his. And he had taken. Hadn't asked her, approached her, even kissed her affectionately. He hadn't kissed her at all. Without a word, he had rolled on top of her, roughly pulled up her nightdress, done his business, and rolled off. It had taken approximately five minutes or less. He was now lying on his back, his snores reminiscent of a large pink farmyard animal that lived in a sty, and if this grunting continued she would never get any sleep.

She sighed painfully as her eyes traced the shadows on the ceiling and settled on the large one in the corner by the window. The picture it formed suddenly leapt out at her. It was of an old woman; large nose, thin lips and jutting chin. It looked like Ida. And she was wagging a gnarled finger. 'It's your duty,' she seemed to say.

Well, Grace had done her duty, one that was required by Bernard at the most a dozen times a year. It didn't matter to him what her needs were – if after the act she herself was fulfilled, content – he'd never once bothered to ask her.

She wondered if there were any other women like herself who were equally as unfulfilled, had to quash their needs, their desires, their expectations – and all because their husbands, the men who were supposed to love and cherish them, couldn't be bothered to ask, or to be truthful didn't really care.

Bernard snored loudly and turned over on his side. His breathing became shallow and for the time being at least the snoring subsided. She turned in the opposite direction, pulled the covers around her and closed her eyes.

Chapter Four

Clara Smith closed the book, sighed softly and lifted her head. Dickens's *Great Expectations* had been stimulating as ever. It was at least the tenth time she had read it and probably would not be the last. Books were expensive and although she could afford new ones, she had to be careful if her money was to last.

It hadn't always been like this, having to be careful. In her youth she had had means at her disposal that had given her a very comfortable life. Books and such like had been taken more or less for granted. But those times were long past and seemed a lifetime away.

This story though, out of all the books she possessed, was her favourite. She felt very close to the character of Miss Haversham. The woman had been cheated of her happiness, just as Clara had been.

She smoothed a delicate bony hand over her snow white hair which was neatly pulled back into a bun at the nape of her neck and gazed around the immaculate room where not a speck of dust was left long enough to settle. The furniture, all second hand, had been chosen with care, and since it had been in her possession, treated with the love usually lavished on heirlooms.

She eyed the piano that graced the wall adjoining her own house with the Wilkinses'. An overwhelming desire to play a piece of Chopin overcame her. It would help to rid her of the awful melancholy feeling that had been with her for several days now. But she wouldn't. It was too late in the evening and she had too much consideration for her neighbours – and from what she had gathered from over the garden wall when no one realised she was there, that poor Mrs Wilkins had enough burdens to carry, being married to her overbearing husband, without Clara adding to them by being discourteous. Besides, she had a terrible headache herself and one that would not go despite continual doses of Beecham's pills and Epsom fruit salts.

She rose stiffly and walked slowly across to her bookcase, carefully slotting the book back into its allotted place. She would choose another later and begin it before retiring to bed. That way she had something on the go when she rose in the morning.

She stood to the side of the front window and stared through the white netting curtains. The street was beginning to quieten down. Women were gathering their children and taking them inside, ready to be scrubbed and put to bed. In some cases just put to bed without being scrubbed. Men no longer walked towards the pub on the corner; they were already there, probably on their second or third pint of beer as they caught up with the day's chat with their cronies.

It had been a hot day for the end of September, sticky and oppressive, but the good thing for her was that it had filled the street with people. Noises of laughter, crying and shouting had made her feel she wasn't entirely on her own.

Clara sighed heavily. She hated this time of an evening when the street was shutting down for the night. This was when her four walls really closed in on her. Soon it would be winter. The streets would be empty and the thought of the long winter months stretching ahead made her shudder.

Clara Smith was lonely. She had been lonely for the past

thirty-eight years. She had not been born to be lonely. It had come about by the way her life had been shaped, the path she had trodden when still a young woman. But she had no one to blame for her situation but herself and her own wrong judgement.

She moved away from the window. She needed to busy herself, that was what she needed to do, had striven for over the past thirty-eight years. Being busy stopped minds wandering and dwelling on things best forgotten. Clocks could not be turned back, lives could not be lived again, however much it was wished for.

The announcement of war three weeks before had unsettled Clara. It had brought back memories of events before another war had disrupted the world, memories which she had fought hard to forget. Now they were unleashed and invaded her like unwelcome visitors. Feelings she had long ago managed to bury, surfaced and haunted her every moment. Her only solace was reading. Lost in her books, she could forget for a while.

She ran her hand again over her throbbing temple, feeling beads of sweat on her brow. She really did feel terrible. She would take some more pills and go to bed. Maybe a good night's rest would cure whatever it was that was ailing her.

As she climbed between the spotless white sheets and gratefully rested her head on the snow white pillows, she suddenly wondered, should she die during the night, how long her body would lie undetected.

Earlier in the evening, in the house next-door to Clara's, a young girl had slowly climbed the stairs, careful to mind the holes in the worn lino so as not to spill the tea in the handleless cup she was carrying.

Inside the bedroom, she stole across the bare wooden floor and stood before the bed.

'Mum,' she called softly. 'It's time to get up.'

Madge Cotting slowly opened her eyes and stared up at her eight-and-a-half-year-old daughter, Jessica. She rubbed her hands over her eyes and stretched herself, yawning loudly.

'Ohhh,' she groaned. 'It ain't, is it?'

She pulled herself up, ran her hand through her dishevelled dyed blonde hair, then gratefully accepted the cup of weak tea that was being thrust at her.

She noticed Jessie grinning. 'What's split your face, girl? Won the pools or somethin'?'

'Wish I had, Mum, then you wouldn't have to go to work tonight and leave us.'

'Ah, don't start that. I have to work, you know I do. You didn't answer my question. What yer laughing at?'

'You. Your hair looks like a bird's nest.'

'So would yours if you'd bin tossing and turning all day. I couldn't get to sleep. It was too 'ot and the racket coming from the street didn't 'elp.' Madge took a long gulp of the scalding liquid and grimaced. 'Ran out of milk again I see. You should have gone and scrounged some off the neighbours. Pass me fags, there's a love.'

She grasped the packet from Jessie's hand and lit a Woodbine, inhaling the smoke deep into her lungs. She coughed long and loud, swallowing the phlegm. 'That's better. Another cuppa and I'll feel almost human.' She yawned again and patted the dark blue eiderdown. 'Sit down and tell yer old mum what you and our Tony got up to today.'

Jessie sat down. 'Nuffink much.' She averted her gaze from her mother. 'We 'ate it 'ere, Mum. Can't we go 'ome? All the kids laugh at the way we talk, and they eat funny fings. Faggots! A' you seen 'em, Mum? They're disgustin'. I wanna go back 'ome. I miss all me friends.'

Madge slammed the cup down on to the orange box at the side of her bed. 'How many times do we have to go through this? For gawd's sake, girl, we've only bin here two weeks. We can't go home. We had to leave the smoke because of this rotten war looming. I never asked to come to this stinking hole of a town, but this is where we ended up. You and your brother should think yourselves lucky we got this house. It's better than the one we came from. Anyway, other 'vacees ain't been so lucky. They've had to lodge with strangers or got split up. How would you 'ave fancied that, eh? We might not have much but it'll do us 'til this bloody war's over and we can get back to normal.' Her voice lowered and her face softened. 'It won't be for long, love. As soon as the danger's passed we'll go back, I promise.'

Jessie's face lit up. 'You mean that, Mum?'

'I said so, didn't I? Now, out me way while I get up and dressed or I'll be late. And we can't have that, can we?'

Jessie shook her head. 'I'll get your dinner.'

'What we got?'

Jessie grinned. 'Faggots.'

Madge eased her long legs out of the bed and stood up. She pulled off her nightdress and examined herself in the long piece of cracked mirror propped up against the wall. She ran her hands over her shapely hips and cupped her breasts. Not bad, she thought. Not bad for a woman of thirty who's had two kids. Her daughter was right though, her hair was a mess and she had better do something about it or it might turn her customers right off and then where would she be?

At the thought of her customers she secretly smiled. So far as everyone knew, even her children, she worked the twilight shift in the plaster factory on the Abbey Lane. Laborious work for terrible pay and no way to earn the kind of money she was after. Only she didn't work there and never had, but the lie was far better than the truth. This way she kept a respectable front. Neighbours watched out for the kids and when hand-outs were offered they were top of the list.

This war was going to be the making of her. Being evacu-ated was the best idea she'd ever had and she was going to milk it for all it was worth. The government had even paid their train fare and the good souls of Leicester had given her this house. It wasn't much, but it was far, far better than she'd had in the East End of London.

It was a pity really that she had had to bring the kids along. She would have preferred a free rein. Madge smiled to herself. But without them she would not have been evacu-ated in the first place, and besides, Jessie was just as good as having a housekeeper. With her doing the work, it left Madge free to do her own job at night and lie in bed all day. Bliss, she thought, utter bliss to what they'd left behind.

She shuddered at the memories of the damp, bug-infested, tiny rooms she had been forced to occupy with her children when their father had abandoned them to go off with the tart from across the road. The building was practically derel-ict; the stinking toilet at the bottom of the yard had been shared with several other families; the water had had to be fetched from a standpipe and carried in a bucket, and in winter everything froze. Nothing had changed since the turn of the century. And they said that England was a land fit for heroes! Who had said it? That's what she wanted to know. That bit of England hadn't been fit for anyone.

Still, that was all behind her now, the war had seen to that. She was going to save every penny she could, take all she was offered, and when the time came to return, things would be far different. It was all thanks to her friend, Avril. It was Avril who had taught her everything she knew and there had been a lot to learn in this game. Madge was just annoyed that she hadn't thought of this line of work before. It was all so simple, providing you had the know how. But more importantly, you had to have the nerve, which she had plenty of.

She hummed to herself as she walked down the stairs. Sitting at the table she tucked hungrily into the faggots and peas her daughter had prepared. She had a long night ahead and one that would use all her energies so better to fill her stomach. It wouldn't do for her clients to hear loud rumbles during the session.

At ten o'clock precisely she was sitting in a darkened rented room off the Woodgate, just down from the notorious Robin Hood pub, far enough from her own area so as not to be recognised.

On a table, the tools of her trade were spread, ready for her first client. She was dressed for the part right down to the wooden painted bracelets on her wrists. She heard the tap on the door, waited for a moment, then slowly rose.

'Here we go,' she said, smiling at the thought of her purse filling with money.

After their mother had left for work Jessie looked across at her seven-year-old brother sitting at the old pine table reading his *Boy's Own* comic. The table, like the rest of the sparse furniture, bedding and crockery had been presented to them by the authorities. Any other bits they had acquired had been donated by kindly neighbours and the Voluntary Services. To Jessie, this house and everything in it was heaven to what they had left, but it still wasn't home to her and never would be.

She stole towards Tony, grabbed the comic and pulled him to his feet.

'Come on,' she announced.

He pulled an angry face and made a grab for the comic. 'Gimme that back, our sis. I was reading it,' he cried, jumping up and down in temper.

'You can't read. You just look at the pictures.'

'I can so. Now gimme it back.'

'What's that say then?' she said cockily, pointing to a bold heading.

Tony stopped jumping and sniffed disdainfully. 'How can I read it when your finger's in the way?' he replied, studying his bare feet.

'Told yer. Told you you couldn't read. Anyway you can look at the pictures when we come back.'

'Back? Where we goin'?'

Jessie smiled secretively. 'I'm gonna get us some supper.'

Tony's face lit up. He would follow his sister anywhere if food was at the end of it.

She locked the house behind them and silently they stole down the entry.

'Where we going, Jessie?' Tony enquired.

'The allotments.'

'Eh! What for?'

'You'll see. Now, shush. Someone might hear us. And keep a look out for the bobby. Don't want to end up in the nick, do yer?' she threatened.

Tony hurriedly shook his head, clamped his mouth shut and grabbed hold of the back of his sister's skirt.

It was nearly dark by the time they arrived at the deserted allotments. Plenty of produce had still to be gathered and Jessie had a good look round before she made her choice.

'We'll have a couple of them cabbages and some carrots.'

Tony, never having seen vegetables before in their natural habitat, stared agog.

Jessie turned on him. 'Well, get pulling.'

Tony stared at the enormous green things protruding from the ground.

'Pull?' he gawped.

'Oh, God love me,' she groaned. 'I suppose I'll have to do it meself and you're 'sposed to be the man of the house. Just keep a look out, I'm warning you. And while you're looking, see if you can find an old sack.'

She bent down and yanked with all her might. The cabbage wouldn't budge. Taking several deep breaths she tried again. Thankfully this time she had success. The cabbage left the ground with speed and she fell flat on her back, flattening a row of young Brussells sprouts.

Armed with two cabbages, several pounds of carrots and some sticks of rhubarb, complete with huge leaves, they departed for home, the old sack Tony had found tucked at the side of a wooden shed carried between them.

Tipping their ill-gotten gains on to the kitchen table, she picked the smallest cabbage and wrapped it in newspaper. Tony looked on bemused, wondering what on earth he was going to get for his supper from this lot. He had eaten some things in his time but he drew the line at cabbage, carrot or rhubarb sandwiches.

The next thing the little lad knew he was standing at the side of Jessie as she knocked on Mrs Wilkins's back door.

Grace, who had just been thinking of going to bed in order to be out of the way when her husband came back from the pub, raised her head, wondering who could be calling at this time of night.

She tentatively opened the door, mindful to obey the black-out regulations, and stepped back in alarm as the cabbage plus several sheet of crumpled newspaper was thrust at her.

'Mum told us to give you this.'

'Oh! Why . . . er . . . thank you. Thank you very much,' she said in pleased surprise, accepting the gift.

She looked down at the two poorly dressed mites in front of her, their clothes and faces covered in a dusting of dry mud.

'Is your mam at work?' she asked gently.

They both nodded.

Grace tutted. 'Would you like a cuppa and something to eat?'

Grinning broadly, they both nodded again.

'Come away in then.'

Jessie turned to Tony, grinning mischievously. 'See,' she whispered. 'I told you I'd get us some supper.'

A sandwich which Grace had prepared earlier for Bernard, plus a slice each of cold apple pie and two mugs of tea, were quickly demolished.

Grace, elbows resting on the table, chin in hands, silently watched them, her maternal instincts wreaking havoc.

The weekend after the declaration of war, the City of Leicester had opened its arms and welcomed thirty thousand evacuees, the majority from London, the rest from Sheffield.

Grace had pleaded with Bernard for them to do their bit and take two in, but he had stood firm. This problem was nothing to do with them. If other folks opened their doors, more fool them and he hoped they had locked away any valuables.

His bigoted attitude had not stopped her from going down to the station when the trains were due in. She had stood helplessly by as wave after wave of bewildered little lost souls alighted on the platforms, brown paper parcels tied up with string tucked under their arms, name tags pinned to their coats.

Her heart had gone out to each and every one of them. She longed to take them all and wipe away their tears, soothe their fears. But Bernard had said no.

Deep in her heart, Grace knew this was one thing for which she would never be able to forgive him. These children, having been plucked from their homes, away from their loved ones, urgently needed security, love and reassurance – things she had plenty of. And he had denied her, and not only her but also the children.

Luckily others did not share Bernard's opinions and soon all were safely housed and being cared for.

Grace smiled tenderly at the two before her. These children were luckier than most, they at least had their mother with them even if she did have to work such unsociable hours, her pay hardly feeding them.

She strongly resisted the urge to leap up, gather them into her arms and cuddle them, reassure them both that hopefully their situation would not be for long; that as soon as the threat of bombing was over they would return to their own familiar streets, back to the arms of the rest of their loved ones.

Her smile broadened as Tony, who had the face of an innocent angel framed around with a thatch of straw blond hair, wiped crumbs from his mouth with the back of his hand and patted his stomach.

Jessie nudged him. 'Say yer manners,' she hissed.

'Eh? Oh!' He beamed across at Grace. 'Ta very much, missus.'

Grace returned the smile. 'You're very welcome.'

Jessie pushed her plate away, rose and grabbed her brother's hand. 'We'd better be off.'

Grace rose also. 'You don't have to. Why don't you stay awhile and we can have a chat? You can tell me all about London.'

Jessie hesitated. Begrudgingly, she liked Mrs Wilkins. She was a pretty woman with a lovely smile, welcoming. She would have loved to stay and avoid going back to the empty cheerless house, but it was no use getting friendly. They were going back home soon, so it would be a waste of time. Besides, Jessie didn't want to bump into that husband of hers. She knew he thought them no better than dirt. She could see it in his eyes whenever their paths crossed in the street. She had only brought Tony tonight because she had seen Mr Wilkins going out earlier.

'I've got to get Tony to bed,' she said firmly.

'Ah, sis,' he grumbled.

'I understand, Jessie,' Grace cut in. 'Some other time. You're always welcome.' She did not want to scare off the little girl with the wary eyes. She wanted the child to feel she could knock on her door any time she wished and be welcomed. It worried Grace that they were both returning to an empty house and she wished she could offer to accommodate them for the night. She would without hesitation, left to herself. She would get them cleaned up and dressed in some of Charlie's old nightclothes and tucked between clean white sheets on a makeshift bed on the settee in the room at the front. But she knew Bernard would have a fit and it would be the children who suffered, being made to feel so unwelcome, which was the last thing they needed.

She opened her mouth to offer to walk them home when the door burst open and Bernard strode through. He looked at the children, at the table, at Grace, then back at the children.

'Bit late for you to be out, ain't it? I'd get off home if I were you.'

Grace froze in humiliation at his icy tone. She opened her mouth to challenge him, but before she could say a word, Jessie had hauled Tony to the door. She looked at Grace and smiled. 'Thanks, missus.' She flashed a scowl of hatred at Bernard, then they were gone.

Grace shot to the door. 'Take care now,' she called out into the darkness.

She stood for a moment, trying to calm her anger, before she turned and stared over at her husband, face set grimly. 'How could you, Bernard?'

'How could I? How could I what?' he said innocently. 'I'm right, they shouldn't be out at this time of night. I was only showing concern for their welfare.' He looked hard at the table and especially at the empty apple pie dish. 'I shan't bother with a sandwich. I'll have a piece of that apple pie left over from dinner.'

Grace walked slowly to the table. 'Well, you're out of luck,' she said lightly. 'The children have just eaten it.' She turned towards him holding the pie dish, knowing that he knew fine well what had happened to the pie and that was why he had asked. 'I can make you a cheese sandwich,' she offered.

'I don't want a cheese sandwich, Grace. I want some apple pie.' He slowly inhaled, lips tightening. 'But I suppose in future, me the breadwinner,' he said, stabbing his chest, 'will be lucky to get anything if we're going to be feeding the street.'

Grace swallowed hard. He was going to milk this for all it was worth and she felt powerless to stop it. 'You're exaggerating Bernard. The children had a piece of bread and cheese and the remains of the pie. That's not feeding the street. Anyway, it's the least we can do. This war isn't their fault. It's none of our faults. The least we can do is try and make their stay in Leicester a happy one.'

Bernard glared. 'I thought I told you these people are not our responsibility? Good God woman, we have a hard enough job to feed ourselves, let alone half of London. Now listen to me and listen good. This will not happen again. I will not go hungry for the sake of two waifs who have taken you for a right mug. If they need feeding, let their own mother do it. Your family should come first.' He looked condescendingly at her. 'It comes to something, it does, Grace Wilkins, when strangers come before your own family.' He marched towards the door. 'I'm going to bed. Now heed what I've said. I don't want a repeat of this. I shan't take it so kindly next time.'

She stared after him, body sagging as every last drop of feeling she'd had for him drained from her.

Chapter Five

The following Friday at midday a preoccupied Grace was returning home after delivering Ida's dinner. The old woman had been particularly difficult, unjustly complaining that Grace was late, and had turned her nose up at the delicious stew and dumplings placed before her. It was cold, the meat fatty and the dumplings hard. 'Kids could play football wi' these,' she had sniffed disdainfully. But regardless, she had soon snatched the plate and gobbled up every mouthful, and scraped the bowl clean of the steamed jam pudding and custard that followed.

But it was not her complaints about the food that were troubling Grace as she turned the corner of her street, so much as the fact that Bernard's mother was stepping up her campaign to move in with them. This bothered Grace more than anything else she could think of. She felt she could cope with most things if she had to – war, famine, earthquakes and floods – but never, under any circumstances, could she face the thought of living with Ida.

As she neared her house, loud wails of anguish suddenly rent the air and stopped her in her tracks. So powerful were they that all thoughts of Ida flew from her. She stared around, wondering where they were coming from. As more followed, she quickly realised they were issuing from the Rudney household. Whoever was screaming must be in terrible pain,

71

like a trapped animal in great distress.

She spotted Willy sitting in the gutter, idly swinging a sacking bag of marbles, seemingly oblivious. The string on the bag suddenly broke and the marbles scattered. Muttering under his breath, Willy jumped up and began to gather them.

'Is that your mother? What on earth is wrong?' Grace shouted to him worriedly.

Willy nonchalantly lifted his head and nodded absently. 'She's havin' one of 'er fits. I wish she'd hurry up and get it over 'cos I'm starvin'. I want me dinner.'

Grace stared at him. 'Fit? What kind of fit? Is she ill?'

Willy shrugged his shoulders. 'I dunno. Just a fit. Summat to do wi' me brothers. Our Polly told me to clear off out of it 'til she's calmed down.'

Grace turned back and stared towards the house. The screams were no angry fit of temper, of that she was sure. Something was dreadfully wrong with Mrs Rudney. Her instincts told her to rush in and offer to help but she hesitated for a second, unsure whether she would be interfering in something that was none of her business. As yet another cry rang out her mind was made up for her. She flew down the entry.

The back door was wide open and, without waiting, Grace knocked and rushed in.

Bessie was prowling around the table in the living room, her thick brown hair escaping from its pins, flabby arms flapping wildly, a mixture of profanities and screams of anguish spurting from her mouth. Her usually jolly face was ashen and drawn, her eyes and nose red from crying. Polly was pressed up against the far wall, Maureen huddled into her side. On the floor by the door which led to the stairs and front room, in a puddle, having wet himself, sat Bobbie. In sympathy with his mother, he was breaking his heart. The two older boys, Dennis and Barry, stood shamefaced by the table, shuffling their feet.

On spotting her neighbour, Bessie rushed over and threw herself on her, wailing loudly, burying her head in Grace's shoulder, tears quickly wetting her blouse.

Grace dropped her gas mask and placed her arm around her, looking enquiringly at all the others. 'What on earth has happened?'

Bessie pulled her head back, jerking a podgy finger towards her sons. 'It's them. It's them pair a' buggers. They've only gone and joined up.' She thrust her tear-streaked face into Grace's. 'What am I gonna do? Oh, Mrs Wilkins, what the 'ell am I gonna do?'

Grace took a deep breath, mind racing wildly in order to choose her words very carefully. She quickly realised that it was up to her as an outsider to take charge of the situation. Someone had to before murder was committed.

She guided Bessie towards a chair and sat her down. 'You two had better get back to work,' Grace told the boys. The look of relief on their faces was not lost on her. As they shot out of the door, she turned to Polly and Maureen. 'Take Bobbie outside and stay out while I calm your mother down.' She suddenly remembered something Willy had said when she spoke to him outside. 'Hold on a minute.' She grabbed the bread knife from the table and quickly cut large chunks from a loaf. Finding a dish of dripping, she spread the bread thickly, adding a sprinkling of salt. She slapped the slices together and handed them over. 'Sorry, girls, but you'll have to make do with these for now. Mind you give some to Willy.' She hurried across to the kitchen and lifted the lid on the huge pan bubbling on top of the stove. It was vegetable soup and smelt delicious. She replaced the lid and turned down the gas. 'Your dinner will keep for later. Oh, and don't forget your gas masks.'

The girls nodded, and like their brothers before, relief spread across their faces. Maureen grabbed the gas masks; Polly scooped up Bobbie and they hurried out.

Grace quickly mashed a pot of tea and poured out a mug. She ladled in two huge spoons of sugar and placed the mug on the table in front of Bessie, who by now was sobbing noisily into the bottom of her floral wraparound apron. Grace sat down next to her and placed her hand gently on her arm.

'Have a sup of tea, Mrs Rudney, it'll do you good.'

Bessie raised her head, sniffing loudly. 'Oh, what am I gonna do? I can't bear it, I really can't. The thought of me boys going off to fight them Germans.' She shuddered violently. 'Tom'll go mad when he finds out.'

Grace patted her arm. 'Drink your tea,' she ordered firmly. She picked up the mug and placed it in the plump fist. Bessie's hand shook as she bought the mug to her lips and some of the tea slopped on to her apron. When she had drained the last drop, Grace poured her another.

'Mrs Rudney, I can imagine what you're going through, but make no mistake – what your boys have done is a grand thing. You've raised them up to be good, honest lads who want to do their duty.' She paused and smiled kindly. 'And you know, this is also their way of showing their regard for you.'

Bessie shuddered as a sob caught at the back of her throat. 'Is it? 'Ow?'

'By going off to fight they're protecting you and the rest of their family from the enemy. It's their way of showing their love.'

Bessie gawped in surprise. 'Oh! Oh, yes, I see. I never thought on it like that before.'

Grace patted her hand. She paused and eyed the woman in concern. 'Besides, it's done now and there's nothing you can do but grin and bear it. You have to be brave and send them both off with a smile on your face.'

Bessie shook her head vigorously. 'I don't know whether I can do that.'

'You have too, Mrs Rudney. Before those lads go off to
war you have to let them know how proud you are of them.
You'll never forgive yourself otherwise.'

Bessie slowly nodded and raised red-rimmed eyes. 'Yes,
yes, you're right. And I do feel proud, really I do. But 'ow
come I just want to bash their 'eads together and tell 'em
how bloody stupid they are?'

Grace smiled ruefully. 'Because you're hurt, Mrs Rudney.
You're hurting because they did something without consulting you first, and you're worried because you know deep
down they really don't understand what they're going off to
face. To them this is all an adventure. At this moment, they
don't see the danger. You just want to protect them like you
used to when they were little boys.' She paused and lowered
her voice. 'You feel the same as any mother would. The most
difficult thing we have to face is the fact that our children
have grown and don't need us in quite the same way as they
used to. I don't know who suffers the most during this time
of change, the mothers or the children. But it doesn't matter
how old they are, to us mothers they're still our babies and
that's not wrong, Mrs Rudney. Don't reproach yourself for
still caring.'

Bessie stared at her wide-eyed. 'Yer right, Mrs Wilkins.
For 'ow big they've got, I still feel the need to tuck me boys
into bed at night and give 'em a cuddle.' She tutted loudly.
'Only problem wi' that is, I'm usually in bed these days
before they are!'

Grace nodded, smiling in agreement. 'It's the same with
me and Charlie. I keep having to remind myself that's she's
old enough to take care of herself and make her own
decisions. How else is she ever going to cope when she
marries and has children if she doesn't learn about life and
make her own mistakes? After all, Mrs Rudney, we aren't
going to be around forever, are we? As much as we'd like to

be.' She took a deep breath and sighed loudly, gazing absently around the room. 'You know, lots of mothers across the country are going through the same as you today. Mothers with boys the same age as your sons, and just as much loved, are having to cope as well. It's tough, Mrs Rudney, but it's something we could all face in the future if this war really develops.'

Bessie wiped her hand under her nose and managed a watery smile. 'Just seems like yesterday I wa' chasin' my ones out the 'ouse wi' me broom up their backsides for summat they'd both done. Always up to summat, were my lads. Now look at 'em. A strapping six foot and still causing me 'eartache.'

Grace laughed. 'And they will 'til you're six foot under.'

Her eyes caught the clock on the fireplace. Bernard would be home any second expecting his dinner on the table, but she could not leave Bessie, not while the woman was in this state. Charlie always took a packed lunch to work so she wouldn't be home until gone six. Well, Bernard's dinner was all ready and waiting to be dished up. It wouldn't hurt him for once to help himself, considering the circumstances. She swiftly shut off thoughts of him and turned her attention back to her neighbour.

Bessie leaned over and grabbed her hand, gripping it tightly. 'Oh, Mrs Wilkins, I'm so glad yer came in today. I don't know what I'd 'ave done wi'out yer. You've made me look at things like I've never done before. I can't say as I feel any better, but you've certainly made me realise that as far as me boys are concerned, they're old enough to know their own minds and I should stop interfering.' She looked at Grace questioningly. 'But that don't mean to say I 'ave ter stop lovin' and worryin' about 'em, does it?'

Grace shook her head. 'No, it doesn't. We just have to learn to give them more breathing space and keep our loving and worrying more to ourselves, that's all.' She smiled warmly. 'I'm glad I came in too, Mrs Rudney. Sometimes it's catastrophies like these that bring people together.'

'Put like that, I'm surprised it's took ten years for you to be sittin' in my kitchen.' Bessie guffawed loudly. ''Cos I've had more castastrophes in this 'ouse than the Pope's had confessions.'

Grace chuckled. She suddenly felt a great affection for this large jolly woman sitting beside her. A woman who could still laugh despite the trauma she was facing. Women like her were to be envied. Everybody suffered from life's battering one way or another, but people like Mrs Rudney knew how to ride the bad times and bounce back. It was an inborn instinct. The likes of Ida and Bernard and several other mealy mouthed residents in the area could learn a thing or two from the Rudneys and be the better for it.

Grace felt an inner glow spread through her. She suddenly realised that the fact she was sitting in this homely kitchen after years of being on little more than nodding terms with the occupants was no accident, it was fate. She knew then that this was the beginning of a friendship, and this knowledge was very welcome on her part. She could only hope that Bessie Rudney felt the same towards her.

'Would you like a drop of soup?' Grace asked. 'It'd do you good to get something in your stomach.'

Bessie shook her head. 'I couldn't eat 'ote at the moment, ta. But I bet the little 'uns are starving, bless 'em.' She made to rise. 'I better get 'em summat before all 'ell lets loose.'

'Don't worry about them. I've sorted that for the time being.'

Bessie looked at her, relieved. ''Ave yer? Ta. I'm very much obliged.' She eyed the tea pot. 'I will 'ave another cuppa though.' She looked hopefully at Grace. 'What about yerself?'

She nodded. 'I'd love one, thanks.'

Just then a shadow crossed the doorway. Both women looked up and saw a bewildered Tom staring at them both.

Grace rose hurriedly. 'I'd better be going,' she said, flustered.

He raised his large hand. 'Don't go on my account, Mrs Wilkins, I've only popped in on me way past to drop off this.' He put a brown paper parcel on the table and addressed Bessie. 'Bit of cod I managed to pick up.' He studied her face, suddenly becoming worried. 'What's up, Bessie? You look like you've lost a shillin' and found a tanner.'

'Oh, worse than that. It's them lads of yourn. It's what they've gone and done what's upset me.'

Tom tutted loudly and ran his hand through his light brown hair. 'What this time? They ain't gone and got the sack, 'ave they?'

Bessie rose and spread her hands on the table. 'Worse than that. They've joined up, that's what!' Her eyes filled with tears again which rolled down her plump cheeks.

Tom tightened his mouth and closed his eyes. He quickly gathered his wits and rushed to his wife, throwing his arms around her, pulling her close.

'Come on, gel, pull yerself together. We both talked about this and knew it was on the cards. They're good lads, Bessie, as good as you'll get. And I don't know about you but I'm proud. They'll give them Germans a run for their money all right. I wouldn't like to be on the receiving end when our lads face 'em.'

She gave a deep-throated chuckle. 'Yer right, Tom.' She looked towards Grace. 'And so a' you, Mrs Wilkins. I'm just a silly old woman, thinkin' of meself.' She took a deep breath and dried her eyes. 'Right, who wants a dish of soup?'

Tom grinned broadly. 'I think I can manage that. And you, Mrs Wilkins? I bet you could do with a bowl of our Bessie's soup. Makes the best soup this side of Scotland she does.'

Bessie nudged him playfully in the ribs. 'Yer daft sod,' she said, laughing. 'Mek yerself useful and cut the bread while I dish up.'

Tom was right, Grace thought as she tucked in. Bessie's soup was the best she had ever tasted, and much to her neighbour's delight asked for the recipe.

As Bessie gathered the dishes, Tom leaned over and whispered to Grace: 'Could you stay wi' her for a bit? I don't like to ask only I 'ave to get back to work.' He looked across at his wife. 'She's trying to hide it, but I can see she's still upset.'

Grace nodded. 'Course I will.'

She could see by Tom's eyes that he was just as upset as his wife but was managing by sheer willpower to conceal it. She thought of Bernard again and wondered what his reaction would be if he knew that she was in with the Rudneys, a family he abhorred, having just shared their food. But she didn't need to wonder, she knew. He would be furious to learn she was mixing with what he called 'scum'. And how wrong he was! By rights he should be proud to have neighbours such as these, and it was his loss that he thought otherwise.

It touched Grace deeply to have witnessed the loving scene between Tom and Bessie, and saddened her to realise it would never enter her own husband's head to act in such a way to her regardless of how upset she was. He would just grunt and tell her not to be so stupid.

Her mind was made up. Regardless of how Bernard felt, this time she would truly defy him. If Bessie wanted to be her friend then she would be, and Grace herself would be grateful of it. She felt she needed Bessie more than Bessie needed her. What Bernard didn't know wouldn't hurt him. The only problem she faced was making a plausible excuse for her absence at lunchtime.

Tom broke into her thoughts as he smiled gratefully at her. 'Thanks, Mrs Wilkins. It's much appreciated.'

His eyes lingered on Grace for a moment. As much as he loved his Bessie, he could not help but admire this attractive woman. Like his wife, he also wondered how she had ever come to saddle herself with such a bigot as Bernard Wilkins. The man must possess something, he thought, but God knows what it is.

He rose and said his goodbyes, telling Bessie that he had a load of machine parts to deliver to a factory in Birmingham and didn't know what time he would get back. He kissed her on the cheek, nodded at Grace and left.

Bessie eyed Grace guiltily. 'I'll understand if you 'ave to get back, me duck. I'll be fine now, 'onest.'

She smiled. 'If it's no trouble to you, I'll stay for a bit. I've nothing that needs doing which can't wait.' She settled back in her chair. 'To be honest, this makes a change for me.'

Bessie scrutinised Grace's face. 'D'yer know, I used ter think you were a stuck up so and so when I first moved in. But you ain't, a' yer? You're a really nice woman.'

Grace blushed embarrassedly. 'Why, thank you, Mrs Rudney. I'll take that as a compliment. And I happen to think you're very nice too.'

'Well, yer right there, gel,' Bessie agreed. 'You keep company wi' me and yer won't go far wrong.' She folded her arms and shuffled her bottom further back on her chair. 'We must do this more often, Mrs Wilkins. A few minutes outta our day for a cuppa ain't gonna 'arm anyone.' She gave a deep-throated chuckle. 'And I don't need an excuse to stop doin' me chores.'

Grace smiled warmly. 'I'd like that very much. Especially now. Us neighbours will all need each other for support if we're going to get through this war for however long it lasts.'

'Yer right there, me duck. I remember the last war like it

were yesterday. Me and Tom were about fourteen when it started . . .'

As the pair sat reminiscing, outside on a low wall at the bottom of the street the young members of the Rudney family had finished their sandwiches and were staring around, bored. Bobbie, who had been plonked in the large green coach pram on leaving the house, had fallen asleep.

It was the last weekday of the autumn half-term break and none of the children was looking forward to going back to school the following Monday. The next long break would be Christmas and to their young minds that seemed a lifetime away.

Polly slid off the wall and grabbed her gas mask out of the pram. 'I'm off to Wendy's for a bit. You can look after Bobbie and make sure our Willy don't get into trouble, our Maureen, Mam's had enough for one day.' She kicked Willy with the toe of her plimsoll. ''A' you listening? Stay outta trouble or else,' she warned.

She made to walk off, but Maureen jumped off the wall and grabbed the back of her cardigan, pulling her back. 'That ain't fair, our Polly, I always get lumbered. You 'ave 'im for a change.'

Polly raised her head scornfully. 'Just do as you're told, or I'll tell Mam it were you that sneaked that last bit of rhubarb pie that she wa' saving for Dad's supper last week.'

Maureen's mouth clamped shut. Oh, how she hated their Polly. Her sister always seemed to have some bit of information stored up to blackmail her with.

She angrily kicked at a stone on the ground then grabbed hold of the pram handle and released the brake. 'Come on, you,' she shouted at Willy.

He slid off the wall. 'Where we goin', sis?'

''Ow do I bloody well know? Just come on.'

Willy gawped. 'You swore,' he said accusingly.

She clipped him round the head. 'No, I did not.'

'I 'eard yer, I did,' he accused, rubbing his head. 'You said "bloody".'

'I bloody did not! And if yer say 'ote ter Mam, I'll say you swore an' all.'

Willy stared at her, defeated. He'd lost again. But that was nothing new. He never won anything up against his sisters.

The exchange was quickly forgotten. Armed with his wooden Airfix glider plane and sword, Willy skipped happily at the side of the pram. As they turned the corner of the street they collided with the two evacuees from number eighty-six.

'Whatchit!' Jessie spat, grabbing her brother.

'Whatchit yerself,' Maureen hissed back.

The two girls eyed each other, unaware that the two younger boys were huddled together examining each other's toys.

'Where yer off then?' Maureen casually asked.

'What's it to do with you?' Jessie replied cockily.

Bessie had ordered her younger children to do their best to make all the evacuee children they came across welcome, especially the two in their own street, so Maureen thought she had better make the effort just in case it got back to her mother.

She slowly stared around then brought her eyes back to Jessie. 'I'm off for a walk if yer wanna come?'

'Where to?' she asked nonchalantly.

Maureen shrugged her plump shoulders. 'I dunno. Round the street.'

'We can do that by ourselves. Besides, I've better things to do.'

Maureen eyed her, interested. 'Oh! What things?'

Jessie thought rapidly. Secretly she would have liked nothing more than to have tagged along with the plump, pleasant-faced girl who lived with the large family further down the street, but she had the house to tidy, the washing to sort and the dinner to prepare. 'Just things.' She grabbed hold of Tony. 'Come on.'

He pulled back. ''Ang on a minute . . .'

''Ang on nothin'! Just come on.'

She stalked off, leaving Maureen staring after her. Finally Maureen turned back and grabbed the pram as an idea sprang to mind. Sod her, she thought. She'll be sorry she never came with us when she finds out where we're going.

A picture of Abbey Park rose before her. Her parents had taken them all one Sunday afternoon the previous year when the annual Abbey Park Show had been in progress. There had been swings and stalls, acrobats and jugglers. A huge striped tent had been filled with flowers and vegetables, and her parents had treated them all to candy floss on sticks.

It had been a wonderful afternoon and Maureen had often relived every moment in her dreams. Well, that's where they would go now. It didn't occur to her that the park was at least two miles across the town or that she didn't know the way, and far worse than that was the fact that none of the younger Rudneys was allowed to wander out of the area without first consulting their parents.

Without a thought on any of this she stepped jauntily forward, Willy skipping happily behind her.

They had to ask the way several times and it was well over an hour later before she pushed the pram through the large iron gates. By now Willy had began to grumble about his tired legs and Bobbie had woken with a thirst and had begun to howl.

Luckily a discarded baby bottle of water was still in the pram. She spat on her fingers and wiped the rubber teat, cleaning off most of the fluff, then pushed it into his mouth.

As they walked further inside, Maureen surveyed the area in dismay. No sign of any show was apparent, but more alarming was that most of the land the park occupied was in the process of being dug up for the growing of vegetables or the erection of deep trenches for shelter during possible air raids.

Regardless, she continued pushing the pram down one of the tarmac paths. They had come this far, they might as well have a rest by the River Soar which weaved its way through the middle of the park. It was just a pity they had no money for a cake from the pavilion. She was starving and had no doubt Willy was too and would soon start complaining.

Arriving at a grassy bank by the river she parked the pram, settled down on the grass and slid off her holey plimsolls to air her hot tired feet. If she had realised the park was this far away from home she would never have come. They had still to make the journey home and that thought did not please her.

Willy squatted by her side, plane and sword aloft, playing dive bombers, stabbing his sword in the air as he fought his imaginary enemy.

Maureen lay back on the grass, folding her arms at the back of her head, gazing up at the warm September sun. All around her the noises of men working, birds chirping, Willy playing and Bobbie chattering away to himself as he watched the proceedings going on around from his vantage point high in the pram, faded into the distance as she fell into a dreamy doze.

After a while the noises drifted back and she yawned and stretched herself. She lazily smiled as she focused her eyes. Her dream had been very pleasant. School had been abandoned because the teachers had all disappeared and the sun had been ordered to shine for the winter. Raymond, the lad she sat next to in class, had suddenly shown an interest and she was playing him along.

'Willy,' she said, folding her arms again at the back of her head, squinting skywards, 'we'd better get goin' in a minute.'

Still engrossed in his imaginary game, he rolled over on his front and aimed his gun at the submarine that had surfaced on the distant water.

'Rat-tat-tat-tat – boom!' he shouted, smiling broadly as the German Captain waved both hands in the air in surrender. He grimaced and narrowed his eyes. He didn't like the smile spread across the Captain's face or the foreign-sounding noises he was making. It was a trick, it had to be. He beckoned his army forward and raised his gun again. 'Rat-tat-tat-tat – boom! Yes!' he cried in jubilation as the hand grenade he had thrown hit the target and the submarine began to sink.

Maureen sat up. 'Willy, stop mekking such a racket. It's driving me mad.' She looked around, her eyes widening in alarm. 'Where's the pram?' she demanded. She leaned over and grabbed Willy by the hair, pulling him upwards. 'Where's the bloody pram and our Bobbie?'

Willy was shaken back to reality. He stared at his sister for a moment then slowly gawped as the truth dawned. Speechless, he turned and pointed across to the river. No wonder the Captain looked happy. It was their Bobbie, and the submarine was the pram which must have rolled down the bank and into the water and was now caught in the current, gathering speed as it headed towards the weir.

Maureen jumped up, face wreathed in horror. Quickly she sized up the situation. Below the weir was a torrent of swirling white water and very shortly the pram, complete with her little brother, would be plunged headlong into it. Bobbie, unaware of the danger he was facing, was waving and chuckling happily.

She began to jump up and down, screaming hysterically. 'Me brother! Help, HELP! Me little brother's gonna drown. For God's sake, someone, HEEELPPPP!'

Her frantic screams attracted several workmen digging close by. Dropping their tools, they ran across and one plunged straight into the water, another swiftly following suit. Hindered by water weed and discarded rubbish, their progress was slow. Maureen started to wail in anguish. Willy was so shocked he was frozen to the spot. A crowd had gathered and was watching the proceedings with macabre interest.

The pram bobbed closer and closer towards the edge of the weir. The crowd held their breath. Maureen's life flashed before her. If anything happened to her little brother she would die – that's after her mother had killed her first. The man nearest the pram made a grab for it inches from the edge of the weir and held it against the current. Several moments later the other man reached them and scooped up Bobbie.

Maureen sank down on the grass and the crowd breathed a sigh of relief and began to disperse. The men slowly waded back, dragging the pram and carrying a sopping Bobbie. He was howling in protest. They had spoilt his fun.

Safely on the bank, Maureen threw herself on the men, crying uncontrollably. 'Oh, Misters, Misters, thank you! You've saved me brother.'

The dripping men collapsed, catching their breath. 'Put the brake on next time, love. The young 'un might not be so lucky again.'

Maureen grabbed Bobbie and cuddled him tightly. 'I will, Mister, I will.' She looked down at her brother and frowned hard. 'He's soaking,' she exclaimed, her mouth drooping in horror. 'Oh, me mother! How am I gonna tell me mother?'

The taller of the men began to laugh. 'I wouldn't be in your shoes, gel. Not for all the beer in the Red Lion, I wouldn't.' He awkwardly rose and shook himself. 'Me wife works in the pavilion. Go up and tell 'er I sent yer. She'll dry the young 'un off. In the meantime, I'd think of a good excuse if I were you.'

Maureen nodded. 'Ta, Mister.'

She put Bobbie in the pram which was covered in green slime and had several new dents in its side received on its perilous journey. The gas masks were also soaking wet. She turned on Willy and struck him round the head. 'This is all your fault.'

He cried in protest. 'Me!'

'Yes, you. If you hadn't been playing your stupid game nonc of this would've happened.' She pulled him by the ear. 'Come on, let's get to the pavilion before our Bobbie gets pneumonia. And you'd better think of summat good to tell our mother, 'cos she's gonna kill you if she finds out you nearly drowned him.'

Without waiting for Willy to respond, she grabbed the handle on the pram and strode off.

The kindly woman at the pavilion came up trumps. While Maureen and Willy cleaned down the pram as best they could, she washed and changed Bobbie into a pair of old shorts and a jersey belonging to her own son. The clothes were too big, but they served the purpose. As she sent the subdued pair on their way she made Maureen promise that the clothes would be returned.

As they neared home, she decided she would not tell her mother what had transpired. With a bit of luck they might just get away with it.

Back at the house, Grace and Bessie had talked the whole afternoon away. It had done both of them the world of good. and their friendship had been sealed. Grace suddenly realised the time and jumped up.

'I must be going,' she said in alarm.

Bessie rose also. 'Come again, Mrs Wilkins. Don't leave it another ten years.'

Grace smiled. 'I won't. But you must come to me next time.'

'I will that. Ta for the invite.'

Bessie walked with Grace to the front door and looked up and down the street. 'I wonder where my kids 'ave got to. It's not like them to stay out for so long wi'out stormin' in demandin' food.'

Just then Maureen and Willy pushed the pram around the corner and Bessie smiled. 'I knew they couldn't be far away.'

Maureen drew the pram to a halt before her mother. She planted a smile on her face. 'Hello, Mam. Hello, Mrs Wilkins.'

'Hello, Maureen, Willy,' Grace replied. She patted Bobbie's head. 'He looks tired out. You must have had a good afternoon.'

Willy looked down and studied his feet and Maureen smiled nervously.

'We did, ta very much.' She looked cautiously up at her mother, who was leaning casually against the doorframe, her plump arms folded under her ample bosom.

Bessie gazed down fondly at her son in the pram. She frowned quizzically. 'What's he doin' dressed in them clothes? Whose are they?'

Maureen gulped in horror. She hadn't thought of that. Oh, God, that was the one thing she'd forgotten about.

Bessie righted herself, her face grim. 'You, in,' she hissed, stepping into the street to allow them inside. 'I think the two of you've got some explainin' to do.' She tutted loudly and turned to Grace. 'I dunno. I need eyes in the back of me 'ead wi' my lot. 'Cos as sure as me name's Bessie Rudney, I know them kids 'ave been up to no good.'

Grace bit her lip to hide her mirth. 'I'll see you soon, Mrs Rudney.'

Bessie nodded. 'I'll look forward to it.' She stepped back inside the house. 'And if you hear screamin', ignore it. It's only me committing blue murder,' she shouted before she slammed shut the door.

Arriving back at her own house Grace quickly let herself in. The acrid stench of burning filled the air and she froze. The oven was still on and the oxtail casserole inside was burned to a cinder. Controlling her anger, she scraped the tin clear of what she could and filled it with water, hoping that it was not ruined as well as the dinner.

As she placed the kettle on the stove and lit the gas beneath it the door opened and Bernard strode through. Without a glance in her direction he took off his cap, walked through to the living room and sat down in the chair.

She stood for a moment, then followed him through, busying herself at the table. 'Your tea won't be long,' she said lightly.

His silence unnerved her as intended. Finally he spoke, slow and clear.

'It isn't my tea I'm concerned about, Grace, it's what happened about me dinner.'

She shuddered at his tone. Taking a deep breath, she turned to face him, clasping her hands. 'I'm sorry I wasn't here to see to you, Bernard, but your dinner was all ready to dish up.'

He rose from his chair and loomed menacingly over at her. 'But that's your job, not mine. I work in that factory to buy the food for you to dish up, remember? Or have you conveniently forgotten?' He narrowed his eyes and glared at her. 'Where were you, Grace?'

She gulped, mind racing frantically as it searched for a plausible excuse for her unauthorised absence. Slowly she lifted her head and stared straight up at him. Be damned, she thought angrily. Why should I make excuses and lie for doing nothing wrong? Damn him for making me feel like a criminal. 'I've been with Mrs Rudney,' she said boldly.

'I see,' he replied, shaken for a moment at the assertive tone of her voice. 'And being with that woman is more important than seeing to your husband, is it?'

Grace fought to stop her legs shaking, her momentary feeling of bravado draining from her. She fought to hold on to it. 'In this case, yes, it was, Bernard. The poor woman has had a dreadful shock and I spent the afternoon comforting her. Her sons have joined up, you see.'

He thrust his face into hers. 'I know what those two have done, all right. It's all over the factory what the Rudney boys have done. Right little heroes. Mr Janson himself even made the announcement. Well, they didn't give a thought to who's going to do their work while they're off adventuring, did they?'

She froze. She knew Bernard to be selfish, but in view of the circumstances this was carrying things too far. For once she couldn't keep her feelings to herself. He was wrong to be acting like this. She raised her head. 'Adventuring! Oh, Bernard, I hardly feel that risking life and limb could be called "adventuring". Besides, you've always said the Rudney lads have never done a day's work since they've been apprenticed at Janson's. I would've thought you'd be glad they're going.'

Bernard's face glowed red in anger. 'Don't you back answer me, Grace Wilkins.'

She clasped her hands even tighter. 'I wasn't. I was just stating a fact. You're always saying they should be got rid of. Well, now you've got your wish, Bernard. Only Mrs Rudney isn't of your mind. After all, they are her children. She was in a right state and I couldn't turn my back on her. I'm sorry you went hungry, but all you had to do was dish it up.'

His chest heaved in temper. 'Oh, I didn't go hungry, Grace,

far from it. I had a meal at the pub and right tasty it was too. I shall be docking the price of it from your housekeeping.'

She gawped. 'But that's not fair, Bernard. I hardly cope on the money you give me as it is.'

He smiled condescendingly. 'You should have thought of that before you went galivanting off to do your do gooding. You're a married woman, Grace Wilkins. You've got your own commitments to honour before anything else. But to my mind you can't even meet them properly, let alone advise neighbours on how to handle their problems.' He stopped for breath and stared down at her. Worry assailed him. His wife had dared to speak out. She had never done that before. It was that Rudney woman. She was putting ideas into Grace's head. Well, he would have to put a stop to that nonsense before it went any further and he had the perfect way of doing so. The only problem was that he himself didn't really want to resort to it for his own reasons. But then, he couldn't have his wife getting out of control.

He decided to issue a warning first.

He leaned forward and stabbed a finger into her shoulder. 'If this kind of thing happens again, I'm going to do something I should have done a long time ago. So be warned.' He spoke coldly.

She shuddered. 'Do? Do what?'

He smirked. 'You'll see.' He turned from her, sat down in the armchair, picked up the newspaper and shook it out. He looked over at her. 'Well? Is a starving man going to get anything to eat or what?' he asked sarcastically.

Chapter Six

October 1939 blasted in furiously and put an abrupt end to
the long lazy heat wave. Winter clothes were hurriedly
unpacked and smoke billowed continually from chimneys.
Steaming washing hung from cradles suspended from kitchen
ceilings and condensation dripped from already damp walls.
For the majority of the women of the city the six monthly
nightmare had begun. Thousands of men were preparing for
battle in Europe but the fight for warmth and food in hungry
bellies was the one being waged at home.

For the City of Leicester the war raging in Europe had still
not fully been felt. The expected aid raids had not transpired
and a few people had stopped bothering to trek to the shelters
during the nightly warnings. If they were going to die then
best do it in the comfort of their own beds, was the feeling.
The cumbersome gas masks at first religiously carried everywhere were now defiantly left at home. The only visible
evidence that anything was amiss was the steady stream of
men boarding troop trains heading for training camps, leaving behind distraught loved ones, and the arrival of another
ten thousand evacuees who once again found a welcome and
a home with the residents of the city and surrounding areas.

Many people were starting to hope that Leicester, because
of its location in the heart of England, might escape the
attention of the Luftwaffe. Dance hall managers rubbed their

hands as, regardless of the blackouts, a steady stream of pleasure-seeking customers began to drift back into their establishments once more.

But despite the lack of any real evidence of war in their district the people of Leicester did not rest on their laurels, breathing sighs of relief, but wholeheartedly threw all their energy into supporting the war effort.

Factories that had once dressed the fashionable turned to producing parachutes and forces clothing; vehicle manufacturers to munitions and weaponry; wireless producers to radar. The Land Army was formed and women, unused to manual work, rolled up their sleeves, grabbed their tools and began to dig, sow and harvest, feed animals and husband them, always willing, always with a smile.

For Bernard Wilkins, the upsurge of patriotic feeling did nothing but kindle contempt within him. But more alarming than anything for him was the change he was witnessing within his wife. He could not quite put his finger on what was causing this change, but felt deep down it had something to do with the Rudney woman. He did not welcome it and felt threatened. For over twenty years he had controlled Grace easily, but that was no longer the case. He knew if he wasn't to lose control he would have to be very vigilant and harsh in his treatment of her.

A chilly morning saw him huddled over his workbench, slowly grinding away at a piece of metal that, when finally finished, would become part of the firing mechanism for a heavy artillery gun. The piece of work did not interest him, its end use did not concern him, his mind was filled only with thoughts of escape from his inevitable call up.

He turned and glowered at the Rudney boys, beavering away at their machines. They were just waiting for instructions to report to the training camp, but regardless, their pride in their work would be carried through until the last.

'Put some more coke on the stove,' he grumbled gruffly. 'Thought it was your job to watch it. Any lower and it'll be gone out. Bloody wasters,' he hissed under his breath.

He turned back and missed the two-fingered gesture offered by Barry.

From the corner of his eye, Bernard glanced scathingly at the younger man sitting adjacent, concentrating fully on his task in hand. He sighed with irritation. The man had been given the job that should have been Bernard's. When old man Grimble had retired, the position of Foreman of the Grinding Section should automatically have passed to himself. Instead, Janson had offered it to Frank Wilby, a man half his age, hardly out of his apprenticeship. In Bernard's mind this act was unforgivable. Not only was he conscious of the sniggers behind his back, but by Wilby's promotion his own one saving grace of being acclaimed a key worker in the company, and therefore ineligible for fighting, was taken from him.

He mulled over this problem very carefully and gradually the spark of an idea began to form. If Wilby went, the job of Foreman would become vacant. Because of enlistment there was no other man left working in the factory capable of handling it. Only Bernard himself. Janson would have no other choice. Grinding was not a job learned overnight. It was specialised.

His eyes glinted in satisfaction. He had his answer. It had been a long time coming, but answer he had. He just had to make sure it worked.

He waited until the Rudney boys were out of earshot then turned to Frank, eyeing the young man for a second before he spoke. 'How's Mrs Wilby?' he asked casually.

Frank turned and looked at him suspiciously. Never had Wilkins asked after his wife. 'She's . . . er . . . fine, thanks. And your wife?' he asked automatically out of courtesy.

'Grace? Oh, bearing up. She's not happy about me joining up but as I told her, I have to do my bit for King and Country. Not gonna have anybody labelling me a shirker.'

Frank gawped. 'You! Joined up? Mr Janson's not said anything. And shouldn't you have told me? I'm yer foreman.'

'I'm telling yer now. I was keeping it as a nice surprise.' He held up the piece of metal he was working on and made a great show of inspecting every minute detail. He slotted it back into place inside the machine. 'What about yerself?'

'Me?'

'Yes. When a' you gonna do the decent thing?'

'Oh! Oh, well, I talked it over with Mr Janson and he says I'm a key worker, see. Says I can't be spared. To be honest, I was relieved. Not that I'm against doing my bit,' he said hastily, 'but with Hilda 'aving so much trouble carrying the baby . . . Well, I'll still be with her, won't I, when the time comes.'

Bernard laughed scornfully. 'He's a clever bastard is our Philip Janson. Key worker indeed! He's fooled you good and proper. Kept you stringing along just as he intended.'

Wilby frowned. 'What d'yer mean?'

Bernard turned fully round on his stool, giving him his full attention. 'I happen to know through Gladys his secretary that he's already got someone lined up to do your job when you go. Grimble's coming back at half the pay, only the silly beggar broke his leg so can't start for another few weeks.'

Frank laughed wryly. 'Don't be daft! Grimble's just about ready to croak.'

'Ah, old Grimble might be, but young Grimble ain't. Didn't you know about young Grimble? He used to work here years ago alongside his old man, then left for pastures new. Well, them pastures didn't turn out to be quite so green and what with the war and everything, he's back. Janson got wind and snapped him up. He's well in his fifties so too old to fight. He's right glad of the work, I can tell yer, and the pay's better than nothing at all. And as for all the other jobs . . . women are gonna be hired and trained, they say. Again on a lot less pay.' He grinned. 'So bob's yer uncle. Everyone's happy. 'Cept you, a'course. You're out on yer ear. Same as me, I expect. Only I ain't gonna give him the satisfaction.'

Frank shook his head. 'You're talking a load of twaddle, Wilkins. Mr Janson would never do that kind of thing. He's a gentleman.'

'Gentleman, is he?' Bernard scoffed. 'Then how come your name's top of the list the War Office sent for names of eligible men working here that could be spared for duty?'

Again Frank shook his head in disbelief. 'No, I don't believe yer. Anyway, the likes of you would never get to see a list like that. Them sorta things are private.'

'Private a' they? Not to someone who's "friendly" with Janson's secretary.' He winked knowingly. 'If yer know what I mean? Actually being truthful, I don't think she intended me to see it. I'd slipped up to see her when Janson went out earlier and while we were . . . chatting, the telephone rang. I just happened to glance at what she was typing when she was answering it.'

Frank stared at him blankly for several moments, trying to remember when Wilkins had slipped away from his work-station. He couldn't have gone without asking. But then he must have if he had seen the list. He grimaced. 'And my name was top of the list, yer say?'

Bernard crossed his heart. 'Should God strike me dead. I do not lie.' He smiled inwardly. Frank Wilby was taking the bait, but he had better make doubly sure. 'You're not the only one that's been taken in by him. There's plenty others. He sacked three blokes once for daring to ask for their rights. All with young families and nothing else coming in.'

Frank frowned deeply. 'Mr Janson did that! Why?'

'They only wanted their pay made up to what others doing the same job were getting, that's all. Janson laughed at them and had them thrown off the premises.'

'No!' Frank spat, comradeship with his fellow workers surfacing.

'He got rid of my wife too. Well, she wasn't my wife then, just my fiancee. But he got rid of her all the same. Put her on a job she couldn't cope with until in the end I made her leave for her own sanity. She ain't worked since. Lost her confidence, see.'

'Why? Why would Janson do that?'

''Cos he's got a grudge against me, that's why.'

That was true, Frank thought. Janson's loathing for Wilkins was legendary. But as all this had transpired before he had joined the company, he had not known the true reason why. He took his chance to find out.

'Why does he bear a grudge?'

Bernard lowered his head, eyes filled with mock sorrow. 'Because of his daughter.'

'Daughter? I didn't know he had one.'

'Oh, yes. He's got a daughter all right. Mrs Cecily Hammerton. Only before she became Mrs Hammerton, she fell for me. Got it really bad, she had, and I returned the favour. Good-looking woman was Cecily Janson. Still is as far as I know.'

'What happened?' Frank asked.

'Janson put a stop to it, that's what. I wasn't good enough for his only daughter, was I? Me, a lowly factory worker. He threatened me with the sack and said if I didn't get out of her life he'd make sure I never worked again and Cecily would be disowned.' He shrugged his shoulders helplessly. 'Well, what could I do? I had my old mother to support and poor Cecily would lose her inheritance. I had no alternative but to agree. Broke both our hearts it did. Next thing I knew was that my poor Cecily had been forced to marry the son of an old family friend and had moved up to somewhere in Yorkshire. They've got a mill.' Bernard glanced quickly at Frank who was looking very thoughtful. A discreet smile of satisfaction hovered on his lips. 'Then there was the other business . . .' He paused, frantically searching for another plausible lie. He was saved by the sight of Gladys's shapely body making for the stairs across the other side of the factory. Knowing he held Frank's attention, he winked broadly and waved his fingers in an intimate greeting.

Frank turned and saw her ascending the stairs. He looked back at Bernard. It must all be true, he thought angrily. Bernard had to be on more than friendly terms with Gladys to get away with a gesture like that, and what about those stories he'd just told? No one could make up tales like that.

'Course, you can always ask Janson yourself about the list,' Bernard continued. He paused, narrowed his eyes and folded his arms across his chest. 'But personally I wouldn't give him the satisfaction. He's had things his own way for far too long, has Mr Janson. It's about time us workers made a stand.'

Just then the clerk from the despatch office poked her head out of the door and bellowed across the drone of machines. 'Frank. FRANK! Mr Janson wants a word. Can you pop up?'

Bernard's heart thumped madly. Frank could possibly confront Janson and ask to see the list and then it would take only seconds for him to realise that all that had just been said was lies. Janson would also be aware of what Bernard was up to. He had to act, and quick.

'That'll be Janson going to give you the news. Maybe Grimble's recovered enough to take up the job.' He grabbed hold of Frank's arm. 'Don't let him do it to you, Frank. Don't let the bastard walk all over yer like he's done to all the others. Get in before he does.'

Fired up, Frank switched off his machine, jumped up from his stool, ripped off his brown overall, screwed it into a ball and threw it on the floor. 'Yes, I will. I'm gonna go and join up now. Let's see his face when I come back and tell him.' He leaned over and grasped Bernard's hand, shaking it hard. 'Thanks, pal. Thanks for the warning.'

'No need to thank me,' Bernard said, smiling. 'Us workers have to stick together. Now get off before he catches you.'

Frank grabbed his coat from the locker and was gone.

Bernard returned to grinding his piece of metal, congratulating himself on his cleverness.

Ten minutes later Philip Janson appeared at his side. He looked around. 'Where's Frank?'

Bernard raised his eyes. 'Dunno, sir. He grabbed his coat not five minutes ago and shot out. Don't know where to.'

Philip looked puzzled. 'Did he? It's not lunchtime.' He rubbed his hand thoughtfully across his chin. 'Tell him I'd like to see him when he returns. I have scheduling to discuss.' He made to walk away, then stopped and looked intently over Bernard's shoulder. 'Good God, man,' he fumed. 'That order should be ready for shipment by now. You've not even half-finished.'

Bernard's hackles rose. He turned his head and stared straight into Philips's eyes. 'You want it done properly, sir, don't you? These bits are part of a firing mechanism. Wouldn't do to make an error with these, would it, sir? Not when our lads' lives will be depending on them when they're in conflict against the enemy.'

Philip held his temper. 'No. It wouldn't. I'll . . . er . . . see if I can get somebody to help you.'

He turned and strode away.

Bernard stared after him, smiling. From the corner of his eye he caught sight of the Rudney boys who between them were pushing a skipful of metal parts ready for machining. They were laughing at some silly joke.

Bernard scowled. 'Oi, put yer back into it and stop capering about! And put some more coke on the stove, it's bloody freezing in here.'

Barry pulled the skip to a halt and turned to his brother. 'One of these days I'm gonna flatten that bloke, so help me God.'

Dennis nodded. 'And I'll help yer.' He suddenly grinned, his eyes twinkling mischievously. 'He wants more coke on the stove, does he?' He nudged Barry in the ribs. 'Well, come on, brother, let's give the man what he wants.'

Grace lifted the lid on the pan of stew, gave it a stir and turned the gas down a fraction. It smelt delicious, she just hoped that Bernard did not notice that she had had to use ox tail instead of the usual shin beef. Going back into the living room she untied her apron, folded it neatly across the back of a chair and gazed around the room. The table was set, the treacle tart in the oven and the custard powder and sugar just waiting for the boiling milk to be added.

She had nothing else to do today apart from some shopping. Bernard needed some new razor blades and the elastic in his underpants had slackened and wanted replacing. Nothing urgent. Nothing that couldn't wait until tomorrow. But she would get those things today just to have an excuse to leave the house; she would go as soon as he had finished his lunch and returned to work. She would also drop in to see her parents. That should fill her afternoon.

She walked back into the kitchen, lifted the lid of the pan again and gave the stew another stir. Time was hanging heavily and she wished the lunch hour was past so she could get out of the house.

Her ears pricked and she raised her head. She could hear

crying. It was only faint, but someone was crying and it sounded like a child. She pulled on her coat and went out to investigate.

She found Tony huddled in the entry between Miss Smith's and his own house. He was dressed only in a thin shirt, short trousers and a pair of worn down boots with no socks. The sight of his pathetic figure saddened Grace deeply and she squatted down beside him and placed her arm around his shoulder.

'Tony,' she said softly, 'what's the matter, my love?'

He raised a grubby tear-streaked face and shuddered. 'I've locked meself out. I've lost the key.'

Grace smiled tenderly. So the poor little mite had come home from school and couldn't get in. 'Well, that's easy done. I did it myself only the other week,' she lied. 'Why didn't you come and tell me? You can always knock on my door, you know that.' She rose and pulled him gently to his feet. 'Come on. Come and get a warm and something to eat. I bet you're starving.'

He looked up at her, sniffed loudly and nodded.

'Come on then.'

He pulled back from her and instinctively she knew why. He was worried Bernard was around. 'It's all right, Tony. I'm in on my own at the moment and I would welcome your company.'

He instantly relaxed and held out his hand. She led him towards her house where, after washing his face and hands, she sat him at the table and placed a plate of piping hot stew and potatoes in front of him.

She sat down opposite and watched him tuck in hungrily, wiping his plate clean with a piece of bread. He pushed his plate away and drank noisily from his mug of tea. Finished, he looked across at her and beamed, showing gaps where his front teeth had fallen out.

'Thanks, missus, that were lovely.'

'My pleasure.' Grace felt a warm glow. It felt nice to have her food so much appreciated. She studied him for a moment. He looked so ragged and uncared for, her heart went out to him. 'Where's your coat, Tony? Did you leave it at school?'

His head jerked up in alarm, then dropped as he stared intently at his empty plate. 'Haven't bin to school,' he muttered.

'You haven't?'

He shook his head. 'Jessie says it ain't worth it. Reckons we ain't gonna be here long enough.'

'Oh! Oh, I see.' She paused for a moment, choosing her words carefully. 'Where is Jessie, Tony?'

'Down the market. Gone to see if she can get a job.'

'And your mother? Is she in bed?'

He nodded. 'She goes mad if we wake 'er. She needs her sleep, see. So I daren't knock on the door.' He rubbed his hand under his nose. 'Jessie told me not to go out and I wasn't to answer the door 'case the school man came round.' He raised his head and looked at her worriedly. 'But I had to go to the privy. I couldn't hold it no longer. I locked the door like she telt me but the key fell out me pocket and down a crack in the slabs and I can't get it out.' His eyes filled with tears. 'I'm gonna be in trouble, ain't I?'

Grace shook her head. 'No, no, Tony, don't worry. Things like this happen.' She scraped back her chair, stood up and held out her hand. 'Come on. Let's see if we can get that key.'

He jumped from his chair, grabbed her hand and smiled up at her gratefully.

With the aid of a piece of wire the key was prised from between a deep crack in the slabs. Tony held it to him lovingly.

'Ta, missus. I won't get in trouble now, will I?'

'What's goin' on?'

They both raised their heads to see Jessie standing in the toilet doorway, her childish face thunderous. Straightening up, Grace saw her shiver as the icy cold whipped through her thin cotton dress. Her hands were thrust deep into the pockets of her holey cardigan and her shoulders were hunched. Like her brother's, her laceless boots were worn down and a sockless toe was peeping out.

'It's all right, Jessie. Tony had an accident. He dropped the key . . .'

Jessie grabbed hold of his hand and wrenched him to her. 'I told you, didn't I? I told you not to leave the house,' she said angrily.

'It's all right, Jessie,' Grace soothed. 'He just had an accident, that's all. Look . . . would you like to come to my house and have something to eat and a warm? I have a pan of stew all ready.'

Jessie's mouth watered at the thought. She had been out since early that morning badgering the market traders for any kind of work, but with no luck. They had all wanted to know her age and why she wasn't at school. She remembered the stale loaf of bread on the table and the tiny scrape of marge left in the wrapper. Her mother had been in a foul mood for the last couple of days and hadn't handed over any money and Jessie dared not ask her for any.

She worried for an instant how her mother would react when she rose later and found nothing to eat or any coal with which to light a fire. Oh, but the invitation to a plate of stew sounded so inviting. Her stomach grumbled loudly. But instead of accepting the invitation like she wanted, she raised her head stubbornly and tightened her mouth. She wasn't going to be beholden to anybody.

'No fanks,' she said sharply. 'We can feed ourselves, ta very much.'

Grace's heart sank. She knew the child was hungry but pushing her would only make her grow more distant.

She smiled. 'As you wish. But should you change your mind, my offer still stands.'

Jessie looked at her blankly, turned and pulled Tony down the yard. Grace followed, meaning to return to her own house.

As they approached the back door and Grace the gate, the door was yanked open and a dishevelled Madge Cotting stood on the doorstep, pulling her dressing gown tighter round her shapely body. She reached inside her pocket and pulled out a packet of cigarettes. She lit one and dragged hungrily on it, surveying the scene before her as she did so.

'What's going on?' she snapped.

Grace eyed her tentatively. The last thing she wanted to do was get the children in trouble with their mother. 'Young Tony locked himself out that's all, Mrs Cotting.'

Madge eyed her son and daughter sharply and moved aside. 'Get in, both of you. Fancy causin' our neighbours trouble.' As the children shot past, she smiled sweetly at Grace. 'Kids! I dunno. Can't turn your back for five minutes.'

'It was no bother,' Grace responded. 'Any time I can be of help, please let me know.'

'Thanks, Mrs Wilkins. I might take you up on that.'

Grace deliberated for a moment then commented: 'Er . . . Mrs Cotting, the children haven't been to school. Did you know? Only the Board Man will soon get wind and be round.'

Madge planted a look of surprise on her face. 'Ain't they? Little buggers. Don't worry, I'll sort it.'

Grace smiled tightly. There was something about this woman she couldn't quite fathom and didn't quite like. She pulled the gate open. 'I'll leave you to see to the children then.'

Thoughtfully Grace made her way home and Madge

walked inside her house, slamming the door shut.

She stared at the children standing hesitantly by the empty fireplace. Without a word she lowered herself down on a chair at the table and drew deeply on her cigarette.

'Mum . . .' Jessie hesitantly began.

'Don't start,' she snapped. 'I ain't in no mood for none of your lies. Just get me a cuppa.' She shivered, put her cigarette into her mouth and pulled her thin dressing gown tighter around her body. 'It's bloody freezing in here. Why ain't the fire lit?'

Jessie gulped. 'There ain't any coal, Mum, or tea.'

Madge sighed heavily. There hadn't been much in the first place so she wasn't surprised to be told they had run out. But knowing her light-fingered daughter who possessed her own cunning ways she had thought the lack of provisions would not be a problem. She ran her fingers through her matted hair. Things hadn't been going as well as she had thought they would. Avril's idea might not be the money maker first envisaged. Her clients had dwindled alarmingly. People were tightening their belts even further as this war deepened. The couple of pounds in her purse wouldn't go far. Regardless of whether she had clients or not she still had to pay the rent on her room. And she needed that new dress . . .

Her eyes misted over as a vision of Jacky rose before her. Oh, but he was handsome. He had money too. She daren't ask how he acquired it, knowing instinctively the source wasn't exactly honest. But money was money in her mind, however it was gained.

She had met him quite by accident. Fed up with waiting for a knock on the door of the room she rented, she had gone over to the pub for a quick slug of gin to boost her morale. She liked her gin. If given a choice between her fags and her gin, she would face a real dilemma. Just as she had been about to leave, Jacky had come over to her and offered her a drink.

She had accepted, but not before she had made a great point of letting him know she wasn't used to being picked up. But since he looked a decent type, she would just have the one.

She hadn't told him what she was doing for a living, or about the kids. He must never find out about the kids. That would really put him off. He was taking her out tomorrow night for dinner then on to a night club. It was a long time since she had been taken out on what she would term a proper date and she knew if she played her hand properly she could land him. They were both each other's type in more ways than one. But there was one nagging problem that could scupper the whole evening. She had nothing decent to wear. She didn't even have to make a decision. The money in her purse went towards a new outfit. The kids would survive by some means or other.

She turned her head and looked towards the children waiting expectantly. 'I ain't got anyfing, Jessie love. Go and see what you can scrounge off that nice Mrs Wilkins. Ask her for a bucket of coal and a spoon of tea.' She rose and made for the stairs. 'Tell her I'll sort her out at the end of the week when I get paid. Now I'm off back to bed.'

Jessie pouted. 'Do I have to, Mum?' She wouldn't admit it but she liked Mrs Wilkins and the thought of begging filled her with shame.

The resigned look on her mother's face gave her her answer. Still grasping Tony's hand, Jessie sullenly left the room.

Back in her own house, Grace hurriedly cleared away the evidence of Tony's visit. She had just finished when the door opened and Bernard walked through. Without a word he took off his outdoor clothes, swilled his hands under the tap and sat down at the table.

She put a plate of stew and potatoes in front of him along with two thick slices of bread.

'Had a good morning?' she asked lightly, sitting down opposite and raising her knife and fork.

'The usual,' he grunted back. He was preoccupied with thoughts of Frank Wilby. He wouldn't be happy until he had heard from the man himself that he had successfully joined up. Only then could he rest easier. He swallowed a mouthful of food, looked down at his plate, then glared over her. 'What's this muck?' he hissed.

Grace put down her fork. 'It's stew, Bernard. I couldn't get the usual shin beef so I had to settle for ox tail.'

He pushed his plate away. 'What? All the butchers in the area sold out, had they?'

Grace held her breath. The stew was delicious. As usual he was just being awkward.

'I had to take what I could get, Bernard. Please don't let it get cold.'

'Cold or hot, I can't eat that.' He looked disdainfully at his plate. 'It ain't fit for pigs, ain't that.'

Grace forced a forkful down as a feeling of apprehension rose. Why did he have to be like this? What pleasure did he get from it all? Why couldn't they just enjoy their meal together like any other family?

He grabbed at a slice of bread from a plate in the middle of the table, slapped on a chunk of butter and spread vigorously, causing the bread to break up. 'Fine thing, ain't it? Work like a navvy all morning and come home to slops.' He looked across at her patronisingly. 'It ain't much to ask, Grace, to come home to a decent dinner. Twenty years of cooking and you still can't do it right.'

She held her breath. He was waiting for her response, willing her to back answer him so he would have the excuse he needed to have a go at her.

She was saved by the back door opening and Charlie charging through. She dropped her gas mask on the floor and flopped down at the table, face wreathed in excitement.

Grace had never been so glad to see her daughter. She scraped back her chair and stood up.

'What a nice surprise, Charlie. It's not often you get home for dinner. Have you time for some stew? It'll save me hotting it up for you later.'

Charlie smiled appreciatively. 'Please, Mum. It smells wonderful.'

'Might smell it,' Bernard grumbled as he took a bite of bread. 'Tasting's another matter.'

Charlie ignored his remark. 'I've come home to tell you the news.'

Grace put a full plate in front of her daughter and looked at her enquiringly. 'News?' she asked, sitting down again.

'I've got a job in a munitions factory. I start on Monday.'

Bernard froze and glared at his daughter angrily. 'That you ain't, my girl. You already have a job in the offices at the Co-op.'

'Yes, and I've hated every minute of it. But that's not why I left. I want to do my bit, and working in munitions *is* doing my bit.'

'You should have discussed this with me first.'

Charlie lowered her fork. 'Why, Dad? What I do for a living is my decision. As long as you get my board money, which I've never failed to give you.'

Grace picked up the tea pot. 'Bernard, another cup?' she asked, trying to defuse the situation.

Ignoring her, he scraped back his chair and stood up, laying his large hands flat on the table. 'While you live in my house, what you do is my business. You're under age for a start.'

Charlie laid down her fork. 'Only by a few months.' She narrowed her eyes. 'If making my war effort is going to be a problem for you, Father,' she said icily, 'I'll just leave home.'

Grace's face fell in alarm. 'No, Charlie, no!' she cried, and looked at Bernard beseechingly. 'Bernard, please. We should be proud Charlie is doing her bit. Now please, please, let's finish our dinner.'

His face reddened angrily. He opened his mouth to speak but a noise from outside grabbed his attention. He turned and stared out of the window leading on to the yard. Like lightning, he shot out of the door.

Grace and Charlie looked blankly at each other then hurriedly rose and followed him.

A yelp was heard. Bernard, his face triumphant, emerged from the coal shed pulling Jessie along by her ear.

'Caught her red-handed I did. Stealing our coal!' He let go of her ear and bent down, thrusting his face into hers. 'That's right, ain't it? You were stealing our coal? You thief!' He turned to Charlie. 'Go and fetch the constable.'

Grace shot forward and gathered the girl to her, her mind racing frantically. 'Bernard, she wasn't stealing the coal. I said she could have it.'

Charlie moved to her mother's side. 'She did, Dad. I was there when she said it.'

Bernard glared at his wife. 'You what! You said she could help herself to my coal?'

Grace's back stiffened. 'Yes, I did. They haven't got any, Bernard. The house is freezing. Her mother will repay it when the coal man's been.'

He froze. He was outnumbered here and he knew it. He also strongly suspected that Grace and Charlie were lying. He felt the urge to explode at Grace for going behind his back, but quickly decided to temper his tone. He had an audience. He stared down at the child looking defiantly back at him, then turned to Grace. 'That was a silly thing to do. Why, we've hardly enough for ourselves.' Hard eyes turned to Jessie. 'I don't know what my wife was thinking of when she told yer to help yerself. I'm sure the coal merchant will help you out if you go round and see him. And that way there won't be any need to pay us back, will there? Now off you go.'

Jessie broke free from Grace and shot off. Bernard stared at his wife. 'It's all very well trying to be charitable Grace, but I draw the line at us going without.' He turned, strode into the house, grabbed his coat and made his way out of the front door, slamming it hard behind himself.

Charlie turned to her mother but before she could speak Grace held up her hand, shivering as a blast of icy wind cut through her clothes. 'Don't, Charlie. Please don't say a word.'

Respecting her wish, Charlie sighed heavily and together they walked into the house.

Inside she turned to her mother. 'Mam, you are pleased for me about the job, aren't you?'

Grace planted a smile on her face and slid her arm around her daughter's shoulder. 'Yes, of course I am. You'll enjoy it. And all those new people you'll meet.' She paused and searched her face. 'But please, no more talk of leaving, eh, love?'

Charlie shook her head. 'No, all right. But I can't promise I won't if he goes at me like that again. You might have to put up with it, Mam, but I don't.'

Back at work, Bernard wiped beads of sweat from his brow. He was all hot and bothered with worry. Frank had still not returned and Bernard could not for the life of him think what was keeping the man. For God's sake, how long did it take to do the business and get back to break the news of his heroic action? Once that had happened, he himself could relax, safe in the knowledge that he could sit out this war without fear of reprisals for his lack of a uniform.

Sweat dripped down the sides of his face and on to his oily brown overalls. He was obviously more worried than he gave himself credit for, or else he was sickening for something. His back felt as though it was on fire. It was freezing cold outside, but to Bernard it felt as though he was sitting in the middle of the Sahara Desert at noon dressed for Arctic conditions. He would be glad when this business was all settled and he could get back to normal.

A scream of terror shook him rigid and he spun round to see Gladys, armed with the wages box, standing to one side of him and staring wildly across the factory floor. He turned further in the direction she was staring.

Bernard's jaw dropped in disbelief and his eyes bulged in sheer horror. He leapt up from his stool and flattened his back against his workbench.

The stove, several feet away, was glowing molten red.

His eyes travelled the length of the pipe which ran upwards and through the wooden roof. The whole lot, apart from about a foot at the top, was glowing red. He stifled a scream of fright. The whole lot looked ready to explode. Regardless of whether it did or not, the roof was in danger of catching fire and if it did, the factory could end up as cinders.

On hearing Gladys's scream, Philip Janson, who had been inspecting some documents in the despatch office, came running. Spotting the stove he stopped abruptly, shocked. Gathering his wits, he turned to Bernard. 'For God's sake, don't just stand there, man! Get some buckets of water. We'll have to climb on the roof and empty it down the pipe. Quick, before the roof catches fire!' He spun round to Gladys. 'Go and telephone the fire brigade.'

Two hours later, the fire brigade having done their job and the factory floor still being mopped clear of several thousand gallons of water, an angry Philip Janson faced Bernard Wilkins across his desk.

'Don't blame the Rudney boys, Wilkins. According to them they were only following instructions from you.'

Red-faced and tight-lipped, Bernard narrowed his eyes. 'I didn't tell 'em to climb on the roof and fill the chimney stack with coke.'

Philip shook his head. 'Wilkins, have you never been young?' he hissed. 'Your constant complaints of feeling the cold and telling them to bank the stove put the idea into their heads. To them it was a bit of fun. They didn't stop to think of the consequences.'

'Oh, and I'm supposed to stand over them all the time, am I? It ain't my fault if they ain't got the sense they were born with. And by the way, Mr Janson, I'm not the Foreman. You gave that job to Frank Wilby. Only he ain't here, is he? Some Foreman who just ups and offs without warning,' Bernard added sharply.

Philip clenched his fists in anger. If this tale was being related to him by another he would have laughed, seeing the incident as extremely funny. He could just imagine the Rudney boys climbing on the roof and tipping several buckets of coke down the stack, laughing themselves silly. But he knew their foolish actions had only been taken as a direct result of Wilkins' continual sniping. Fed up, they had decided to get their own back on him. He couldn't blame them really. But the consequences had nearly been the end of his factory, and Wilkins was right – where was Frank Wilby? It was so out of character for the man just to walk out like that. A more conscientious worker Philip had never come across. He was deeply worried, knowing there must be a very good reason for Wilby's actions.

He inhaled deeply. 'Just go, Wilkins, get out of my sight. But be warned. If anything like this happens again I shall not be so lenient. I look to the older employees to guide the young apprentices. Remember, they're human beings, here to learn a trade – not to be used as skivvies at your beck and call. In future, if coke needs putting on the stove, you're just as capable of doing it as they are.'

Bernard stared at him coldly, then turned on his heel and left the room.

Philip shook his head. If Frank Wilby had been here this wouldn't have happened. Thank God he had had the foresight to give him the job of Foreman and not Wilkins. Wilkins couldn't organise a Sunday school picnic without upsetting everybody. His manner towards his fellows left a lot to be desired.

For a fleeting moment he thought of Grace and guilt for her situation rose within him. He still could not help but feel responsible for her marriage to Wilkins and wondered worriedly how she had fared living with such a man for the last twenty odd years.

He remembered fondly the pretty and intelligent sixteen year old who had sat before him; the one thought highly of by the rest of the staff; the one with a very promising future had she been allowed to pursue it; the one he had tried his hardest to sway from associating with Wilkins.

Sadness at his failure had lasted for many years after he knew they had married. Philip felt entirely to blame. He firmly believed Wilkins had turned his attentions on Grace in direct retaliation after the showdown regarding Cecily, and due to her youthfulness and inexperience Grace had not been able to see his true nature until it was too late and the deed was done.

Philip sighed deeply. He supposed that, like himself, she

had just got on with things and shouldered her responsibilities. He had seen that quality in her many times whilst she had been working for him.

His eyes settled momentarily on the picture of his own wife that sat on his desk: a handsome woman with a determined chin. In some respects his life had not been as happy as he would have wished. Events beyond his control in his youth had shaped his future. He did know something of what Grace must have gone through, the difference being she had been in love with Wilkins when she had married him. The circumstances surrounding his own marriage were entirely different.

He had never loved Katherine the way a man should. The only woman he had loved, for whatever reason, had walked out on him and he still did not understand why she had done so. Nearly forty years later he felt the pain, but not quite so intensely as once he had. For a moment he wondered just how she had fared, how she was, what she was doing. But mainly if she was happy.

His head jerked up as Gladys came into the office carrying a cup of tea. She smiled at him warmly.

'Thought yer could do wi' this, Mr Janson.'

He returned a grateful smile. 'Thank you, Gladys. You'll make someone a good wife.'

Before she departed she gazed momentarily at the handsome man who did not look his sixty years despite his iron grey head of hair and the tired lines around his kindly brown eyes. I could have made you a lovely wife if only you weren't already married, she thought sadly. She didn't like Katherine Janson one little bit, thought her a haughty bitch. But bitch or not, she doubted such a man as Philip Janson would ever have looked in her own direction. She was just Gladys the efficient secretary; she wasn't supposed to have any interest in her boss outside working hours.

As she closed his door, she collided with the woman in her thoughts: Katherine Janson.

She glared at Gladys disdainfully. 'You really should look where you're going, Gladys. I cannot abide clumsiness.'

Without further ado she pushed open her husband's door and glided through.

'Hello, darling. I thought I'd get a lift home with you. Tea at The Grand was not up to its usual standard, but I suppose I shouldn't complain in the circumstances. Anyway, Muriel Hotten-Smythe and myself have decided to form a committee. We're going to organise parcels for the boys at the front. Knitted things and what not. What do you think, darling?'

Philip looked across at her, surprised. 'That's an excellent idea,' he said lightly. 'Anything that makes life a little easier and lets our lads know that we back home are behind them, can't be a bad idea.' But for the life of him he could not see his wife knitting.

Katherine was a pampered lady right down to her delicate Nottingham lace gloves. A woman who would faint at the thought of having to make a cup of tea for herself. He couldn't blame her. She had been brought up surrounded by doting monied parents and servants who had catered for her every whim. She was a woman who was used to getting her own way over everything. If she didn't everyone suffered, one way or another.

Philip watched her thoughtfully as she peeled off her gloves and sat gracefully down in the chair to the side of his desk, crossing her still shapely legs. This war, he knew, was going to have a profound effect on his wife in more ways than one. For a start, the people who waited on her, whether it be at home or serving tea in hotels, were not going to be around. They would be doing their bit for the war. How was she going to take to having to fend for herself? Not kindly, he knew. But she'd have to learn as would the rest of her gentried friends.

He ran his fingers through his hair. 'I shan't be able to leave here for a while yet, Katherine. We had a catastrophe today and one of my foremen has gone missing.'

She pouted generous pink-painted lips. 'Oh, darling, surely not? I've asked the Brodericks over for a game of bridge, and you haven't forgotten Cecily and the family are arriving tomorrow? Let the people you pay sort things out.'

Philip hid his dismay. He could not stand the pompous Brodericks whose main topic of conversation was the gradual decline of the upper classes. The thought of spending a night in their company, watching them stuff down expensive food that would feed a family of his workers for a week, sickened him. But he was looking forward to seeing his daughter and grandchildren and that thought lightened his mood. 'I can't leave just yet, Katherine. Don't forget that half my experienced staff have joined up. I've hardly anyone capable left to whom I can delegate responsibility.' He rose and walked round, placing his hand on her shoulder. 'I'll be home tonight as soon as I can. And don't worry about the rest of the weekend. I wouldn't let anything spoil Cecily's visit. We see too little of them as it is.'

She looked up at him, a resigned smile on her face. 'All right, dear, but don't be too late.'

'As soon as I can, I promise.'

Sighing deeply, she pulled on her gloves, rose and kissed him lightly on the cheek.

He watched thoughtfully as she walked out of the room.

Chapter Seven

After Charlie had returned to work and the kitchen had been tidied, Grace stared out of the living-room window distractedly. In her mind's eye she could still picture the scene earlier. Bernard's treatment of the child disgusted her beyond belief. Did he not realise that the family had nothing and that was why the child had resorted to stealing? They themselves hadn't much, but it was a sight more than the poor evacuee family possessed. Would it have hurt him to have spared just a few lumps?

The thought of those poor little mites huddled together inside that cheerless house distressed her deeply. Regardless of her own growing reservations about their mother, she knew she would have to do something for the children. She thought of Bessie who would probably have some old clothes from her own children, or if not, would know where Grace could acquire some. And she would take that bucket of coal. Damn Bernard and his callousness! To cover her tracks, whilst he was out of the house she would keep the fire burning as low as she could without going out. That way he would hopefully never realise what she had done.

She moved away from the window and stood before the mirror hanging over the fireplace, absently tidying several loose tendrils of hair that had escaped from the roll across the nape of her neck. She gazed at her reflection. Since becoming friendly with Bessie her life had become more bearable. The jovial woman and her family were a joy to know, but despite their growing friendship and the void it was helping to fill, for Grace it wasn't enough.

She felt an inner panic rise as she remembered Charlie's desire to do her bit for the war effort. What if her beloved daughter had to move away? What if the major salvation of her life was no longer around to care for and protect? What would she do? How would she cope? She felt a dreadful desire to beg Charlie never to leave her. Demand that she stay at home so she would not be left alone with Bernard. But that was selfish. Charlie had her own life to live. Grace could not ask her daughter to pay for mistakes she herself had made.

She sighed heavily and fingered the fine crow's feet beginning to form around her eyes. It suddenly hit her that life was passing her by. She would be thirty-nine years old very soon, and what had she achieved? According to Bernard, nothing. According to him she wasn't even capable of running her own household without him checking her every move, though she knew deep down he was wrong. She knew if she allowed herself to be honest that he had always striven to make her feel inferior to cover his own inadequacies, to prove her total need of him. She didn't really need him to survive as he always maintained, it was the other way round.

She raised her chin and stroked her neck. The thought of being left with only Bernard filled her with such fear. She needed more. She needed to do something. Something that would make her feel useful and worthwhile. Surely to God even with her limited experience she had something useful to offer? If she could just find out what, living with Bernard might not be so bad.

She felt a flicker of resentment settle. When she had fallen in love and delightedly agreed to marry, she had not envisaged for a moment that her life would amount to nothing more than caring for her husband and the many children she had hoped to have. She had thought they would grow together, develop, and when the children left for homes of their own and they reflected in their old age, they would be proud of their achievements and feel fulfilled.

As things stood now, apart from the raising of Charlie there would be nothing to reflect on, no feeling of fulfilment, and this thought frightened Grace.

She shivered, a cold feeling settling upon her, and suddenly she knew she could not carry on with life the way it was. Today's episode was the last straw. This realisation hit her like a cold slap on the face and she stepped back as though struck.

She felt confused and turned from the mirror, clutching the back of the chair. Why was she feeling like this? Why today? Was it the weather? This war? Was it the worry that soon Charlie might leave? Or was it that she was finally being honest with herself? Regardless of the whys and wherefores, somehow today these concerns that for years she had managed to suppress had surfaced despite herself.

She took a breath and raised her head. The time had come. The time to do something had arrived. She didn't want to leave this world having made no mark, no impression on others' memories other than as that poor woman married to Bernard Wilkins. How she went about altering her situation she did not know. How she summoned the courage to confront Bernard and make her stance she did not know. All she knew was that she herself had to do these things for her own peace of mind.

Grace suddenly felt an inner strength begin to grow and raised her head. She was going to get a job. How she didn't know. What she didn't care. As long as it was a job which would make her feel useful, that she was doing her bit. Bernard, whether he liked it or not, would have to come to terms with the new Grace Wilkins, because regardless of his actions, this time she was not going to back down.

The loud thump on the front door made her jump. She gathered her wits and went to open it.

'Mornin', Mrs Wilkins.' Mr Murray, the Prudential Insurance man, addressed her jovially, doffing his hat. He shuddered with cold and stamped his feet on the icy pavement as he put down his large black briefcase and opened his ledger. 'We're in for a bad 'un this year, mark my words, Mrs Wilkins. I ain't known an October as cold as this for a long time. I'd stock up on coal if I were you.'

Grace grimaced at the mention of coal. 'I'll just get my book.'

She handed over the blue-covered booklet and her shilling and waited patiently as he marked it off. He handed the book back, picked up his briefcase and doffed his hat.

'See yer next week then, Mrs Wilkins.'

''Bye, Mr Murray.'

She made to shut the door but he stopped her. 'Oh, you haven't seen Miss Smith, have you? Only I can't get any reply.'

Grace peered in the direction of her neighbour's house. She frowned. 'She's maybe out or gone away somewhere?'

He shook his head. 'Not Miss Smith. She only goes as far as Vinny's shop, and that's only occasionally. She gets most of her stuff delivered. Even the Bank Manager calls, I've seen 'im.' A worried frown settled on his face. 'I've been collecting her insurance for the last thirty-five years and it's the first time I've ever known her not to be in.'

Grace looked at him thoughtfully. It suddenly struck her how little she knew about her neighbour.

Miss Smith had been in residence long before Grace and

Bernard had arrived. In the early days, the then young Grace had striven to make her acquaintance over the garden wall but all Miss Smith had ever done was nod in reply and hurry back inside her own house. Disappointed, Grace had soon learned to respect the older woman's desire for privacy and long ago stopped asking if there was anything she could do or Miss Smith needed when she was going to the shops.

Now Mr Murray had mentioned it, she realised she hadn't caught sight of Miss Smith for a while.

She raised her eyes, worried. 'I'll pop around and make enquiries.'

Mr Murray smiled. 'Thank you. It'd put me mind at rest. I'm quite fond of the old gel.'

Grace hid a smile. Miss Smith was at least ten years younger than Mr Murray, who was approaching seventy if he was a day. She watched as he walked towards the Rudney house and raised his hand to knock. Before his fist touched the wood the door flew open and Maureen fell out into the street, Bessie's voice bellowing after her.

'When I tell yer to get to the butcher's I don't mean tomorrow, I mean today! And remember, I want a piece of ox tail cut as near to the neck as possible. And a bone for the dog.'

Maureen turned and scowled. 'We ain't gorra dog.'

'We do if yer want soup next week,' Bessie shouted, arriving on the doorstep. She suddenly spotted Mr Murray and folded her flabby arms under her huge bosom. 'Er . . .'ello, Mr Murray. I weren't expectin' you today.' She leaned out of the doorway and waved to Grace. ''Ello, me duck. Comin' in for a cuppa later?' Grace smiled and nodded in acceptance. Bessie turned back to Mr Murray. 'I'll have to square wi' yer next week.'

He shook his head. 'You said that last week, Mrs Rudney.'

'Did I? Well, it ain't next week yet,' she said indignantly.

'I'll square wi' yer then like I said.'

She turned, marched inside her house and shut the door.

Mr Murray shook his head, collected his briefcase and walked off down the street.

Grace chuckled, turned and looked again at number ninety-one, the residence of Miss Smith. She would go and see the older woman. Check if everything was all right. The worst the woman could do was shut the door in her face. Grace suddenly clamped her hand over her mouth in shock. Ida's dinner! With all that had happened she had forgotten all about it.

She shot back inside the house. Her mother-in-law was not going to be pleased about this oversight, regardless of Grace's explanation.

'Oh, ignore the silly so and so!'

'Mother!' Grace gawped in surprise at her own mother's outburst.

'Well, Grace, the woman would try the patience of a saint. She should count herself lucky she has a daughter-in-law like yerself to bother about her.' Connie placed her hands on her bony hips. 'Next time she speaks to you like that, throw the dinner in the bucket and tell her to fend for herself in future. That'll soon shut her up.'

Grace hid a smile. Her mother was right, but then she wouldn't have to bear the reprisals for such an action.

As soon as she had remembered Ida's dinner Grace had rushed round, to be greeted by a torrent of verbal abuse. No amount of explanation on Grace's part would appease the older woman. According to Ida, Grace had left a poor crippled woman starving for days and just wait until her son got to hear! Yes, just wait, Grace thought. He would make a real issue of this. She sighed deeply. 'Any more tea in the pot?' she asked her mother.

Connie grinned. 'For you, me darlin', I'll personally squeeze the tea leaves.'

She picked up Grace's mug and drained the pot, added a measure of milk and two spoons of sugar and gave it a vigorous stir. She pushed the mug towards her daughter and sat down at the table, resting her arms on the top. 'So what else is on yer mind apart from that old crow?'

'Mam!'

'Well, she is. She brings out the worst in me she does. But no more talk of 'er, she ain't worth my breath.' She looked Grace in the eye. 'Well?'

She smiled fondly. 'Never could fool you, could I?'

'Not likely. I've only got to look at your face. So what is it?'

She told her mother about her desire to get a job.

''Bout time, our Grace. You've been stagnating far too long. I've always said you're wasted.' Connie turned and addressed her husband. 'Ain't I, Arthur?' She tutted at the sight of him fast asleep in the armchair. 'He's goin' in early today.' She shook her head. 'That job's getting too much for him, Grace. He'll have to pack it in, before it packs him in.'

Grace frowned deeply. 'He's all right though, ain't he, Mam?'

'Yes, 'course he is,' she replied lightly. She couldn't let her daughter know how worried she was about Arthur. All he seemed to do these days was sleep after his long night shift and he was complaining of pains in his chest. No, she couldn't unburden herself on Grace. The girl had enough on her plate without them adding to her problems. 'Anyway, about this job. Have yer thought what you'd like to do?'

Grace leaned her elbows on the table, clasped her hands tightly and rested her chin against them. 'I don't think it's a case of what I'd like to do, Mam. I think it's more what I'm capable of. And with my limited experience of working, I don't think I've many choices.'

'Don't yer? Oh! I'd a' thought you'd have plenty.'

Grace frowned quizzically. 'Do yer? How come?'

'Well, you got all that experience when you worked at Janson's.'

'Mam, that was over twenty years ago.'

'So? You haven't the kind of brain that forgets things easily, Grace. And besides, with all our men going off to war, women are having to do the work. I read the papers, yer know. Industry's really suffering at the moment. They'll jump at someone like you. Anyway, you won't be the only one applying without experience.'

Grace looked at her thoughtfully. 'No, I won't, will I? There must be many women in my position.'

'I'll say. And being honest, I expect the extra money would come in handy. I know you ain't got it easy, gel.'

Grace smiled. 'We manage, mam. But you're right, the few extra bob could be put to good use.' She jumped up from her seat, rushed round and hugged her mother. 'Mam, I love you. You're a wonderful woman.'

'Yes, I know,' laughed Connie. 'Your father's always saying so.'

Grace kissed her fondly on the cheek. 'What about coming round on Sunday, like you used to? I miss our teas, Mam. The walk ain't that far and you could both take it slowly. Charlie and I could come and meet you.'

Connie reddened, flustered. Her daughter had caught her unawares. She hurriedly began to tidy the table. She had missed the afternoons also, more than she ever dared let on to Grace. She and Arthur would like nothing more than to accept the invitation but after what Bernard had let slip about going without all week to provide the food, neither of them would be able to eat without feeling choked. 'Er . . . that would've been nice, love. But . . . well, let's face it, if you start workin' you'll need all your spare time.'

'Mam, what's to say I'm even going to get a job? And if I did, there's nothing I'd like more than to spend my spare time with you both.'

'Grace,' Connie spoke sharply, 'let's leave things as they are for the time being, eh?'

She nodded reluctantly. 'All right, Mam, you've made your point.' She sighed deeply. 'I'd better be off. I've a few things still to do.'

'Okay, me darlin'. And I 'ope one of them is finding that job. Eh, and don't let anyone put you off.'

'I won't, Mam. Don't worry, I won't. Say cheerio to Dad for me.'

She picked up her bag of shopping and departed.

Arriving at the Rudneys', she rapped on the door. It was yanked open and Bessie pulled her inside.

'Come on out of the cold, Gracie love. I've just mashed.' She poured a pint mug full of thick brewed tea and pushed it across the table.

Grace unbuttoned her coat and sat down. She'd drown in tea soon, she thought, if she drank much more.

'Thanks, Bessie. This is grand.' She relaxed back in her chair. She felt so welcome in Bessie's cluttered kitchen, remnants of the large family scattered about. The remains of dinner were still sitting in the large pot sink by the door and a pile of ironing lay half finished. Hanging from the cradles suspended from the ceiling dripped another load that, when dry, would be added to the lot half done. With her large family to care for, Bessie's work was never finished. But it was a workload she enjoyed. That fact shone from her rotund, red-cheeked face.

Bessie scooped up Bobbie and sat him on her lap. Resting his head on the soft mounds of his mother's huge bosom, Bobbie settled large innocent eyes on Grace and watched her intently as he sucked hard on the dummy in his mouth.

The sight of the child lying content in his mother's lap brought to mind the two evacuee children. 'Bessie,' Grace began. 'Do you happen to have any old clothes of your children's that would fit the two 'vacee children at number eighty-nine?'

Bessie shook her head. 'By the time my kids are finished wi' their clothes, they ain't even fit for the rag and bone man.' She noticed Grace's crestfallen expression. 'Eh, it ain't your job to dress them kids, it's their mother's.'

'I know that, Bessie. But somehow I get the feeling she doesn't bother about them all that much.'

'Huh, well, I've never liked the look of 'er meself. Summat about that woman I can't fathom.'

Grace looked at her keenly. 'Why, Bessie?'

She shrugged her fleshy shoulders. 'I dunno. Just instinct, I suppose. Anyway, if yer that bothered I could ask around for yer. There's always someone with an old frock or two lying about. Mind you, things are gonna get tight, believe me. People are gonna be wearin' their own clothes 'til they fall off their backs. I remember the last war. Me mam had a right job clothing us. And food! God, it wa' a nightmare. What we ended up wearing, rags 'ud 'ave been an improvement.' She paused thoughtfully for a moment. 'Eh, I tell yer, we could always pay a visit to the WVS place down the road. I hear they started collectin' clothes and stuff for the war effort, 'case things get tight.' She chuckled loudly. 'Might even get summat for ourselves, eh?'

'Oh, Bessie, that'd be smashing. I'm sure young Tony hasn't a coat and I'm worried he'll freeze to death.'

'That's settled then. If I can't get n'ote from me pals, we'll visit the WVS. We'll soon get those kiddies sorted out.'

Bessie took a long drink from her mug and placed it down. 'A' yer 'eard about Hilda Wilby?'

Grace shook her head. 'No. What about her?'

'She lost the baby.'

Grace's jaw dropped in shock. 'Oh, no. Poor Hilda. Her and Frank were so desperate for that little mite. What happened?'

'Seems Frank went and joined up and the news so upset Hilda she went into labour. Born dead it was. Poor little sod. Well, she were only seven months gone. It didn't stand a chance, did it?'

Grace grimaced. 'Whatever made Frank do such a thing? Hilda only said the other week as we both waited to be served in Vinny's that Philip Janson told Frank he was a key worker. As such there's no way he'd be allowed to join the forces. Hilda was delighted. She'd been worried sick he'd get his call up papers.' She looked at Bessie quizzically. 'Why would he change his mind? Doesn't make any sense.'

'Well, 'e did, whatever the reason. And things don't look good for Hilda neither. Seems she's right poorly.'

Grace sighed sadly. 'I'll ask Bernard about it when he comes home. He must know something, Frank being his Foreman. I wonder if there's anything I can do for them.'

'Shouldn't think there is. She'll 'ave all the help she needs in the 'ospital and with the rest of 'er family. She's one of twelve, yer know.'

Grace nodded thoughtfully. 'I will visit though when she comes home.' She gazed fondly at Bobbie who had fallen asleep in his mother's arms. She felt deeply saddened for Hilda and the baby she had lost. She would have been distressed beyond belief had she known her own husband's part in the tragedy.

Grace noticed Bessie had grown distant. 'Are you all right?'

Bessie looked at her blankly. 'Eh? Oh, yes, yes, I'm fine, me duck.' She paused thoughtfully, then took from her apron pocket two brown envelopes which she slid across the table. 'These came today but I couldn't bring meself to hand them over to the boys at dinnertime. Besides, they were laughing themselves silly over summat. I dunno what, but I bet it were summat they'd bin up to that they shouldn't 'ave. I 'adn't the 'eart to spoil the mood though.'

Grace stared down at the official-looking envelopes. 'I wonder when they have to report?'

'Monday. Both of 'em do.'

Grace raised her eyebrows.

Bessie grinned wickedly. 'I steamed 'em open. Well, I've a right to know summat like that. I'm their mother, ain't I?'

'Yes, you are,' Grace agreed, although she did not agree with Bessie about opening her sons' mail. 'How do you feel?'

'Feel?' She sighed deeply and absently smoothed the top of Bobbie's head. 'Devastated. But like you said, I've got to put a brave smile on me face and send 'em off 'appy.'

Grace smiled warmly at her. 'That's the spirit.'

'Yeah, well, I suppose there'll be enough time for crying after they've gone. But there's some things I won't be crying over.'

'Oh, what's that?'

'The fact I don't have to do their washin' for a while! Those boys of mine get filthy rotten at Janson's. They came 'ome at lunchtime lookin' like they'd fell down a coal 'ole.'

Grace laughed loudly. 'Yes, I suppose I shall have to prepare myself for that.'

'What, going down a coal 'ole?'

'No. Washing my Charlie's dirty overalls. She's starting in the munitions on Monday.'

'Is she? Well, good for 'er. I've always liked your Charlie. She's a good gel. She'll go places that one, you mark my words. 'Nother cuppa?'

Grace shook her head. 'No, thank you.'

Bessie refilled her own mug and took a gulp. 'Seems Monday's a red letter day for both of us, doesn't it? I know,' her eyes twinkled brightly, 'let's me and you go to the pictures on Monday afternoon. Eh, what d'yer say? I don't know about you, but I'm fed up to me back teeth of the blackout and these false air raid warnings and I'll need summat to cheer me up after seein' me boys off. And I think we deserve a bit of pleasure, don't you?'

'Pictures!'

'Yeah. Come on, Gracie Wilkins. When was the last time you enjoyed yerself for a couple of hours?'

Grace frowned hard. She couldn't remember.

'That's what I thought,' Bessie answered for her. 'Well, pictures it is. I won't take no for an answer. It'll be my treat and we'll 'ave a quarter of chocolates 'an all. My Tom's gettin' plenty of overtime, so a few coppers can be spared for enjoyment. He's working late again tonight delivering a load of machine parts to Coventry.'

A slow smile spread across Grace's face. Going to the pictures with Bessie sounded a wonderful idea and it would be something to look forward to. But she wouldn't let Bessie pay. She had enough looking after her own family. They needed Tom's overtime money, of that Grace had no doubt. She would somehow put the few coppers by herself. How she did not know, but she would do it. 'It's a date,' she said, and rose and gathered her bags. 'I'd better be off. Oh!' she exclaimed loudly.

'What's up?' Bessie asked worriedly.

'I've just remembered, I promised Mr Murray the Prue Man I'd look in on Miss Smith.'

'Miss Smith? Why, what's up with 'er?'

'I don't know. But Mr Murray is worried about her. And after he mentioned it, I realised I hadn't seen her for several days.'

'Well, I shouldn't worry too much. Nobody ever sees much of the old gel as it is. She'll probably send you packin' with a flea in yer ear. Tell yer not ter be so bloody nosy. D'yer want me to come with yer?'

'No, it's all right. No point in both of us getting a telling off. But thanks for the offer.'

Bessie rose, laid Bobbie gently on the peg rug by the hearth and followed Grace to the front door. Bessie eyed her neighbour closely as she stepped out into the street. 'You look different, Gracie Wilkins.'

Grace hitched up her shopping bag and turned to face her. 'Different?'

'Yeah, you do. But I can't put me finger on it.' It was on her mind to ask if Grace had given Bernard the heave-ho, but she thought better of it.

'Well, actually, Bessie, you could be right. I've made a decision today,' she said proudly.

'Oh, only one? By the looks on yer, I'd say you'd made a few.'

Grace grinned. 'One at a time is enough for me.'

'What is it then?' Bessie asked, intrigued.

'All in good time, Mrs Rudney. When I've got it settled in my own mind, then I'll tell you.'

'Spoilsport!' Bessie chuckled. 'But mind you hurry up, 'cos I'm itching to know what it is.' She suddenly grimaced at the sight of Maureen and Willy racing round the corner on their way home from school. She leaned against the door frame, folded her flabby arms under her big bosom which wobbled alarmingly, and tutted loudly. ''Ere we go. "What's for tea, Mam? We're starvin' ".'

Maureen arrived first, panting and out of breath. 'What's for tea, Mam? We're starving.'

Bessie looked at Grace. 'What did I tell yer? Think of n'ote but their bellies, my lot.' She bent down and pushed her face into Maureen's. 'A slice of fresh air, spread wi' last year's jam.'

132

Grace chuckled at Maureen's look of disgust. 'I could eat that myself,' she said, licking her lips, and winked at Bessie. ''Bye. See you soon.'

Chapter Eight

Grace cupped her eyes with her hands and peered through the back window of number eighty-nine. White net curtains obscured her view. She stepped back into the yard and looked up at the house. The blank windows stared back at her. After knocking several times and getting no response, it was her opinion that Miss Smith had gone away. It was usual for neighbours to inform each other of their plans, but as Miss Smith had never been on more than nodding terms, if she had gone away and told no one then this would be nothing untoward.

Grace frowned. Only it was like Mr Murray had said, it had never been known for Miss Smith to go away. Not even for a day. So why now, in this bitterly cold weather?

Shivering, she dug her hands deep into her pockets and looked around the slabbed yard. It was empty apart from a metal dustbin at the side of the privy. Nothing lurking in dusty corners, nothing propped against walls. Like the house itself, it appeared unlived in, void of any occupancy.

She knocked the back door again. The sound echoed back. That was it, she thought, Miss Smith had definitely gone away. She turned towards the gate then stopped. Something was niggling her but she didn't know what. Instinctively she returned to the back door and tried the knob. It turned. Grimacing deeply, Grace pushed the door open. Surely Miss

Smith would not have gone away and left the back door unlocked?

Hovering on the threshold, she peered into the gloomy interior. She suddenly felt like an intruder, invading the privacy of this old lady who had, for whatever her reasons, chosen to live a hermit-like existence. Would she take kindly to a neighbour barging in unannounced? But what if something was wrong? Could Grace live with herself if she walked away now? What also if Bessie was right and the old lady was extremely annoyed at this invasion of her solitude? Grace deliberated for a moment, torn between consideration for Miss Smith's privacy and her own strong need to satisfy herself that no misfortune had befallen her neighbour. She chose the latter course. Now she had ventured this far she would not rest easy until she was happy in her own mind that all was well, and would just have to accept responsibility for any outcome.

Grace stepped inside the house. 'Hello? Miss Smith?' she called. 'Are you there?'

Still no response. She shivered. The inside felt colder than outside and the air smelt musty, tinged with damp. She glanced around. Against the yellowing whitewashed wall was a small pine table; to the side a single wooden chair. On top of the table was a tea tray lined with an embroidered cloth on top of which sat a single cup and saucer, milk jug, sugar basin and tiny tea pot, all clean and ready for use. Above, screwed to the wall, were two narrow shelves. On the bottom was a dinner plate, tea plate and bowl, two small saucepans and a frying pan. The shelf above was empty.

The pantry door, next to the cream and green gas cooker, was closed. Fixed to it was a clean roller towel edged in red. The pot sink was empty and a beige string knitted dish cloth was folded neatly on the edge. The single brass tap protruding above dripped rhythmically, the drops of water echoing loudly as they hit the bottom of the sink.

Grace shuddered violently. Without going any further, she could sense the loneliness that prevailed; it clung to the air and penetrated her own being.

She walked towards the door leading through to the living room and called again. 'Miss Smith? Hello, Miss Smith. Are you there?'

The deafening silence was overwhelming.

Again she glanced around, a feeling of foreboding encroaching. Apart from the large blackleaded fireplace and a Victorian leather horsehair sofa the room was bare down to the floorboards, as though the occupants of the house had hurriedly departed and left the sofa behind.

Taking a deep breath, she made her way across and opened the door by the stairs leading to the front room, steeling herself for what she might find inside.

As she stood on the threshold her mouth fell open in surprise. Never before had she seen such a beautiful room and happening on it so unexpectedly filled her with shock.

Covering the floor was a colourful Chinese patterned rug. Red flocked wallpaper lined the walls. A solitary red leather wing back armchair sat to the side of the fireplace. By the window which looked out on to the street was a what-not filled with china and porcelain ornaments. Dominating the room was a mahogany bookcase sited against the side wall. It was crammed with books.

Avoiding a walnut occasional table, covered by a delicate white lace cloth in the centre of which sat a figurine of a shepherdess and several miniature silver snuff boxes, she walked over and ran her fingers gently across the spines. Miss Smith was obviously a great reader. The shelves were filled with all manner of titles, many of which Grace had never heard of before. There was Dickens, Austen, Woolfe and Hemingway, and many more, all placed in alphabetical order by author and title.

She longed to withdraw a book and leaf through it, but

stopped herself. She was an intruder, here uninvited to check on Miss Smith's welfare, nothing more.

Carefully she made her way out and ascended the stairs, calling out as she rose upwards. An icy fear settled on her and she began to wish she had accepted Bessie's offer to accompany her.

The three doors leading off the short landing were shut. She made towards the far one, knocked and tentatively opened it. This room was even barer than the back room. It was completely empty, save for the blackout curtains hanging at the sash window.

She quickly closed the door and made her way towards the next. Knocking again, she called out Miss Smith's name and turned the knob. The door was stiff and it took several attempts to push it open. The stale dusty air inside hit her full force and she gasped for breath, her eyes not believing what they were seeing. Thick cobwebs hung down from the ceiling like layers of lace curtains and dust lay thickly. Her eyes darted around in shock. The room was furnished for a child.

Through the cobwebs she could see faded sprig print curtains hanging at the window, matching paper on the wall. In the recess by the fireplace was a pine tallboy on top of which stood a basin and jug so covered in dust the pattern and colour were obscured. In the centre of the room was a wooden cradle.

Grace's hand flew to her mouth. The room had obviously been sealed for many many years. Why? Quickly she shut the door and rested her back against it, many different possibilities flying through her mind. The horror of what she had seen was quickly pushed aside at the sound of a moan so low it was hardly audible.

Pulling herself together, she rushed towards the third room, and without knocking, opened the door. In a bed across the room lay Clara Smith.

Grace moved over and stared down at her. Clara's breathing was slow and shallow, her pallor deathly. Her blue-tinged lips were cracked and rimmed with congealed blood. Instinctively Grace placed her hand gently on the woman's forehead. Her skin was burning to the touch.

Without further thought she rushed from the room and down the stairs. Rummaging around, she found an empty pudding basin and filled it with cold water, doing likewise with a cup. Back inside the bedroom she sat gently on the edge of the bed, slipped her arm underneath Clara's head and raised her carefully upwards. Placing the cup to her parched mouth she let the water slowly trickle inside. The old lady spluttered, most of the water pouring down the side of her chin and wetting further her already sweat-soaked thick white nightdress. Undeterred, Grace patiently persisted and gradually Clara managed to swallow several mouthfuls. Grace gently laid her head back on the pillows and, wetting a hand towel she had found next to the basin on the dresser, dabbed her forehead.

She shook her head in consternation. The old lady was very ill and needed more than the limited care Grace could offer. She needed a doctor.

Never having had much need for one herself, and not knowing who if anyone had attended Miss Smith in the past, she took the risk of leaving the old lady for a few minutes and asked for help from the nearest surgery she knew of on the Evington Road.

It seemed an age before the doctor arrived, Grace growing more anxious as the minutes ticked by. Finally a dark-haired Yorkshireman arrived whose age Grace guessed to be around her own. After showing him into Miss Smith's bedroom she retired to the kitchen and patiently awaited his verdict.

He joined her finally, his face grave. Silently he washed his hands under the cold water tap and dried them on the roller towel. He turned to face her, his ruggedly handsome face filled with anger.

'Why was I not called before?'

Grace was shocked at his tone. 'I'm . . . er . . . sorry, doctor. I didn't know she was poorly.'

'Poorly! My good woman, that old lady upstairs is more than poorly, she's at death's door. I'll be amazed if she makes it through the night. She has pneumonia and I'm not surprised, this house is like an icebox. For the love of God, get a fire lit in the bedroom, and she needs nourishment. Beef extract will do for a start. By the looks of her I'd say she hasn't eaten for days.' He opened his black bag, sorted through it and selected a bottle of pills. He thrust them at Grace. 'Get two of these down her immediately, crush them up if necessary in a little milk, but make sure she takes them. Then two every three hours. Keep sponging her with cold water, the fever needs to be broken. I'll be back later to check on her.' He pressed his bag shut, grabbed it up and headed for the door. As he reached it he paused, turned and narrowed his eyes. 'I'd be ashamed of myself if I were you. You should never have let your mother become so ill before calling me. Are you that worried about paying my bill? Well, I'll tell you this, it's a darn sight cheaper than a funeral.'

Grace's face reddened. 'She isn't my mother, doctor. I'm only her neighbour.'

'Well, I don't think much of your neighbourliness.' He eyed her coldly. 'Can you get hold of a relative? She's going to need constant care for the next few days. That's provided, of course, she survives the night.'

Grace bit her bottom lip. 'I don't know if she has any.' Humiliation rose at the doctor's look of disgust. 'Don't worry, I'll stay with her.'

Without another word he turned and departed.

Grace stared after him. How rude! But she had no time to dwell on his arrogant manner, Miss Smith needed her.

Painstakingly she carried out all of the doctor's instructions. When the bedroom had been heated sufficiently, she took it upon herself to sponge the old lady down and change her sodden nightdress as the smell emanating from her was not pleasant, but more importantly the woman herself must be far from comfortable. Single-handed this proved to be a very difficult task, but finally, with careful manoeuvring, Grace achieved success.

Carrying a chair up from downstairs, and having refreshed the water in the bowl, she sat down and gently began to sponge Clara's forehead. She looked at the old lady, deeply concerned. She was desperately ill and Grace herself was suddenly filled with such shame.

Over the years she should have got to know her better. She should have persisted in her neighbourliness. If she had done, then the situation now might not be so desperate.

A solitary tear settled on her lower eyelid and overspilled to roll down her face. The pathetic figure lying in the bed saddened her so deeply. Why had she practically cut herself off from humanity for all these years?

Grace raised her head. She could hear her own name being called.

Depositing the basin on the floor, she went down the stairs to find Bessie hovering just inside the kitchen door.

'I saw the doctor arrive,' she whispered. 'I'd 'ave come sooner but I'd to wait 'til our Maureen came 'ome from her pal's before I could leave Bobbie. What's 'appened, Gracie love? Is the old gel all right?'

Grace shook her head. 'No, she isn't, Bessie. She's very poorly. She's got pneumonia. The doctor seems to think she'll be lucky to make it through the night.'

'Oh, dear,' Bessie replied gravely, shaking her head. 'Is the doctor sending 'er to 'ospital or what?'

'He never mentioned the hospital.'

'Oh! Maybe 'e thinks there's no point then. Poor old duck!' She took Grace's arm. 'Come on, let me 'ave a look at 'er.'

Grace showed her through to Miss Smith's bedroom. Silently they both looked down at her.

'Mmmm.' Bessie frowned. 'She does look at death's door, don't she?' She shook her head sadly. 'I bet she was a good-looking woman when she was young. I wonder why she shut herself off like she did.' She raised her head and looked at Grace. 'It ain't natural, is it?'

She shrugged her shoulders. 'Who's to say what's natural and what isn't? At the moment, Bessie, I'm more concerned with doing what I can for her now.'

Bessie looked ashamed. 'Yes, yer right, Gracie love. What's the plan?'

Grace sat down on the chair and picked up the basin, beginning to bathe the burning hot forehead once more. 'I haven't made any plans as such. The doctor's calling back later. I'm just going to sit with her and do what he tells me.'

'Well, you'll need 'elp wi' that. We'll take it in turns. And what about food?'

Grace looked up at her enquiringly. 'Food?'

''As the old lady managed anythin'?'

'I gave her some Bovril as the doctor ordered. She's kept that down.'

'Did she? Well, that's a start. I wonder if she'd manage some of my soup? It'd do 'er more good than Bovril. I've a drop left in the bottom of the pan. I could strain it but it'd still have all the goodness in the liquid. It might 'elp to build up 'er strength.'

'Oh, Bessie, that's a good idea. Anything is worth a try.'

She beamed. 'Right then, I'll go and get it. And what about yerself? I bet you could do with a cuppa.'

'That'd be nice, thank you.'

Bessie left and returned fifteen minutes later. 'Now it's a bit 'ot,' she said, handing over a tin tray to Grace on which sat a chipped pudding basin filled with steaming yellow liquid. She put a mug of tea on the floor by the chair. 'I put two sugars in. You'll need energy yerself.'

Bessie sat on the bed propping Clara gently against her shoulder. Grace blew on a spoonful of Bessie's soup and spooned it carefully between Miss Smith's lips. It was a painstaking process but eventually they managed to get some of the soup down the sick woman.

Bessie laid her back against the pillows and together they tucked her up.

Bessie shook her head. 'Well, the bit she's managed is better than n'ote. At least her body'll 'ave some sustenance to work on.' She looked across at Grace. 'Oh, by the way, I seen your Charlie.' She grinned. 'Well, I think it wa' your Charlie.'

Grace frowned. 'What d'yer mean?'

'You'll see, me duck. Anyway, I explained the position like. She's most concerned, bless 'er. But she says you're not to worry, she'll get her dad's tea ready for when he comes 'ome and then come through and see you. See if she can do anythin' like.'

Grace smiled appreciatively. 'Thanks, Bessie. With all this, I'd forgotten about my own family.'

'Ah, well, that's understandable. Won't 'urt them though to fend for themselves for a while. Like mine. I've left our Polly in charge.' She guffawed loudly, then grimaced as she remembered the sick woman lying in the bed. She lowered her voice to a whisper. 'Knowin' my lot, they'll probably burn the 'ouse down before I get back.'

Grace looked at her, worried. 'Oh, Bessie, you get off, I'll manage.'

'Don't be daft. You can't nurse 'er all by yerself. Besides, I wa' only jokin', my lot are quite capable. Now what else needs to be done?'

They were interrupted by the doctor entering. Without a word he walked towards the bed and felt Clara's forehead. He tutted loudly and turned to Grace. 'I'm trying to organise a nurse but I'm having a little difficulty. Most of them are involved in the war effort.'

'That's all right, doctor,' Bessie butted in. 'We can do any nursin'.'

He turned to her. 'And who are you?'

'A neighbour, like Mrs Wilkins 'ere.' She nodded at Grace. He glared at them both scathingly. 'I see.'

The tone of his voice made Bessie's hackles rise. 'And what d'yer mean by that, doctor?'

Grace took a breath. 'He doesn't think much of our neighbourliness, Bessie.'

She raised her eyebrows, annoyed, and folded her arms tightly under her vast bosom. 'Oh, don't 'e!' She glared at the doctor. 'You think 'er state is our fault, do yer? Well, let me tell you summat, doctor. I've lived in this street for the past ten years and I've bin lucky to get a nod out of Miss Smith 'ere. We've all done what we could to get to know 'er. Every year we've invited 'er in for Christmas dinner and every year she's refused. Very politely like, but refused all the same. My Tom even offered to clean 'er windows and the kids to run errands. But you can't go on forever. If the old gel wants to live like an 'ermit, who a' we ter dispute that? Now what d'yer call that, doctor, if it ain't neighbourliness?'

He took a deep breath. 'I ... er ... owe you ladies an apology, I didn't realise.'

'No, you didn't,' Bessie erupted. She glanced quickly at Grace, then back to the doctor. 'Now if yer tells us what needs doin', we'll mek sure it's carried out. We want the old duck to live as much as you do.'

He nodded. 'Keep sponging her forehead with cold water and get as much fluid down as possible, and any nourishment that you can. Soup would be ideal.'

'We've already done that,' Bessie said in a superior way. 'And Mrs Wilkins 'as washed 'er and changed the bed. We're going to take turns in sittin' with 'er.'

He looked at Grace, surprised. 'Oh, good.' He made for the door. 'Remember the tablets. Then it's just a case of praying, I'm afraid. I'll be back some time in the morning.'

Grace followed him down the stairs and held the back door open for him.

He hovered for a moment, 'Look, Mrs Wilkins,' he began, 'I'm sorry for my remarks earlier. They were out of order.'

She gave him a smile. 'It's all right, doctor, I understand.'

He searched her face. I wonder if you do? he thought. I wonder how you would cope seeing the poverty I do day after day? People dying because they can't afford to pay their rent let alone buy nourishing food. And medicine for the sick. Well, most of the time that was out of the question.

It was hard for him to believe that 1940 would soon be upon them. In the last fifty years, life had changed dramatically. Remote parts of the world had been explored and conquered; the motor car had been invented; the aeroplane; the telephone. People could sit by their wireless in the most northern parts of the country and hear broadcasts from London. But still there were deaths for such simple illnesses as measles, while the poor could not afford more than the most basic food.

To him it didn't make sense. And harder to understand was that, after the atrocities of the Great War not twenty years before, here they were again, on the brink of possible destruction. Their little island was once more faced with the struggle for democracy. Had the Prime Minister not said only a short time ago that no halt would be called until the aggressor was beaten?

Many more intelligent and worldly than himself, hoped, believed even, it would be all over by Christmas. But not him. He knew, deep down in his bones, that a long bloody battle stretched for years ahead in front of them, and all on the whim of one man. The Germans had already sunk the *Royal Oak* with the loss of eight hundred and ten men. Women were already without husbands and sons and it had hardly begun. How many more dead, he wondered, before it was over?

It wasn't only the fighting men who would suffer, it was people like this good woman facing him. Admittedly, the war had yet to touch this part of the country, they had still to face the nightmare of the air raids, the devastating destruction caused by bombs – not only to buildings but also innocent lives. He himself had no doubt it would come. Then these people would have to summon all the courage they had, find a resourcefulness they hadn't known existed and fight their battle at home. As things stood he didn't know which was worse. Either way, at home or on the front, it would be a battle for survival.

How could he begin to explain to this woman, the true reasons for his rudeness when they had first met? His worries and fears for the future? If indeed they all had one. He couldn't. It wouldn't be fair to unburden himself upon her as he would have liked to do, in the hope she would truly understand and forgive him. Like her and thousands of others he would have to soldier on, keep believing that in the end faith and courage would pull them through.

He took a deep breath and patted her arm. 'I'll be back in the morning.'

Chapter Nine

Grace rubbed eyes gritty from lack of sleep, shifted her aching body in the uncomfortable wooden chair and looked in concern at the woman in the bed. Her fever was raging and she was delirious.

Though she had nursed Charlie through scarlet fever and the measles, Bernard through numerous colds and a bout of pleurisy, Grace had never felt so helpless. She wished she could do more than bathe the burning forehead and spoon liquids into the parched mouth. And pray. She had done her fair share of praying for the old lady as she had sat by her bed.

Bessie had been forced to leave towards nine to see to her own family but had only done so on a promise from Grace that at the slightest need she would be fetched, regardless of the hour. Since then Grace had sat on her own in the darkness, shadows dancing eerily around her, cast by the flames from the fire she kept continuously stacked. The unfamiliar sounds in the house unnerved her and for a worrying moment she visualised ghosts of long dead occupants gliding around the empty rooms, especially the one next to this, decorated for a child and left abandoned. It didn't need much imagination to realise that the child it had been intended for was dead.

Her eyes settled on Clara again and her heart went out to her. Her grief must have been unbearable for her to have done such a thing. She remembered her own joy the day Charlie had been born. How would she have felt or acted had her baby died? The thought was so terrible it didn't bear thinking about.

She froze in horror at a sound from across the room. Her eyes darted towards the door. In the light cast by the fire she could see the knob turning. Her heart drummed loudly in fright. She watched, hardly daring to breathe as the door slowly opened and a head popped around it. Grace let out a gasp of relief.

'Charlie! Oh, you scared me nearly to death!' She looked at her daughter hard. 'It is you, isn't it?'

Charlie closed the door gently and tiptoed towards her, sitting down on the chair Bessie had vacated earlier. She tucked her dress around her legs. 'Yes, it's me, Mam.' She patted her hair. 'I've had my hair cut in the Liberty style ready for starting my new job on Monday. Do you like it?'

Grace looked her over and smiled in admiration. 'Yes, I do. It suits you. Makes you look really grown up, and prettier if that's possible.' She took her daughter's hands. 'I'm so proud of you, really I am.'

'Are you, Mam? And you don't mind about my job in munitions?'

Grace shook her head. 'Everything is all over the place at the moment, love. We all have to do our best, however we can.' She squeezed her daughter's hand affectionately. 'Whatever you do is fine by me.'

Charlie sighed loudly. 'I wish Dad would say the same. I doubt I'll ever please him. If I married the King of England, surrounded by luxury beyond belief, he'd still find something to criticise me for.'

'Charlie!'

'I'm sorry, Mam, but it's true. Anyway, I don't care what he thinks any more.' She sensed her mother's distress at the direction in which the conversation was heading and thought it best to change the subject. She looked at Miss Smith with concern. 'How is she?'

Grace shook her head. 'No change. She's still burning up and delirious.'

'What's she been saying?'

'Nothing I can make out.'

'Poor old girl,' Charlie said tenderly. 'I wonder if she's any family?'

Grace grimaced. 'I like to think that there's somebody out there who does care for her. But how we go about finding them, I don't know. Anyway, Miss Smith might not thank us for meddling in her affairs. At the moment all I want is for her to get better.' She let go of Charlie's hands and rubbed her brow wearily. 'Anyway you, madam, shouldn't be here at all. You should be sleeping. You have to go to work in a few hours. It's your last day at the Co-op. You don't want to be late for that. The girls might have a few surprises for you.'

Charlie laughed. 'I doubt it, Mam. They're a right miserable bunch. Anyway, I couldn't sleep, I'm too excited.' She glanced around the dark room, shuddered at the eerie shadows and settled her eyes again on the figure in the bed. 'Ain't you scared, Mam, sitting here by yourself?'

Grace smiled warmly. 'No,' she lied. 'I don't believe in ghosts. Now off you go.'

'In a minute. I'll sit with you for a bit.'

'As you wish.' Grace took her hand again. She was glad of Charlie's company for however long. 'How's your dad?' she asked tentatively.

Charlie avoided her eyes. How could she tell her that her father's face had turned thunderous when she had told him that her mother was nursing the old lady next-door? He had grudgingly eaten the sandwich she had prepared and then gone off down the pub, afterwards returning and going straight to bed. He hadn't said a word on the subject and that was what was most disconcerting. Her father usually had plenty to say. She presumed he would when he got Grace on his own but decided it was best not to worry her mother, who had enough on her mind.

'He didn't say anything.'

Grace frowned. 'What, nothing at all?'

She shook her head. 'No. I made him a sandwich and he went down the pub. He got back about eleven and went to bed.'

'Oh, good,' said Grace, relieved. The last thing she needed was for Bernard to have one of his tantrums and come round causing a scene. But then, she thought, he wouldn't do that. He would wait until he got her on his own. Oh, well, if she could get the old lady through this, then Bernard's wrath would be well worth it. She patted Charlie's hand. 'Go to bed, my love. There's no point in us both sitting here. I'm fine, honest. Mrs Rudney's promised to come in about six to relieve me, so I'll see you before you go to work.'

Charlie nodded. 'Okay, Mam, if you're sure? She's a good egg, isn't she?'

'Who?'

'Mrs Rudney. I know what some people say about her, that she's loud and her kids are unruly sometimes, but there's a lot of love in that house and she's got a heart of gold. They haven't much themselves but she'd give you the dress off her back if she thought you had more need of it. It's a pity more people aren't like the Rudneys. The world would be a happier place.'

Grace stroked her chin thoughtfully. 'I didn't realise you knew them so well. But, yes, what you say is true. The more I get to know Bessie and her family, the more I value her friendship. I'm just sorry I didn't try to know her before.' She shook her head and smiled, light from the fire dancing on her face. 'If her lads joining up has done nothing more, it's brought us together.'

'Out of evil comes good, eh?'

They both lapsed into silence then Charlie began to laugh softly.

'I shouldn't tell you this, Mam, but I bumped into Barry on the way home from work.'

'Barry? Barry Rudney?'

She nodded. 'Me and him have been friends for years. Ever since they moved into the street in fact. We used to walk to school together. We'd always meet round the corner past Vinny's shop in case . . .' She paused. They both knew what she had been going to say. In case Bernard saw and put a stop to their association. 'Dennis used to tag behind,' she continued. 'Barry stuck him in a dustbin once and wedged the lid. He didn't half get into trouble for being late for school! And there was the time Barry never got his homework done because he was helping his dad load his lorry to earn some extra money. I let him copy mine. The teacher realised and we both got the cane.'

Grace's mouth dropped open. 'You never said.'

'No. Well, us kids have our secrets.' Charlie smiled broadly. 'There's some things parents are best not knowing.'

'I see,' Grace said, trying to sound severe. 'And what else did you get up to that you haven't told me?'

'Oh, nothing that'd land me in jail, so stop worrying.' She sighed softly. 'I suppose you could say Barry was my childhood sweetheart. I shall miss him as a friend when he goes away, but I've promised to write.'

Grace squeezed her hand. 'I bet he'll look forward to your letters. Anyway, what were you going to tell me? You said you met him on the way home from work?'

'Oh, yes.' Charlie fought to control her mirth, mindful that there was a very sick woman lying in the bed. 'Well, it seems both he and Dennis got fed up with Dad moaning about the stove in the factory. Grumbling that they kept letting it go out. So they climbed on to the roof and filled the stove and the chimney right up with coke.'

Grace raised her eyebrows. 'They never!'

Charlie giggled. 'The whole place could have gone up. The fire brigade was called and had to hose it down. Mr Janson went bananas.'

'I bet he did.'

'Dad got a right ticking off. Mr Janson blamed him for putting the idea into the lads' heads. Barry said it was hilarious, and you can't blame them, Mam. Dad's always having a go at them. In a way it serves him right.'

Grace agreed but couldn't voice her opinion. Bernard was after all her husband, and as such she had to show him loyalty. 'Regardless, we'd better not let your father know we heard all about this.' She smiled. 'Hitler should be warned, I reckon. I don't fancy his chances if the Rudney boys get within shooting distance.'

'Me neither,' Charlie agreed wholeheartedly. She yawned loudly. 'I think I will get to bed. Is there anything you need before I turn in?'

'Yes, you could come with me to freshen up the water in the basin.'

Charlie glanced around her, then settled eyes filled with merriment on her mother. 'I thought you said you weren't scared of ghosts?'

Grace woke with a start. The room was still dark, lit only by the glow from the fire. She sat for a moment and focused her eyes, wondering what had startled her as she dozed. Strange noises were coming from Miss Smith. It must have been her ramblings, thought Grace. She stretched out and reached for the wet cloth. Squeezing out most of the water, she laid it across the old lady's forehead.

Suddenly Clara's eyes flew open. She stared at Grace wildly. Her arm reached out and she grabbed Grace's wrist, gripping it tightly. 'Is that you, Katy? Tell me. Please tell . . . baby . . . not dead? Katy . . . Katy . . . please. Baby . . . not dead.' She let go of Grace's wrist and sank back against the pillows, wailing loudly in anguish before her voice tailed off in a whimper.

Grace gently took her hand and stroked it tenderly. 'Shush,' she soothed. 'It's all right, Miss Smith. Go back to sleep.'

Her eyes fixed on Grace as panic appeared in her ashen face. 'Who . . .?'

'It's me, Miss Smith, Grace Wilkins from next-door. You're very ill. But don't worry, I'm here to look after you.'

Clara let out a long slow sigh and closed her eyes. For a moment Grace thought she had breathed her last. She leaned over and placed her ear next to the woman's lips, sighing with relief when she felt the hot breath. She ran her hand over Clara's forehead, feeling sure it was cooler. Only slightly, but anything was a good sign.

Satisfied that the old lady was sleeping, she rose and banked up the fire, glad of the fact that Miss Smith had an ample supply of coal. She would have dreaded having to conceal from Bernard the amount needed to keep this fire going as well as the bucketful she had given to the Cottings.

She sat back in her chair again and looked at the deathly face on the pillow. So the poor old dear had had a baby that had died. Her assumption had been correct. The room next-door had been left as a shrine and the old lady's way of coping, she presumed, had been to shut herself off, living like a hermit.

Grace shook her head sadly. How awful to lose a child. The pain of loss must be dreadful. But, she wondered, who was Katy? Whoever she was, was she dead also? Grace doubted she'd ever find out. The old woman had kept her distance for all these years, she couldn't see things changing now. The only change Grace could envisage was the one brought about by herself. If hopefully Miss Smith conquered this illness, then Grace would be much more diligent in future. She would keep a close eye on her without her knowledge.

Bessie arrived as promised just after six and a desperately tired Grace returned home. She would see to Bernard and Charlie's breakfast and have a couple of hours' sleep, then return to relieve Bessie. She also had Ida to see to. Somehow she would have to find the time to fulfil that duty as well. A sick neighbour was not a good enough excuse for abandoning her mother-in-law.

She let herself into the kitchen. Bernard was lighting the gas beneath the kettle. She could hear Charlie moving around upstairs.

Grace unhooked the frying pan from a nail on the wall. 'I'll have your breakfast ready shortly, Bernard,' she said lightly, fighting fatigue. She would have liked nothing more than to drink a cup of tea and crawl into bed.

He glared at her, turned his back and walked from the room.

Her shoulders sagged wearily. Please, she screamed inwardly. Please, Bernard, don't start. I haven't the strength.

Charlie appeared and took the frying pan from her. 'Go to bed, Mam,' she ordered. 'I'll get Dad's breakfast and bring you up a cuppa. Go on.'

Grace looked at her gratefully and opened her mouth to protest.

'Do as you're told, Mam. You're exhausted.'

Grace didn't need another telling. She hugged her daughter tightly and headed for the stairs, ignoring Bernard as she passed him where he sat at the table waiting for his breakfast.

She undressed and climbed between the inviting sheets, still warm from her husband's body. She didn't hear Charlie come in several moments later with the promised cup of tea. She was sound asleep.

Grace woke with a jump and grabbed hold of the tin alarm clock, scanning its face through sleep-blurred eyes. It was just past eleven.

Diving out of bed, she hurriedly washed, dressed, and ran a brush through her hair, grabbing it up and pinning it into a bun at the nape of her neck. Dinner was a scratch affair left in the oven with a scribbled note of instructions for Bernard. Not that lifting the dish out of the oven and transferring it to a plate needed instructions but Bernard's mood was going to be bad enough thanks to the time she was spending at Miss Smith's. The note, she hoped, would ease a little of the tension.

Before she went to take over from Bessie, she called upon a neighbour of her mother-in-law's. Persuading the woman to keep an eye on Ida whilst she was otherwise occupied was not an easy task, not even after an offer of money which Grace worried about finding. It was quite apparent that she was not alone in finding her mother-in-law a trial. But thankfully the neighbour eventually agreed, if only on the promise that as soon as the invalid was better, Grace would resume her duties.

When she arrived at number eighty-nine Bessie was just showing the doctor out. He smiled at Grace as she came through the gate.

'The fever's broken. I'm hopeful she's going to be all right.'

'Oh, thank God, thank God!' cried Grace, relieved.

'Well, it's thanks to you two ladies. She'll still need constant care for a while, though.'

'That's all right, doctor. We'll manage,' Bessie said.

'Right. Well, I've told Mrs Rudney to carry on with the liquids and the tablets, and I'll pop by tomorrow.'

Grace and Bessie thanked him. When he'd departed they went up to Clara's bedroom. The old lady's pallor was not quite so ashen and her breathing was a little more even. She looked to be in a peaceful sleep. Grace turned to Bessie.

'I'll manage for a while if you want to get home?'

She nodded. 'Okay, me duck. I've a few things to do. When I come back, I'll bring yer summat ter eat.' She paused for a moment and rubbed her hand over her double chins. 'A, yer seen that room next-door? It's like summat out of a horror film. And the front room downstairs . . . I ain't never seen such a palace.' She puffed out her chest. 'I wasn't bein' nosy. I was lookin' for . . . well, I was just lookin'. But that room next-door. Well, it's weird, ain't it?'

Grace nodded. She could understand Bessie's curiosity. 'Yes, I've seen it. But the reason for its state is entirely Miss Smith's. I don't think we have the right to question, and I don't think we should tell anyone else either.'

Bessie shook her head. 'No, I agree. But it's still weird.' She sniffed loudly. 'I'll be off then, me duck. Be back about oneish, okay?'

Grace nodded and settled down in the chair by the bed.

It wasn't Bessie who arrived just before one o'clock, it was her husband Tom. Grace was surprised as his large frame tiptoed into the room, carrying a plate filled with a thick crust of bread and a noggin of cheese.

She gratefully accepted the food.

'I told Bessie I'd drop this in. She thought you'd be famished by now. She's gonna be a bit late.' He lowered his voice to a whisper. 'She's been summoned up the school.'

'Oh!' Grace mouthed in alarm. 'Nothing serious, I hope?'

Tom shrugged his broad shoulders. 'Something and

nothing. Our Willy's refusing to go down the bomb shelter when they have the mock air raid drills. And twice 'e's forgotten to take 'is gas mask to school.' He smiled broadly. 'That son of mine reckons it's all a waste of time. But the Headmaster doesn't, so our Bessie's gone to sort it out.' He looked down at Miss Smith. ''Ow's the old gel today?'

Grace followed his eyes. 'A bit better, I think. She is not rambling so much and her temperature is definitely down. The doctor's been again and seems to be satisfied.'

'Oh good, good.'

Grace wrung her hands. 'He's been several times now. I'm afraid to ask for the bill.'

'Eh, don't you go worryin' about that. If the worst comes, we'll have a whip round in the street. I don't care 'ow proud the old gel is.'

Grace smiled up at him warmly. 'You're a good man, Mr Rudney.'

Tom blushed scarlet. 'No more so than yerself, Mrs W.' He raised himself up to his full six foot one and thrust his hands deep into his trouser pockets. 'If you want a break for a bit, I'll sit with 'er. I've got a bit of spare time. A load I was scheduled to deliver ain't ready yet.' He didn't tell her that the load was from Janson's and not finished due to the slackness of her husband.

'That's nice of you, Mr Rudney, but don't your two boys go away in a couple of days? You'll be wanting to spend as much time with them as you can.'

Tom nodded. 'That's true, I do. But a few minutes won't 'urt.'

'It's all right really, Mr Rudney.' She didn't want to tell him that she'd prefer not to go home in case she bumped into Bernard who would be having his dinner. She was putting off the inevitable. 'And tell Bessie not to hurry back.' She grinned. 'After she's finished sorting the Headmaster,' she said, visualising Bessie's verbal attack on the poor unsuspecting man. 'I'm fine, honestly. My Charlie will pop round when she gets home from work, so it's not as though I'm coping on my own.'

'I'll tell 'er what you said,' Tom replied gratefully. 'To be 'onest, Miss Smith's illness 'as kinda took the edge off the boys' leaving, if you know what I mean? It's been good for my Bessie 'aving her mind occupied by summat else. She likes nothing more than to feel needed.'

'She's been a Godsend, Mr Rudney. I'm sure Miss Smith wouldn't be so much improved if it hadn't been for Bessie's nursing.'

'Well, she's doin' this as much for you as she is for Miss Smith.'

Grace looked up at him, confused. 'Me?'

'Oh, yes. Right fond of you is my Bessie, and she's that honoured that you're her friend.'

'Honoured? But I don't understand.'

'Bessie's always said that you're a lady, Mrs Wilkins, and she's not the only one around these parts to think that.' He shuffled uncomfortably on his feet. 'I just want you to know that if ever you need any 'elp, don't you 'esitate to call on me.'

'Oh, Mr Rudney, I won't. Thank you.' She rose from her seat and stood before him. 'But there's something you have to understand. It's not Bessie who should feel honoured, it's me. She's the most wonderful friend I could ever wish for. You and your family have welcomed me into your home, and I'll never forget that.'

Tom blushed scarlet. 'Right, I'd better be off then. You sure you don't need anythin'?'

'I'm sure, Mr Rudney. And please thank Bessie for the food. Tell her I'll see her tomorrow, after the boys have left. And tell them I wish them all the best.'

'I'll do that.'

She watched as he departed, a warm glow filling her. Fancy Bessie thinking her a lady! Grace shook her head. She would have to have a talk with her when they next met and set her straight.

Charlie looked up at her father as he re-entered the room. 'Who was that at the door?'

He lowered his bulk into the armchair and picked up the Sunday newspaper, shaking it out. 'If it'd been for you, I'd have told yer.'

Charlie scowled, hatred for the man sitting opposite glinting in her eyes. 'I only asked, Dad. There's no need to be so nasty.'

'You watch your mouth! Think you're big now you're going to be working in munitions, don't yer? Well, you'll see, my girl. You'll soon wish yer were back doing yer old cushy job.'

'I'm not afraid of hard work.'

'Huh. You don't know the meaning of the word.'

Charlie fought down her temper. If it wasn't for her love for her mother, she would have left this house long ago.

Bernard lowered the newspaper. 'Did your mother condescend to say when she'd be back?' he snarled.

If she had any sense she'd never come back, thought Charlie. 'No. Miss Smith's still very ill, Dad,' she said evenly. 'If it wasn't for Mam, I expect she'd have died. Mrs Rudney's been doing more than her fair share too, but she's a family to look after.'

'And your mother hasn't?'

Charlie bit her tongue. 'I'm going to pop round in a minute. Do you want me to give her a message?'

'No. I'll tell her myself when she comes in. Whenever that is,' he added sarcastically.

'Tell her what?'

'Charlotte, the message was given to me so I'll be the one to pass it on.' He stared at her piercingly. 'Are we going to get any tea today or what? I don't suppose your mother has given any thought to that.'

Charlie clenched her fists. Only a couple of hours ago, her father had eaten a substantial dinner prepared by Grace on a fleeting break from her nursing duties. He had come in from the allotment, leaving his muddy boots in the middle of the kitchen, the produce in a heap on the table, and complained bitterly what a hard morning he'd had. He may have, Charlie mused. But his stint of gardening, pulling a few carrots and digging up some spuds, was not as physically wearing as her mother's nursing.

Slowly, she rose and walked into the kitchen where she snatched the frying pan from the hook on the wall, fighting the urge to smash it down upon his head.

Chapter Ten

Grace rubbed weary eyes and stretched her legs. Several nights sitting in a wooden chair and the strain was telling on her. She was so tired, her body so stiff, she could have wept. Thank goodness for Bessie, she thought sincerely. Without her neighbour's help, she could never have managed to give Miss Smith the constant nursing needed. But poor Bessie was suffering herself now. The usual merry twinkle in her eyes had dulled since waving her boys off to catch the troop train for training camp. Was that only yesterday? It seemed a lifetime ago.

After seeing them off, Bessie had joined her in the bedroom and cried enough tears to fill a bucket. No words of comfort on Grace's part had helped to ease her pain. As a mother herself, she knew Bessie would not rest peacefully until her boys returned home, the war over. But no one, not even the Almighty himself, could give any guarantees. All she could do was join all the other mothers praying their sons would be spared.

Absently she leaned over and straightened the covers on Miss Smith's bed. The patient did seem better, though, that was one consolation. Tenderly Grace scanned the lined face. It took several moments for her to realise that a pair of faded blue eyes were staring back at her.

'You're . . . you're the lady from next-door,' a cracked voice said.

Grace instinctively took hold of her hand and stroked it. 'Yes, that's right. Grace. Grace Wilkins. How are you feeling, Miss Smith?'

'Feeling?' She paused, fighting for the energy to speak. 'Not very good, my dear.'

'That's understandable. You've been very ill, Miss Smith. the doctor . . .'

'Doctor?'

'We had to get the doctor,' she said, worried. 'He didn't think you'd make it at first.'

Clara eyed her, alarmed. 'Am I going to die? You can tell me the truth.'

'No, you're going to be fine. Honestly.'

Clara sighed in relief. 'Not that I mind dying.' She spoke huskily. 'In a way it would be a blessed relief, my dear.' She gave a watery smile. 'And you've been looking after me?'

'Yes. Myself and Mrs Rudney.'

'Mrs Rudney? Oh, yes, the jolly lady with the children. I know who you mean.' Her eyes grew troubled. 'But she has enough to do without caring for me. And so have you, my dear.' She took a painful breath. 'But all the same, it was very good of you both. I'm so sorry to have put you to all this trouble.'

Grace felt shocked surprise at the older woman's manner. She had never expected such a sweet-natured reply. 'It was no trouble, Miss Smith. I speak for both of us when I say it's good to see you on the mend.' She patted her hand. 'But please, try to rest. I can tell you everything when you're a little stronger. Can I get you anything now? A drink maybe?'

Clara smiled gratefully. 'A cup of tea would be nice, if it's no trouble? Thank you.'

'It'd be my pleasure. I won't be a moment.'

Aided by Grace, Clara managed several sips of the sweet, milky tea before exhaustion overcame her and she sagged

162

against the pillows and fell asleep.

It was just after four in the morning when she awoke again. 'I wasn't dreaming then?'

The soft voice, coming so unexpectedly, shook Grace rigid. 'Pardon? Oh, Miss Smith, I'm sorry, I must have dozed off.'

'You should be in bed yourself.' She reached out her hand and grasped Grace's. 'But I'm so glad you're here, my dear. It's such a comfort. I'm so fortunate to have such good neighbours. I don't deserve you, really I don't. I never even so much as passed the time of day.'

'It's not wrong to want your privacy, Miss Smith. And we all respected your wishes.'

She smiled, ashamed. 'But that's just it, my dear. Privacy is the last thing I wanted, and as for respect . . . I don't deserve anyone's respect after what I did.'

Grace stared at her, bewildered, as the old lady's eyes dropped and she fell asleep again.

She was still sleeping peacefully when Bessie arrived just after seven. 'I'm sorry I'm late. 'Ad a job gettin' the kids up this mornin'.' She looked down at Miss Smith. ' 'Ow's the old duck?'

Grace smiled warmly. 'She's been awake and had a sip of tea.'

'Oh, 'as she? Good. She's on the mend then. That's a shame,' she added, plonking down on the chair beside Grace's.

She frowned. 'Why do you say that?' she asked, shocked.

Bessie's face grew serious. 'Well, with 'er on the mend, the doc won't be calling.' She turned to Grace and raised her eyebrows. 'I'd say he's taken rather a fancy to you meself.'

'Bessie!'

'Speak as I find, me. And I definitely reckon 'e's took a shine.' She shuffled her bottom more comfortably on the chair. 'Best get off then, gel, and get some sleep. You look fair knackered. Now don't you worry about rushin' back, I've got me dinner prepared. I've only to bung on the spuds and slice up the leftover mutton. And don't you worry about Miss Smith 'ere. She'll be all right wi' me. I'll get her whatever she feels like when she wakes up. Now go on, get ter bed.'

Grace yawned. 'Thanks, Bessie. I'll be glad to see my bed.' She smiled fondly at her friend. 'How are you?'

'Me? I'm fine,' she said, just a little too lightly.

Grace had too much respect for her to probe further. Bessie was putting on a brave front, but it was obvious she was missing her boys. Grace rose. 'I'll be off then.'

Bessie withdrew her knitting from her large black bag, put the ends of the silver pins under her armpits and settled back to do a few rows, keeping her eyes peeled for any signs of movement from her charge.

As Grace arrived at her back door, Charlie was just coming out.

'Hello, Mam. I was just going to drop by and say cheerio. You've just missed Dad. He went not ten minutes ago.'

'Did he? He's early.'

'Oh, I'd just be thankful, Mam. He wasn't in the best of moods because he had to get his own breakfast.'

Grace sighed heavily, then leaned forward and kissed Charlie on the cheek. She stepped back and surveyed her daughter. Under her coat she wore a pair of brown trousers and a loose-fitting white blouse. Her thick chestnut hair was hidden beneath a red turban-style scarf. Grace smiled proudly.

'Well, I never thought I'd see the day my daughter went to work in trousers! But I must say, they suit you.'

Charlie laughed. 'Thanks, Mam. But regardless of whether they suit me or not, a skirt would be no good in this job. All that bending and lifting. It's hard work and a bit boring, but

I love it. And I've met some smashing people. There's all sorts of women working in the factory, Mam. Most of them are like me and never done this kind of work before so we're all mucking in together. Once I've done my training, I'll be working really long hours, but it'll be worth it. And the money's better than I was getting.'

Grace could see excitement shining from her daughter's eyes. Charlie pulled on a pair of thick hand-knitted gloves and wrapped the ends of her scarf around her neck. 'But the main thing is . . .'

'. . . you're doing your bit,' her mother finished for her. 'Well, you'd better get off. You mustn't get sacked for being late, must you?'

Charlie laughed. 'No, Mam. I'll see you tonight.'

'Take care.' Grace leaned over and kissed her on the cheek. Then again. 'And one for luck.'

Charlie grinned. 'I'll need it, Mam.'

Grace stood and watched Charlie disappearing down the entry, her heart filling with a fierce pride. Her girl was achieving something. She had never seen her daughter look so excited about anything. Then, shivering with cold and fatigue, she walked slowly into the kitchen and mashed herself a welcome mug of tea before climbing into bed.

Chapter Eleven

Bernard tried to keep his delight from showing on his face. 'So what you're saying, sir, is that you're giving me the job of Foreman, is that it?'

Philip Janson sighed heavily. The last thing he wanted to do was give Wilkins this job, but he had no choice. He had been shocked and dismayed to learn that Frank Wilby had joined the forces. And he had not been the only one. His poor wife had been so upset that she had not only lost her baby, but nearly her life. Philip himself had insisted Frank spend his remaining few civilian days with her. In view of his wife's health and what he faced in the future, he could not expect the man to work. That left him with Wilkins and he was far from happy with the fact.

'That's right,' Philip nodded.

Bernard sniffed disdainfully, purposely delaying the words of agreement. He wanted Janson to beg, wouldn't be satisfied with anything less. He rubbed his large hands down the front of his brown overalls. 'I see. Well, I'll have to give it some thought.'

'Thought?' Philip hissed, annoyed. 'Have you forgotten there's a war on, man? We haven't time for thought.' He narrowed his eyes. The bastard was playing games with him. Well, he'd turn the tables. 'Look, Wilkins, if you're thinking of joining up, don't be afraid to tell me. I wouldn't dream of coming between a man and his duty. Don't worry about your loyalties to me. I'll just get on to the Ministry of Employment and see if they can find someone suitable for the job.'

Bernard's jaw dropped in shock. He suddenly saw all his clever plan disintegrating. 'Eh? Oh, no, sir, it's nothing like that. No, I'll take the job. After all, you need my skills. It'd tek a new chap a while to settle in and we have all these orders to fill. No, Mr Janson, sir, I accept. I'll get down to it now.'

Philip tightened his lips. 'You see you do. I'll be keeping an eye on you myself, Wilkins.'

He turned and made to walk away but Bernard stopped him.

'Er, excuse me, Mr Janson? Just one thing.'

Philip turned. 'Yes?'

'This job. It's classed as a key job, ain't it? I'm only asking out of curiosity like?'

Philip stared at him, then froze as realisation hit him full force. He suddenly saw it all. Deep down he had known there had been something very fishy about all this business, Frank joining up like that out of the blue. Now he knew. It had been Wilkins's doing. The job was what he had been after all along. It was his security against being conscripted.

Blind rage filled him. Rage he fought hard to control. Wilkins had once again been up to his tricks. He had manipulated Frank into enlisting so he could get his job. Wilkins had never considered the consequences, as usual his actions had been entirely selfish. But Philip knew he had no proof of all this so couldn't even voice his suspicions. Wilkins would laugh in his face.

With a huge effort he forced himself to turn and walk away. He knew if he stayed he would be hanged for murder.

Bernard turned towards his machine and rubbed his hands in glee. His plan had worked out perfectly. He was safe.

* * *

Grace returned to Clara's just after twelve, feeling refreshed after her few hours' sleep. As usual she had left Bernard's dinner cooking in the oven. All he had to do was dish it up. They had not crossed paths over the last several days and it occurred to her that she had not missed him. Sooner or later, though, Miss Smith would be well enough to fend for herself and things would get back to normal. Grace shuddered as she turned down the entry. The thought was not appealing.

She found Bessie settling Clara more comfortably in her bed. The old woman looked frail propped up against the large white pillows, her greying hair in dire need of a wash and comb. Grace decided if Clara felt up to it she would tackle the job later.

Bessie beamed at her. ''Ello, Gracie love.' She finished straightening the bed covers and stood back. 'There, that's better, ain't it?' she said to Clara, then turned to Grace. 'I've given 'er a nice wash down and was just about to mash a cuppa.' She looked over at Clara. 'Do yer reckon you could eat summat?'

Clara smiled wearily. 'Tea would be lovely, thank you. I might be able to manage something later.'

'Right yer are then. Tea it is.' She gathered together the bowl and washing materials.

Grace took them from her. 'Give those to me, Bessie. I'll see to the tea. You get back home to see to your family's dinner.'

Clara coughed painfully. 'Mrs Rudney,' she extended a limp hand, 'thank you. Thank you so much.'

Bessie smiled broadly. 'My pleasure, me duck. Eh, and less of the Mrs Rudney. It's Bessie to me friends. And this 'ere is Grace.'

Their patient smiled. 'Then you must call me Clara.'

'Clara, eh?' Bessie took hold of the proffered hand and shook it. 'Nice ter meet yer, Clara. Now I'd best get off

169

and feed me starving brood, and I've a bit of shoppin' to get. I'll be back later.'

During the next couple of hours Clara dozed on and off. When she finally fully awoke again, Grace was relieved to see some colour in her cheeks. She made her as comfortable as possible then settled herself down on the chair.

'You look much better,' she said sincerely.

Clara took several painful breaths. 'I feel it.' She managed a weak smile. 'Although I don't think I could run a marathon yet.' She settled grateful eyes on Grace. 'I don't know how I can repay you and Bessie, my dear.'

'Repay?' She frowned disapprovingly. 'You getting better is all the payment we'll accept.'

Tears sprang to Clara's eyes. They overspilled and ran down her face. 'I don't deserve this, really I don't!'

'Hey, hey, no need for this, Clara. You're just feeling low through being ill, that's all.'

Clara sniffed and wiped her eyes on her handkerchief. 'I'm not, Grace. You should have left me to die.'

She stared at her in horror. 'Why? Why do you say that?'

Clara lowered her eyes. Suddenly she had an overwhelming desire to unburden herself to the pretty younger woman who had given up her time to care for her. Thirty-eight years of isolation, cutting herself off from humanity, had not eased her guilt or the pain of her loss. But she couldn't endure such self-denial any longer. She knew wrongs could not be put right, but knew also that she could not let herself go through the rest of her remaining years without a friend, someone to speak to, turn to during her bouts of loneliness.

She raised her eyes and searched Grace's face. But would this young woman want to be her friend if she knew the truth? Clara blew her nose and wiped her eyes. She would have to take the chance. Grace, she knew from conversations overheard in the garden, had not had an easy time of it. In view of that she might just extend a little sympathy towards Clara.

'I had an affair with my sister's fiancé,' she blurted. 'And I had his baby.'

Grace stared at her. 'Oh, I see.' She reached over and took Clara's hand. 'What you've done in the past, Clara, ain't anything to do with me. If we're honest, we've all done things we know not to be right.' She sighed softly. 'And whatever you've done, you can't go on paying for ever.'

'If I live to be a hundred, my dear, I don't think I'll ever put right the dreadful wrong I did.' Her eyes filled with tears which she wiped with her handkerchief. 'You see, I hurt so many people.'

'And you think that living like a hermit has made a difference?'

'No.' She shook her head wearily. 'It only resulted in my own loneliness, but I felt I deserved to be punished.'

Grace stroked her hand tenderly, feeling this woman's pain fill her being. 'The baby died, didn't it?'

Clara stared at her wide-eyed. 'You know?'

'I saw the room and guessed.' Grace took a deep breath. 'Don't you think losing your baby was punishment enough?'

Clara nodded. 'I suppose it was God's way. I've never got over it. It was a little girl. She would be approaching thirty-eight if she had lived.'

'Thirty-eight! You've shut yourself off for thirty-eight years?'

Clara nodded.

'Oh, but that's terrible.'

She tightened her grip on Grace's hand. 'Let me tell you the story, Grace. Then you can decide yourself whether it's terrible or not.'

'You don't have to, Clara.'

She smiled wanly. 'I'm being selfish, my dear. I feel the

need. Please let me do this. I know it won't clear my conscience, nothing will do that. But at least you'll know the truth. I feel I owe it to you.'

'You owe me nothing, Clara. But I'll listen.'

'Thank you.'

Her mind drifted back over the years to when it had all begun.

'I was seventeen when I first met my sister's fiancé. I was still away at school.' She smiled at the look on Grace's face. 'My family are – were – wealthy. My true name isn't Smith, my dear.' She took a deep breath. 'My father was a strict disciplinarian. He ruled me and my sister with a rod of iron. Our lives were all planned out and we would follow those plans to the letter. My mother agreed with anything he said. She had had to do what her father told her, so why shouldn't we? But regardless, I had a wonderful childhood, filled with love and anything I could ever want.

'My sister was rather wilful and very trying at times and found my father's rules somewhat difficult to keep. She had secretly met a man she worshipped and was going to marry him regardless of what my father said. She wrote to me at school. Long letters full of love for this man, and how she was going to run away with him. And I couldn't blame her. Why shouldn't she follow her heart? But my father would have strongly disapproved and made her give him up. The man's family were what he termed tradespeople and a daughter of his did not marry among tradespeople.

'I came home for the summer holidays, and on a supposed trip to town we met up with him. She wanted me to meet him, she was so proud.' Clara's eyes grew misty. 'The moment I saw him, I fell in love. I tried to hide my feelings, but when you're young and inexperienced in matters like this, it's not always possible.'

'Did your sister know how you felt?'

'Oh, no, my dear. How could I tell Katy I was in love with the man she planned to marry? But it seemed that her fiancé felt the same about me. He wrote when I returned to school, and young and foolish as I was, I arranged to spend a week with him in Brighton. I told my Headmistress that I had been summoned to care for a sick aunt. Lies, you see, all lies. But we had a wonderful week. He told me he loved me and wanted to marry me.'

'And what of his feelings for your sister?'

'Well, that's it. He said that it was all her doing. That he did not love her and had no intention of marrying her, that they had only ever been friends. I believed him. I wanted to so much. I knew the hurt Katy would feel, but to me it wasn't fair that she should make him marry her just because it was what she wanted. She'd always been strong. Always got her own way. So when he explained how things truly were between them, I could fully understand what had happened.'

'So did he explain to her about you and him?'

'He wrote and told me he had. He said she was distraught, had threatened suicide even, though I couldn't see Katy doing that. But once he had managed to calm her down, he said, he'd made her see reason. That it would never have worked between them regardless of his love for me. I felt so bad for hurting her. She was my sister and I loved her so much. I wanted to see her myself, but she had told Phips she never wanted to see me again.'

'Phips? Oh, I see. That was his name?'

'It's what I always called him. Anyway, Phips and I decided it best to be discreet. We would wait until I was twenty-one. It seemed such a long time, but I'd be old enough to marry who I wished. But more importantly, it was only fair to Katy. During that time she'd have a chance to meet someone else.'

Grace smiled. 'That was good of you both.'

Clara swallowed back tears. 'Then I realised I was pregnant. Oh, it was dreadful. To be unmarried and pregnant was unforgivable. I know Phips would have stood by me if I had told him, but I panicked, you see.'

'Well, what did you do?'

'I wrote and told my sister.'

'Oh, I see.'

'She was the only one I could tell. My mother would have died with the shame, my father commit murder, so she was the only one. She came straight down to the school. Told me she knew nothing about me and Phips. That he had never spoken to her about us. That until she had received my letter she had thought herself still engaged to him.'

'So this Phips had strung you both along?'

Clara lowered her head and nodded. 'Yes. Katy said he could only be after our money. By seeing us both he was hedging his bets, so to speak. Only I went and got pregnant. After all these years I still can't believe that all the things he said to me were just lies. I couldn't believe he would do such a thing.

'I wanted to go and confront him myself, but Katy begged me not to. She didn't want me to make a bigger fool of myself than I already had. She said that once she had finished dealing with him, he would never hold up his head again. She was marvellous. Told me not to worry, that everything was going to be all right. It made my guilt even worse. If she had disowned me, threatened to kill me even, maybe I could have coped better. As it was she took charge. She said that what had happened must be put behind us for the sake of the baby. We had both fallen for a rotten apple and we mustn't let it come between us.

'I was so relieved. I needed her strength. The thought of having this baby on my own frightened me to death. She said I was to leave everything to her. She would break the news to my parents and give them time to get used to the idea. In the meantime she bought this house for me, choosing it because we would not be known in the area. We were both to live here until I had the baby.'

'Your sister sounds a wonderful person,' Grace said sincerely.

'Yes, she is – was. I haven't seen her for such a long time. Not since I sent her away. But I'll come to that in a minute.' She took a deep breath and smiled wanly at Grace. 'Katy was true to her word. She stayed with me the whole time.'

'What about your parents? Didn't they wonder where you both were? Especially when you left school. The Headmistress must have contacted them, surely?'

'Katy dealt with all that. I had no idea what excuse she used and did not ask. I was just glad that she was taking care of it all. I don't know what I'd have done without her. It was decided that when the baby was born we would go and see my parents together. Katy promised me that everything would be fine and told me not to worry. So I didn't.

'To help take my mind off things we started to furnish the house. It was such fun. To someone like myself who had everything done for them, it was a game, like playing grown ups when a child. But it soon got to a stage when Katy thought it best that I didn't go out. Just in case someone did happen to recognise us and my parents got to hear of my condition, before we had told them ourselves.

'It was winter time by then anyway. That's when we would sit by the fire, roasting chestnuts and toasting tea cakes, and make plans for when the baby came. As the months went by I gradually grew to love the child inside me. Regardless of what Phips had done, this baby was innocent. As far as I was concerned it had been conceived out of love and I began to want it so much. If the worst happened and my parents did disown me, I had money from an inheritance – enough to support us both as long as I was very careful.'

Clara twisted the edge of the sheet between her hands and stared absently across the room. 'I will never forget the night the baby was born. It was bitterly cold, the snow piled up against the windows. The midwife, whom Katy had organised, had a job to get through. It was a difficult birth but when my daughter arrived I was overjoyed. She was the image of Phips and looked so healthy. I held her to my breast and she took her first feed. I fell asleep the happiest woman alive. I think I secretly hoped that once he got to hear of the baby then all would be well. That he did truly love me and somehow what Katy had told me had been a mistake.'

Clara shuddered, tears springing to her eyes. 'But my hopes and happiness were short-lived. My baby died that very night. I wouldn't believe it, couldn't believe it. She had been so beautiful, so healthy. I thought I would go mad, the pain was unbearable. I was so upset Katy wouldn't let me see her body. She was worried the shock would kill me. She was so frantic for my health she took it upon herself to visit my parents and Phips.' She bowed her head. 'None of them wanted to know. I think Phips was the hardest to bear. I still couldn't accept that all he had said to me had been lies, but I had to believe it then. He must have hated me to turn his back at such a dreadful time. Not even a visit to offer comfort. After all, it was his child I had borne.

'I thought given time my parents would mellow, but they must have gone to their grave despising me for what I did.' She looked at Grace beseechingly. 'I could never act in such a way. Especially not to my own daughter. They may all have thought my sins so terrible to cast me aside like that, not even affording me the chance to explain.'

Grace sadly shook her head. Whatever Charlie did, regardless of whether she herself understood it or not, she would have to stand by her. 'Having a baby out of wedlock is a mortal sin in some people's eyes, Clara. And it's always the women who are branded, regardless of the circumstances.'

Clara sighed forlornly. 'Yes, Grace, and I have suffered ever since. But then, I had sinned so terribly. I had stolen, to all sense and purpose, my sister's fiancé. Which was wrong whichever way you look at it. And then I'd had his baby. The baby's death was God's way of punishing me.

'I did write to my parents to beg their forgiveness. Katy took the letter, but told me my father ripped it up without even reading it. He told her the shame I had brought on the family was too great for him ever to forgive, and that went for my mother as well. I told Katy she must leave the house and go back to my parents. I knew that if she was to make peace with them her only hope was to sever all ties with me. I had to force her to agree. But she knew I was right.'

'And you've never seen your family since?'

'No. For nearly thirty-eight years, I haven't.'

'Oh, Clara. That's so sad. Are you sure they haven't tried to contact you in any way?'

'I'm sure. Katy knew where I was. If any change of heart came about, she knew where to contact me.' Clara sighed. 'Anyway, it's all too late now. My parents would both be dead, and what became of Katy or even Phips I do not know.' She eyed Grace pitifully. 'Now do you understand why I feel unworthy of anyone's friendship?'

Grace ran her hand over the top of her head thoughtfully. 'If you want the truth, Clara, no, I don't.'

Clara's mouth fell open in shock. 'You don't?'

Grace shook her head. 'To put it bluntly, you fell in love with the wrong man. You're not the first or the last woman that will happen to. The way I see it, you did your sister a favour)by exposing this Phips for what he was. It was unfortunate you fell pregnant but when we think we are in love, we do things out of normal character. I personally think you've been too harsh on yourself.'

Clara stared at her in surprise. 'You don't think I deserve to be punished for what I did?'

'None of it was really your fault, Clara. Falling for your sister's fiancé was not something you did deliberately, and the baby dying wasn't your doing. As for your parents' behaviour – they acted in the only way they knew how.'

Clara clasped her hand to her mouth. 'Oh, Grace, I've never looked at it all in that way. I just felt so much blame, I couldn't see things any differently.'

'Well, it's not too late, Clara.'

'Isn't it?'

'No, of course not. I'm sure your sister would be delighted to make contact with you again. After all, it was you who forced her to sever all ties. She probably has a family herself who would be thrilled to meet their auntie.'

Clara shook her head. 'I don't know about that. I've been on my own so long, I think I would find it very difficult.'

Grace smiled warmly. 'Why don't you take a small step at a time?'

'How?'

'You could start by just saying hello to people. That doesn't take too much courage. Then when you feel a bit braver, you could accompany me and Bessie up the town. I'd like to take you to see my own mother. She'd be delighted to make your acquaintance. Then, you never know, after a while you might feel you can contact your sister. I would always come with you. If you wanted me to, that is. But it's all in your own good time, There's no rush.'

Clara stared at her thoughtfully. 'You would help me with all this?'

'Yes, 'course. I'd be delighted.' Grace smiled at her warmly. 'I'm just sad, Clara, that this business has gone on for so long. Please don't waste your life any further. To be honest, at the moment people have far too much on their minds with this war to worry about something that happened forty years ago. And besides, no one in this area knows except for me and I won't be telling anyone, you can rest assured on that.'

Clara exhaled slowly. 'Oh, Grace, how wrong I have been.' She raised grateful eyes. 'It's taken you to point out my error of judgement.'

'Clara, you did what you thought best at the time. The only mistake you made was deciding that nobody would want to know you when in fact I'm sure the opposite is the truth. But forget about the past, Clara. Think of the future. If you want my help at all, I'll be there for you, and I know Bessie will as well.'

Her eyes filled with tears. 'Oh, Grace, thank you, thank you so much. You are a good woman.'

Grace grinned broadly, her eyes twinkling. 'I suppose, as Bessie would say: "I have my uses sometimes." ' She rose and stretched herself. 'I'll make you a cuppa. I could do with one myself.'

When Grace departed, Clara laid her head back on the pillows and stared up at the ceiling. Had her thirty-eight years of isolation really been for nothing?

An overwhelming sadness enveloped her. All those years she had lost, cooped up inside these walls, feeling burdens so great at times she thought she would die under the pressure. It had taken the young lady from next-door to make her see the error of her ways, that what had happened in her youth was something that had happened before to others and would continue to happen long after she was gone.

She herself had more than paid her debt. Grace was right. For however many years she had left she owed it to herself at least to try and live them.

She took a deep breath as Grace re-entered the room armed with the tea-tray, a feeling of hope, something she had forgotten existed, filling her. 'I will take your advice,' said

Clara, smiling. 'One step at a time.'

Grace's eyes lit up in pleasure. 'And you won't be on your own, remember that.'

As Clara sipped at her tea she made another decision. 'Grace, I know this might be an imposition but I would like to ask your help in one other matter?'

'Yes, if I can.'

'When I am well enough, would you help me to clean the room next-door? I have finally to bury the ghost, and tackling that will help me to do it, I hope.'

Grace took her hand. 'Yes, of course. I think that would be a good idea.'

For Grace, the thought of sleeping in her own bed for the first time in over a week was a very welcome one. But despite her tiredness and aching body and the inevitable showdown with Bernard for her prolonged absence from her wifely duties, the outcome of Clara's illness was well worth it.

Her introduction back into society would not happen overnight. The process would be slow, and Grace had no doubt at times difficult as the elderly woman learned once again to trust those around her. But regardless of how long it took, Grace herself would be there for her.

As she made to turn down the entry to her back yard, she stopped, remembering several items she needed from Vinny's shop. She might as well go now before it closed. As she made her way towards the corner shop she knew her decision was only delaying her inevitable meeting with Bernard. She had to face him sooner or later.

Malcolm Vincent was just pulling down the blind on the door when he spotted her. He let the blind spring back and opened the door.

'Just caught me, Mrs Wilkins. Is it much that yer want only me supper's on the table?'

'I'm sorry, Mr Vincent, I didn't realise it was that late. But I would appreciate just a couple of things to tide me over 'til the morning.'

Malcolm stood aside to allow her entry and walked behind the long dark wood counter. He pulled on his white apron and tied it around his back. 'Well, it's understandable, Mrs Wilkins, considering your burdens at the moment. Running back'ards and forwards like you must be. It never rains but it pours, eh? Now, what can I get yer?'

'Just a loaf and some salt, please.' She eyed him sharply. 'I would like to point out that nursing Miss Smith back to health was no burden, Mr Vincent. And I don't like to feel folks thought it was.'

He picked out a loaf and the salt and put them on the counter. 'I never meant that, Mrs Wilkins. We were all sorry to hear about the old gel and only too glad to know she's recovering. No, I was meaning yer father. The worry must be a burden to yer on top of Miss Smith.'

Grace put the groceries into her bag and pulled out her purse. 'My father? What about him?' she asked in bewilderment, handing over a florin.

Malcolm raised his eyebrows, surprised, as he accepted the money. 'Why, his stroke of course. What did you think I was meaning?'

'Stroke?'

'Yes, it happened on Sunday. Ada Harper told me. She'd popped round to your house wi' the message.' He eyed her sharply. 'Didn't you know?'

Grace clasped her hand to her mouth in shock. 'No, I didn't,' she whispered faintly.

Abruptly she turned on her heel and fled.

'Eh up, yer change!' Malcolm shouted after her.

Charlie gently closed the back door and slipped off her shoes.

She eased across the blackout curtain, mindful to check for chinks. It wouldn't do for the air raid warden to come snooping around and shout that a light was showing. He would wake her father and that was the last thing she wanted. He would without doubt manage to spoil her good mood. She rested her back against the door and stared across the darkened room. She didn't know what she had enjoyed most. Seeing *Gone with the Wind* for the fourth time, lusting after Clark Gable, or the time spent in the company of her escort.

She decided it was the latter. Andy Watlin was living and breathing, not a celluloid picture of an inaccessible film star living thousands of miles away in America. She might have gazed longingly into Clark Gable's eyes on the large screen as he had whispered endearments to Vivien Leigh, wishing all the time that he was doing it to herself, but it had been Andy's arm she had felt slip around her shoulders; his lips that had kissed hers goodnight when he had left her just moments ago. Besides, she had read that Clark Gable had bad breath. She shuddered. For all his good looks and money, that was enough to put any woman off.

She tiptoed across the kitchen and into the living room, her mind filled with her forthcoming date with Andy. She had met him in the munitions factory on her very first morning and knew by the way he had looked at her that it was only a matter of time before he asked her out. He had, that lunchtime as she had sat with the rest of the girls on her shift, eating greasy stew and potatoes in the overcrowded, noisy canteen.

Beryl Mills had been green with envy. She had earmarked him first. Since then, miffed to the point of extreme annoyance at what she saw as a rebuff, Beryl would scowl deeply and point her nose in the air every time her own and Charlie's paths crossed.

But the simple fact of who won and who lost was not really

an issue. Andy would not be around for much longer. He was only waiting for his call up papers then he would be gone, like the thousands of other young men before him, leaving all the women behind to wait, worry and wonder, when, if ever, they would come back. Already accounts of atrocities abroad were headlining the news.

The sight of uniformed men and women, laden down with backpacks heading towards the station, milling around on the platform, saying their goodbyes to loved ones, was now a common occurrence, made only the more painful when amongst the crowds embarking were people you knew.

Andy would be amongst those men soon and she would be saying her goodbyes just as she had done to Dennis and Barry. Charlie felt strongly that it was up to her as well as his other friends to make his last remaining days at home happy ones, days he would remember when he was in the thick of it, wondering what it was all about.

Her thoughts of Andy and his like were hurriedly dispelled. She froze in the doorway as she spotted the huddled shape in the armchair, lit only by the dying embers of the fire.

She rushed across and knelt on the peg rug. 'Mam! Whatever's the matter?'

Grace's head jerked up, her face streaked and eyes red from crying. 'Oh, Charlie, Charlie!' she wailed, throwing her arms around her daughter's neck and burying her face in her shoulder.

Charlie's heart thumped painfully in bewildered anticipation, wondering what on earth had upset her mother so badly. She pulled back from Grace's grip and stared into her face. 'Mam, what's happened?' she demanded.

'It's . . . it's just everything, love,' she sobbed. 'Your grandad . . .'

'Oh, Mam, no!' Charlie erupted. 'He's not . . .'

'No, no. He's going to be all right.' She shuddered as a

wave of misery swept over her. 'He had terrible chest pains and your grandma thought the worst. But the doctor put her right. It was indigestion, thank God. But he has to cut down on his work. It's too much for him at his age.' She sniffed loudly and wiped her eyes with the back of her hand. 'But you know your grandad.'

'Yes, the stubborn so and so.' She stared at her mother worriedly. 'But if he's all right, why are you so upset?'

'Because . . . because of your father,' whispered Grace.

'Oh, him,' Charlie hissed. 'What's he done now?'

'It's what he didn't do, Charlie. He didn't tell me about my father when he knew he was ill.'

Charlie sank back on her haunches, exhaling deeply. 'Oh, Mam! How could he?' She clenched her fists tightly as realisation dawned. 'That was the message he got on Sunday. It's Tuesday now and you've only just found out? I don't believe this, really I don't.'

'Nor do I, Charlie. Why? Why does he do this to me? Does he hate me that much?'

A footfall on the stairs alerted them both. Bernard entered the room dressed in his pyjamas and dressing gown, running his hand over his balding head and yawning loudly. He flicked on the light switch. 'What's going on down here? Can't a man get any sleep? I have to get up for work in the morning.' He glared at Grace, who was blinking rapidly, as light assailed her eyes. 'Oh, you remembered where you live then?' he said harshly. 'Are yer back for good or is this just a passing visit?'

Charlie sprang up. 'Don't speak to Mam like that!'

'I'll speak to yer mother as I like. She's my wife. And what time of night do you call this to be coming in? You'll stay in, my girl, 'til further notice.'

'Like hell I will.'

'Stop it! Stop it!' Grace cried, jumping up from her chair. 'Hasn't enough damage been done without causing more?'

Bernard's lip twitched. 'And what damage are you referring to, may I ask?'

'The damage you've done by not telling Mother about Grandad's illness. He could have died,' Charlie erupted.

Bernard looked at her blankly. 'Has he died?'

'No. But that's not the point.' Charlie put her arm around her mother's shoulder and pulled her close. 'Mam only heard through Vinny. You should have told her yourself when you first knew about it. Why didn't you, Dad?'

Bernard's jaw clamped shut. Charlie was right. What plausible excuse had he for not telling Grace, other than his own desire to use the situation against her? If he let this argument slip, his grip on her would be loosened.

'How could I tell her when she wasn't here? If she had been at home, like she should have, this would not have happened.' He took a deep breath and raised his head. 'I was only protecting you, Grace.'

She stared at him. 'Protecting me? How?'

'News like that is very upsetting. I didn't want to come barging into a strange woman's house. I waited for the moment when you came home and I could be of comfort.' He looked at her condescendingly. 'But you never came home when I was here, Grace, so how could I? I hope this teaches you a lesson. Maybe you'll think twice in future before you go offering your services willy-nilly. Now if you don't mind I'm going to bed.' He turned on his heel and headed for the stairs.

He stopped, turned and paused. He was about to do something that he really didn't want to do. But it would once and for all have Grace exactly where he wanted her and put a stop to any fanciful ideas he had a strong inkling she was getting.

'Oh, by the way. All this rotten business with your father and Miss Smith has got me to thinking. It's made me realise how short life is.' He smiled at Grace patronisingly. 'And how good you are, my dear, at looking after old people. I'm fetching my mother tomorrow. She's coming to live with us.'

He fought to stop laughter erupting at the look of horror that filled their faces. 'I'm really thinking of you, Grace. It will be so much easier on you having me mother living here, than running between the two houses. After all, you're not getting any younger yerself, are you? And she'll be company for you now Charlotte is working such long hours at the factory.' He yawned loudly. 'Good night.'

Chapter Twelve

Grace smiled broadly in greeting, then shivered as the back door shot open and Bessie charged through, instantly followed by a blast of arctic wind. January 1940 was setting the record as the coldest this century. Canals and rivers had frozen over for the first time in years. People slid to work instead of walking. It was so cold, the freezing blast that followed Bessie decreased the heat in the tiny kitchen by at least ten degrees in the short time it had taken her to enter and shut the door.

'My God, it's bloody cold out there,' she said, stamping her feet and rubbing her hands together.

'I noticed,' Grace replied, eyes twinkling as she turned over the pastry she was rolling. 'Sit yourself down, and I'll make you a cuppa. The kettle's just about boiled.'

'Lovely,' her friend said, slapping a newspaper parcel on the table.

Grace eyed the parcel. 'What's that, Bessie?'

'A bit of liver fer yer tea.' She leaned over and whispered, 'Our Tom got it from one of 'is buddies down the pub. Two nice big bits so I split it between us.' She straightened up. ''E's on 'is way ter N'thampton to deliver a load so I've no idea what time 'e'll be 'ome.'

Grace smiled gratefully. 'Thanks, Bessie, but I can't take it. You'll need it yerself.'

'Oh, shut up, Gracie Wilkins. What a' friends for if they can't share a bit of good fortune?' She smacked her lips together. 'We're gonna 'ave ours fried wi' onions tonight and I'm lookin' forward to it. Love a bit of liver, I do.' She pulled out the chair to the side of the small table and sat down, eyeing the pastry. 'What yer makin?'

'Meat and potato pie. Though it's more spud than meat.'

Bessie folded her flabby arms under her ample bosom. 'Regardless, I'd mek the best on it, gel. A' yer heard the news?'

'What news?'

'Rationin's started. Butter, sugar and bacon for a start. But mark my words, it won't be long afore there's more.'

'Oh, dear,' Grace groaned. 'Things are going to get hard just as we feared. Bernard takes three sugars in his tea. He isn't gonna like this one bit.'

'Well, that's tough for him. It won't 'urt 'im to cut down. Everyone else'll 'ave too.'

'Who's come?' a voice shouted from the living room.

Bessie tutted loudly. 'There's n'ote wrong with 'er hearin', is there?'

'Shush, Bessie, she'll hear you.'

'I couldn't give a damn.' She tightened her lips grimly. 'I don't know 'ow you put up with 'er, Gracie.'

She sighed deeply. 'It's a case of having to. She is Bernard's mother.'

'I've me doubts on that.'

'Doubts? What d'yer mean?'

Bessie shook her head. 'I personally can't see that old trout doing anythin' that'd result in the conception of a baby.'

Grace spluttered in mirth. 'Oh, Bessie, don't!'

'It's true, I can't.'

If Grace was honest she couldn't either, but respect for her elders, whether she liked them or not, stopped her agreeing with Bessie. Just then her mother-in-law appeared in the doorway, leaning heavily on her walking stick.

'Didn't you 'ear me callin'?' She eyed Bessie scathingly. 'Oh, it's you.' She sniffed disdainfully. 'Can't yer see Grace is busy? And I suspect you've enough to do in yer own 'ouse.' She tightened her lips to two thin lines. 'So I expect you'll be wantin' to get off.'

Grace glared at her in humiliation, then opened her mouth to protest. Bessie stopped her by placing a hand on her arm as she rose from her chair.

'I was just going anyway, me duck.' Her eyes twinkled wickedly. 'Tea'll be ready in five minutes then, Gracie,' she said loudly. 'And bring Clara wi' yer. We'll 'ave a nice little natter. Just the three of us.' She inclined her head towards Ida. ''Bye, Mrs Wilkins. I 'ope yer mouth gets better soon.'

'Me mouth?' Ida scowled. 'There's n'ote wrong wi' me mouth.'

Bessie raised her eyebrows in surprise as she pulled open the back door and another icy blast shot through. 'Ain't there? Well, I'm shocked, I must say, 'cos I'd a thought you'd 'ave 'ad a right nasty taste in it with the amount of bitterness that comes out.' She winked at Grace. 'Five minutes,' she said, pulling the door shut behind herself.

Ida shook with anger, so much so that she nearly overbalanced on the step that led into the kitchen. 'I don't know how you can mix with scum like that!' she spat.

Grace took a deep breath as she slapped the top layer of pastry over the filling and began edging it round. 'Who I make friends with is none of your concern, Mrs Wilkins.' She raised her head and looked at Ida squarely. 'And you were rude to her yourself.'

'I was not. I was stating a fact. You are busy.'

'But that's for me to say, not you. Bessie actually came to bring us some liver which I thought we would have for dinner tomorrow. But being as you dislike her so much, you obviously won't want any.' She fought to hide a smile at the look on Ida's face. 'And while we're talking of food, I'll need your ration books.'

'Me ration books. What for? They're mine they are.'

'Yes, I know they're yours,' Grace said evenly. 'That's why I want them. Rationing has started and if you want feeding, I suggest you hand them over. And you'd better tell me where exactly you registered for what.' She wiped over the table and untied her apron. 'Now I'm off out for a while. Would you please put the pie in the oven about twelve?'

'Me? You're expectin' me to do that when you know fine well I'm an invalid? You're unfeeling you are, Grace Wilkins. Fancy expecting me to do that?'

Grace eyed her sharply. 'Well, I do expect it, Mrs Wilkins. I've a few errands to run and I won't be back in time and it won't hurt you to do a little something around the house. After all, I do everything else.'

Ida glared at her piercingly. 'Well, I never! My Bernard was right about you. He said you'd do anythin' fer the neighbours at the expense of yer own family.'

'Bernard said that, did he? Well, I expect he'd be interested to hear how you climbed the stairs and had a rummage round the drawers in my bedroom. You being such an invalid and all.'

Ida stared at her indignantly. 'I did not!'

'Didn't you? Well, how come you knew about the red headscarf I keep under my underwear? My mother bought that for me several Christmases ago and I've never worn it. I overheard you telling Ada when she called on you yesterday that you thought it disgusting that I should own such a scarf. There's no way you could know about it unless you climbed the stairs and went through my drawers.'

Her eyes lingered on Ida for a moment. When Bernard

had announced his intentions regarding his mother Grace's heart had sunk and she had bitterly resented the fact that he had made his decision without even consulting her and Charlie. Their feelings on the subject had not even been considered. He had instructed her to clear out the front room to make way for his mother's bed and anything else she wanted to bring with her.

For years this announcement had been the one Grace had been dreading but had hoped would never come. Her mother-in-law's arrival at any time would have been hard to accept and live with, but coming now, it had prevented any plan of getting a job. Going to work was out of the question now. She knew this without even mentioning the subject to her husband. He would call her thoughtless even to consider leaving this defenceless old woman alone for so long on her own.

As much as she tried not to, she could not help but feel resentful towards Ida, and her self-centred attitude and bigoted opinions did not help matters. Grace just thanked God for her neighbours. Without Bessie and Clara to break the monotony and make her smile, life would be unbearable.

She turned from Ida and took her coat from the back of the door. 'Now don't forget, about twelve, gas mark five. Or your son won't be pleased to come home and find his dinner not ready. I'll be back in time to put on the spuds.'

Clara was delighted to see her but a bit sceptical about a visit to Bessie's.

'Now come on, Clara,' Grace said encouragingly. 'You're well over your illness and it's only a short walk. It'll do you good, and I'll make sure you get back all right.'

Clara eyed her cautiously. 'I'd like to come,' she said hesitantly. 'Bessie's a grand girl and she does make me laugh with all her tales.' She paused, worrying if she was up to the visit, but more worried that if she kept making excuses, the offers could dry up. People only had so much patience after all. 'Yes, all right, I will. Just let me get my coat.'

Grace beamed in pleasure and before Clara could change her mind the pair were shutting her back door and heading for the entry, Clara bringing a packet of Nice biscuits to eat with their tea.

Grace paused by the entry gate. 'Can you hear someone crying, Clara?'

She listened. 'I can. I think it's one of the Cotting children. It's certainly coming from that direction anyway.'

'You're right, it is.'

They found Tony huddled on the back step, shivering with cold, tears of misery pouring down his face.

Grace knelt down and placed her hand on his bare knee. Clara hovered at her back.

'Tony,' she spoke softly, 'what's the matter, pet? Why aren't you wearing the coat I got you? You'll perish in this weather. And why aren't you at school?'

He raised his tear-streaked face to Grace. 'Jessie's gone to the pawn wi' me coat 'cos we had no money for the gas, and I've locked meself out and she's got the key.'

'Where's your mother, Tony?'

'Me muvver!' He sniffed loudly and wiped his grubby hand under his nose, raising worried eyes. 'Dunno. We ain't seen 'er for two days.'

Grace glanced quickly up at Clara, then back to the little boy, frowning worriedly. 'Come on, Tony. Come with me.' She took his hand and pulled him. He pulled away from her.

'I can't. What if our Jessie comes back? She'll be mad I've gone.'

'Don't worry about Jessie, my love. I'll speak to her. Now we must get you into the warm.'

Clara took her arm. 'Bring him back to my house, Grace. Poor little mite.'

She smiled worriedly. 'Thanks, Clara, but I feel we'd be better taking him along to Bessie's. She might have some warm clothing I can borrow for him 'til we can get his own sorted out.'

Bessie placed three mugs of steaming tea on the table and glanced over at Tony huddled by the fire, eating a thick slice of bread and dripping, wrapped in a grey blanket reading one of Willy's tattered comics. Bobbie was lying flat on his back to the side of him, fast asleep. She shook her head. 'Poor little tyke. Where's 'is mother, that's what I wanna know? 'Ow could any woman leave 'er kids like that?'

'There might be a valid reason, Bessie. We should wait and see what she says when she comes home before we jump to conclusions.'

'You would say summat like that, Gracie. You see the good in everybody. Well, not me. The woman's up to no good mark my words.'

'Grace is right,' Clara said softly. 'We must wait to hear what explanation Mrs Cotting gives before we make assumptions.'

'Huh!' Bessie mouthed, unconvinced. 'Well, as regards clothes, I could lend a couple of our Willy's old pullys, but I'll need 'em back. I was gonna undo 'em and re-knit a cardy for our Bobbie.' She glanced at her son lying flat out on the rug, and shook her head. 'I tell yer, if that little lad of mine grows much more, 'e'll outgrow 'is strength.'

Grace and Clara laughed at her remark.

'Our Tom reckons I feed 'im too much,' she continued. 'But I can't stand skinny kids.'

They all froze and instinctively looked upwards as the loud wail of the air raid warning sounded. 'Oh, my God,' Bessie groaned. 'Not again. Quick, in the pantry!'

Grace jumped up. 'I'd better get back to Bernard's mother. Make sure she's all right. I'll take Tony with me.'

'Oh, sod 'er!' Bessie shouted over the wail as she scooped

up Bobbie with one arm and grabbed Tony with the other. 'Surely she's got the sense to get under the table or summat? Just get yerself in the pantry, Gracie.'

Crammed in the limited space of the dark pantry, the three women squatted on the stone floor, scarcely daring to breathe as the wail of the sirens continued. Tony was pressed into Grace's side; Bobbie, undeterred by all the noise, was gazing around him, a finger firmly planted up his nose.

Bessie tutted loudly. 'D'yer know, gels, I've seen more of the inside of this pantry since these bloody air raids started than I've done in the ten years I've lived in this 'ouse.' Her eyes twinkled brightly in the darkness. 'And if I'd 'ave known I wa' gonna 'ave such distinguished company, I'd 'ave asked our Tom to spruce it up a bit.'

A terrified Clara and Grace spluttered with mirth.

'Oh, Bessie, don't. I'm too frightened to laugh,' Grace said, shivering.

'And me,' chipped in Clara.

'Arr, rubbish! It'll be a false alarm again, you mark my words. I reckon they do it to keep us on our toes.'

Within the gloomy interior of the pantry they lapsed into silence, each filled with her own private fears.

Grace was worried about her parents, her daughter, and the thought that at any moment a bomb could drop and that would be the end of them or herself. She smiled. If that happened, though, at least she was with friends.

A wicked thought fleetingly crossed her mind, one which she severely scolded herself for having. Wouldn't it be a miracle if a bomb dropped on her house when the only occupants were Bernard and his mother? The release from her bonds would be instant. But how terrible she could think that!

Since the day Ida had moved in, she had set out to rule the roost. Every movement Grace and Charlie made was questioned in the belief on Ida's part that she should be consulted and give approval, even for a visit to the shops which was timed to the minute. She was rude to visitors, the few they did have, and turned her nose up at any meals placed in front of her, before gobbling them up.

All in all her arrival had tied Grace securely to the house. In one fell swoop all her dreams of liberty had been cruelly squashed.

But worse than that was the terrifying thought that Charlie was losing all patience at the constant jibes and questions on her friends and whereabouts; that one day very shortly she would announce she had had enough and was moving out. That was the one thing Grace could not bear and consequently most of her waking hours were filled with keeping the peace and shielding her daughter from Ida's wicked tongue. It was hard and sometimes nigh on impossible, but at least this way Charlie's inevitable departure would hopefully be stalled.

Clara smiled to herself in the darkness. Several months ago, to have a friend had been an impossible dream. Now she had two of them, and if her end was about to come, she could think of no better people to meet her maker with. With Grace and Bessie's help she was learning, albeit very slowly, to venture forward, constantly reminding herself that never, never could she return her life to the way it used to be. Though if she did die now at the hands of the mad German, at least her last few months had been happier than any she could remember.

Tony was worried about his mother's disappearance. He knew she wasn't the kind of mother other children had. One that cooked tasty dinners that were ready just when your belly was starting to rumble; gave a cuddle after a fall; tucked you into bed at night and read a story; was always there, day or night. But for all he felt his mother was lacking, he loved her. He pressed himself further into Grace's side, seeking reassurance from her warm body. Her arm tightened around him and for the first time in his short life he felt secure. Suddenly the pain and anguish of his mother's absence seemed worthwhile if he could feel the comfort of this lady's arm around him. Momentarily he wished that *she* was his mother.

Grace looked down at him in the near darkness and smiled. 'All right, my love?' she asked, squeezing him tightly. 'Don't worry, as soon as this is all over, we'll find your mam and Jessie.'

He nodded up at her, his wish growing in strength. Mrs Wilkins acted just like the kind of mother he longed for, but for all that it still did not stop the gnawing ache settling in his stomach for the woman who had given birth to him.

Bessie, knowing her youngest children would be safe in the bowels of the school air raid shelters, watched over by the formidable school ma'ams and the military-type Headmaster, had managed to push all worrying thoughts of Dennis and Barry to the back of her mind and was thinking solely of her beloved husband Tom. He was out on the road somewhere driving his loaded lorry.

Suddenly she missed him dreadfully. She desperately wanted the feel of his strong arms around her for comfort. Like many others in the city who until now had been glad of their location in the heart of England, she felt suddenly afraid that the war was escalating, that very soon not only German planes would be turning their attention to their little island but the land army too and then they'd know no peace at all, just like the poor people in Europe.

What if that was happening now, she thought, and her Tom was a target for a gunner as he drove unsuspecting along the open roads? She shuddered, pulling her son closer to her, then silently scolded herself severely. She, Bessie Rudney, who had always taken everything as it came and handled it in her own inimitable fashion, was not about to wish misfortune upon herself. If it did happen then she would face it. It was no good getting upset and making herself ill worrying about things that might never transpire. Her Tom would come home safe, as would all her children. They dare not do anything else because otherwise they'd have to face her wrath.

She took a breath and raised her eyes upwards, scanning over the packed shelves filled with various tinned foods, packets of Symmington's soups, jars of Bovril, evaporated milk, and other items she had stockpiled, afraid to use them just in case supplies dried up altogether. A tickle of mirth caught the back of her throat. She began to laugh. She laughed so loud it drowned out the wail of the sirens.

All eyes were upon her, wondering what on earth was making her so merry.

'It's them,' she guffawed, pointing upwards. 'If we stay in 'ere and a bomb drops, it won't be the blast that kills us, it'll be them tins landing on our 'eads!'

She struggled upright, hitching Bobbie up in her arms. 'Come on, you lot. It's more dangerous in 'ere than it is outside. I'm gonna mash a cuppa.'

Instantly, Grace and Clara saw the wisdom of Bessie's observation and hurriedly followed her out, dragging Tony behind them.

She was right. The air raid was thankfully yet another false alarm.

Thanking Bessie for her hospitality, Grace saw Clara safely home and, hand in hand with Tony, still wrapped in Bessie's grey blanket, went in search of his sister Jessie and their mother.

They found Jessie in the Cotting living room, huddled by a tiny fire burning in the grate. On the table was a loaf of bread, a slab of deep yellow-coloured marge and a lump of cheese. These meagre items, along with the coal for the fire, were obviously the result of pawning Tony's coat, thought Grace.

On seeing her brother enter, Jessie leapt up and fell upon him, hugging him fiercely.

'Oh, our Tony, where yer bin, where yer bin? I've bin that worried. I told yer not to move, didn't I?'

On realising Grace was standing in the doorway she pulled back from her brother and eyed her neighbour warily, mouth set firm.

'He's been with me, Jessie love,' Grace said kindly. 'He was locked out.'

Jessie stared down at him. 'Wadda you mean, locked out?'

He raised scared eyes. 'I was, Jessie. I wa' locked out, honest.'

She shook her head. 'The door weren't locked, it'd stuck. Mam sez it's 'cos the wood gets swollen in winter and doesn't fit properly. You 'ave to give it a good shove, that's all.' She grabbed his hand tightly, pulling him close, before looking over at Grace and raising her head proudly. 'I'm sorry if he's bin a bother. I'll take care of him now.'

Grace smiled. 'He was no bother, Jessie love.' She glanced over the sparsely furnished room, her eyes settling momentarily on the foodstuffs on the table. Instinctively she knew that these few items were all they possessed and would not go far. She shuddered. The air in the room was damp and she knew that the small fire in the grate was the first that had been lit there for a while. She looked across at the two pathetic figures standing by the table and her heart went out to them both. She forced another smile. 'Look, Jessie, I can see you ain't had time to prepare a hot dinner. Why don't you and Tony come back with me now? I've a meat and potato pie in the oven. It won't take me a minute to boil a few spuds.'

As the invitation left her mouth she instantly worried how she would divide the pie between them all. But dividing the food was of lesser importance than the reaction she would receive from Bernard and his mother. But suddenly she didn't care what they said, these children needed warming and feeding and, even more urgent than that, showing some love. 'Well, Jessie, what do you say? I make a real tasty pie so I've been told.'

Tony's eyes lit up in delight and he licked his lips as he looked up at his sister expectantly.

Jessie's mouth watered. She hadn't eaten a decent hot meal for days. But accepting this invitation, as much as she wanted to, would be letting her mother down, she felt. She bit her bottom lip anxiously. Where was her mother? The worry and fear that were rapidly growing as Madge's absence lengthened was getting too much for Jessie's nearly nine years to cope with. She desperately wanted to confide in this lovely kind woman who lived two doors away. To share her burden would be such a relief. But she couldn't. Pride and allegiance to her mother stopped her. She tightened her grip on her brother's hand and yanked him closer. 'No, fanks, missus. I can manage.'

Grace's shoulders sagged, but before she could find words to persuade the girl to change her mind, the back door slammed and Madge Cotting appeared in the living-room doorway.

'What's going on?' she asked, unbuttoning her coat as she advanced into the room. She groped for her packet of cigarettes and hurriedly lit one, drawing deeply on the smoke, her wary eyes falling on Grace.

Grace quickly scanned the woman. She was dishevelled, as though hurriedly dressed, remains of makeup streaking her face. She took a deep breath. 'The children were worried, Mrs Cotting. Tony said you hadn't been home for two days.'

For a fleeting moment fear glinted in Madge's eyes. She

quickly shook her head. 'As though I'd leave me kids,' she said defensively, walking towards the table and placing her handbag on top. She looked Grace straight in the eyes. 'You shouldn't believe anything our Tony sez. He's a little liar.' She looked across at her son. 'Ain't yer, our Tony?'

His head drooped.

'Well, answer me!' she barked.

He nodded. 'Yes, Mum.'

'See, 'e even admits it. I told 'em I'd got an extra shift. Didn't I, Jessie?'

She looked at her mother blankly then hurriedly nodded.

Grace narrowed her eyes. She knew the woman was lying.

Madge smiled brightly. 'I appreciate your concern, Mrs Wilkins, real neighbourly of you it was. It's right warming for me to know when I'm slaving at my machine, I've good neighbours at home.' She turned towards her children, pulling a handful of coins out of her pocket. 'Here, Jessie, go and get some chips and a couple of pies, and when you come back we'll make a list of the other things we need. I got paid today.' Jessie took the money and shot out of the door. Madge turned back to Grace. 'I'm forgetting me hospitality. Would you like a cuppa or somefing?'

Grace shook her head. 'No, thanks. I have to get back and see to my husband's dinner.'

'Rightio. I won't keep you then.'

Madge saw Grace to the door and shut it firmly behind her. She sat down on a chair by the table and eased off her shoes, realising that in her hurry to get dressed she had put on her best pair, the ones she had been out dancing in the previous night. She hoped the Wilkins woman hadn't noticed. She raised her eyes to her son, still wrapped in Bessie's blanket, standing rigid by the table.

'Come 'ere, you,' she said, extending her arms. He slowly inched over and she pulled him close. 'Wadda you go and tell her that for, eh? I've told you and Jessie often enough, you don't tell nosy neighbours any of our business.' She planted a kiss on his cheek and ruffled his hair. 'I have to work, Tony love. Without the bit I earn we'd be on the streets. And if you go round telling people I ain't bin home they'll get the authorities and you'll be put in a home. You wouldn't like that, would yer?'

Tony's eyes filled with tears and he sniffed. 'No, Mum.'

'No, 'course you wouldn't. She eyed him searchingly. 'Have you bin to school?'

He shook his head. 'Jessie pawned me coat to get some coal and some fings to eat.'

'Oh, gawd,' she groaned. 'You know I told yer you'd 'ave to go after what Mrs Wilkins said last time.'

Madge sighed heavily. She'd have to use money she intended for other purposes to get the coat out of the pawn. She couldn't risk others poking their noses in again and moaning she neglected her kids. Accusations such as that attracted attention from sources she would sooner not alert.

Blast! she thought angrily. She herself needed new face powder and stockings. She couldn't expect a man like Jacky to take her out without decent stockings which were getting scarce now and, when found, expensive. Well, she'd just have to wangle things somehow. With a bit of luck she might get a few clients tonight. With their money in her purse she could get her own purchases and Tony's coat.

She smiled at him. 'Don't go worrying about that silly old coat. I'll give Jessie the money to get it out. Now you can have the rest of today off, but you must go to school tomorrow else the Board Man'll be round and then we'll be in trouble. A' you listening to me, Tony? Don't bunk off school again whatever happens, 'cos I can't promise they'd let me have you back again if they took you away,' she added, wanting to scare her son. She couldn't care less whether they went to school or not, but the misdemeanour could jeopardise her plans.

He stared at her, scared witless. He'd heard what happened to children in those homes. He'd been read a story once by a teacher back in London, something about water and babies, if his memory served him correctly. The children in the book had lived in a home and had been locked in cold dark cellars for days on end, without food or water, and been forced to climb chimneys to clear soot. Many boys much younger than himself had burned to death. He shuddered in fear. Suddenly he didn't care how cold and hungry he was in the future, he would go to school regardless. No Board Man was going to drag him away from his sister and mother and put him in a home.

'I'm sorry, Mum,' he blurted, tears rushing down his cheeks. He lunged forward and hugged her tightly. 'I won't tell anybody anyfink again and I will go to school, Mum, I promise.'

She wrenched herself free from his embrace and slapped him playfully on his bottom. 'That's my lad,' she said, smiling and fingering the grey blanket. 'That'll do for yer bed.'

'But it's Mrs Bessie's. She says I've got to take it back, and the pully she lent me.'

'Oh, she didn't mean it. She's got plenty and won't miss them old things. Now go and take it up and put it on yer bed.' She yawned loudly. 'When I've eaten my pie and chips I'm gonna get my head down for a while. I hope I can trust yer not to get into any more trouble today?'

He nodded at her and she watched silently as he left the room, then took a deep breath and reached for her packet of cigarettes. That was a narrow one. She hadn't counted on the Wilkins woman sticking her nose in where it wasn't wanted. She'd reckoned on Jessie's resourcefulness to handle the matter of her absence. But, she supposed, Jessie did her best. After all she was only eight. Her daughter had a long way to go before she had learned as many tricks as Madge herself knew.

She leaned back in her chair and smiled to herself. The fun she'd had! It had been well worth the lies she had just told.

She blew a plume of smoke and watched it swirl in the air, feeling a warm rush race through her body. She had promised herself she would land Jacky and she had. He was truly smitten. Hadn't he told her just last night as they had lain side by side in his king-sized bed in the flat he owned on the Belgrave Road. They had both smoked Turkish cigarettes, drunk a few large scotches, and she had snuggled provocatively against him, pampered beyond belief by the feel of satin sheets against her bare skin, something she had only dreamed of previously.

She had more than liked the luxury this man could give her, was hungry for it and wanted desperately to live in the surroundings he could offer, money seemingly unlimited. Didn't she deserve that after all her years of struggle? She shuddered, cold fear settling upon her. What would he do if he saw where she really came from? And especially the kids.

She shuddered again. Children of any age or description did not figure at all in the life of a man such as Jacky McCoughlin. He mixed with people the police watched like hawks but could never pin anything on.

When he moved, it was quickly. He had to in order to secure the dubious deals he was into. She knew through keeping her ears and eyes open that the black market figured heavily in his healthy bank balance, and thus it could only swell as the war worsened and need for the items he procured and supplied grew.

If she became his woman, which at this moment she desired to be above all else, he would expect her to be at his side, looking the business, all the time. How could she manage that with two children to look after, children he knew nothing about? If ever he found out he would dump her as quickly as he had picked her up.

She ground out the stub of her cigarette on an empty plate. Somehow, until he asked her to move in, or dare she hope marry him, she must keep all this a secret.

And if she did pull it off, what about the kids then?

She stroked her chin thoughtfully. No way on God's earth could she let go of this opportunity, she would be mad to do so. It was something she had dreamed of since a child as she had fought for a space beside her ten brothers and sisters on the lumpy, lice-ridden mattress, counting the cockroaches that climbed the damp walls and listening to her mother and father screaming at each other in the adjoining room.

She shuddered at the memory. But what about the kids? She took a deep breath. Well, maybe they would be better off in a home or being fostered. That way she herself could have the best of both worlds. She could keep her new man and visit the kids when she could manage without Jacky's knowledge. He need be none the wiser.

She jumped as Jessie appeared with a newspaper parcel. Marge smiled, good-humoured after making her decision. 'They smell good. Give our Tony a shout, he's up the stairs, and let's tuck in before these get cold. And put some more coal on the fire, Jessie love, it's freezing in 'ere.'

As Jessie obediently complied Madge unwrapped the parcels and divided the food. Yes, she thought, as things stood the kids would be far better off without her, and she them.

Chapter Thirteen

Charlie wiped a stream of sweat from her brow as she manoeuvred another tray of shell cases on to the conveyor belt on their way towards the inspection girls. The inside of the factory was hot as a greenhouse, heated to Regulo 6 by the relentless August sun beating down on the corrugated iron roof.

The sun, it seemed, was making up for its rest during the long dreadful winter. From the onset of summer it had gradually heated to this intensity. It hadn't rained for over two months now and the ground outside was parched to a cinder. Charlie raised her eyes, wishing that somehow the roof could be lifted just a little to allow even the smallest waft of welcome air inside. If it didn't cool down soon, she'd be done to a turn, crisp at the edges.

Regardless of the heat, the constant stream of sweat that poured and the ache of tired muscles, she, like the rest of the workforce, laboured relentlessly, often not stopping even to drink their tea. Now more than ever the munitions their factory supplied were urgently required. Several days ago, on 13 August, the battle for Britain had begun in earnest. For the people of England, August 1940 changed the history of their island. It began with the horrific bombing of London.

From the moment the news of the fight in the skies began to filter through, the mood of the people of Leicester changed. The illusion that the war would not reach their island, let alone their own city, was shattered.

Families who had previously scoffed at air raid warnings would rush to gather their belongings as soon as they sounded, no longer prepared to take a chance. Weighed down with pillows, blankets, flasks of tea and sandwiches, they would rush to the shelters and dugouts, not emerging until the all clear sounded.

The brave declaration that it would all be over by Christmas now rang hollow.

Charlie felt a tap on her shoulder and turned to find Sybil Gamble standing behind her, hands resting on the metal handlebar of a large trolley on which sat a pallet of finished shell cases she was delivering to the despatch area. On one of the shells, marked in large black lettering was: HITLER, THIS ONE'S FOR YOU!

'A' yer heard the latest, Charlie?' she shouted over the drone of the machines. 'London got it bad again last night. Apparently the whole of docklands is on fire. Fire brigades from all over have been called in to help.'

Charlie gaped at her in horror. 'Oh, my God, Syb.'

'I know, it's bloody awful. I just keep thinking of those poor people. I feel so 'elpless.'

Charlie clenched her fists. 'We ain't being helpless, Syb. We're doing our bit making the munitions to fight back. And remember, Leicester's took in over thirty thousand evacuees and given them shelter. So in our way we are doing our bit.'

Sybil grinned wryly. 'Yeah, yer right.' She patted the shell case bearing Hitler's name. 'Let's hope this does its job. Blow the bastard to smithereens! Anyway, coming fer a drink tonight after work? Wash the dust outta our throats.'

'Haven't you to get home?'

'Nah, me mother-in-law's got the kids. It won't 'urt her to keep 'em a bit longer.'

Charlie paused thoughtfully. All she really wanted to do was get home and wash the grime from her body, eat her meal and climb into bed for a good night's sleep – providing, of course, that a warning did not sound. But if she was truthful home was the last place she wanted to go. Since Ida had moved in, life there had grown steadily worse. Her grandmother and father between them made life very difficult and Charlie wondered how her own mother put up with it all. Her decision was quick.

'Yeah, I'd love to, Syb. But I'm on 'til seven.'

'Me too. I'll meet you at the gates just after. Okey doke?'

'Okey doke.'

Sybil placed two half pints of bitter on the table and scowled deeply. 'I'm sure the landlord waters the beer. It's like bloody cat's pee. No 'ead at all.'

Charlie picked up hers, took a large gulp and placed the glass back down, wiping her mouth with the back of her hand. 'I don't care, Syb. My throat's that parched it tastes like nectar.' She opened a packet of crisps, sprinkling them liberally with salt from the tiny blue twist of paper inside, and offered the packet to Sybil.

'No, ta. I've to think of me figure even if you ain't.'

Charlie grinned to herself. Sybil had a figure to match that of Rita Hayworth and the hairstyle to go with it. She turned men's heads wherever she went. No one would guess she was well into her thirties with three children. She caught Sybil eyeing a group of soldiers on leave and nudged her arm.

'You're married,' she said, laughing.

'Yeah, to a sailor. And you know what they say about sailors, Charlie gel? A woman in every port. Well, I wouldn't. put it past my old man to have two, the lecherous old git! What's good for 'im is good for me. 'Sides, I'm fed up wi' waiting for 'im to come 'ome on leave, I could do with a bit of fun. I've no doubts 'e's 'ad 'is share.' She glanced over at the soldiers again. 'The dark 'un's a bit of all right, and his mate's definitely got eyes for you.'

Charlie tutted nonchalantly, picked up her glass and downed the contents. 'Well, he can look as much as he likes. At this moment, I'm too hot and tired, and to be honest I can't be bothered. Another?'

Sybil drained her glass and handed it over. 'Ta, me duck, and I'll have a gin as well, being's you're payin'.'

When Charlie returned with the drinks, Sybil looked at her, frowning.

'What's the matter, gel? You ain't your usual ray of sunshine. Is it a bloke?'

Charlie shook her head. 'I wish it was that simple.' She sighed deeply, not really wanting to air her family problems in public, but suddenly she felt the need to. 'Sybil, I've got a female relation that'd make Attila the Hun look like a saint, and to be honest I'm just about at the end of my tether with her.'

Sybil shook her head. 'You can't possibly 'ave, Charlie. That honour belongs to me.'

She stared at her. 'Honest?'

'True as I'm sitting 'ere. My mother-in-law is that bad she even charged me baby-sitting money for watchin' her own grandkids while I had to go to 'ospital to get me wisdom tooth pulled. Bloody cow, she is.'

'She never?'

Sybil took a sip of her gin. 'Listen, gel, I could tell you stories that'd make yer 'air curl. She's never forgive me for marryin' her son and she never will. I personally detest the woman but I need 'er so I can come to work. But I tell yer, she meks me pay for the privilege.'

Charlie gawped. Maybe Ida wasn't so bad after all.

'What's your old gel like then?' Sybil asked.

'My grandmother? Huh, she's just an interfering old devil and my father's as bad. I don't know how my poor mother puts up with it all. You remember Andy, don't you?'

'Andy? Young lad, worked in despatch. You were seein' him, weren't you, before he went away?'

'That's him. I quite liked him. On the Saturday before his departure he asked me to go to the pictures and, without thinking, I asked him to come to tea.' She shook her head. 'Never, never again will I do a stupid thing like that! I must have been crazy.'

Sybil looked at her, intrigued. 'Why, what happened?'

'My mother, bless her, made a cake – and you know how hard that is now rationing's taken hold.'

'Only too well. We've money in our pockets and nothin' in the shops to spend it on. To be honest, I'm getting fed up meself wi' the queuing and when you get to the front they've bloody sold out.'

Charlie laughed. 'Fact of life now, ain't it? Anyway, a lovely cake it was and some paste sandwiches. My dad, aided and abetted by my grandma, proceeded to pick the food to bits. Insinuated it wasn't fit for human consumption while my grandmother pushed her plate away with a look on her face that would turn fresh butter rancid. Then they started on Andy. What were his prospects? What did his mother and father do? et cetera, et cetera. Andy got redder and redder whilst my mother and I slid further down in our seats, we were so embarrassed. As soon as he was able, he shot out of the house as quick as his legs would carry him. I never saw him again after that.'

Sybil grimaced at her. 'I know what I'd 'ave done.'

'Oh, what?'

'Emptied the tea pot over 'em.'

Charlie laughed wryly. 'Syb, I'd have liked nothing more. But it wouldn't have been worth the moment of pleasure. I can just about take their attitude 'cos I'm out of the house most of the time, but it wouldn't have been fair on Mam. She has to put up with a lot more than I have to take.'

Sybil took a gulp of her drink. 'Well, if you ever fancy getting out you can always come and bunk in with me. It ain't the Ritz but at least you'd be shot of them two.'

Charlie stared at her. 'Do you mean that?'

'I don't say things I don't mean. You'd be company for me. As long as you don't mind kids, that is? Mine are the devil's offspring.'

'I bet they're little angels compared to my father and grandmother. Anyway, thanks, Sybil. I'll bear that in mind. No offence meant, but it would have to be the last resort because of my mother.'

'I understand. I'll air the bed ready though, just in case.'

Sybil turned her attention back to the bar. 'I do think 'e's rather nice. D'yer fancy another drink?'

Charlie laughed. 'What, so you can chat him up?'

'No 'arm in it, is there? Give the man something to remember when 'e's back fightin' the Germans.'

Charlie shook her head. 'Another time, if you don't mind. I want to pop in and see my Granny and Grandad Taylor before I go home.'

'Suit yerself,' Sybil said sulkily, draining her glass. 'I'll see yer tomorrow then.'

'Aren't you coming?'

'What, and miss an opportunity like this? Listen, gel, I'll be a long time dead. Go on, get off, I'll see yer tomorrow.

Connie Taylor was delighted to see her granddaughter. 'Come away in, Charlie, my old love. Yer just in time for a quick chat with yer grandad afore he goes to work.'

Charlie kissed her grandmother warmly on the cheek, then grimaced hard. 'He's still at it then?'

'It'd take more than the fright of a stroke to stop yer grandad from workin'. 'E'll be there, boots black, 'til the building falls down.' Her grandmother sighed. 'Charlie love, yer grandad would go mad if 'is time wasn't filled. 'E needs to work, especially now. 'E's only a caretaker, but it makes 'im feel 'e's doin' his bit. 'Sides, being honest, darlin', we need the money. But don't tell yer mother, promise? She'd fret herself silly.'

Charlie sighed heavily. 'I promise, Gran.'

'Good, now let's get you a cuppa. I expect it's just a quick visit. You young 'uns . . . rush, rush, rush! Never a minute to spare. Still, we love to see you, gel, regardless how long.'

Albert grinned in delight as she entered and beckoned her over. 'Come and sit 'ere, Charlie gel. Come and see what I'm mekin'.'

She sat on the stool at the side of his chair and inspected the wooden puppet closely. 'Oh, Grandad, it's beautiful. You are clever.'

'Yeah, I am, ain't I? When it's finished, I can sell it for five bob. Not a bad return from a bit of old wood I picked up in the factory yard, is it?'

'It sure isn't,' she agreed heartily, accepting the mug of tea her grandmother handed her. 'Any news, Grandad?'

He eyed her eagerly. 'I'll say. We bagged seventy-eight Nazi planes to thirteen of ours last night. Not bad eh? If this carries on, our lads'll soon whip those Germans into shape. Anthony Eden made a marvellous speech. It's a pity you never got here earlier, you could have listened wi' us.'

Charlie frowned. She didn't want to tell her grandfather she had been in the pub. 'Well, we're well in front of our orders in the factory. The boss personally thanked us all today and said we could be proud of ourselves.' She grinned wickedly. 'I doubt that Hitler realised what he was taking on when he challenged us British.'

'Well said, young Charlie,' Arthur spoke proudly.

He turned from her and resumed his carpentry.

'Got yerself a nice boyfriend then yet?' Connie asked.

'Grandma!' She grimaced. 'Fat chance of that whilst this war's on. The only men left are either too young or old enough to be my father.'

'Yeah, I suppose. Well, let's 'ope they're all back soon, eh? I'd like to see you happily wed, gel, before I cop it.'

'Gran, you've years in you yet.'

'Not so many, gel. But I'll do me damnedest to stick around for a while. Anyway, how's the job goin'?' Connie asked, sitting in her armchair and picking up her knitting.

'Busy and hot.'

'Ah, can't say as I envy you, stuck in that factory in this weather.'

'You can say that again. I don't mind the work, Gran, but the heat's appalling. All I've done all day is sweat and it's very wearing.'

Connie frowned. 'Charlie! Young ladies do not sweat.'

She laughed loudly. 'Well, this one does, Gran. Bucketfuls.'

Connie laughed with her. 'Oh, deary me, what are we gonna do with you, eh?'

Charlie held her mug out. 'Pour me another cuppa.'

'Cheeky monkey. 'Elp yerself. What about you, Arthur? Arthur?' Connie tutted. 'See your grandad, give him a piece of wood and 'e's in oblivion. Arthur!' she shouted. 'Do you want another cuppa afore you go to work?'

'Eh! Oh, yes please, and I'll have some jam on mine.'

Connie raised her eyebrows in exasperation. 'Told yer, 'e never heard a word I said. Might as well talk to a brick wall.'

Charlie smiled warmly at him, whittling away at his piece of wood. She rose, walked towards the table and picked up the teapot. 'At least his mind's occupied and he's happy,' she said, pouring out the tea.

'Oh, he's happy, me duck. Ain't yer, Arthur?' Her husband didn't reply and Connie sighed, smiling. Her eyes grew distant as the knitting needles clicked rhythmically 'Which is more than I can say for yer mother.'

Charlie stared at her as she pulled a chair out from under the table and sat down. 'What, Gran? What was that you said about my mother?'

Connie shook herself. 'Oh! Oh, nothin', just that I don't think she's very happy. Not that she sez 'ote to me. But I'm her mother, I know these things. I was only thinkin' to meself this mornin' after she'd popped in, that it was a pity she couldn't get a job. She needs summat does your mother, summat to get her out of the 'ouse more, especially now Ida's living wi' yer. That woman is the devil in woman's clothing. She has your mother run ragged. But Grace swore me to say nothin' in case I mek matters worse. Mek matters worse!' Connie repeated ruefully. 'I'd string the woman up given half the chance.'

'And I'd kick the chair away,' Charlie said harshly.

'Eh, yer don't mean that, gel? You ain't the grudging kind, never have been. Anyway, a job is just what she needs.' Connie sighed deeply. 'You see, young Charlie, she never really had the chance to see any of the wide world. At your age she was married with you as a toddler. It's a pity. Not about you, me duck,' she added hastily. 'But yer mam had good prospects at Janson's. Shame she had to give it all up. I reckon she'd have made somethin' of 'erself.'

Charlie looked at her thoughtfully. 'Well, it's not too late. She could get a job easily if she wanted.'

Connie shook her head. 'Not whilst yer father's got a say she wouldn't, and definitely not while that mother of his is around playing the invalid. Invalid indeed! I don't believe it for a minute.' She looked at her granddaughter thoughtfully. 'I always used to think that my Grace was happy with

213

Bernard, but these last few months I've begun to wonder. You know sometimes, Charlie, we don't see things that are under our noses.'

Charlie gnawed on her lip. As much as she would have loved to open up to her granny and tell her exactly how things were, she couldn't. Her mother did not want her own mother to know her situation. Grandma was old, too old, Grace had told her, to have needless worries thrust upon her. Charlie had to respect her mother's wishes and deep down she agreed with her. If her grandparents did know the full truth it was not as though they could do anything to ease her mother's burden. Except, maybe, string Ida up as her grandmother had suggested!

She sat silent for a moment then took a breath, her eyes twinkling. 'I've had a thought, Grandma.'

Connie stopped her knitting. 'Oh?'

'Well, factories are crying out for workers. Posters have gone up all over the town, and they're using all sorts of incentives to entice people. I reckon it'll be compulsory soon for able bodied persons over a certain age regardless of whether they want to or not. Anyway, I was thinking, if my mam won't go after a job, what if a job came to her?'

Connie frowned. 'Eh?'

'It's just an idea, Gran. Let me investigate. It might take a while with having to work all hours in the factory, but rest assured I'll tell you all when I find out more.'

Connie grimaced. 'I wish you wouldn't do that, our Charlie. I shan't be able to sleep for wonderin'.'

'Grandma, you're always telling me that you fall asleep as soon as your head touches the pillow.'

'Ah, well, maybe I do. But I shan't tonight.' Her eyes caught the battered tin clock on the mantel. 'Eh up, Arthur, a' yer seen the time? Arthur, the time.'

His eyes flew to the clock and he jumped up, the tin tray

holding his work tools and pieces of wood falling on the floor with a clatter. 'Oh, look what yer made me do now! Did yer have to shout?'

'If I didn't shout you wouldn't 'ear me. The Germans could drop a bomb and the 'ouse could blow up and you'd still be working away,' she said, eyes twinkling affectionately.

Charlie jumped up and began to clear the mess, which was quickly done.

When her grandfather was ready and about to leave, she hooked her arm through his. 'Come on, I'll walk with you to the end of the street.'

Arthur kissed Connie on the cheek. He looked at Charlie proudly, patting her arm. 'See, Connie. I ain't too old yet to land a pretty young gel.'

Chapter Fourteen

Bernard raised his eyes as the double doors of the public house burst open and two women hanging precariously on the arms of airmen fell through. They were all roaring drunk by the looks of them. He eyed them disgustedly as they weaved their way towards the bar and ordered their drinks. He felt it unseemly that women should be allowed in public houses. They should be at home where they belonged.

One of the women leaned her back against the bar and stared around, tapping her foot to the sound of the piano being banged with gusto by a middle-aged woman, hair wrapped in a turban, having come straight from her shift at the sock factory down the road. A cigarette hung from her lips, the ash falling on to the keys. Two other women leaned on the piano, holding their drinks, along with several soldiers. All were singing loudly and out of tune: 'We'll Meet Again', followed by 'Roll out the Barrel', then 'We'll Hang Out our Washing on the Siegfried Line'. On the long seat running the length of the far wall sat several elderly men, a group at the end around a table engrossed in a game of dominoes, seemingly oblivious to all the noise and goings on around them.

The pub was packed to bursting, the air filled with swirling cigarette smoke and the smell of stale beer. Only Bernard noticed these things. Everyone but him was having a good time.

Bernard had not had a good day. His new role of Foreman was not easy. Philip Janson was forever breathing down his neck, and since he'd taken over from Frank Wilby the workload had doubled. Orders had to be fulfilled on time or the official from the Ministry came down to see why.

But how was he supposed to cope with a staff of three half-baked apprentices who spent most of their time plotting capers, usually against himself, and one skilled grinder brought out of retirement for the duration?

Conversation going on around him broke into his thoughts. It was all about the war. He had come to the pub for a peaceful pint and all he could hear was talk of the war. He was getting sick of it. His eyes fell upon a woman with her back against the bar. She was staring at him scornfully. Her scrutiny unnerved him. He watched her as she narrowed her eyes and nudged the other woman next to her.

'What d'yer reckon, Hilda? Coward or what?'

Hilda turned her attention to him. 'Coward, I reckon. Oi!' she shouted loudly over the din. 'Where's yer uniform, eh, mate? Left it at 'ome 'ave yer?'

Bernard cringed as several faces turned and stared across at him. This was not the first time he had been challenged for his lack of uniform. He had got beyond the stage of trying to inform his detractors that he had a key job. They only saw it as an excuse. He held his breath as the two airmen and a group of soldiers at the other end of the bar also turned and stared across, as did the old men playing dominoes. The pub fell silent.

Bernard gulped. Trouble was brewing, and he didn't like trouble. He liked instigating it, but hated the thought of being the brunt of it. Hurriedly downing his pint, he grabbed his paper and headed for the door, shouts of 'coward' and 'traitor' still sounding when he reached the pavement.

He leaned his back against a wall further down the street

and raised his eyes skywards, studying the heavens. It was well after ten. Long past the time when he was usually making his way home. But he did not want to go home. Before his mother had come to live there he had been the head of the house; now Ida had assumed that responsibility and he was finding himself no match for her. She was treating him like a little boy again. Bernard shook his head. Offering her a home had not been one of his better decisions, regardless of why he had done it. But it was too late to go back. She would never be budged now until they carried her out in a box, which he hoped would not be long.

He had never been overly fond of his mother and his tolerance was wearing very thin. Still, she was serving her purpose which was to keep his wife in her place, so he supposed in a way it was all worth it.

But this latest episode in his local pub tonight had upset him greatly. For the first time thoughts of whether joining up might have been the better option began playing on his mind.

He took a deep breath, put his paper under his arm, stuck his hands in his pockets and slowly walked down the road, his mind filled with seeking a solution. He couldn't go through the remainder of the war frightened to step outside his door for fear of reprisals. He'd never for a moment bargained for this.

The total blackout made journeying anywhere at night highly dangerous as unexpected obstacles loomed suddenly. Happening upon the lamp-post and banging his head, nearly knocking himself senseless, did not help Bernard's mood. He stumbled, stunned for a moment, then rubbed his sore head, muttering a profanity that would have shocked even the men in the factory. He then kicked the lamp-post with his booted foot, questioning why someone had inconsiderately put it there.

Arriving at the corner of his street, he stood and stared down. It appeared in the darkness like a long dark endless tunnel, silent and eerie. He shuddered. Suddenly it felt alien, as though he didn't belong. But he did belong. He belonged, he felt, more than anyone who lived here.

His sudden mood of desolation was the result of this latest episode in the pub, one he had been frequenting for the last twenty odd years. And it wasn't those women's comments that were bothering him, it was the old timers. He had sat and drunk amongst those men for years. It had been their looks of disapproval that were making him feel like this. It wasn't fair. He shouldn't be made to feel an outcast. Didn't those stupid old fogeys realise that if it wasn't for the likes of him, the forces would have no ammunition to fight with?

He knew without doubt that if he had been wearing a uniform he'd have been welcomed with open arms wherever he went, with pats on the back, drinks thrust upon him. But he wasn't joining up, risking his precious neck, just to receive that kind of treatment. Well, there was only one thing for it. He would just have to stay in in future. He shuddered. The thought of night after night sitting in his mother's company did not appeal one bit.

Bernard hunched his shoulders, stuck his hands into his pockets and turned. He felt the need for a walk to clear his head, prepare himself mentally for the trying times ahead until this blasted war was over and things got back to normal.

The night air was warm, the sky clear, and as he aimlessly walked he worried for a moment. This was a good night for an air raid. He just hoped to God it did not happen. The last thing he needed tonight was to be cooped up with strangers in an airless shelter, singing patriotic songs, sharing flasks of lukewarm tea with well-meaning women and mardy kids annoyed at being dragged from their beds.

He supposed, though, they were lucky. Although Leicester lay in the flight path of the bigger cities of the Midlands and further northwards – Birmingham, Manchester and Liverpool – it was those locations the Germans were after, not Leicester, so the threat of being blown to smithereens had never become a reality. Despite the fact that Coventry, a near neighbour at twenty-five miles away, had only a few nights ago received a heavy barrage, the people of Leicester were still living in the belief that they were safe.

For a moment he wondered why. Didn't those stupid Germans realise that Leicester's numerous factories produced many of the components their enemy used to fight back at them with? Not only that but some of the clothes they wore, the parachutes they used, and some of the food they ate – all produced or grown in and around the Shires.

He sniffed disdainfully. But why should he worry? He had more pressing matters to deal with.

Spinney Hill Park loomed eerily ahead and he stared across at it for a moment. He hadn't realised he had walked so far.

Two air raid wardens snatching a crafty cigarette leaned against a tree. One spotted him and flicked on his torch, shining it in Bernard's eyes. He quickly flicked it off.

'Come on, mate, ain't you a home to get off to? You shouldn't be prowling the streets at this time a night.'

Bernard stared over at him. He wanted to tell the man if he wanted to walk the streets at any time of night, war or no war, then that was his business. But he could not be bothered with the confrontation and continued his walk. He had better get home, he supposed. He was tired and this aimless walk was solving nothing.

As he turned down a jitty that wove between the backs of two rows of terraced houses, he did not see the pair of feet belonging to a body propped up against an unlit lamp-post until he had fallen over them and was sprawled flat out upon the hard ground.

It took him several moments to gather his wits. His head

smarted from the second bump it had received that night and he could feel the trickle of blood.

He pulled himself upright and glared across in the darkness. The body was that of a soldier. Clutched in one hand was a half-empty bottle of whisky, on the floor to the side the remains of his supper and chips. Bernard glared at him. He had suffered torments because of his lack of a uniform. Just look at the way this man was treating his. What would the old timers in the pub say if they could see this man collapsed in a drunken stupor in a darkened alleyway? Bernard tightened his lips. They would more than likely carry him home, give him a bed for the night and a hearty breakfast before sending him on his way. But they'd do nothing like that for him. Nor would they think to thank him for all his hard graft in the factory.

In frustrated temper he lifted his boot and kicked the man's leg hard, feeling no remorse for doing so. The soldier did not move. He was obviously so drunk his feelings were numbed. Grinning to himself, Bernard bent down and prised the half-empty bottle of whisky from his clutches. This man had obviously had enough of this for one night and wouldn't remember what he'd done with the rest when he finally awoke, feeling as if a train had run over his head.

Hiding the bottle in the inside pocket of his jacket, he turned and continued his journey. His footsteps began to slow to an eventual halt. He turned and stared back, running his hand over his head. An idea was dawning. He stood rigid. It was such a good idea, one that if he dared carry though would put a stop to his torments once and for all.

Slowly he retraced his steps and stood before the soldier, staring down at him. A grin spread across his face. This drunken soldier was the answer to his prayers. It was just a pity Bernard himself would never be able to thank him for what he had unwittingly done.

An hour later he rubbed his hands in pleasure and patted the piece of sacking under which was hidden the soldier's uniform. He smiled broadly, feeling the need to laugh out loud but not daring to just in case anyone heard him. It was not very likely at this time of night but he could not take the chance.

The soldier had not moved a muscle as he had been stripped of his uniform. Bernard would have loved to have been around when he finally awoke to find himself dressed only in his underwear, but wouldn't like to be around when the man had to face his superiors and explain its loss. Well it was his own stupid fault for getting in such a state and allowing it to happen.

All he himself had to do now was make sure it was well hidden, and his allotment shed was just the place. This was solely his domain so concealment was not going to be a problem. When he did dress in it all he had to do was make sure no one in the vicinity recognised him.

He had already tried it on. It was a little tight but he felt sure no one would notice. Oh, what fun he was going to have! He visualised the free drinks, the unwarranted praise, the women's eyes. He liked the thought of that the most. It was surprising how a uniform turned a woman's head. A thought suddenly struck him and he frowned. If he was seen too often, wouldn't people query why he wasn't away fighting? Ah, but that was easy. He would say he was injured. A walking stick would solve the problem. A practised hobble aided by a walking stick would quieten questioning tongues. He smiled. He knew exactly where to lay his hands on one.

Chapter Fifteen

In early-September Grace stared in surprise at the man standing on the pavement outside her door. He took off his trilby hat and smiled warmly at her.

'Mrs Wilkins? You don't recognise me, do you?'

She frowned. He did look familiar but that was as far as it went. He held out his hand. 'Janson. Philip Janson.'

'Oh, my goodness me!' she gasped, wondering what on earth her husband's boss was doing on her doorstep. She suddenly realised she was forgetting her manners. 'Mr Janson, I'm so sorry.' She stood aside. 'Please, come in.'

Philip stepped over the threshold and followed her down the passage. They arrived at the living room and he glanced around. The room was badly in need of decoration, very dull and uninviting, but regardless of its sparseness was spotlessly clean. But cleanliness was what he would have expected from a woman such as Grace.

He nodded a greeting at Ida sitting bolt upright in the armchair. It struck him suddenly that the witch-like woman glaring back must be Bernard's mother. Although this woman was thin in the extreme with a face to match that of a withered prune, and Bernard himself a large hefty fellow, the likeness was still remarkable. It was the eyes, he thought. Cold humourless grey eyes that showed a lack of character. They both possessed them.

Poor Grace. Fancy having to live with two such people. Still the proposition he had come to put to her might help ease her situation.

His eyes dwelt upon her. She had changed greatly since the last time he had seen her. Her youthful figure had blossomed to a shapely maturity, her teenage prettiness to a ripe beauty. Bernard was indeed a very fortunate man to have kept such a woman. Philip wondered if the man himself realised this. He doubted it. Knowing Bernard as well as he did, he doubted very much he took much notice of her. It was a shame. Married to the right man, Grace would have gone far.

As these thoughts occurred to him, Grace hovered uncertainly, worried whether she should offer him a cup of tea. With rationing biting deeply there was not much in the caddy and she didn't have fresh milk, only Carnation.

'My husband is out at the moment,' she said, finding her voice. She extended a hand towards Ida. 'This is Mrs Wilkins, my husband's mother. Mrs Wilkins, Mr Janson, Bernard's boss.'

He moved towards her and held out his hand. He shook hers hastily, not liking the feel of the thin bony claw in his grasp. He hurriedly turned back to Grace. As he did so all their attention was caught by the appearance of Charlie.

'Oh, Charlie – Charlotte,' Grace corrected herself. 'This is Mr Janson, your father's boss.'

She smiled in greeting and walked towards him, her hand outstretched. They shook firmly, a glance of recognition fleetingly exchanged.

'What can I do for you?' Grace asked nervously as memories suddenly returned – memories of herself as a young girl sitting before this man in his office. He had been very carefully trying to warn her about Bernard and she in her innocence had misinterpreted his intentions. She forced the

226

memory away. 'As I said, my husband is out. Would you like to leave a message?'

'Well, actually it's not Mr Wilkins I've come to see, it's yourself.'

'Me? You've come to see me? Why?'

'Sit down, Mr Janson,' Charlie said, pulling out a chair. 'Would you like a cup of tea?'

'Er, no, thank you.'

Grace recovered her composure. 'What did you want to see me about, Mr Janson?'

He smiled at her warmly. 'I've come to offer you a job.'

'Job!' Ida erupted. 'She can't go ter work, she's already enough to do. She's got me ter look after, and my son. Oh, and her daughter,' she added, catching Charlie glaring at her out of the corner of her eye. Ida folded her bony arms. 'She can't do that properly if she's at work.'

Charlie fought hard to keep her temper. 'Grandma, my mother can speak for herself.' She beamed across at Grace. 'Mam, this is a wonderful opportunity. A job's just what you need.'

'She don't need no job,' Ida erupted again. 'And it's not 'er yer should be askin', it's 'er husband.'

'Mrs Wilkins,' Grace spoke sharply, 'please stop interfering. Mr Janson is talking to me.' She turned back to him hesitantly. Was this really true? Was she being offered a job? A glow spread thought her. She wanted to pounce on him, hug him in gratitude. Something she had longed for, for such a long time, was within her grasp. Bernard couldn't possibly deny her this, not when the boss himself had asked her personally.

Suddenly the door opened and Bernard came in. He stopped abruptly, frowned, looking at each in turn then settling his attention on his boss, wondering what on earth he was doing in this room. Never in all the years he had worked for the man had he visited Bernard's home.

The atmosphere was charged, he felt it as soon as he entered. For an instant he worried about the stolen uniform, then squashed that.

No one knew he even had it, he had made certain of that. He had only this very night as he sat on an old wooden stool in his shed fingering the material, finally made up his mind to go out tomorrow wearing it for the very first time. His decision had filled him with excitement, thrilled him beyond belief at his forthcoming adventure. He couldn't wait to see eyes upon him as he walked into a public house he had yet to choose. One a good way away from his familiar haunts. All he had to do was secure his mother's walking stick without her knowledge. It would only be thought she had lost it and Grace would just have to get her another one.

He cleared his throat. 'Is there a problem in the factory, Mr Janson?' he asked cautiously.

'Not to my knowledge – other than the fact that if we don't step up production and get orders out on time, the Ministry will be down on us. But I'll speak to you about that in the morning. No, it's your wife I came to see.'

'My wife? Whatever for?'

'About a job, Dad,' Charlie said, closely watching her father's face. He wasn't going to like this one little bit.

When she had approached Mr Janson with her idea, he had asked her if her father knew. She had been truthful and explained the situation, telling him she thought her mother was wasted and that her years of being at home had sapped her confidence so as to stop her from approaching him herself.

Surprisingly Philip had instantly agreed with her when she had been prepared to make a stand and plead her mother's case. He explained how women like Grace were in great demand right now. They might not have years of work experience, but experiences gained raising families, juggling money around to pay bills, dealing with everyday life in fact, were all things which could be put to good use in the working environment. He had several openings that he had been unable to fill due to lack of suitable applicants. Grace, whom he knew from her years of working for him previously, was a very capable woman, just the kind he needed now.

As Philip looked at Bernard he knew he had a fight on his hands. But then, he had known that from the moment Charlie had first approached him about a job for her mother. But this time Wilkins was not going to get his own way, oh no. If Philip had to stand here all night and plead his case, he was not leaving until it was agreed that Grace would work for him. In some way, he thought, his giving her a job might put right a little of the wrong he felt he had done her in the past. If he hadn't come down on Bernard all those years ago, the man might never have married her in the first place.

He was right. Bernard was outraged by the prospect of losing Grace to the workplace. As much as he fought not to show his feelings, his temper rose and his face grew thunderous.

'That's not possible, Mr Janson. My wife has enough to do at home looking after her family.'

'Bernard, just a moment,' Grace began.

He spun to face her. 'I'll deal with this, Grace, thank you.'

'I've already told 'im that,' Ida erupted.

Bernard for once was glad of her interference. 'You can see for yourself, Mr Janson, my mother couldn't possibly be left on her own.'

Philip looked at the scrawny old lady, a smug expression on her gnarled face. 'Why ever not?' he asked.

Bernard gawped. 'Why ever not?' he repeated. 'She's an invalid,' he said, pointing to the walking stick by the side of which sat an empty glass and a bottle of stout.

'Oh, I see.' Philip's mind raced. If this woman was an invalid then Bernard had a point. His gaze fell on Ida again, and he saw the malicious glint in her eye. It was then he remembered that this woman was Bernard's mother, a man who was a past master at lying. He had to have got his talent from somewhere. Philip decided to take a chance. He had nothing to lose, but Grace did. He took a breath. 'Well, she didn't look much of an invalid to me when I saw her yesterday walking up Green Lane Road carrying a bottle of stout. Admittedly she wasn't walking very quickly, but then she's an old lady, isn't she?'

Ida's head reared back indignantly. 'I never went there yesterday,' she spat. 'It wa' the day before and it weren't stout, it were light ale.' Suddenly she froze, realising what she had said, then wondered how the hell Mr Janson had recognised her when to her knowledge she had never met him. Before she could voice her queries, her angry son interrupted her.

'Mr Janson, my wife is not coming to work for you. Her place is here. She knows that better than anyone.'

'Dad, it's up to Mother . . .'

'Shut up, Charlotte, this is none of your business.' Bernard took a deep breath. This unexpected situation was getting out of hand. If only he had been forewarned about it he could have thought it through. As it was . . . Think, man, think! his mind screamed. A glimmer of an idea came to him. It had better work. He turned to Grace and made a great show of staring pityingly at her.

'My wife wouldn't be of any use to you, Mr Janson. She's only a housewife. I'm trying to spare her the humiliation of you sacking her when you find out she's useless.' Grace stared at him, horrified. 'I'm sorry, my dear, but it had to be said. Now if there's nothing else, Mr Janson, I wish you good night.'

For Grace, Bernard's remarks were the final straw. She couldn't believe that her husband was belittling her in front of this man, and not just him, her own daughter and mother-in-law as well. Is that what he really thinks of me? I'm just a housewife, and a useless one at that? Well, enough is enough! she thought angrily. After over twenty years of devoted service, during which time her own needs and desires had been buried, she had come to the end of her tether. She was no longer prepared to be subservient, conforming to Bernard's own selfish wishes.

She tightened her lips defiantly and raised her head. 'Just a moment,' she said sharply. All eyes flew to her. 'Only a housewife, am I? Well, I might be only a housewife, but I've still got a brain – and one I can put to good use if Mr Janson is willing to take the risk. And I might be your wife, Bernard, but I'm still a person in my own right. I could work and still perform my wifely duties. Other women do.' She took a deep breath, trying to still her shaking legs, hardly daring to believe that at long last she was daring to make a stand. 'Mr Janson, I appreciate your offer of work. Thank you very much for thinking of me.' She turned to her husband standing rigid, his anger apparent by his knuckles showing white as he clenched his fists. 'We could do with the extra money, Bernard, and I'm sure I can manage to organise things so that neither you nor your mother suffers at all.' She turned back to Philip. 'When would you like me to start?'

A deafening silence fell.

Charlie held her breath, watching her father's face turn as black as thunder. He was that angry, she thought, he looked about to explode. But she knew he wouldn't, not in front of Mr Janson. 'Oh, good on you, Mam,' she cried, bounding over and hugging her tightly.

Grace pulled away, embarrassed. 'Charlie, not in front of Mr Janson,' she whispered.

Philip smiled at the show of affection. He had taken a shine to Charlotte Wilkins the moment the pretty young woman had walked into his office several days ago and put forward her proposition. He liked her forthright manner and the way in which she acquitted herself. He felt she had great prospects, showing all the qualities her mother had. He had no doubts Charlie would go far, providing the same thing didn't happen to her as it had her mother. It was a pity she was happily employed in the munitions factory, he could have found a place for her also.

'Don't mind me, Mrs Wilkins. I've a daughter myself, although she's much older than you my dear,' he said, addressing Charlie. Out of the corner of his eye he caught a look of hatred cross Bernard's face at the mention of Cecily.

Ida too could not control herself. 'Yes, and we'd have bin related if it wasn't for my stupid son marrying Grace instead!'

Bernard's face burned red as he squirmed in embarrassment. 'Mother . . .'

Ida would not be quietened. 'No, it has to be said, Bernard. What you did was a daft thing, turning' down Mr Janson's daughter like that.'

Philip tightened his mouth. So Bernard had not only spread malicious rumours at work, he had carried them home as well. He looked across at the man and suddenly a flicker of a smile touched his lips. After all these years of suffering in one way or another at Bernard's hands, a most unexpected opportunity had arisen to get back at him, and Bernard's mother had unwittingly given it to him. Philip didn't feel any pleasure at being able to do so, just a great desire to put right a few of all the wrongs Bernard had done other people.

'Is that right, Wilkins? Were you talking marriage with my daughter? Only she never mentioned anything to me, and neither did you when I had you in my office and asked you to stop spreading rumours about her to the other workers in the factory. As far as I know the only man my daughter was ever on intimate terms with was Edward Hammerton, and she's been happily married to him for the past twenty years.' The look of horror on Bernard's face was not lost on him and to make him squirm even more Philip could not help but add: 'The next time Cecily comes to visit you'll have to come over and renew your acquaintance.' He smiled at Grace. 'And bring Mrs Wilkins with you.'

Bernard froze. He could feel eyes burning into him, waiting for him to speak.

Ida stared at him, confused. The story that Bernard had told her and the one Philip was telling were contradictory in the extreme. 'I don't understand none of this. You told me yer were gettin' engaged to Cecily Janson. Were yer or not?'

Bernard squirmed even more. His lies had caught up with him after years and there was nothing he could think of quickly enough to redeem the situation.

Grace gnawed on her bottom lip, choosing to stay silent. She'd known all along that Bernard had lied about it. Let him get out of this one himself, she thought, and looked at Charlie, warning her to stay silent.

Ignoring his mother's question, he looked straight at Philip. 'It was all long ago and best left alone. But thanks for the invitation.' Finding his feet he walked over and opened the door. 'It's getting late, Mr Janson. I expect you need to be getting home.'

Philip picked up his hat. 'I'm away on business until Friday, Mrs Wilkins. Come to the office then, at your convenience, and we'll discuss it further.

Grace smiled warmly, trying to stop her excitement from showing. 'I'll look forward to it.'

After hustling Philip out, Bernard, face ashen in anger, grabbed his coat.

'Where you goin'?' Ida asked, stunned. 'Ain't you gonna

sort out this business of 'er working? You ain't really going to allow it, are yer?' She grimaced. 'And what about this Cecily business? I think you've some explainin' to do, my lad.'

Bernard narrowed his eyes, feeling the redness of embarrassment creeping up his neck. 'Shut up, Mother. Don't yer think you've said enough for one night? I just hope to God for your sake you ain't lost me my job, raking up the past like that. Mr Janson knew nothing of this. You heard what he said. Now I just hope he don't go and question Cecily and cause her any trouble. We parted 'cos we both felt it best. Anyway, I don't need to explain things to you. I don't need to explain things to anybody. I'm the master in this house and don't none of you forget it.'

Ida shrank back. 'I'm sorry, son.'

'I should think so.' He breathed freely, feeling at least he had managed to salvage the situation to some extent. He turned on Grace, narrowing his eyes icily. 'And as for you working . . . Well, I ain't got much choice, have I? Not now Mr Janson's asked you personally.' He stared at her accusingly. 'I reckon you planned all this to try ter make me look stupid. Well, you'll be the stupid one when yer have ter give it all up 'cos yer can't cope. And don't come running ter me for sympathy. But at least there's one good thing. Working at Janson's, I'll be able to keep my eye on yer.'

With that, he marched out of the door.

Grace stared after him. His last remark had taken the pleasure right out of being offered this job. She set her mouth grimly. She wasn't going to let him do this. Her job being at the same place as her husband's was immaterial; she was still going to be doing something useful and earning her own bit of money. She smiled to herself. Maybe some of it could be used for some paint to brighten up the house.

Her eyes fell on her daughter and lit up as she rubbed her

hands together. 'Come on, Charlie, let's celebrate.'

'Celebrate? Oh, good, how?'

Grace laughed. 'I'll mash a pot of tea. But first, if you don't mind, I have to pop out.'

'Out? Where to?' demanded Ida.

'Just out,' Grace replied. She leaned over and whispered excitedly in Charlie's ear. 'I just have to go and tell Bessie the news.'

She grinned. 'I understand, Mam. She'll be thrilled, you'll see. I'm so proud of you. Eh, and don't worry about her,' she whispered, nodding at Ida. 'If she starts, I'll sort her out.'

Bessie pulled Grace inside the kitchen, looking at her expectantly.

'Well?'

She controlled her excitement. 'Well, what?' she asked casually.

'Eh, don't you start messing wi' me, Gracie Wilkins,' Bessie replied, pretending annoyance. 'You look like yer've won the pools. Now out wi' it?'

Grace grinned broadly and clapped her hands together. 'I've got a job, Bessie. Can you believe it?'

Her rotund face broke into a beam of delight. 'Well, I never. Eh up, Tom!' she shouted, grabbing Grace's hand and dragging her through to the living room. 'Gracie's gorra job. What d'yer think of that, eh?'

Tom, who was sitting at the table eating a doorstep of a sandwich and reading his paper, looked up, as did Polly who was lolling in the armchair. Willy, Maureen and Bobbie were already in bed. 'Well done, Grace love,' said Tom, enthusiastically.

'Yeah, well done,' piped up Polly.

'Oh, thank you,' she beamed. Then her face fell. 'I'm sorry, Mr Rudney, I didn't realise you were home.'

He frowned at her. 'What's with the Mr Rudney lark? It's Tom to me friends. And it makes no difference whether I'm here or not, you're welcome any time you like. Now sit down, gel, and tell us all about it. Pass me a mug, Bessie, for a cuppa for Grace. Come on, out with it all before Bessie bursts.'

Grace felt an inner glow. No one dared come into her house when Bernard was at home, except Bessie of course. She was game for Bernard at any time, that was part of the reason he detested their friendship so much. The rest of his resentment she knew was because he felt the likes of Bessie were beneath them.

She sighed. It was a shame her own husband could not welcome her new friends as enthusiastically as Tom was now welcoming herself. He was such a nice man, a good husband and father, and in his own way an attractive man. Bessie was a lucky woman.

She pulled out a chair, accepted her mug of tea and imparted her news.

'You won't go wrong there, Grace,' Tom said knowingly. 'Janson's is a good place to work and the boss himself a fair man. He'll see you all right.'

'And if you want an 'and any time, Gracie, don't be afraid ter ask. I can always get you some shoppin' or see to Ida. That'd 'elp a bit, wouldn't it?' Bessie offered.

'Oh, Bessie, you are kind. But I'm not sure about Ida. She's a handful.'

Bessie guffawed loudly. 'She's no match for me, Gracie love. Just let 'er start and she'll get what for. And if you ask me, it'd do the old trout good.'

Grace tried to hide a smile. Bessie could be right. She was just the kind of person to put Ida in her place.

Grace stayed longer than intended and decided against visiting Clara, not wanting to disturb her as it was after nine and the older woman she knew would have locked up for the night and settled down to read one of her books. Her news could wait a little longer. But she knew that, like Bessie, Clara would be delighted for her.

After Grace had left, Bessie's face grew serious and she turned to her husband.

'Do yer think 'e'll let 'er?'

Tom frowned. 'Do I think who'll let who what?'

'Him – Wilkins. Do yer think 'e'll let Gracie go to work?'

'I can't see how he can stop her. He's her husband not her jailer.'

Bessie pursed her lips. 'I'm not so sure.'

He nodded knowingly. 'I know what yer getting at. Well, it'll be up to Gracie, love. She'll have to stand her ground, there's no doubting that. But I think she's got it in her. She might not have a few months ago, but for some reason I've a feeling she has now. It's you,' he said, grinning. 'You've taught her well. She's seen how you browbeat me.'

'Ged away wi' yer, yer daft beggar,' she laughed.

He held out his arms and gathered her to him. 'Now how's about you and me having an early night?'

She looked up at him blankly. 'I didn't realise it were Friday?'

He burst into laughter. 'Now who's a daft devil? Whenever have we had a roster for a bit of loving, eh, woman?'

She beamed up at him, double chin wobbling in mirth as she slapped him playfully on his arm. ''Elp me wi' these dishes and you might get yer wish.'

Next day all thoughts of Grace's impending job were to be pushed to the back of Grace and Bessie's minds as, like the rest of the people of Leicester, illusions that the war would not reach as far as their city were shattered.

Just before noon, through a break in the clouds, a lone Dornier 17 Luftwaffe plane released eight high explosive bombs over the gasworks on the Aylestone Road. Luckily the target was missed but extensive damage was caused to shops and houses in the district. But far worse than that, six people lost their lives and many were injured, some very seriously.

Shock waves flew round the city and a new more frightening fear raged within. Was this attack just an isolated incident or the first of many?

Chapter Sixteen

Clara gazed at Grace in awe. 'A job? Oh, I say, a job. I'm so pleased for you. I'm not surprised you forgot to tell me after that terrible bombing raid yesterday. Oh, but it's good news.' She shuddered, a look of deep sadness crossing her face. 'Those poor people who died. I feel so sorry for their relatives. Their deaths were so pointless.' She sighed deeply, then her face brightened. 'But a job. Oh, Grace, it is good news, isn't it? If I can do anything to help . . . Yes, I can. I can get the dinner going for you each day. That would help you, wouldn't it? Well, let's face it dear, I can't see your mother-in-law lending a hand, can you?'

'Oh, Clara, I couldn't expect . . .'

'Nonsense, dear. It would give me a great deal of pleasure. Now what did your husband say about it all? Was he pleased?'

Grace lowered her head.

'Oh, I see. I take it he wasn't pleased then?' She smiled reassuringly. 'Oh, well, it's something he'll just have to get used to. This war is going to change many things which lots of people aren't going to like. Where is this job then?'

'It's where Bernard works. You know, the tool makers.' She raised her head proudly. 'His boss came to see me personally.'

'Oh, really. I bet you felt honoured. So where is this exactly?'

Grace stared at her, then her face relaxed into a smile.

'Oh, of course, you wouldn't know where Bernard works. It's Ja—'

Just then the back door burst open and Bessie filled the doorway. 'Come on, Gracie, quick. Vinny's got some tinned tomatoes. Our Polly seen 'im sneaking 'em round the back. Let's get in quick afore the news gets round the neighbourhood and there's none left.' She spotted Clara and grinned. ''Ello, me duck. 'Ow's you then?'

'Very well, thank you. Grace was just telling me about her job.'

'Yeah, great innit? Just what our Gracie needs, is a job.' She turned her attention back to Grace. 'Oh, and talking of yer job, I need to speak ter yer about summat.'

'Oh, what?' she asked.

Bessie waved her hand excitedly. 'It'll keep. We need to get round to Vinny's. A' you coming Clara?'

She rose. 'I might as well. I'm quite partial to tomatoes.'

'Who's there?' Ida shouted through.

Bessie grimaced. 'Big ears is awake then?'

Grace spluttered. 'Bessie, stop it.'

'I'm only sayin',' she said, taking Grace's coat from the back of the door. 'Get this on and 'urry up about it.'

They reached the shop just as a small crowd was gathering. News such as this travelled fast. Bessie pushed her way through, entered the shop and marched to the counter, Grace and Clara following behind.

The shop, which before the war had started had shelves filled with everything from tinned salmon to scrubbing brushes, now looked decidedly bare. The shelves were filled, but the display packets were empty. The food that did get through was not in the shop long enough to be allowed shelf life.

Malcolm Vincent moved away from the bacon slicer where he had been slicing Spam as thinly as possibly to make a quarter of a pound look more substantial. He wiped his large hands on his stained white apron and smiled broadly in welcome. 'Yes, ladies, and what can I do fer you?'

Bessie squared her shoulders ready for battle. 'We'd all like a tin of tomatoes, please.'

Malcolm sniffed. 'Now you know I ain't got none, Mrs Rudney. I told yer that last week.'

'As you said, that were last week, Mr Vincent. This is this week and we'd like three tins of tomatoes.' She snatched the others' ration books and banged them down on the counter along with her own.

Malcolm shifted uneasily on his feet. 'I ain't got any, Mrs Rudney.'

Bessie looked at Grace and Clara. 'I really will have to tek my young Polly to the opticians. The poor gel is seein' things.'

Grace took the hint. 'She's never, poor girl. And what is she seeing?'

Bessie sadly shook her head and looked Malcolm squarely in the eyes. 'Tins of tomatoes. Two cases of 'em being sneaked round the back.'

He reddened and tightened his lips. 'Now look 'ere, Mrs Rudney, don't yer know there's a war on?'

Bessie's eyes bulged in anger. ''Ow dare you, Malcolm Vincent? 'Ow dare you ask me if I know there's a war on! I've seen off me two lads, remember. They've just been sent to India. I don't know when I'm gonna see 'em again and you 'ave the nerve to ask me if I know there's a war on. Bloody cheek!'

'I'm sorry, Mrs Rudney. I was . . . er . . . forgetting meself.'

Bessie thumped her fat fist on the counter. 'Forgetting yerself! I thought at the least you'd lost yer brain the way yer just spoke ter me.' She folded her arms under her bosom and planted her feet squarely. 'Now you look 'ere, Malcolm Vincent. We all know what your little game is. You're gonna hoard those tomatoes 'til they're that scarce you can put the price sky high. Well, we ain't standin' for it, are we, gels?'

Grace and Clara shook their heads, the latter somewhat timidly. Clara, who had never been faced with a situation like this before, was finding it daunting, but for the sake of her new-found friends would muster the courage to stand firm.

'Now I'll tell yer, Mr Vincent. You either sell us those tomatoes, and at the right price, mind, or I'm sure the authorities 'ud like to 'ear about this.' She turned to Grace. 'Did you 'ear about that bloke that got done for sellin' an eightpenny comb for one and six? A good hefty fine 'e got and an eye kept on 'im in future.'

'Serves him right,' Grace responded.

'It sure does,' echoed Clara.

'Well, you'll get more 'an that done ter yer,' Bessie continued. 'If you try 'ote like this again, I'll personally mek sure none of the women in this street shops 'ere again. War or no war.'

Malcolm held up his hands. 'Okay, okay, you win.'

Bessie, Grace and Clara smiled broadly in victory.

'Thank you, Mr Vincent,' Bessie said. 'That's three tins for us and . . .' She turned and marched towards the door, yanking it open. 'Come on, gels, it's tomatoes 'e's got.'

Bessie was nearly pushed over in the stampede. The last thing she remembered seeing was Malcolm's ashen face as he turned and rushed into the back, returning double quick weighed down by two cases of tinned tomatoes.

In Bessie's living room Grace wiped tears of mirth from her eyes. 'Oh, my goodness, Bessie, it was worth getting out of bed this morning to see Vinny's face when you let all the street through his door.'

Bessie filled her mug with a fresh brew of tea. 'Yeah, well, those tomatoes'll taste twice as nice seein's we never nearly got 'em.' She filled Clara's mug and pushed it towards her. Her mouth tightened grimly. 'Meks yer wonder whose side some people are on when they pull dirty tricks like that.'

Grace and Clara voiced their agreement.

Clara studied Bessie's face. 'Are you all right, Bessie dear? Only you seem a bit down.'

'Me? I'm all right.' She shook her head sadly. 'No, I'm not really. It was tellin' Vinny about me lads. To be 'onest, I'm right worried about 'em. India!' She looked at Grace and Clara with tears in her eyes. 'Well, it's the other side of the world, ain't it? Tom's told me not to worry, but I can't 'elp it. I'm their mam, ain't I? And I know Tom's as worried as I am, only 'e's trying to be brave for my sake, bless 'im.'

'He's right though, Bessie love,' Grace said kindly, placing her hand on top of hers and patting it reassuringly. 'You have to try and put them to the back of your mind. Worrying yourself silly won't bring them home any quicker.'

Bessie sniffed loudly and wiped the back of her podgy hand under her nose. 'Yer right, Gracie. But it ain't 'alf 'ard.' She suddenly grinned, her whole face lighting up. 'I know I had summat to speak ter you about. Pictures.'

'Pictures?' queried Grace.

'Yeah, pictures. We never went, did we? Clara 'ere decided to go sick and it put the kibosh on it. Well, let's go. Let's all of us go before Gracie starts 'er job. We'll go Sat'day afternoon.'

Grace clapped her hands together. 'Yes, that's a wonderful idea. I'll look in the *Mercury* and see what's on. I quite fancy something with Gracie Fields or the Crazy Gang. Or, what about *Gone with the Wind*? My Charlie's seen it four times and she's says it's lovely.' She turned to Clara. 'You will come, won't you?'

'Well, er . . .'

'Course she will. It wouldn't be the same wi'out 'er.'

Clara smiled. 'All right then, I'd love to.'

Grace drained her mug and rose. 'I'd better be going. Ida's lost her walking stick and I've to go to the hospital and see if I can get her another one.' She ran her hand over her head. 'Though for the likes of me I cannot think what she's done with it.' She looked hard at Bessie. 'And don't you say anything.'

Bessie raised her eyebrows innocently. 'I wasn't goin' to.'

As it was the trip to the pictures had to be postponed once again. Philip Janson asked Grace to start her job first thing Monday morning and she had to get herself organised quickly.

On entering the offices for her interview she had looked around in surprise. Nothing seemed to have changed since the day she had left over twenty years previously on marrying Bernard. The offices were still cluttered with overspilling filing cabinets, piles of ledgers and trays on desks filled with paperwork that still needed to be worked on. Some of the desks, however, were now vacant, the male clerks who occupied them having gone away to war.

Grace smiled as she happened upon the tea lady in the corridor, pushing her heavy trolley.

'Hello Sadie. How are you?'

She pulled the trolley to a halt and stared quizzically at the woman addressing her. Her face suddenly broke into a large, near toothless grin. 'Well, I never! It's young Grace Taylor. Well, 'ow are yer, me duck?'

'Fancy you remembering me! I'm very well, thank you. And I must say it's good to see you're still here after . . . how many years is it?'

'Fifty-two years, girl and woman.'

'Good lord! Is it that long?'

Sadie raised her aged head proudly. 'Sure is. Janson's couldn't function wi'out my cups a' tea and buns. And I still 'elp wi' the dinners.' She looked at Grace shrewdly for a moment. 'You left ter marry that Bernard Wilkins, din't yer? 'Im that's Foreman in the grinding department. Miserable old git 'e his. I often wonder 'ow you cope, gel.' She sniffed disdainfully. 'What yer doin' 'ere?'

'I've come for an interview about a job.'

''Ave yer? Well, good for you, gel. We need people like you 'ere. It'll be nice to see a smiling face once more in the offices.' She grabbed the handle of her trolley. 'Good luck.'

'Thank you.'

Philip was delighted to see Grace and after sitting her down and asking Gladys to get them a drink, explained that there was so much work to do that defining her position would be difficult.

Grace smiled and reassured him that she would be happy to do whatever was required as long as she was able.

'Don't worry on that score,' he said. 'I have no doubt whatsoever as to your capabilities.'

As she had left he had watched her walk across the yard from his window, feeling positive that with the minimum of training, Grace Wilkins would soon be holding her own.

Although the details were vague, now her job was confirmed Grace made plans. The major housework, washing and ironing, would all have to be tackled on a Saturday afternoon and on Sundays; the rest of an evening after work. She would be tired, but as least it would be a fulfilling and satisfying tiredness.

Her only reservation was about Bernard. Much to her surprise he had said nothing on the subject after Philip Janson's visit. From previous experience she had expected his wrath to explode and to have a major battle on her hands. This had not transpired. Bernard seemed to be very preoccupied and had begun to spend a lot more time at his allotment. What he found to do in the dark, she had no idea.

Chapter Seventeen

It was two weeks into November. The splendid autumn of that year had reluctantly given way to the winter dampness and fog that Leicestershire was famous for. Grace had been at work for just a month and had enjoyed every moment of it. Her working hours flew by and she found it hard to believe that only four weeks had passed since she had tentatively arrived for her first morning of work after a break of twenty years, having hardly slept a wink the previous night. She need not have feared. The years might never have been and she quickly settled in, listened well, asked endless questions, and was soon working away under her own steam.

Within a couple of weeks many of the employees in her department who had been there years were coming to her for help, asking her advice on how to handle matters, and she was filled with delight. They all looked forward to hearing Grace's cheery voice, receiving her helpful tips and listening to her infectious laughter. It brightened the office which was desperately needed during these very desperate and troubled times.

Sadie had just plonked a welcome cup of tea on her desk and pushed away the heavy trolley when Philip appeared at Grace's side.

'Everything all right?'

She smiled up at him. 'Yes, thank you. I've just scheduled

a new order from the Ministry.' She pushed a piece of paper towards him. 'I've made a few adjustments to the progress through the factory. I was about to take it to Mr Thomas and see what he thought.'

He scanned his eyes across the paper and frowned. Pulling a chair up, he sat down next to her and studied the schedule in depth. When finished he raised his eyes to her. 'Did you do this all by yourself?'

'Er . . . yes.'

'How?'

'How?' She paused nervously. 'Well, I . . . er . . . found out how we tackle things now by looking over some old schedules, then by talking to people in various departments. It struck me that part of the process was duplicated and that by switching things around, precious time could be saved. If you look, the raw metal visits the galvanising department twice. Once when it first comes into the factory and then after it's been ground. Well, after doing some checking, I realised that this was wrong. That the running order hadn't been updated since the factory began and was pointless because the quality of the raw materials today is far superior to what Janson's used to get at the turn of the century.' She eyed him warily. 'Have I done wrong, Mr Janson?'

'Wrong! Grace, I wish I had more employees who used their initiative.'

'Initiative! Oh, I never got given any of them. Should I have collected them when I first started?'

He looked at her bemused, then smiled. 'I was talking about commonsense.'

She felt foolish and her mouth fell open. 'Oh, I see.'

He patted her hand. 'I'm very pleased about this, my dear. You're to be congratulated.' He rose and returned the chair. 'Take the new schedule straight to Mr Thomas and tell him

I have personally authorised its instigation. And in future, Grace, if you find anything like this again, come straight to me with it.'

She beamed. 'I will, thank you.'

'No, thank you.'

A warm glow filled her as she returned to her work.

Bernard stood in his garden shed and smoothed his hands over the uniform. He studied himself in the piece of broken mirror he had smuggled in. His eyes stared proudly back. He had painstakingly sewn a false hem on the bottom of the trousers, also managed to lose a little weight which he felt suited him, and the uniform was now a perfect fit. Well, rationing had seen to that. The food allowance is hardly enough to feed a dog let alone a working man, he thought. But grudgingly he had to admit to himself the meals Grace managed to rustle up with the limited ingredients available were palatable.

Tonight would be the seventh time he had ventured out wearing the uniform and he was getting braver, no longer feeling apprehensive about being recognised. The city was filled with servicemen of all descriptions; one more uniform made no difference. But he knew, should anyone find out the deceit that lay behind it, his life here would be finished. But there was no chance of discovery. He had covered his tracks too well and was far too careful.

Once again he was looking forward to seeing sympathetic eyes upon him as he hobbled through the door of the public house across the other side of town. A sly smile crossed his lips as he wondered how many free drinks he would have thrust upon him, how many willing ears would listen to his account of how he'd received his terrible injury. A mere broken leg had escalated to a bullet wound with splinters of shrapnel the doctors had still to remove. This injury could last for an age, with complications added if and when necessary.

All in all the procuring of this uniform had opened up a new life for Bernard. It made him feel important, a somebody; wearing it gave him a thrill the likes of which he had never experienced before and for this reason he selfishly wanted the war to continue.

For the first time in an age he was really enjoying himself. Enjoying himself so much that when he was in the house he was so preoccupied with where he would venture next, he hardly had time to notice what was going on around him. Little did he realise that his wife and daughter, although bemused by the change in him, welcomed it gladly. It was only his mother who wasn't pleased. Ida no longer seemed to have an ally to back her snide remarks and mischief-making. Not that it stopped her.

He wiped condensation from the shed window and peered through. The allotments appeared empty. It was too dark and cold for any sensible person still to be lingering. Picking up the walking stick he had stolen from his mother, he opened the shed door, checked around and ventured forth.

So preoccupied was he that he didn't see the slight figure slip from behind the shed and, keeping a safe distance behind, adroitly follow him.

The Robin Hood on the Woodgate was his next chosen venue. He had frequented The Salmon at the back of St Margaret's church on the last four occasions and felt ready for a change. The Robin Hood sounded just the place, albeit one he wouldn't normally have dreamed of drinking in. It was well known in Leicester as a meeting place for villains but this did not deter Bernard. He was a big man now, in others' eyes a soldier, a person to command respect. As time was passing he found himself wishing the uniform had belonged to a commissioned officer. Still he was in no position to be choosy. A common soldier's uniform was far better than nothing.

The public bar was packed when he pushed open the door and hobbled through. The burly barman gruffly took his order and thrust a pint of bitter towards him. Bernard placed his money on the counter.

'I'll pay for that,' said a husky voice.

Bernard smiled in gratitude and turned towards the person the offer had come from. His eyes opened wide. It was a woman, not an attractive one but not what Bernard would have termed ugly either. She would, he guessed, be around her middle-forties, with a shock of dark brown hair, sprinkled with natural grey streaks. She smiled at him through heavily made-up hazel eyes, crossed her thin legs seductively and patted the stool next to her. 'Take a seat,' she said, noticing his walking stick. 'Can yer manage?'

'I can, just about, thank you.'

The woman began chatting. She told him of her husband, how he had died in the evacuation of Dunkirk. Bernard commiserated with her. He himself had been a part of the nightmare, he said, knowing himself lucky to get out alive when many thousands had not. He had waded out into the sea, up to his neck in freezing water, German bullets whizzing past his ears, when he had been plucked from the icy waters by a grocer from Bournemouth, manning a tiny pleasure craft hardly suitable for cruising a mill pond let alone the open seas. He had been fortunate just receiving the injury to his leg, severe though it was, and the guilt of his comrades dying would never leave him.

All the time he spoke she stared at him, eyes filled with deep sympathy.

She studied the badge on his shoulder. 'You didn't know my husband, did you? Walter Thompson? He was in your outfit.'

Bernard shook his head. 'No, sorry. Can't say as I did.'

She sighed. 'I'm being daft even to think you would. No one can know everybody. It's just that . . . well, I'd like to know exactly what happened when he died. The telegrams don't tell yer that, do they? They just say . . . well, that they're dead, not how.'

He looked at her kindly. 'I'm sure he didn't suffer.'

She threw back her head. 'I 'ope to God the bastard did! He used to beat me black and blue. I 'ope his death was long and painful. That's why I want to speak to someone that was there. I 'ope 'e lingered right 'til the last in excruciating pain. The kinda pain 'e put me through every time 'e felt like it.'

Bernard gawped as she downed her half pint of bitter. ''Nother?' she asked.

He went to offer to pay then changed his mind. Why should he? he thought. This woman seemed willing enough.

As she tried to attract the barman's attention he swivelled around on his stool, mindful of his 'injured' leg, and stared around. Two rough-looking characters were huddled in a corner deep in conversation and Bernard wondered if they were striking a deal of some sort. Several gaudily dressed women, obviously prostitutes, were weaving amongst the crowd, propositioning any man they came across. Bernard sneered. One thing he wouldn't pay for was sex.

He averted his eyes and gazed through the crowds to the far side of the room. A fleeting glimpse of a woman momentarily caught his attention. She looked familiar and he frowned, wondering where he knew her from, if indeed he knew her at all. The crowd closed again and his view of her was gone. He realised his companion was talking to him.

'Well?'

'Sorry, well what?'

'I asked if yer fancy coming back to my place?' She licked her lips and batted her eyelashes. 'A widow woman gets kinda lonely, yer know.'

Bernard held his breath. He felt a stirring in his groin and a tingling sensation in his stomach. It had been a long time since he'd been propositioned and the thought excited him.

His eyes lingered on her. She wasn't that bad-looking for her age, although beneath her coat he could tell her body was a little on the scrawny side, but he supposed with the lights off it wouldn't matter.

It was then that he realised that light or no light this woman would know instantly that there was no injury to his leg. He couldn't risk having a romp under the sheets, much as he desired it, for fear of discovery. If only he'd thought to bandage his leg, he could have got away with it. Blast! he inwardly fumed. It was sod's law playing its hand.

'I can't, I'm sorry,' he said reluctantly.

'I see. Married, eh?'

'No, no, widowed like yerself,' he lied. 'Only the doctors have warned me against any strenuous activity in case me stitches break open.'

'Oh! Oh, I see.' She looked at him longingly. 'But that don't stop us still enjoying each other's company, does it?'

Bernard pursed his lips, beads of sweat glistening on his forehead. 'No, I suppose it doesn't.'

She drained her glass, uncrossed her legs and slipped off the stool, grabbing his hand. 'Come on then. I only live up the road.'

Two doors away a figure lurked in the shadows, keenly watching every move Bernard Wilkins and his companion made. When the door closed, the figure emerged, smiled to itself, and hurried off down the street.

Holding his boots in his hands, Bernard emerged from the widow's dismal room in the attic of a nearby terrace just after twelve, worn to a frazzle. Hardly over the threshold she had pounced on him, and the last two hours had been spent fighting off her fearsome advances, his injuries seemingly forgotten. He'd only escaped on a promise to return the following night. He had never been so frightened in all his life and had no intention of returning. A romp was one thing but fighting off a sex-crazed female was another.

As he tiptoed down the stairs towards the first landing a door opened and a figure emerged. It was a soldier and for fear of discovery Bernard slunk back into the shadows, hardly daring to breathe. As he waited he felt this situation was worse than the one he had just escaped from. He was beginning to wish he had not bothered to come out tonight at all.

'Thanks again, Madam Zena,' the soldier said, putting on his cap.

A woman dressed in a long flowing robe, her neck and arms bedecked in costume jewellery, emerged out of the dimly lit doorway and shook his hand, the silver and gold coloured metal bracelets on her wrists jangling. 'My pleasure,' she said with a hint of an accent. 'You'll be all ze better for tonight. Trust me.'

'Oh, I do, Madam Zena, I do. I'll be back and I'll bring me mates an' all. I'll tell 'em a quid, that right?'

'Yes, zat's right. For what I do, zat's cheap.'

'I know. I know. Good value fer money. Tomorrow night then, same time.'

'I'll look forward to it.'

The soldier nodded vigorously, turned and made his way down the dimly lit stairs. The woman stepped further on to the landing and watched his departure. As she turned to walk back inside, Bernard had a full view of her face, lit by the room beyond. He gawped in recognition. It was the woman he had caught a glimpse of in The Robin Hood, and no wonder she had looked familiar. It was Madge Cotting, the evacuee woman from number eighty-nine.

He waited until he heard the door click shut then inhaled

sharply. The dirty cow! he fumed. Madge Cotting was no more than a common prostitute, the scum of the earth. She had fooled all the neighbours into thinking she worked the night shift in the plaster factory. And they in turn had taken pity on her, even helping to clothe and feed her kids, when all the time she was earning her money having sex with men!

But worse than this discovery was the fact that a woman of ill repute resided in the same street as he did. That he could not, would not, tolerate and he would make sure she didn't for much longer. He'd make sure everybody knew what she was up to.

Checking the coast was clear, he tiptoed down the stairs and out into the street where he leaned against a wall and pulled on his boots.

Inside her rented room Madge hurriedly changed her clothes and only moments later was outside on the landing, locking the door. She had to get to the club for twelve-thirty where Jacky would be waiting for her after his business meeting. It was already five past.

Jacky was tiring of her. Already his eye had begun to roam and she knew it was only a matter of time before she was dumped for some faceless tart. Her being late would not help the situation. He wouldn't be pleased. Jacky was not a man most women dared mess with. But then, Jacky was soon to realise that Madge herself was not like most women.

Right from their initial meeting, she had known he was no saint. Normal working men did not wear cashmere coats and own luxurious flats; they could not afford to eat steak paid for from a permanently fat bankroll stuffed in their pocket, while the majority of the rest of the population of Great Britain were having to manage on rations.

How he earned the money had intrigued her and right from the start she had kept her ears and eyes open. And she had learned well. Protection rackets and prostitution were what kept him in luxury, and thanks to the war his finances had benefited further from branching out into the black market. There wasn't much that Jacky couldn't lay his hands on by one means or another – providing, of course, you could pay.

But for all that, even she had been surprised at the sort of company he kept. He mixed with some of the nastiest men this side of London, men whose faces adorned the posters in police stations the length and breadth of the country and Madge had no doubt that his face would at some time or other join them.

Madge was no saint either, and saw no reason why she should not profit from her knowledge. If she was about to become history, Jacky was going to pay and the money received would finance her future. The police, she felt sure, would be very interested in what she could tell them and Jacky would have to cough up dearly for her silence.

She stopped suddenly, eyes glinting brightly. Why wait any longer? She was tiring of all this running around, being on hand when he wanted her, lying low when he didn't, and the lies she had had to tell to cover up. Not only to him about her position at home but also her neighbours.

She smiled to herself. Wouldn't they all, in one way or another, get a shock if they knew the truth? Especially her neighbours. Gullible fools that they were, believing she worked the night shift in the plaster factory when in truth the money she earned was from telling people's fortunes, her clients mainly soldiers desperate to be told they would live to tell their tales, that their sweethearts would be faithful – and any other things she could think of that she knew they wanted to hear.

Avril had taught her well, having herself learned all the tricks from a gypsy.

Madge's thoughts returned to Jacky. It wasn't even as though the man was helping her financially. If he had done, just a little, she would have been able to give up the fortune-telling lark before she ran the risk of being exposed as a con when her prophecies failed. But Jacky kept a tight hold on his money. Not one present had he bought her in all the time they had been friends. Well, she had had enough. Why should she wait until he gave her the boot, why not turn the tables and do it to him? And she would do it tonight. Get it over and done with. The sooner she got her money, the sooner she could get away from this stinking hole and head back home where she belonged.

For a fleeting moment as she hurried down the last of the stairs and across the short span of corridor towards the front door she thought of her kids. Her decision regarding them was unchanged. Meeting Jacky had opened her eyes to the kind of life she wanted more than anything. She had liked the feel of silk sheets against her skin; of eating in posh restaurants; of being in a nice home. The money she would extort from him would help a little towards getting what she wanted, but to keep it up she would have to find another wealthy man and couldn't hope to do that with two kids tagging behind. And her looks wouldn't last for ever. She would be sad to hand them over to the authorities but it was for the best. They needed a proper home; proper parents. She had never been that to them. To be truthful, given a choice, she would never have had them in the first place.

Reaching the front door, she pulled it open and rushed out into the street.

Outside Bernard had just straightened up after tying his boots and was about to move off when the door behind him burst open and a figure charged through, colliding slap-bang into him, sending him flying. He landed heavily on the pavement, scraping his chin, and yelled out in shock.

The collision threw Madge backwards and she tripped on the doorstep and fell into the hallway.

It was several moments before each gathered their wits.

Madge scrambled up first and straightened her clothes. She peered in the near pitch darkness at the figure still sprawled on the ground. She could just make out it was a soldier, and she laughed. 'I 'ope you weren't coming to see me, mate? I've finished for the night. I could possibly manage you tomorrow.'

Bernard's face turned thunderous at the very thought. He awkwardly rose, picked up his mother's walking stick and, out of practice, leaned heavily upon it, staring at her angrily. 'I wouldn't spit on you, let alone cross your doorstep.'

Madge raised her eyebrows at his unexpected exchange. 'Eh!'

Bernard sneered. 'Don't play the innocent with me, Madge Cotting. I know your game. Women like you make me sick.'

She frowned hard. Who was this person? And what did he mean, people like her? But more to the point, he had called her by name. 'Do I know you?' she asked warily.

'Know me? I'll say you know me all right!' He pushed his face towards her. 'Know me now, do yer?'

'Oh, it's Mr Wilkins. And what brings you to these parts? Out for a stroll? I'd have said it was a bit cold for that myself.'

'Don't you be bloody sarcastic with me. And whether I'm out for a stroll or off to rob a bank, it's got n'ote to do with you. But what you're up to's got everything to do with me, 'cos I'm the silly beggar that's helping to feed your kids.'

Madge smiled as she brushed her hand over her coat. 'Yes, I meant to thank you for that. Right neighbourly of you. You Leicester people are really generous, I must say.'

'Neighbourly!' he spat. 'More like the bloody mugs you've took us for.'

'Yes, well.' Madge gave a grin. 'You could have a point

there. But regardless, I'm grateful anyway. Now if you don't mind, I have to rush.'

Bernard's temper rose at this woman's nerve. Worse, she was mocking him. Well, she had better watch out, she was dealing with Bernard Wilkins, not some idiot she'd picked up off the streets. 'Off to meet a client are we?'

'No, actually, I'm not. But if I was, it's got nuffink to do with you.'

'Oh, but it has, Mrs Cotting. Very much so. Prostitution is against the law. I'm sure the authorities 'ud be very interested in your activities.'

Madge stared at him, then it dawned on her just what he thought she was doing. She was angry. How dare he make assumptions? The corner of her mouth twitched. 'Oh, that's what I'm doin', is it?' Anger erupted inside her and she stepped towards him and poked him hard in the shoulder. 'Well, report me and we'll see who has the last laugh, shall we? 'Cos, truthfully, I couldn't give a monkey's. In fact, you'd be doing me a favour.' She inclined her head towards the house. 'This is my work address, number four, second floor, and if they want to interview any of my clients, they'd be willing, I'm sure. Think very highly of me, do my clients.' She laughed loudly, then stopped abruptly as something she had noticed earlier registered fully. She scanned her eyes over him and nodded in satisfaction. 'Before you shoot off down the police station, just answer me a question. Since when did you join up?' She eyed the walking stick. 'Injured in the line of duty, were we?'

Bernard froze, face turning ashen. In his delight at discovering her, he had forgotten about his attire. He stared at her, horrified. She had him and he knew it. His mind, usually so active, was blanked.

Madge felt a glow of satisfaction spread through her. This bigoted man standing before her, the one accusing her of being a prostitute, was guilty of a far worse misdemeanour than he thought her guilty of. And he was going to be sorry. Like Jacky, he was going to pay, and dearly.

'I know what your game is, Mr Wilkins. Impersonation is a grave offence, especially that of a soldier. All those poor blighters getting their heads shot off, and I bet you ain't even been inside the recruiting office. Shame on you, Mr Wilkins! I'd expect the least you'll get is prison. And another fing. You'll never be able to walk down your street again. Folks don't forget things like this, 'specially the women.'

Bernard gawped. The situation he found himself in was dire. His heart thumped so painfully he thought it would burst through his rib cage. How was he going to get out of this unscathed? He had judged her wrong. Madge Cotting was no pushover. His usual manipulative tactics were not going to work this time.

'What a' yer going to do?' he whispered.

'Well, I'm not quite sure yet. You'll have to wait and see what I come up with.' Her eyes glinted wickedly in the darkness. 'But you can be sure I'll let you know, whatever it is.'

At this Bernard's temper boiled up and over. Without realising what he was doing, he raised the walking stick and brought it down heavily on the side of her head. She stumbled and fell back against the wall of the house, banging her head again.

She yelled out in pain as her hand flew to her forehead and she felt the trickle of blood.

Above them a window shot open and a head poked out. 'What's goin' on down there?' a voice shouted.

Bernard stared up wildly.

Madge righted herself and stared up also. 'It's okay, Brenda, it's me, Madge. I tripped over the doorstep and banged me head. Bloody blackout.'

Brenda laughed, "As it knocked some sense in ter yer, gel?'

Madge lowered her gaze and stared across at Bernard. 'Oh, I'll say, Brenda.' She raised her head again. 'Go back to bed.'

'Right yer are. See yer tomorrow.'

'Yeah.' Madge wiped the blood off her temple with her handkerchief. 'You'll be sorry you did that, Mr Wilkins. Bloody sorry.'

Bernard's throat dried. He was sorry. He was sorry he'd ever stolen this blasted uniform, sorry he'd ever clapped eyes on this dreadful woman, he was even sorrier at this moment that his mother had given birth to him. His whole way of life was disintegrating around him and he was powerless to stop it. A vice-like grip twisted his stomach. His future, if indeed he had one, lay in the hands of this woman and he had made the whole situation doubly worse by striking her. Why? Why had he done that? Turning abruptly on his heel, he fled.

Madge, grinning to herself, turned in the opposite direction and hurried off down the street.

Chapter Eighteen

The next four days were a living nightmare. Bernard performed his duties in a daze, constantly looking over his shoulder, constantly aware that at any moment the authorities could grab him and march him off to face – God knew what. He was in hell and the uncertainty that faced him was driving him mad. He couldn't eat, couldn't sleep, and his pinched, ashen face was telling the tale.

Since that night, he had seen not a glimpse of Madge Cotting nor her children. Not that he himself had ever seen much of her as it was. What was she playing at? Whatever she had planned, why didn't she just get it over with? At least he'd be put out of his misery.

Grace was deeply concerned over Bernard. Never had she seen him so jumpy. He looked ill to the point of collapse but any enquiry or offer of help was harshly snapped at and ferociously rejected.

Ida tackled her. 'What you done ter my son?' she demanded.

'Nothing, nothing. I don't know what's ailing him.'

'Well, I do,' she spat, folding her bony arms under her scrawny chest. 'It's yer job. You've humiliated 'im, that's what yer've done.'

'Oh, Mrs Wilkins, don't be silly. Lots of women work and Bernard can't deny the money's handy. Besides, I happen to like my job.'

'Just as I thought. Thinkin' of yerself as usual. Don't matter ter you that 'cos you work, we're all suffering, does it?'

Grace turned on her. 'And how are you suffering, Mrs Wilkins? And your son for that matter? The house is clean, the washing done and the meals prepared. You tell me, what's changed, apart from the fact that I'm happy? That's what you don't like, isn't it? You don't want me to be happy, do you?'

Just then Charlie charged in. She dropped her bag on the floor and collapsed in the chair. She looked at her mother then her grandmother enquiringly. 'What's going on?'

Grace turned towards the table and picked up the teapot. 'Nothing. Your grandmother and I were just discussing my job. She was just saying how well everything is working out.' She turned and looked Ida in the eye. 'Weren't you, Mrs Wilkins?'

She mumbled something inaudible under her breath.

Charlie studied her grandmother for a moment. She wasn't convinced that the wizened creature staring back had said that at all. As usual Grace was covering up to spare Charlie.

She gratefully accepted the mug of tea her mother had poured. 'Thanks, Mam. Has anyone called for me?'

'Why? Who you expectin'?' Ida demanded.

'Just a friend, Grandma,' she replied sharply.

'No, no one's called, Charlie,' Grace said, cutting thick slices of bread. She grimaced at the unappetising appearance of it, greyish in colour because of the unrefined flour the bakers were having to use. She scraped it sparingly with marge and added two thin slices of spam, cut the sandwich in two and handed it over to her daughter. 'Off out tonight?'

'Yes, hopefully. Derek is calling any time so I'd better get a move on. I want to be ready when he knocks on the door. We're going to the pictures.'

'Oh,' Grace said, impressed. 'How did you meet him?'

'In the blackout, funnily enough. We literally bumped into each other.'

Grace laughed. 'As good a way as any, I suppose, to meet a nice young man. He is nice, I hope?'

Charlie grinned. 'Very, Mam. So stop worrying.'

Grace tried to hide her dismay. Not that she minded Charlie going out, far from it. She wanted her daughter to enjoy herself. She worked hard, long hours in the factory, and deserved some relaxation. It was just the worry of an air raid. Most nights now the warning sounded. The scramble for cover and the hours spent listening to the drone of enemy planes flying overhead were taking their toll. Although no bombs had dropped since the incident in August, the threat was still there and if the Germans' Luftwaffe did decide to target their city she would sooner have Charlie close by her.

She sensed her mother's thoughts. 'Don't worry, Mam. If an air raid starts, we'll be straight down a shelter.'

Grace managed to smile. She herself had been meaning to go to the pictures on several occasions over the last two months and every time arrangements were made between herself, Clara and Bessie, something happened to prevent the outing. Still, she supposed, with a bit of luck she'd get there one day and would appreciate it all the more.

'Who's this Derek, when 'e's at 'ome?' Ida asked.

Charlie sighed. 'I've already said, Grandma, a friend. Actually 'e's a policeman if you really want to know.'

'Huh,' was Ida's response. She looked across at Grace. 'Don't I get a cuppa tea then?'

Charlie rose. 'I'm off to get ready. If Derek calls, will you tell him I'll meet him outside Vinny's shop, please mam?'

'Oh, but he can come in and wait . . .' She was stopped by the look on her daughter's face. Charlie did not wish any friend to step inside the house whilst her father was around. Not after the last episode. She knew Charlie had still not

265

forgiven Bernard for humiliating her. 'Don't worry, love, I'll give him your message.'

Charlie smiled gratefully, gathered her things and ran up the stairs.

'Ashamed of us now, is she? Don't want 'er friends meetin' 'er family.'

Grace sighed heavily. Sometimes she wished Ida would keep her petty thoughts to herself. She wanted to turn round and tell her mother-in-law the reason for Charlie's reluctance: the carping attitude of Bernard and Ida herself to any visitor who crossed the threshold. Although of late Bernard seemed constantly distracted, his abrupt manner was still enough to send a saint running. But Grace knew her breath would be wasted and also suspected Ida knew exactly the reason, she just wanted to cause trouble as usual.

The back door sounded and Grace went to answer it. It was Clara and Grace ushered her inside, quickly shutting the door and securing the blackout curtains.

'You look worried. Is anything wrong?'

Clara rubbed her hand over her chin. 'I don't really know, Grace dear. I'm not sure, you see. But,'yes, I am worried.'

'Who's there?' shouted Ida.

Grace pressed her lips together in frustration. 'It's just Miss Smith, Mrs Wilkins.'

'What's she want?'

Grace took a breath to calm her annoyance. 'She's come to see me, Mrs Wilkins.' She settled her attention back on Clara. 'I'm sorry for her rudeness. Now what were you saying? You're worried about something. What?'

'The Cottings.'

'The Cottings?'

'Mmm, the Cottings. I feel there's something wrong, Grace.'

'In what way?'

'Well, I haven't seen or heard the mother for several days, and although the house is in darkness, I know the children are still inside. I've just got a strange feeling, Grace, that's all.'

She stared thoughtfully. Come to think of it, she hadn't seen the children for several days herself. She went to work in the dark and came home in the dark, and with the blackout it was extremely difficult to see anything. She could walk right past Charlie and not realise who she was.

'We'll go and check on them. Put your mind at rest.'

Clara looked at her worriedly. 'Do you think it wise? Madge Cotting doesn't take kindly to interference.'

'It's not her I'm thinking of, it's those children, and it wouldn't be the first time she's left them on their own. Come on, Clara. The more I think on what you've said, the more I don't like it.'

She grabbed her coat from the back of the door. 'I'm just popping out for a moment,' she shouted through to Ida.

'Where! Where to?'

Her question fell on deaf ears. Grace and Clara had gone.

Several minutes later Bernard lumbered heavily down the stairs.

''Ello, son. Did yer manage to 'ave a kip?'

'No, I didn't,' he snapped, picking up the teapot. It was empty and he slammed it down.

Ida jumped.

'Where's everyone?' he barked.

She pursed her lips. 'Charlie's upstairs gettin' ready ter go out, and Grace . . . well, she's gone, don't know where to. That Clara Smith came but I couldn't 'ear what they were sayin'.'

'Oh,' he replied blankly.

Ida stared at him. What was wrong with her son? This wasn't like him at all. Usually he would have had a lot to say about Grace's disappearance. He had something on his mind and whatever it was was worrying him deeply. His face was grey, his eyes heavy from lack of sleep and he was losing weight.

'Want to talk about it, son?'

He swung round to face her. 'Talk? About what?'

'About whatever's on yer mind. You needn't worry, son. I know what it is.'

Bernard's pallor was alarming. 'You know! Wadda you mean, yer know?'

Ida folded her skinny arms, as a superior 'I told you' look settled on her face. 'It's 'er and that job, ain't it? If she'd 'ave got any concern for you she wouldn't 'ave taken it. Selfish, that's all she is.'

Bernard exhaled sharply. For an instant he had feared his mother had somehow found out what was troubling him. Grace and her job were the last thing on his mind. At this moment she could work all hours and he couldn't give a damn. His mother, as usual, was poking her nose in to cause trouble. Usually he welcomed it, but not tonight. He glared at her angrily. 'Oh, for God's sake, Mother. Why don't you shut up? It's about time you learned to keep your nose out of things that don't concern you.'

Her mouth fell open. 'Bernard!'

The front door banged loudly and he froze in terror. Who would be calling at this time of night? As far as he knew no one was expected.

'Well, answer it,' Ida instructed. She knew it would be Charlie's friend come to call and inwardly sniggered at the prospect of Bernard's usual probing questions which in turn would upset Charlie and cause an almighty row to follow. Just the kind of distraction she needed after being stuck in all day due to the wet weather. 'Well, go on. Might be the pools man to tell us we've won.'

'We don't do the pools,' Bernard replied, finding his voice.

''Bout time we did then, 'cos 'ow we gonna win otherwise? Go on, answer it before whoever it is thinks no one's in.'

'Get the door, Mam,' Charlie shouted from upstairs.

Bernard held his breath. He would have to go. It would look so suspicious if he didn't. And if he refused, he would have to face the barrage of questions from his mother. With great difficulty he summoned the will to move, each step towards the door coinciding with the painful thumping of his heart.

He reached the door, took the handle and pulled it open.

Bernard's eyes bulged in terror. He shook so hard he had to grab the door for support.

'Hello, sir,' the policeman began.

'H-he doesn't live here,' Bernard stammered. 'He doesn't. They moved. Weeks ago.'

The policeman stared at him bemused. He was even more bemused when the door was slammed in his face.

Her coat folded over her arm, dressed in a smart navy blue suit and white blouse with a Peter Pan collar, Charlie ran down the stairs to find her father standing in the darkened passageway staring transfixed at the closed door. 'Was that Derek?' she asked. 'Dad, was that Derek?'

He turned to face her, but his eyes still saw the policeman.

'It was him. What did you do, Dad?' Her temper rose. 'I hope you didn't send him away.' She yanked open the door and flew down the street calling his name.

She caught up with him outside Vinny's. He smiled. 'I've just had the strangest thing happen to me,' he said, kissing her lightly on the cheek in greeting. 'I must have knocked on the wrong door and this . . . well, madman answered.'

Charlie's lips tightened. 'And what did this madman say?'

Derek laughed. 'Nothing that made sense. Something about "they don't live here, they've moved". Anyway, you're here now and I must apologise for still being in uniform, but, well, it seems we have a murder to solve and a pretty nasty one at that. It's a woman we haven't identified yet so it's all hands on deck.'

'Oh, how terrible,' Charlie said sincerely, before anger at her father returned. 'And you're going to have another . . . but I can assure you, you won't have to look far for the culprit! It'll be me. Wait here for me, please, Derek. I've just to pop home again but what I have to say and do won't take me long.'

'Charlie? What do you mean? Charlie . . .' he shouted after her. But she was gone.

She stormed into the house, finding her father still standing in the passage where she had left him several minutes ago.

'That's it, Father,' she fumed. 'This is the last time you humiliate me like this. I'm leaving home.' She marched straight past him and into the living room. 'Where's my mother?' she demanded of Ida.

'Out,' came the flat reply.

'Where exactly?'

''Ow should I know? You're mother's a law unto 'erself these days. Doesn't give a damn for anybody else as long as she's all right.'

Charlie clenched her fists. 'Don't you speak about my mother like that. You're nothing but a spiteful, narrow-minded old woman. I'm ashamed that you're my grandmother. Give her a message, please. Tell her I've had enough. I cannot live in this house any more and I've gone to live at Sybil's.' She grabbed up a piece of paper and a pencil from the table and wrote a hurried note which she stuck on the mantel. 'On second thoughts, don't bother yourself. The note will explain. Because I won't set foot inside this house again. Not whilst you and he still live here, I won't.' Without waiting for Ida's response, she turned and ran upstairs where she threw all her belongings into two brown suitcases. With difficulty she closed them and struggled down the stairs.

Her father was still standing in the passageway and for a moment Charlie wondered what on earth was wrong with him. Anger overrode this concern and she marched past him and out the door, pulling it to hard with her foot.

Grace and Clara headed straight for the Cottings' house. It was in darkness and they stood for a moment, unsure what to do. Grace took the lead and knocked loudly on the back door.

'If Madge answers,' she whispered to Clara, 'I'll just . . . er . . .'

'Just what?'

'I dunno. I'll think of something.'

They waited. Nothing happened. So Grace knocked once more. When nothing happened again, she tried the door knob. It turned freely and, placing her shoulder against the wood, she shoved it open. She entered, Clara following close behind.

'Jessie, Tony!' she called.

The freezing musty air inside made them both gasp. Grace fumbled around, feeling for the light switch. She located it and flicked it down. Nothing happened. In pitch darkness they groped their way. Grace came up against the table in the living room and banged her knee. She grimaced in pain, knowing a good-sized bruise would appear come morning.

After searching most of the rooms they finally found Jessie and Tony huddled in their mother's bed, the grey blanket procured from Bessie their only means of warmth; a stub of candle their only light. Terrified, they stared wide-eyed as the two women entered, their grubby faces streaked with tears. It was painfully obvious that they had not eaten properly for days; both looked near exhaustion.

Both women were filled with horror at the pitiful sight. Tears pricked their eyes. Silently Grace moved towards the bed. She sat on the edge and gathered them both into her arms, hugging them to her fiercely.

'Come on,' she whispered emotionally. 'Come on, both of you. You're coming with me.'

Fed up with waiting for her son to return and worried about what was taking him so long, Ida struggled to her feet and hobbled out into the darkened passage where she found Bernard staring at the closed door as if hypnotised.

'What's up wi' you?' she demanded. 'Standing in 'ere like a blethering idiot. Come back in where it's warm.'

In a trance-like state Bernard did as he was told and followed her through. He sank down in the armchair and held his head in his hands, his mother's voice not registering on his muddled mind. She was going on about something to do with Charlie and a friendly Polish man who had lice. Oh, shut up, he wanted to scream at her. He fought the desire to hook his hands round her neck and strangle the life out of her – anything to shut her up. He had too much on his mind to listen to her drivel.

'A' you listening to me?' she shouted shrilly, her voice cutting through his muddled thoughts like a knife through butter.

His head jerked up and he glared at her.

'I said, was that Charlie's friend the policeman at the door? 'E's teking 'er to the pictures.'

Bernard gawped. Slowly it registered just what she had said. 'What, Mother? What did you say?'

She tutted in frustration. 'Oh, God love me, I've bred an imbecile.' She repeated her question.

He fell back in his chair, a feeling of immense relief spreading through him. He was safe. For the time being anyway. 'Charlie's friend you say?'

She nodded.

'Taking her to the pictures?'

She nodded again. 'Yeah. Why, waddid you think 'e'd called for?'

'Er . . . nothing, nothing at all. It was just a bit of a shock answering the door to him, that's all. I thought summat had happened.'

'Huh.' Ida folded her arms and thrust out her skinny chest, feeling hard done by. She'd been looking forward to a confrontation. 'So yer don't mind she's gone out wi' a copper then?'

He shook his head vigorously. He didn't care at this moment whether his daughter had gone out with the Chief Inspector himself as long as they left him alone. He rose, walked through to the kitchen and took his coat from the door.

'Where you off?' Ida shouted.

'Just out, Mother.'

He had had a reprieve and he was going to do something he should have done days ago but had been so terrified of what Madge had planned for him, it had slipped his mind. He was going up to the allotment to burn the uniform. Get rid of the cursed thing once and for all. At least then, if she did inform the police of his activities, there would be no evidence around to support her claim. It would be her word against his and Madge Cotting would never be able to match him in the art of lying.

He suddenly felt better, better than he had done for days. Madge Cotting was bluffing. If she had been going to do something, it would have happened by now. The woman was all mouth. After she had threatened him she must have realised that he had as much on her with her prostitution as she had on him. She must have realised that he would not sit back and accept his punishment without divulging what she was up to.

He smiled to himself. Maybe in the end she hadn't fancied the idea of sharing a cell with him. He clicked his tongue several times. Women. When it came to brains they could never match a man, especially a man such as himself. He let himself out of the back door, raised his head and started to whistle a merry tune as he jauntily made his way to the deserted allotment.

Ida heard her son leave. She sniffed in displeasure. She had been left on her own. They had all gone out without a thought for her. Selfish! The lot of them were selfish. When she had been young, the older members of the family laid down the law. Everything had revolved around the grandparents and here she was left alone without a by your leave. Well, sod 'em, she thought. If they could all go out, then so could she. A half pint of stout at the local and hopefully a natter with some other old timers was a welcoming thought. It'd serve them all right if an air raid started and she was blown to bits. They'd be sorry then. They'd have to live with their guilt for the rest of their lives whilst she herself would be up there somewhere laughing down at them.

Struggling up, she grabbed at the note Charlie had left, eyes glinting wickedly, and screwed it up before throwing it into the fire. Then she pulled on her coat, picked up her bag and walking stick and hobbled out of the house.

Just over two hours later, the children washed, fed and tucked warmly in a makeshift bed in the tiny room off Charlie's bedroom, Grace placed two mugs of tea in front of Clara and Bessie.

'Thanks for the loan of the mattress, Bessie,' she said gratefully. 'And the clothes.'

'No bother, me duck. Our Dennis and Barry won't need it at the moment where they are, and the clothes . . . well, keep 'em as long as yer like.' She shook her head. 'Poor little tykes. They were starved. I'll never forget the way they tucked into that soup. Bless their little 'earts, I don't think they've eaten fer days.'

'Me neither,' voiced Clara. 'That Jessie is normally such a proud-spirited little thing, but now, well, all the spirit's been knocked out of her.' She took a sup of her tea. 'What are you going to do, Grace dear?'

'Do?'

'She means, a' yer gonna inform the police?'

'Inform the police? Oh, I don't know.'

'You'll have to, Gracie. That woman's been gone days accordin' ter the kids. She could 'ave just upped and left 'em, or worse, be dead fer all we know. You 'ave ter do summat for the sake of the kids if n'ote else.' Bessie folded her flabby arms, her huge chest heaving in anger. 'The woman deserves locking up anyway, leaving 'em like that.'

Grace stared at her. Her friend was right, she knew she was. She nodded. 'I'll go now, there's no point in delaying. Will you two stay here 'til I get back? I don't want them to wake up and find the house empty. They've been through enough.' She frowned deeply as she rose. 'Though for the life of me I can't think where Bernard and his mother have gone. Charlie won't be in 'til late, she's gone to the pictures.'

Bessie rose also. 'I'm coming wi' yer. I ain't 'aving you traipsing the streets at this time of night on yer own. You'll be all right, won't yer, Clara?'

She nodded, although she didn't like the thought of Bernard and his mother returning to find her sitting in their living room and then having to explain the reason for her presence. But she didn't voice her fears. Her friends were relying on her.

The kindly constable manning the desk took the details, then, asking the ladies to wait, disappeared through the back. It seemed ages before he returned. The constable pulled up the flap on the counter and asked them through. Detective Inspector Crawshaw would like a word, he explained.

Bewildered, Grace and Bessie followed him behind the counter and through several corridors where they were ushered through to a windowless interview room and asked to take a seat. He then left.

'What d'yer think's going' on?' Bessie whispered.

Grace shrugged her shoulders. 'I dunno.'

The door opened and a tall, middle-aged man entered. He smiled at the two women as he sat down on a chair the other side of the table, laying down a sheaf of papers.

'I'm sorry for any inconvenience, ladies, but I just need to clarify some details.'

For several minutes he went over the description of Madge Cotting: where she lived, what she did and anything else they could tell him about her. When he was satisfied he sat back in his chair, taking a deep breath. 'There's no pleasant way of putting this . . .' he began.

Grace and Bessie looked at each other worriedly, then back to the Inspector.

'But we have the body of a woman down at the morgue. She fits your description of this Madge Cotting.'

'Morgue? Did you say morgue?' uttered Grace.

Bessie's jaw dropped.

The Inspector nodded.

Simultaneously, Grace's and Bessie's hands flew to their mouths, eyes wide in shock.

'A bad blow on the back of her head. She would never have known what hit her.'

'And you think this woman could be Madge?' Grace gasped.

'The description fits.' Detective Inspector Crawshaw

cleared his throat. 'We need an identification. I'd like you to accompany me down to the morgue. Although, I'd better warn you, it won't be very nice for you.'

'Eh!' Bessie cried in alarm. 'You want us to see a dead body? I can't. I ain't never seen a dead body before. Only me grandmother's and she don't count, her being family like.'

Grace took a breath. The very thought terrified her. But it was something she knew they had to do.

'Bessie, if we don't go, then it'll be left to young Jessie. I can't put her through that, I just can't.' She took her friend's hand. 'If you can't face it, I'll do it myself. I don't mind, Bessie. I understand how you feel.'

Bessie stared at her. 'No, I'm all right, really I am. We'll go together.'

Grace patted her hand gratefully. 'Thanks, Bessie. 'Cos to be truthful, I'd prefer it if you were there with me.'

Detective Inspector Crawshaw smiled warmly. 'Thank you, ladies. I sincerely hope that the body is not that of your neighbour.'

'So do we,' muttered Bessie.

After seeing Bessie safely back into the loving arms of her family, Grace made her way home. Never, never would she want to go through an ordeal such as that again. Viewing a dead body was the worst kind of nightmare.

The body was Madge Cotting's. They had both instantly recognised her as the sheet had been pulled back, her lifeless waxen features staring back at them. Instantly, within them both, nausea had risen and they had bolted for the nearest lavatory. The police had been very nice afterwards, plying them with cups of tea until they had both calmed down.

Grace sighed deeply. But at least she and Bessie doing the

identification had spared Jessie such a dreadful ordeal, one that would have stayed with her for the rest of her life. But how on earth was she going to break the news to the children, who were still expecting their mother to walk through the door at any moment, full of her usual excuses, and take them home?

Clara was still sitting at the table when she entered.

The ashen look on Grace's face told her that something was dreadfully wrong. Without a word she rose and mashed a fresh pot of tea, mindful that the rations in the caddy had to last until the end of the week.

Grace, perched on the edge of the armchair by the fire, accepted the mug gratefully. Cradling it between her hands she took a sip, then raised her eyes to Clara's.

But before she could speak she heard the back door opening. Bernard and his mother came in. Bernard, a different man now the evidence was destroyed and feeling no longer that the Cotting woman had a hold on him, had met his mother outside the pub. Jauntily hooking his arm through hers, he had escorted her home. Ida, confused by her son's sudden change of mood, was too wise to question it. She had her ally back. Now things could get back to normal, she thought maliciously.

She knew instantly, as did her son, that something was amiss as soon as they entered the living room.

Bernard looked at Clara, then at his wife's drawn face. 'What's wrong?' he demanded.

'It's Madge Cotting, Bernard,' she said, her voice shaking.

His eyes narrowed alarmingly. 'Madge Cotting? Oh, the evacuee woman. What's happened to her?' he asked warily.

'She's been murdered. A blow to her head with a blunt instrument, so the police say. She was found in an alleyway off the Woodgate. They reckon it must have happened last Wednesday night somewhere around twelve or thereabout.

The police said it's difficult to know the exact time.'

Bernard's throat tightened and he fought for breath. His legs buckled and he caught hold of the back of the chair for support. Grace jumped up and rushed towards him, grabbing his arm.

'Bernard, are you all right?'

'Yeah, yeah,' he uttered, shrugging her off. 'Leave me. I'm fine, I tell yer.'

They all stared at him.

Bernard's thoughts raced wildly. He had struck the Cotting woman with the walking stick but not hard enough to kill her – or had he? And it had been Wednesday night, around twelve, when it had happened. But she had been alive when he had left her. Oh God, the police. They would want to interview everyone who had been in the area that night. His eyes bulged in horror. The neighbour . . . The woman who had heard their exchange and opened the window. It was pitch dark but she could have seen him just clearly enough for a description.

Oh, this situation was dreadful, terrible. What on earth was he going to do?

He suddenly became conscious of eyes upon him, accusing eyes, branding him a murderer. His face drained of colour.

'It wasn't me,' he shrieked shrilly. 'It wasn't me, I tell yer.'

He backed away from them, turned and fled from the house.

They all stared after him.

'Wadda you do that for?' Ida spat.

Grace turned to her. 'Do? What did I do?'

'Accused him, you did. Accused my son of being a murderer.'

'I did not,' she said indignantly. 'There's one thing I do know and that is that Bernard's no murderer. Whatever made him act like that was none of my doing.' She sighed deeply, bewildered herself by his strange behaviour. 'It was probably just the shock of hearing that a resident in his precious street has met a grisly end, that's all.'

'Huh,' Ida exclaimed, pulling off her coat.

'I'd better be going, Grace.'

She turned to Clara. For a moment she had forgotten the woman was still there. 'Oh, Clara, thank you. Were the children all right?'

'Sleeping like babies. They haven't woken at all. I did check on them several times. My heart goes out to them, Grace, it really does.'

'Children? What children?'

'The Cotting children, Mrs Wilkins,' Grace said. 'They're upstairs in the bedroom off Charlie's.'

'Upstairs in our 'ouse? Why? They're n'ote to do with us.' She tightened her thin lips. 'Bernard won't be pleased.'

Grace braced herself. 'Mrs Wilkins, those poor little mites have just lost their mother. They've been in their own house for nearly a week with no heating or food, scared out of their wits. What did you expect me to do? Leave 'em there because you feel it's none of my business?' Her eyes narrowed in extreme anger at this wizened old woman's lack of human compassion. 'Maybe we should have left you – defenceless, as you put it – in your own house instead of bringing you here to live with us.'

Ida froze, her tightly compressed lips and the surrounding skin resembling deeply cracked paving. 'We'll 'ave to inform the authorities about 'em first thing in the mornin'. They'll find 'em foster 'omes 'til their own relatives are contacted. In the meantime, I ain't standing no nonsense from 'em. While they're 'ere, they'll do as they're told. And 'ave you thought 'ow yer goin' ter feed 'em? They ain't 'aving my rations. I 'ardly get enough as it is.'

Incensed at her unfeeling attitude, Grace reared back her

head. 'Mrs Wilkins, you say one word out of turn to those children and I'll personally escort you from this house. Is that understood? Those children need love and care, and while they're with us, we'll give it to 'em. And as for food, they can have my share. There, does that satisfy you?' She turned from Ida and walked with Clara through to the kitchen. 'I'm sorry you had to witness that,' she said apologetically.

'Don't say another word, Grace dear. That woman is the limit. Personally I'm proud of you for putting her in her place.'

Grace smiled wryly. 'Thank you. Although I could have done without it.'

'Well, it hasn't been a very pleasant night for you, has it?' She patted Grace's hand affectionately. 'If you have any problems whatsoever with your husband or his mother, you bring those children to me. I'll have them.'

'Oh, Clara. You are a lovely woman, thank you. But on this, I'm standing firm. Bernard and his mother can say what they like, but those children are staying put 'til matters are sorted one way or another.'

After seeing Clara out she returned to find Ida sitting ramrod straight in the armchair. Grace ignored her and busied herself tidying up. For a moment she wondered where Bernard had gone, then turned and looked at the clock. It was just after ten-thirty and her daughter was late. The pictures would have been finished long ago. She hoped Charlie wouldn't be much longer, there was so much she had to talk to her about.

'Did Charlie say what time she'd be home?' she asked Ida.

Ida's beady eyes sparkled. This woman needed bringing down a peg or two, putting in her place, and she had just the weapon to do it with. 'She's gone and she ain't coming back,' she said smugly.

Grace stared over at her. 'Pardon?'

'You 'eard. She ain't coming back. She's left 'ome for good and she told me to tell yer not ter bother trying ter find her. She's had enough of yer.'

Grace frowned in bewilderment, a knot tightening in her stomach. 'Charlie? My Charlie said that? You must be mistaken.'

'Callin' me a liar, a' yer? I'm tellin' yer, she's gone, packed her clothes and everythin'. And good riddance ter the little madam, that's all I can say. No respect.'

Grace sank down in a chair, staring at Ida. She was lying, she just had to be. Grace jumped to her feet and ran up the stairs to Charlie's bedroom. Ida was telling the truth. All Charlie's belongings had gone. She hadn't noticed earlier, her mind fully occupied with the children. Why? What had happened to make her do such a thing? When she had left for the Cottings' house earlier in the evening, Charlie had been her normal self.

She flew back down the stairs. 'Why, Mrs Wilkins? Why did Charlie suddenly do this? Did you or Bernard say something to her? Did you upset her?'

'That's it, blame an old woman. I said nothin' to 'er, nor did my son. She just barged in, suitcases packed, and announced she was off and you weren't to try and find 'er 'cos she'd had enough.'

A groan of despair escaped Grace's lips. No, not her beloved Charlie. This she could not bear. It had to be a mistake. But the look of satisfaction written on her mother-in-law's face told Grace she was telling the truth. Her daughter had gone and by the looks of it for good.

Bernard sat in his allotment shed, shivering, but it wasn't because of the cold. He was shivering in fright for what lay in store for him and all because of that blasted uniform, the ashes of which were still smouldering in the brazier outside. It was all that soldier's fault. If he hadn't got drunk that night, none of this would have happened and he would be back safely at home now instead of fearing for his neck for something he knew he had not done. He had struck Madge Cotting, he could not deny that, but not hard enough to kill her.

The loud wail of the air raid warning sounded and shook him rigid. Within moments the drone of enemy planes flying overhead filled the still night air. Bernard wished wholeheartedly one would offload its cargo and blow him to kingdom come. He didn't want to die but at least that way this nightmare would be ended. But miracles like that did not happen. Bernard knew he had only one choice. He had to get away. As far away from this situation as he could. In normal circumstances he could have leapt on a train, heading for a destination miles away and losing himself, but these were not normal circumstances. Everywhere you went identification had to be shown and explanations given. People were full of suspicion towards strangers. No, there was only one option open to him. He would have to do something he had been striving against since the war started. He would have to join up and it would have to be soon. Now the police knew the identity of the body, they would be swarming around the street like flies. Oh, blast Grace and her interference! If she had kept herself to herself as he had always instructed her to do, then Madge Cotting's body might never have been identified. But again, Grace had disobeyed him, something she was doing more and more of late, and because of that she had landed him in this situation.

He made a plan of action. He'd sit here all night, then go down first thing in the morning. With a bit of luck he'd be shipped off to training camp straight away. The army was desperate for men, they would welcome him with open arms.

But little would they know that he needed the army more than the army would ever need him.

Grace rubbed tired eyes. Her whole body was fatigued to the point of exhaustion. This night was one that would stay in her memory as the worst she had ever lived through. A day that had started just like any other had ended in unforeseen tragedy. But the worst was the fact that that her beloved daughter had gone, her last words according to Ida that she never wanted to see her mother again. This sudden unexpected loss of her Charlie was tearing her to shreds.

And still the dreadful night was not yet over. Not long after Bernard had departed, the Luffwaffe decided to pay a visit.

At the first sound of the siren Ida shot inside the pantry, wedging the door tightly shut behind herself. Grace had gone up to wake Jessie and Tony to take them to the communal shelter two streets away, hoping she would meet her own parents there; hoping her father had the sense to leave his post and seek shelter.

As she had looked down on the children peacefully sleeping, she could not bring herself to wake them. In a few short hours they would both face trauma beyond belief. Let them rest now while they could. Besides, if they could sleep through the racket going on outside, they must be exhausted.

Unable to settle, and feeling nothing more could hurt her that night, she went outside and stood on her doorstep. Between the neverending waves of enemy aircraft, the night sky was lit by the criss-cross paths of the search lights, the air filled with intermittent bursts of firing from the anti-aircraft guns. Far in the distance the muffled blasts of bombs made her jump. As the horizon began to glow deep orange and red she was filled with a dreadful despair for the whole insanity of it all.

She felt a presence at her side and turned to find Tom Rudney. He too was staring across into the distance.

'What is it, Tom?' she asked, worried. 'What's causing that red glow in the sky? It looks to me like the whole world's on fire.'

'It's Coventry,' he said, his voice filled with emotion. 'It's burning.'

'Oh, Tom,' she whispered. 'Those people. Those poor, poor people.'

Bessie, dressed in her nightclothes, hair wound tightly in curlers, trotted up to join them, Tom's old slippers flopping on her feet.

He placed his arm around her plump shoulders and pulled her close.

For several moments they all stared in silence at the battle taking place in the distance.

'I 'ave to go, Bessie.'

She looked up at him enquiringly. 'Go? Go where?'

'To Coventry. Those people need help. I'm goin' to go and round up some of the boys and what transport we can lay our hands on. The transport won't be the problem, it'll be the petrol. But if I have to walk all the way, I'm goin'.'

She cried out in anguish: 'No, Tom, no! You could get 'urt.'

'Don't, Bessie. Offering our help is the least we can do. If it was the other way round, the folks of Coventry would be comin' over to help us.'

She sniffed loudly. 'Yeah, yer right. I'll go and mek yer some sandwiches.'

'I'll make some as well,' Grace offered. 'It won't be much, but it'll all help to keep you going.'

Tom smiled at her gratefully and Grace stood and watched as, arm in arm, her friends made their way back home.

Chapter Nineteen

Madge Cotting's grisly demise went barely unnoticed. On everyone's lips, and filling their thoughts the following morning, was the devastating destruction of Coventry.

With little thought for themselves, Tom and his mates were amongst many willing volunteers who found whatever transport they could lay hands on – some even walking – to travel the twenty-five miles with offers of help. Tension in the city of Leicester ran high. Everyone, man, woman and child, concentrated their efforts on helping their fellow countrymen. Desperately needed supplies were hurriedly put together along with every spare piece of household equipment – most items given by people who could ill afford to part with their precious rations and possessions themselves.

Not only Coventry suffered that night, but also Birmingham, Derby, Crewe, Sheffield – and Leicester. Towards the end of the intensified raid, the aim of which was to wreak havoc across the Midlands, two aircraft dropped twenty high-explosive bombs in Leicester across an area stretching from the Hinkley Road to the Gas Works on the Aylestone Road. Luckily, though not for the people involved, only two in the city lost their lives and several were injured, although damage to housing and factories was extensive. It was known, though, that it could all have been much worse. They had only to look at Coventry to realise that.

Compared to the rest of the country, Leicester had been hit lightly that night, but it had been given a stern warning by the enemy. Nowhere in their small island was safe.

Like the other residents of the city, what little sleep Grace had had that night refreshed neither body nor mind, and like the rest, the early hours of the morning before going to work were filled for her with the gathering of any spare provisions and equipment that could be sent with the volunteers.

Before waking the children she decided that the news she had to impart was better told as unhurriedly and gently as possible. She knew, though, that in whatever way it was broken, it would be devastating and afterwards the children would need time, love and patience to come to terms with their loss. Normality, she decided, was the best approach and so they should go to school. Regardless, the telling of this dreadful news could not be delayed as the police were expected to call shortly to question them.

Bessie and Clara came up trumps as usual. Despite both being caught up with helping the rest of the street in the gathering of items to despatch with the volunteers en route to Coventry, they both offered their support in the care of the children whilst Grace went to work.

Bernard had still not returned and this fact also played heavily on her mind. She sincerely hoped that he had not somehow been caught up in the mayhem caused by the air raid. If he had been hurt though, which she sincerely hoped he hadn't, she presumed she would have been told by now.

She was to find out Bernard's activities when she returned home that night. A hurriedly scribbled note left on the mantel starkly informed her of his acceptance into the armed forces. He was leaving that very day for the training camp. No reason for this sudden change of heart and surge of patriotism, no explanation for the hurried departure when usually men were given several days' notice to report, affording them time to say their goodbyes to their families.

His thoughtlessness hurt Grace dreadfully. Was that all she was worth to her husband? A hurried note?

Ida flew into a rage. Bernard's joining up was somehow connected with Grace. It was all her fault, and if Ida's son was killed or horribly maimed, Grace would never be forgiven.

She had too many worries to listen and take to heart what Ida was accusing her of. Secretly, Bernard's departure came as a relief. Without him she felt she could handle her mother-in-law, and without the atmosphere his presence created, the children would have more chance of peace in their shattered lives.

Despite all her other problems, her deepest concern was for Charlie. During the days immediately after her departure she had had to fight a compulsion to go to Charlie's place of work, stand by the gates and wait for her to leave. She could question her, find out her motives, then beg her to come home. But her daughter was not a juvenile, she was of an age to know her own mind and make her own decisions, and, judging by the way she had abruptly left, not take at all kindly to her mother's presence. She had to be left to work whatever it was out for herself.

This conclusion Grace found hard to stomach but felt it was the right one. Regardless, the continued absence of any news of her beloved daughter's whereabouts or reasons for leaving so abruptly was hard to bear, and the only way she found herself able to cope was to concentrate all her energies on immediate matters and with difficulty push all thoughts of Charlie to the back of her mind.

The day after receiving Bernard's note she suddenly remembered the allotment. What would she do with it? The food it produced she would need more than ever now to help eke out her money. On her way home from work she decided to make a hurried detour and see for herself the place she had always been denied access to. It had been Bernard's domain, his own private sanctuary. But now he was gone, for how long she had no idea, and however much she worried how she could handle it, the task would fall to her. The ground was too precious a commodity to forget about.

She had to ask several men labouring away which plot was his, and on arriving found to her astonishment two young lads, one hoeing, the other digging up potatoes.

She approached with caution. 'This is Mr Wilkins's allotment?' she asked.

The older of the lads, aged she guessed around twelve, straightened up, eyeing her warily. 'What yer say, missus?' he replied, wiping a grubby hand under his nose. He had beads of sweat pouring down his face. His clothes were threadbare. The younger of the boys stopped his task and rushed over to join them.

Grace stepped further forward, glancing as she did so at the other pieces of ground around. 'I was told this was Mr Wilkins's allotment.'

From the shed at the bottom of the plot a woman emerged, carrying a baby. She was as shabby and unkempt as the boys. The baby looked undernourished.

'Wadda yer want?' she shouted, hurrying down the path. 'You two get back ter yer work. I'll deal wi' this.'

'I'm sorry,' Grace spoke apologetically, 'I was told this was Mr Wilkins's allotment.'

'So it wa'. But it's ours now.'

Grace stared at her blankly. 'It is? How come?' As Bernard had left only yesterday, how could this possibly have happened?

She eyed Grace hard. 'A' you from the council?'

'No, I'm Mrs Wilkins.'

'Oh.' She scrutinised Grace thoroughly. 'Mr Wilkins said we could 'ave it,' she said defensively.

'When? When did he say that?'

'Yesterday.'

'Yesterday?'

'Yeah, 'e was 'ere clearin' some stuff and 'e told me lads 'e were goin' away ter war. Brave man, Mr Wilkins. You should be proud of 'im.'

'Er . . . yes, I am. But I still don't understand why he would do that.'

The woman looked surprised. 'Don't yer? Well, my lads 'ave 'elped Mr Wilkins fer years. Before these two it were me older boy. Mr Wilkins paid 'em a shilling a week ter do all the hard work. And we got a chance ter buy cheap some of the stuff growed. And I can tell yer, wi' my old man a cripple it were sometimes all we 'ad ter eat.' She narrowed her eyes. 'Din't you know?'

Grace gawped in shock. 'No, actually, I didn't.'

She rubbed her hand across her forehead, bewildered. She remembered the numerous occasions over the years that Bernard had come home, worn out, complaining bitterly about the backbreaking work he put in, after a full week's work, growing the food that *she* needed. She had cleaned his boots, washed his clothes, felt sorry for the backache he suffered.

He had lied. He had paid others, and only a miserly shilling at that, to do the hard work, whilst sitting back and taking the glory. Then, to top it all, he had had the gall to sell back to them food they had helped to grow. And, she suspected, it wouldn't have been the best of the stuff. That without doubt would have been for his own table.

Grace looked at the woman in embarrassment, a woman whose need was obviously so much greater than her own. At least Grace herself was earning some sort of wage, able to put basic food stuffs on her table. This woman and her family looked as if they had nothing.

'If my husband says the allotment's yours, then so be it. Believe me, I feel you've earned it.'

'And yer don't want no share?'

'No. Whatever you grow is yours, and I'll sort out the details with the council.'

The woman's face creased in delight. 'I'm much obliged.'

Grace turned from her and walked away.

Four days later, on the night of 19 November, Grace was snatching a hurried cup of tea with Clara in Bessie's cluttered but homely kitchen. It was time she could ill afford but Bessie had insisted, and Grace guessed she needed the company of trusted friends. She still had not received any word from Tom and this absence of news was upsetting her greatly. The news of the destruction of Coventry had grieved people greatly, and an added worry was the fact that any night it could all happen again.

The children, the Rudneys as well as Jessie and Tony, were all in Bessie's front room, fully occupied with the sorting of clothing and toys destined for war victims gathered from their neighbours. Polly was organising them all. Even young Bobbie was doing his bit: the testing of toys destined for less fortunate children.

To Grace the occupying of the Cotting children's minds could only help the healing process. The news, as gently as it had been broken, had nevertheless hit them hard. The police had called as expected and been very good with them. On taking Grace aside they had informed her that they had a very good idea who Madge Cotting's murderer was; were on his trail and were expecting to make an arrest very soon. They would keep her informed of their progress.

Tony seemed the least affected, but Jessie had hardly eaten

or said a word since she had learned of the tragedy. She had withdrawn into herself and this troubled Grace but she could only hope that time would be the great healer it was professed to be. As it was her main concern was that the authorities would soon descend and wrench the children from her loving arms, sending them back to their relatives in London. She could only hope that with the terrible bombing of the capital and the subsequent mayhem it was causing, the inevitable would be delayed, giving her time to prepare the children for whatever the future held for them without their mother.

She knew though, deep down, and selfish as it seemed, that she herself needed them. She needed to throw herself into their care. It kept her mind from dwelling on her own daughter and all the other great changes that had happened in her life since the troubles had begun.

'Vinny was tellin' me earlier that 'e's 'eard it's terrible over in Coventry,' Bessie was saying. 'It's worse than anyone ever thought. 'Alf the town centre's gone and the Cathedral's been burnt to a cinder – and all those people killed. They're digging bodies out all over the place. It's dreadful, so it is. Dreadful.' She raised tear-filled eyes. 'And what about my Tom? What if the bombers return and 'e's caught up in it?'

'Don't, Bessie,' Grace said firmly. 'Don't think like that.'

'But I can't 'elp it. It's bad enough the boys bein' the other side of the world, wi'out this worry fer Tom. Not one letter 'ave I received from that pair a' beggars. Wadda they think they're playing at, not tellin' their own mam what's goin' on?'

'They can't, Bessie,' Clara soothed. 'They're not allowed because of restrictions.'

'I don't bloody care about restrictions. I don't want to know army secrets, I just wanna know me lads are safe. I'll scalp 'em both, so I will, when I see 'em again.'

Grace forced a smile. 'You'll get plenty of time to chastise them when they return, Bessie. You'll be able to clip their ears from one end of the street to the other.'

Bessie rose abruptly and in order to occupy her hands began to rearrange the wet washing hanging on the clothes horse around the sparingly stacked fire. Steam from the clothes rose in intermittent wafts, the condensation from which misted all the windows, causing puddles of water on the sills. The Rudney living room, to an outsider, could have been the Turkish Baths.

'I 'ope yer right, Grace love,' Bessie said emotionally. 'I just 'ope yer right.' Her voice rose harshly. 'But it won't be just a clip they'll be gettin', it'll be me bloody boot up their backsides!'

Despite the severity of the situation, Clara burst into laughter. 'Oh, Bessie, you do make me smile.'

'Huh!' she responded, turning round and placing her fat hands on her generous hips. 'Well, I'm glad I do someone, 'cos it's the last thing I feel like today and it bein' me birthday an' all.'

'Oh, it's never!' Grace proclaimed, distressed. 'Why didn't you say?'

"Cos I forgot meself 'til this af 'noon. Anyway there's n'ote to celebrate at the moment, birthday or no birthday. When me family's all back together, then I'll celebrate. Though God knows when that'll be.' A rumpus brewing in the front room resounded through the brick walls. 'Eh, you lot,' she shouted at the top of her voice, 'cut it out or I'll belt the lot of yer.' She shook her head at Grace and Clara. 'Bloody kids,' she grinned. Snatching up the teapot, she disappeared into the kitchen.

Grace shook her head sadly. 'I wish I'd known about her birthday. I could have done something for her.'

'Mmmm, me as well.' Clara mused. 'It's a shame really after all she's done for us one way or another.'

Grace smiled distantly. 'I don't think Bessie herself will ever appreciate what she does for people. Her just being around is enough to lighten your day. She's got her own special way of looking at life and never ceases to amaze me the way she tackles problems and always comes out laughing.'

'Oh, yes,' Clara smiled. 'Bessie and that laugh of hers! There's no need for an air raid warning when Bessie is around.' She paused thoughtfully. 'Well, it's not too late, Grace dear. We could still make her birthday special.'

Grace looked enquiringly at her.

'You could take her out. She needs a distraction for a couple of hours, and so for that matter do you. This last few days you've had more to face than some do in their whole lifetime. It'd do you both good to escape for a couple of hours. I'll stay with the children. It'd be my pleasure.'

'But where could we go? It's pitch black out there, so a walk's out the question, and I'm not much meself for going for a drink.'

'Well, what about the pictures?'

'The pictures?' Grace rubbed her hand over her chin. If she was truthful she had a great deal to do tonight and was so very tired. She'd been up since the crack of dawn, tackling several household tasks before waking the children, getting their breakfast and seeing them to Bessie's to walk to school with Maureen and Willy. She'd done her full day's work at Janson's and returned home to find that Ida had not lifted a finger the whole day. The unwashed dishes still lay in the sink and the washing Grace had put on the line hopefully to dry had been left out in a downpour of rain, whilst Ida, she knew, had sat and watched it.

Her own mother came round whenever possible and did what she could for which Grace was immensely grateful, but Connie's spare time was limited. She had her own house and husband to care for.

For the sake of cheering up Bessie, Grace would gladly do her chores after they returned from the pictures, but there was one major obstacle standing in her way. 'I can't really afford it, Clara. My money hardly goes anywhere at the moment. I've no idea what the position is regarding Bernard yet. I don't know whether he's arranged to send me any of his army pay.'

'Oh, that will all have been sorted when he joined up. You'll get it each week. I don't suppose it's much though, my dear. Anyway the price of tickets for the pictures is no problem. I'll pay for you both. It'll be my treat.'

'But you're not that wealthy a woman, Clara. You need all your money.'

'I have more than you at this moment, Grace, and please afford me the pleasure of doing what I think fit with it.'

Grace stared at her. 'I'm sorry, Clara, I didn't mean . . .'

Clara patted her arm. 'I know you didn't mean anything, dear, and I didn't take offence. But you wanted me to start standing up for myself and I am.' She smiled broadly. 'To be honest, I feel rather proud.'

Bessie returned with the teapot. 'What you grinnin' at, Clara Smith?'

She grinned more widely. 'You tell her, Grace.'

Bessie plonked the teapot on the table. 'Tell me? Tell me what?'

Grace scraped back her chair and rose. 'We're going out, Bessie, so go and get your glad rags on.'

'Out!'

'Yes, out. We're going to the pictures. It's a treat for your birthday. And don't worry about the children, Clara has volunteered to stay with them.'

''As she? Well, in that case, I accept.' She rubbed her hands together. 'Took us a long time, Gracie, but we've finally managed it. Pictures 'ere we come.' She looked at them both excitedly. 'In't I a lucky woman, 'aving you two as me friends?'

Once settled comfortably in their seats, Bessie turned to Grace and smiled broadly. 'Thanks fer bringing me out, gel. It's really cheerin' me up.' She unscrewed the paper bag of the quarter of chocolates she had bought with her rations and offered them to Grace.

'Oh, thank you,' she said, popping a coffee cream into her mouth. 'It's a long time since I've had chocolate.'

'Well, in that case, tek another fer luck.'

Grace stopped her chewing and stared at her. She swallowed the chocolate. 'What made you say that, Bessie?'

'Say what?'

'And another for luck?'

'I didn't, did I?' She gazed at Grace searchingly in the dim light of the picture house. 'You're upset, Gracie.'

'I'm not.'

'You are. And it's what I said, ain't it?' She frowned hard. 'What did I say?'

Grace sighed. 'I thought you said, "And one for luck". It's something Charlie and I said to each other. It had a special meaning between us.'

'Oh, I see.' Bessie took a breath. 'She'll be all right, Gracie love. She's a grown woman, so stop worrying about 'er.'

'I can't help it. I can't understand why she suddenly upped and left like that. And to say I wasn't to contact her! Well, it doesn't make any sense.' She sighed forlornly. 'Both of us have had our kids taken from us one way or another, Bessie. I just hope the good Lord is watching over them, because we can't, can we?'

'The good Lord?' Bessie whispered scathingly. 'The way I feel about the good Lord at the moment, Gracie, is that the great man 'isself is standing up there somewhere pissing hisself laughin' at us.'

'Bessie!'

'Eh, don't you get "'olier than thou" on me, Gracie Wilkins, 'cos 'ow the 'ell am I expected ter feel? The bloody world's gone mad at the moment. If there is a God, 'ow come 'e's lettin' all this 'appen, eh? And don't bother answering that, 'cos you like me ain't got the answer.'

Before Grace could comment the lights dimmed and the music started and a picture house full of people settled back in their seats, eyes fixed on the huge screen in front of them.

Bessie smiled in the darkness and thrust the paper bag of chocolates under Grace's nose. ''Ere, go on then, tek one for luck,' she said with laughter in her voice.

Grace grinned. 'Thank you, Bessie. I will.'

The audience sat in stunned silence as they watched the Gaumont Pathé News pictures of the terrible atrocities taking place outside their small island. The continuing stranglehold of the Germans on European countries; the destruction of ancient cities; the seemingly total disregard for human life, were horrifically displayed. Hearing about these matters was one thing; seeing them unfold before your eyes was another.

The newsreel had hardly finished when the blast of the air raid warning sounded and a notice was displayed on the screen informing them that there was activity in the area and would people quietly leave their seats and head for the nearest shelter?

'I knew it,' said an annoyed Bessie, struggling awkwardly up. 'I bloody knew this would 'appen. You'd think that 'Itler 'ud give us one night of peace, 'specially seein's it's me birthday.'

Jostled amongst the crowds scrambling desperately to get out, they were just about thrown out on to the pavement and were quickly joined by other people from nearby public houses and those working late. They were soon caught up in a throng of confusion.

'No bloody manners, some people,' Bessie hissed angrily, rubbing her leg where someone had kicked it.

'They're frightened, Bessie, that's all. And so am I for that matter.'

The night sky was already lit by search lights, streams of sparks falling behind tracers fired by the anti-aircraft guns, and as they both looked automatically upwards, already enemy planes could clearly be seen flying overhead. Suddenly a shower of incendiary bombs began falling and shouts of panic arose, mingled with alarm bells from all the emergency services.

More terrified people seemed to arrive from nowhere and suddenly the crowd heaved and surged, pushing and shoving each other, desperate to find the nearest public shelter with screams of terror and blind panic issuing forth.

To the side of them the sky began to glow orange and red as flares and dense black smoke billowed upwards. The Freeman, Hardy and Willis warehouse several streets away was ablaze as were a number of other factories and houses to either side.

Grace stared over the top of the buildings in horror. She grabbed Bessie's arm as they were propelled forward. 'This ain't a false alarm, Bessie. It's the real thing.'

Bessie's face had turned ashen. 'Oh, God, Grace!' she uttered, starting to shake. 'They've come to get us proper this time. Oh, Tom!' she wailed. 'Where are yer?' Tears spurted from her eyes and her voice rose hysterically. 'Why is it they're never around when yer need 'em? Typical men.'

Grace grabbed her shoulders and shook her hard. 'Pull yourself together, Bessie. Come on, we have to get home.'

''Ome. Yes, yes, we've got to get 'ome.'

Together they pushed to the edge of the crowd and ran.

A horrendous explosion shook them rigid. 'That was over our way,' Bessie screamed. 'Me kids. Oh, me kids.'

From nowhere hands shot out and grabbed their arms.

'Where the 'ell d'yer think yer going, ladies? The nearest shelter's that way,' an air raid warden shouted angrily. 'D'yer want ter get yerselves killed?'

They both shook themselves free. 'We have to get home,' they shouted simultaneously. 'We've kids.'

Without waiting for his reply they began to run again, blasts from falling bombs sounding closer by the minute.

Grace thought her heart would break through her chest as she gasped for each painful breath, her mind filled with their need to get home. The children and Clara would be frightened out of their wits.

She had almost run the length of Tichbourne Street when she collided with an old lady standing in the middle of the pavement, holding an umbrella over her head.

The collision knocked Grace into a lamp-post and she clung to it, panting heavily.

'Get under, quick,' the old woman cackled, beckoning her over. 'You'll be safe under 'ere wi' me, me duck. Quick, I said. Come on.'

Grace almost laughed at the ludicrous suggestion but it suddenly hit her that Bessie was not with her.

'Bessie,' she shouted, 'Bessie, BESSIE!'

'I'm 'ere, Gracie love,' her breathless voice responded out of the blackness further down the street. 'I've run outta puff. Just you get going. I'll catch yer up. Just 'urry and mek sure the kids are all right.' She drew a deep breath. 'Some birthday, eh, gel? We'll laugh at this day in years ter come.'

Grace righted herself and made to go back for her. A loud whistle sounded and her eyes darted upwards. It took her only a split second to realise where the noise was coming from.

'Bessie,' she screamed. 'BESSIEEEE!'

The blast that followed a second after knocked Grace off her feet, so too the old lady who landed on top of her. Clouds of dust and falling debris fell everywhere. Several more blasts resounded, followed by more falling debris and clouds of smoke from resulting fires. Anguished shouts and screams of terror echoed shrilly as people began to pour from their houses into the street. Grace felt the weight of the old lady being lifted from her together with several pieces of masonry. She was being asked if she was all right.

'Yes, yes. I'm fine. But me friend?'

'The old lady. She's okay. Bit shaken, but she's all right.'

'No, no!' Grace cried, wiping dust from her eyes and with the aid of her helper struggling upright. 'Me friend. She was back down the street . . .' Her voice trailed away and she felt her legs buckling beneath her.

In the direction Bessie had spoken from, lit now by the raging fires, was a gaping crater spewing dust and smoke.

Chapter Twenty

Tom wiped a blackened hand over his even blacker face. He was almost dead on his feet but the terrible plight of the people of Coventry kept him going.

Not one of the volunteers had really been prepared for what had met them. Vast areas of the city had been reduced to rubble and four days later a sea of fire still raged. Bomb damage had severely disrupted public services; what water there was was being distributed by carts and because of the shortages, fires were being left to burn themselves out. Gas mains were ruptured and the telephone system was practically non-existent.

The people of Coventry had been subjected to eleven hours of bombardment and the terror was still apparent on their faces when they emerged the following morning to find their city devastated, but defeatism was very quickly replaced by a fierce determination to get themselves back on their feet again. The volunteers from neighbouring Leicester were welcomed with open arms and the supplies they brought with them gratefully received.

As Tom worked away alongside his mates he sincerely hoped he did not live long enough ever to witness again such sights as he had seen over the last four days. It was thought that near on five hundred people had lost their lives, many of the bodies still to be unearthed. But what had moved Tom the most was the pride in the people of Coventry, and the will they had mustered not to go under.

Nobby Clarke, a workmate of Tom's, squatted down by him and rubbed his hand over the four-day growth on his chin. Like Tom, Nobby was about ready to drop, fatigue plain upon his face.

'Lady in the 'ouse over there 'as made us some sandwiches. She apologises 'cos it's only bread and scrape. She also said that if a couple of us want to bed down in 'er parlour fer the night, we're welcome.'

'You can tell that good lady from me, Nobby, that her 'ospitality is very much appreciated. Bread and scrape at this moment would taste as good as a juicy steak to me.'

'Same 'ere,' grinned Nobby. He stood up and stretched himself. 'I can't say as I won't be sorry to see me own bed though, Tom.'

He nodded. 'Me neither. I miss our Bessie's cold feet.' He too rose and yawned loudly, raising his eyes skywards. 'We can't do much more now. It's too dark. But to be 'onest, Nobby, I don't much care for that sky. It's ideal conditions for another raid.'

Nobby grimaced hard and exhaled deeply. 'Well, let's just 'ope there ain't, eh? I've seen enough ter last me a lifetime.' He cleared his throat of dust and spat on the ground. 'That's what I think of Jerry.' He rested weary eyes on Tom. 'I'll round up the lads.'

He made to walk away but the sight of Nev Bridgenorth hurriedly picking his way over the top of a pile of rubble that had once been several houses, stopped him. 'Eh up, lads,' he shouted as he neared them. 'I've just 'eard word Leicester's gettin' it tonight. And it's bad by the sound on it.'

Tom froze. 'Oh, God,' he whispered. 'Bessie and the kids.' He turned and sprinted over to where all the volunteers had piled their belongings, Nobby following behind. 'We 'ave to get back, Nobby. Round up the lads, quick. I'll fetch the lorry. I just hope we've enough petrol for the journey.'

The journey back was the worst Tom was ever to make. Shortly after leaving Coventry the muffled sounds of distant bomb blasts and retaliatory gunfire rose. The horizon was lit with the now familiar searchlights and clearly visible were swarms of enemy planes relentlessly offloading their cargo.

The perilous journey down narrow unlit country lanes seemed to take forever, on all the occupants' minds the urgent need to get home. Just after midnight the lorry ground to a halt on the breast of a hill just a few miles short of the city.

To the group of bedraggled men standing on the hilltop their home town appeared to be on fire. Huge flames licked skywards and the dull thuds and crashes of falling buildings were carried to them on the cold night air.

Tom was beside himself. Down there, amongst the thick of it, were his beloved wife and children. No words could describe his feeling of remorse for abandoning them at such a time, even though he himself could never have guessed that the city of his birth would be targeted.

'Why?' he whispered hoarsely.

No one said a word. They were all too choked.

Grace's eyes felt heavy and the pages swam before her. She was so dreadfully tired, but many hours would pass before she would see her bed that night. She had all the children's needs to see to; household chores to do; the next day's meal to prepare for Clara to cook and the worry of how she was going to feed all those mouths with so little. Then there was her mother. Oh, Mother, she thought, eyes filling with tears as the memory of the pitiful sight of her parents arriving on her doorstep, their only possessions the clothes on their backs. Nothing had been left of the place they called home after the bombing of Leicester. Everything had been lost. And the very next day, so had her father. He had died in his sleep. The only night in living memory he had not gone to work. There had been no work to go to. The factory, like his home, was gone.

Connie, she knew, try as she might, would never get over the shock of his death.

As much as she had loved her father, it was Bessie's demise that had hit her the worst. Not only had Grace lost her dearest friend, but she felt responsible for her death. If only they had not gone out that night, Bessie would still be alive; her children would still have their mother; Tom his beloved wife. Not that any of them had ever said one word to make her feel this, but nevertheless it was something that would not leave her. But worst of all to bear was the rumour that the blitz on Leicester had all been a dreadful mistake. That Leicester, that night, had not been a target but had been mistaken for another major city further northwards.

Even now, after three months had passed, they all still expected Bessie's larger than life figure to fill the doorway; her bellowing laughter to sail through the air; her scathing comments to chide them; her witticisms to make them laugh. But that would never happen. Bessie was gone, and part of all those close to her had gone with her.

It was true what was said. You never really appreciate what you have until it is no longer there. And that saying, Grace felt, was never more apt than in the case of Bessie Rudney.

Grace's main worry at the moment was Tom. The man was a shadow of his former self. His wife's death had taken the light from his life and Grace did not know how to bring it back again. Maybe it would not have been so bad if they had had a body to bury, but nothing had been left of Bessie after the bomb had fallen.

Tom had heard the news of his wife via an air raid warden

who had stopped him as he raced through the streets on his way home. He disbelieved the man, but the look on Grace's face when he charged into her house was all the confirmation he needed.

Grace had never seen a grown man cry before. Although cry, in Tom's case, was not a word strong enough for the endless torrent of heartbreaking sobs that had poured forth and continued for hours. Eventually he had returned to his own house in the early dawn of that morning, accepting Grace's offer to keep the children, who along with Jessie and Tony were all fitfully sleeping, the girls crammed together in Charlie's bed, the boys on the mattress already borrowed from Bessie in the tiny room next to it.

Three months later, the children were still with Grace and it was beginning to feel to her that they had always been there, so settled were they now becoming. Striving to bring normality into their lives, with deep concern and love Grace was helping them all to heal, although the process was slow.

Ida had not been happy about the arrangement at all, but now Grace had an ally of her own, her mother, who though in mourning herself was making all the difference to Grace's life. Connie helped all she could but she was old, her body not able to do all that her mind wanted.

For Tom, though, it seemed the grief would never diminish. The house that he had lived in with Bessie, the one that had been filled with so much love, had been made into a shrine to her memory. He could not bear the thought of any outside invasion, including that of his own children.

Since the night of her death, nothing had been touched. Even the clothes horse, although now emptied of clothes by Grace, was still propped around the fire, just as Bessie had left it. After finishing his work, which was now any hour of the day or night, Tom would sit staring into the fire, alone with his thoughts, the imprint of his wife all around as he relived memories of happier times before his cheerful, boisterous family had been torn apart so tragically.

The arrival of Christmas, instead of bringing his family together, only succeeded in deepening the void. Striving hard to make it a festive occasion with money so tight and supplies so limited, Grace managed to occupy the children with the making of newspaper chains; the baking of food with whatever she could procure; the decorating of the Christmas tree given to her by Clara – but still she could not manage to lift Tom's mood in the slightest, however hard and with whatever tactic she tried.

He did, though, late on Christmas Eve before locking himself away for the duration inside his mausoleum, thrust at her a brown carrier bag full of oranges and small russet apples; a rabbit; a netting bag of chocolate coins to hang on the tree and a bag of mixed nuts, for which Grace was extremely grateful though she would have been ecstatic if he had joined them or even asked the children to visit him on Christmas Day.

It broke her heart to witness his decline. Tom was such a nice man, caring, considerate, who had been a tower of strength to his family before the loss of his wife. But grief as deep as his affected people in funny ways. She could only hope that he would learn somehow to come to terms with his as so many thousands of other people were having to do.

But at least Grace felt she was doing some good by caring for his children. At least he would not have that burden until he felt more able to cope.

It was now the middle of February and matters had changed little. She wondered how long his mood would continue. But also how long she herself could go on with her punishing routine. A body could only be pushed so far before it broke, and what would happen to them all then?

It was not caring for the children that bothered her: the

mountain of work it entailed; the constant demands for a comforting cuddle and soothing words; sorting out daily events such as the boys fighting over conkers and other unimportant matters, Maureen getting stuck inside the privy and finding that Jessie had nailed shut the door, the constantly ripped and dirtied clothes. It wasn't even the finance needed to provide for them. It was surprising how far a little could be made to stretch when needs must. It was just that she was so tired.

If only, she felt, she could have just one night of uninterrupted sleep, she could manage. Just one, that's all it would take.

She felt a hand rest gently on her shoulder as she slumped over her desk, and jerked upright.

'Go home, Grace.'

She forced her eyes wide open and stared into the kindly face of Philip Janson who was standing by her side. 'I'm all right, really I am.'

Philip shook his head. 'I said, go home, Grace, and that's an order. Go to bed and get some sleep.'

She looked at him gratefully. She was so lucky having such a boss. A more kind and considerate man she could not have wished to work for. She felt her job here to be a privilege. 'But my work?'

'Grace, it will be here tomorrow.'

She smiled wanly, no strength left in her to argue. 'Thank you.'

He watched as she slowly rose and gathered her belongings and his heart went out to her. This woman, he knew, had never had it easy. And just as her greatest burden, that of her overbearing husband, had been lifted by the miraculous development of his going off to war, she had been landed with more. Life didn't seem fair sometimes.

That made him think of his wife. Since war had broken

out Katherine was having to fend for herself, and wasn't taking kindly to the chore. Nevertheless, to give her her due, despite her own deep belief that the war had been started specifically to upset her, she was getting on with it. The numerous organisations she now belonged to benefited greatly from her bullying tactics, and many nights war victims would not have been fed had it not been for Katherine and her army of women volunteers, manning feeding stations, collecting clothes and finding lodgings for the displaced.

He moved to the window and watched Grace walk across the yard, her slow dragging footsteps telling their own tale. She had taken on too much responsibility, but who was he to question that fact? He was only her boss and her work had not suffered in the slightest until today when he had come across her almost asleep at her desk.

He decided to go round and see her later, ask if there was anything he could do to help. He doubted there was anything she would accept, but nevertheless he could try.

Chapter Twenty-One

The freezing wind whipped through Grace's coat as she made her way home. Icicles as thick as hose pipes hung from window sills and guttering; walking was made hazardous by ice on the cobbles. The only people enjoying the weather were the children, who, feet covered with sacking, turned all the ice to glass.

February 1941 was bitterly cold, worse even than the previous year and that had been bad enough. It seemed that the sun had shut itself down in sympathy with people's sufferings, and trying to cope with already dangerous shortages, the weather only added to the misery they were already facing.

Grace, shivering uncontrollably, arrived at her back door knowing exactly what would be facing her inside. A mountain of washing and ironing, floors that wanted sweeping and an evening meal that needed to be cooked. It was also bath night and that meant endless pots of water to be boiled and the fire stacked enough to stop the children catching a chill. The few lumps of coal left in the cellar would not last much longer and supplies, even if you had the money to buy them, were very scarce because of severe rationing of even the most basic of items.

She continually worried about money. Bernard's army allowance hardly paid the rent let alone anything else, and her wages did not go far when it came to providing for all the people she now looked after. Tom, each Friday night, would thrust money at her for his children's keep but Grace severely doubted that with everything on his mind he had thought through how much it cost to keep them fed and clothed, and she hadn't the heart to approach him for more. Not until he seemed improved.

It was not that she minded her burdens, but just a little more income would have made life so much easier. Still, she thought as she pushed open the door, there were many in a far worse state than they were. Families in Europe had far more to worry about than tiredness and lack of money.

As she entered, an appetising aroma coming from the oven hit her full force and she saw pans bubbling merrily on the top of the stove. She frowned quizzically. Walking through to the living room she gasped in surprise. The room was spotless. A huge pile of neatly folded ironing lay on the table and a fire burned in the grate.

Ida was sitting in the armchair toasting her misshapen feet on the hearth. She ignored Grace's presence, something she did a lot just lately. She still fiercely blamed Grace for the fact that her son had left, she blamed her that not one word had been heard from him since. But she knew she had to watch her step. Bernard was not here to back her up. Her fate lay, for the time being, in Grace's hands and this she did not like.

Grace was just about to ask Ida what was going on when the door to the stairs opened and Clara bustled through. For an instant she looked happy and content in her surroundings as though she was mistress of all she surveyed. She looked at Grace in surprise.

'You're home early,' she said, mouth curling into a broad smile of greeting. She moved towards the table and pulled out a chair. 'Sit down, dear, and take the weight off your feet while I make you a cup of tea.'

Too tired to protest, Grace did as she was told. 'Did you do all this, Clara?' she asked.

'Oh, no, dear. Your mother helped. She's upstairs now having a rest.'

A warm glow of appreciation filled her. 'Oh, Clara, thank you so much.'

'No need to thank me, dear. It's the least I could do.' Clara moved aside some of the washing and put down three mugs which she had fetched from the kitchen. She went back to fetch the teapot and then sat down next to Grace. She put her hand affectionately on Grace's arm. 'I hope you don't think I'm interfering.'

'Interfering? What do you mean?'

'Well . . . these last three months I've seen you struggling and I so wanted to offer my help but you seemed intent on doing everything yourself. I couldn't stand by any longer and watch you grind yourself into the ground. What you're trying to do is far too much for anyone so I took the bull by the horns, so to speak, and decided action was needed. I rallied your mother round and we both set to.' Clara's face saddened. 'She's taken your father's death very badly, poor love. She's resting now on the bed.' Clara paused for breath. 'I'm glad you're home early, Grace, but what I really wanted was to have the meal on the table when you returned. You spoiled my surprise.'

'I don't know why yer bothered, meself.' Ida, who had been keenly listening, could not hold her tongue any longer. 'If she wants ter play the samaritan, yer should let 'er get on wi' it.'

Clara, her face thunderous, shot up from her chair, took a deep breath and glared over at Ida. 'No one asked your opinion, Mrs Wilkins, and since you have never lifted a finger to help your daughter-in-law from the day you moved into her house, I should keep quiet, if I were you. Remember, you're a guest here.'

Ida's beady eyes bulged and her thin lips clamped shut. Indignantly she struggled up from her chair and without a word shuffled from the room. The door to the front parlour which was now her bedroom, slammed loudly.

Clara exhaled sharply as she sat back down. 'She could do with a lesson in manners. She's been rudeness itself all day. If I wasn't a lady, I would hit her with the poker!'

For all her tiredness Grace could not help but laugh. 'Oh, Clara, how you've changed from when we first met.'

'For the better, I hope, dear?'

'Oh, definitely. Thank you. Although for what you've done for me today, "thank you" is not enough.'

'It's all I'll accept. You're the woman, remember, who sat by my bed all those nights.' She reached over and poured the tea. 'Now I want you to drink this up then go and have a couple of hours' sleep. I won't take no for an answer. I'll see to the children when they come in from school. The dinner is all prepared. Young Bobbie is over at Mrs Givens's, playing with her young son. She's going to bring him back later.'

Grace's body sagged with the relief of it all.

Clara sensed her thoughts. 'You seem to forget, Grace, that Bessie was my friend too and I feel just as responsible for what happened. It was, after all, my suggestion that you went to the pictures. You took all the blame on yourself. Forgot about me and my need to share part of the burden.'

Grace's eyes filled with shame. 'Oh, Clara . . .'

She raised her hand. 'I'm not blaming you, Grace. Remember, I've been in a similar situation myself. Through guilt, I cut myself off. You, my dear, have done just the opposite. You can't go on working yourself to death and I can't go on watching you do it. So we'll do it together, for as long as we're needed.'

'I *do* need your help. I've been silly trying to do it all myself, and I'm so sorry I pushed you aside.'

'As I said, I understand.'

Grace sighed heavily and took a sip of her tea. 'I'm worried about Tom, Clara. He's out all hours in that lorry and when he's at home he just sits staring into space. I don't think he's slept properly since Bessie died. He looks so haggard.'

'He needs time, Grace. Just give him a little longer, and if he doesn't seem as though he's improving, then we'll talk to him.'

'Yes, all right.'

'I must say, though, you've done a good job with the children. They came bounding in at lunchtime, ate everything put in front of them and bounded out again. I heard them say they were going to go sliding before the school bell went. They'd arranged to meet their friends on the corner. It's so nice to see them all getting on so well. Even Jessie managed a smile today.'

'They still cry in the night, though, Clara, and Willy wets the bed. But not so often now.'

'Children aren't like adults. I don't think for a minute they'll ever get over losing their mothers, but their young minds get so full of other things, they learn to pick up the pieces quicker. Besides, so many children are losing parents in this war, it's becoming commonplace.'

'It's so senseless,' Grace erupted. 'So damned senseless.' Her head fell into her hands and tears filled her eyes.

Clara put an arm around her shoulders. 'Go to bed, Grace. Get some sleep. God knows you need it.'

She needed no more telling. Kissing Clara affectionately on the cheek, she made her way upstairs, stripped off and joined her mother under the sheets, glad of the comforting feel of the body next to her own. Ida meanwhile was sitting bolt upright on her bed, staring icily across the room. How dare Clara address her in such a manner? She herself had a right to speak her mind in her own son's house. She felt the need for a warming cup of tea but would not venture out of her room whilst that woman was still there, she wouldn't give either her or Grace the satisfaction.

She struggled to rise. She'd go down the pub. It came to something, so it did, when you received more of a welcome at the local than you did in your own home. Besides, as she hadn't been for several nights there must be plenty of gossip by now. Nothing got Ida moving quicker than the thought of learning some juicy gossip, true or not.

Gently closing the front door behind herself, she pulled up her coat collar and made to turn into the direction of the pub when a familiar figure emerged out of the darkness and hovered before her.

Ida glared at the woman icily. 'Wadda you want?'

Charlie took a breath. 'I've come to see my mother.'

'Oh, yer 'ave, 'ave yer?' Ida hesitated for a moment, her eyes glinting wickedly. She'd teach Grace a lesson for treating her like an outcast! 'She ain't in,' she said smugly. 'And in any case, the last person she wants to see is you.'

Charlie frowned. It had taken her a lot of soul searching to make this trip. She missed her mother dreadfully and would never have left if it hadn't been for her father and this spiteful woman standing before her. She had been hurt and bewildered by the fact that her mother had not come round to visit her, and the longer the silence continued the more upset she had become until she just had to come herself despite the strong possibility of bumping into her father.

She took a deep breath. 'When is she due back?'

Ida's mind whirled. She suddenly realised that due to leaving home, Charlie would not know that her father had gone away to war. The corners of her mouth twitched in enjoyment. 'Not fer a few days. She's gone away wi' yer father. They get on like a house on fire these days now you're not around. It's a second 'oneymoon they've gone on. Yes, that's it, a second 'oneymoon. Like a pair of spring chickens they are. Before they left your mother told me herself that the best thing that ever 'appened to 'er was your leaving.'

Charlie's face fell. Ida was lying, she had to be. If her mother and father were now getting on better, that was wonderful news, but her mother would never say such a thing. She took a deep breath. 'Well, I'll come back in a few days and she can tell me herself.' She turned and made to walk away but Ida's voice brought her spinning round.

'Yer needn't bother,' she said harshly. 'Don't yer think yer've 'urt yer mother enough? If yer care for 'er, you'll stay away. If she'd 'ave wanted to see yer, she'd 'ave come when I told 'er where you were living.'

Charlie blinked rapidly to quell the tears that stung the back of her eyes. Ida was right. If her mother had wanted to see her, she would have visited her at Sybil's.

'You did tell her where I was then?' she asked.

'A' you calling me a liar?'

Charlie shook her head. 'No, I was just making sure, that's all.'

Ida glared at her smugly. 'Well, hadn't yer best be getting off? No point in staying where yer not wanted.'

No, Charlie thought, there wasn't, was there? She put her hand in her pocket and pulled out an envelope containing a letter she had written to her mother just in case she was not in. She thrust it at Ida. 'Please give her this when she returns.'

Ida snatched it from her. 'I'll see she gets it, but don't hold yer breath for a change of heart,' she snapped.

A deeply distressed Charlie turned abruptly on her heel and was soon lost in the darkness.

Ida watched her disappear then stared down at the envelope in her hand. She folded it in half and pushed it down into her coat pocket. Grace would never see it.

Several hours later, having rummaged through the mending box and selected several items she thought she could tackle,

Clara settled back in the armchair and, eyes squinting, tongue poking out, painstakingly tried to thread the black cotton through the eye of the needle. Her eyes were not as good as they used to be and this small task was going to prove a major obstacle. But she would persevere.

The room that until a few minutes ago had been bursting with life was now calm and peaceful. Grace and Connie were still fast asleep and Ida had not emerged from her room since she had stormed in there. All the children had been scrubbed in the tin bath in front of the fire, Polly and Jessie last of all in order to hide their modesty. They had been fed, read to, played with, and were now hopefully all fast asleep. Well, Bobbie at any rate. The others she knew would be huddled together, the boys in one room, the girls in the other, telling each other their childish secrets, sharing jokes and all the other things that youngsters discussed.

She smiled to herself, even though the cotton once again refused to slide through the eye of the needle. It was so good to see the children getting on with each other. She herself felt strongly that all the traumas each had faced had helped form a common bond between them. To outsiders it would appear they were all one big family. Grace had certainly done a good job here. And, truth be told, she herself had blossomed since her husband's departure and the burdens that had fallen on her. Despite the tiredness, she was thriving on her new life. She smiled to herself. What would Bernard Wilkins's reactions be, she thought, should he arrive home now and find his house filled with children and elderly relatives, plus of course one very willing and friendly neighbour? He would not be pleased, that much she did know.

Running an exasperated hand over her snow white hair, she licked the end of the cotton and tried again. At least, though, Madge Cotting's murderer had now been caught and was awaiting his fate. Jacky something. For the moment his surname escaped her. A villain if ever she had seen one, she had thought, seeing his picture splashed across the paper. The police, it appeared, had been after him for a while and a 'friend' had willingly imparted information leading to his arrest, which had happened not many days after Madge's body had been identified.

At least that episode was over. All that remained was for a relative of the children's to be found, which was proving difficult with the chaos that the city and suburbs of London were facing. Clara knew Grace was secretly dreading this happening, but would have to face it one day.

Her eyes looked sad for a moment. If only Grace could hear from her daughter. Her absence, Clara knew, was causing her friend deep distress. There was nothing that anyone could say to ease her pain. She herself could only hope, as did Grace, that one day she would open her door and find her standing there. Charlie would be welcomed with open arms and Grace's eyes would shine once again. Until that day came, Grace busied her body and mind beyond normal endurance with the care of her adopted children and through her daily work.

A lump of coal settled in the fire and for a moment Clara's eyes fixed upon it, absently watching colourful flames shooting upwards. She felt a comforting glow spread through her body. For the first time in many a long year she felt wanted and useful. It had given her the greatest of pleasure, helping her friend today. It had taken some courage. The last thing she had wanted was to interfere and cause a rift between herself and Grace, but after a long period of deliberation she had decided to take the risk.

She felt her actions had also done Connie the world of good. For a few hours as they had set to and topped and bottomed the house, tackled the mountain of washing and ironing, all the time ignoring Ida's caustic remarks, Connie had been able to forget her loss. And the grateful look on Grace's face had been worth all their efforts. Clara could only hope that the much needed sleep she was getting now was restful to her mind and body.

A tapping noise startled her and for a moment she wondered what it was. Then she realised someone was at the front door. Laying down her mending, careful to mind the still unthreaded needle, she made her way down the passage. She stood hesitantly in the darkness, unsure whether to open the door or not. After all it was not her house, and as it was rather late, who could possibly be calling?

A knock came again. It was an urgent knock, one that needed answering. If she didn't, whoever it was might knock louder and wake the sleeping inhabitants.

She drew the bolts and opened the door a crack. In the pitch darkness the outline of a man was visible. On seeing her snow white head, he doffed his trilby.

'I've called to see Mrs Wilkins.'

'She's indisposed at the moment.'

'Indisposed?'

'She's . . . er . . . sleeping.'

'Is she? Good. Well, maybe you would tell her that I called? I was just checking on her welfare after I sent her home this afternoon.'

Clara pulled the door open further. 'And who may I say called?'

Philip smiled as he held out his hand in greeting. 'I apologise. Philip Janson. I'm Mrs Wilkins's boss.'

Clara's legs buckled and her vision swam alarmingly.

He saw her sway and instinctively reached out and took her arm.

'Are you all right?'

Clara fought to regain her composure. 'Yes, I'm fine,' she said sharply.

'Well, you don't look it. Let me help you inside.'

'No, I'm fine, honestly. It's this cold air. It rather hit me after coming from the warmth, that's all.'

'Well, if you're sure?'

'I'm sure, thank you.'

Philip put his trilby back on. 'I better get off then. My wife will be expecting me.'

Before Philip had a chance to wish her goodnight the door abruptly shut. He stared at it for a moment, not convinced that the woman he had just spoken to had been telling the truth. She hadn't looked well at all. Her face had suddenly turned the colour of pewter and the excuse of the cold hadn't rung true. He dug his hands into his coat pockets. It was strange but he felt somehow he knew her. And her voice . . . He had heard it before, though it was different now, maybe deeper. He shook his head as he turned and hunched his shoulders against the biting wind. It was the blackout. It played tricks with the mind.

He quickened his pace. Since his daughter Cecily and the children had come to stay to avoid the bombing up north, going home had taken on a new meaning. The rambling house was filled with the constant chatter of his grandchildren who dived on him as soon as his key turned in the lock. It was good to have them around. Their lively presence had brought a spark to Katherine's eyes and she was loving every minute of organising their lives. Being a grandmother suited her.

It was Cecily he was concerned for. She was missing her husband dreadfully and was constantly worried for his welfare. All he and Katherine could do was try and make their stay a happy one and hope, like everyone else, that soon the war would end and the pieces of their lives could be picked up and put together again.

A stunned Clara was still standing in the darkened passage when she felt a hand on her shoulder. She jumped.

'The knocking woke me,' Grace said, tightening the belt on her ancient woollen dressing gown. She frowned at Clara in the darkness. 'Are you all right?'

'Eh! Oh, yes. Yes, thank you,' she uttered, her voice shaking. A few minutes ago her past had come back to haunt her. She had seen a face she never thought she'd set eyes on again. In an instant all the dreadful memories she had tried to erase had flashed before her and the anguish she had felt at the time, a pain so great it had taken many years to bury, resurfaced as fiercely as ever.

Abruptly, she turned from Grace, walked through to the kitchen and took her coat. 'I have to get home.'

Before Grace could say a word she had gone.

Grace slowly walked through to the darkened kitchen and rested her back against the sink, her mind filled with confused and worried thoughts. She stood for an age trying to fathom what had happened to cause her friend to act so strangely, so out of character. A faint rustling noise coming from the direction of the living room interrupted her thoughts and she straightened up and poked her head around the door.

Her eyes widened in shock. Rummaging through the handbag she had left on the sideboard was Jessie.

'What are you looking for?' Grace asked curiously.

Jessie, dressed in one of Charlie's old winceyette nightdresses which was trailing on the ground, clutched something in her hand and froze, the handbag falling to the floor with a clatter, spilling its contents.

Grace slowly walked towards her. She looked down at the book in Jessie's hand then raised her head.

'Did you need that for something?' she asked carefully.

Jessie's eyes darted down to the meat ration book, then back to Grace.

Grace's mind raced frantically, wondering in what way it was best to handle this situation. The girl was obviously stealing the precious coupons, but why? And it wasn't the first time she had caught her stealing; there had been the episode with the bucket of coal. Her eyes scanned the pathetic little figure, head bowed, fidgeting uneasily before her. Jessie's first nine years of life hadn't been easy and Grace knew without doubt that stealing to her was just a means of survival; her quick fingers had kept herself and Tony alive when no other alternative had been available.

Grace's eyes softened and a lump formed in her throat. Somehow she would have to explain to Jessie the error of her ways but the last thing she wanted to do was frighten her and undo all the good she felt she had achieved. She gently took the child's elbow and guided her over to the table to sit her down. Sitting next to her, Grace smiled warmly.

'Why did you want the ration book, Jessie?' she asked lightly.

The girl looked down at the book which burned like a branding iron in her hand. 'I . . . I didn't. I . . . I was looking for . . . for . . .'

Grace placed her hand gently on Jessie's cheek. 'It's all right, love. Just tell me the truth. I can't help if you don't tell me the truth. Now why did you need the book?'

Head still bowed, Jessie gulped. She had stolen many times in the past and this was the first time she'd been caught. She didn't like the feeling. It had seemed so simple, so easy, to slip her hand inside the handbag when its owner had not been looking and slide out the book inside. The precious coupons it held she could sell for over ten shillings.

She really didn't know why she had done it. She'd only come down for a drink of water. But the handbag had leapt out at her and from habit she had relieved it of its burden.

Suddenly she felt so guilty for what she had done. It wasn't as though she could have spent the money. Anything new, even a hairgrip, would have stood out like a beacon, especially to Maureen's keen eyes, and demands as to how it had been acquired would have proved extremely difficult to answer even for an accomplished liar like Jessie.

A feeling of dreadful remorse filled her. How could she ever have contemplated stealing from Grace? The woman who had taken in her brother and herself, given them a home, showered them with love and cared for them since their own mother's death, doing in fact much more than she had done.

She suddenly remembered the times she and Tony had gone cold and hungry, and shivered. Not once had this happened since arriving in this house. Not once had Auntie Grace left them to fend for themselves. She shuddered again as she remembered the fear that she had experienced each time her mother had abandoned them, the strength she had had to muster for the sake of her brother. Sometimes, when alone in the dark, she had wondered how she had done it.

She glanced at Grace through her lashes. This woman had never done anything to warrant Jessie stealing from her, just the opposite in fact. She suddenly felt terribly ashamed. All she wanted to do was die, die horribly for the terrible thing she had done. She raised her head, feeling for the first time in her short life compelled to tell the truth . . . well, maybe not all. 'I were going to sell the coupons.'

Grace searched her face noticing two fat tears roll down her cheeks. 'You need money, Jessie, is that it?'

She nodded.

'Why, my love? Why do you need money?' Her face clouded over. 'Are you in trouble?'

The answer took its time in coming because Jessie needed that time to think of a good excuse. Grace waited patiently.

'No, I ain't in trouble. I wanted a special dress for the Sunday school party,' she finally whispered. 'I've nuffink to wear.' Well, it was true, she hadn't. The only decent dress she did have had been second hand when Mrs Bessie had offered it from the pile donated for war victims. It was too tight now, and cut underneath her arms.

A gasp of anguish escaped Grace's lips and she swallowed hard to rid herself of the lump in her throat. Her arms quickly enveloped Jessie and she pulled the girl gently to her. 'Oh Jessie. Jessie love,' she whispered, distraught.

As she cradled the now sobbing girl in her arms, Grace's mind raced. She had thought the children, with the exception of young Bobbie, understood that there was nothing to spare for items other than necessities. Each second hand pair of shoes had to be budgeted for; woe betide her if two of them needed to be shod at the same time. But Jessie needed a dress. All girls of her tender years needed to feel special once in a while and a dress was just the thing to do that. And not only Jessie, Polly and Maureen too. Oh, God, what was she to do?

Grace pulled gently away and held the girl at arm's length. 'You know what you did was wrong, don't you, Jessie? Taking anything that doesn't belong to us is not right. In future, my love, please come to me. If I can't afford what you need then you'll have to do what everyone else does in our position, and that's go without.'

Jessie nodded. 'I'm sorry,' she sobbed.

Grace hugged her tightly. 'There, there now. I understand why you did it, Jessie, but no more, there's a good girl.'

Jessie nodded and raised her tear-streaked face. 'A' you going to get rid of me?'

Grace's face fell in alarm. 'Rid of you?' she uttered, shocked. 'My goodness, no, child. Why should I do that?'

'Because I tried to steal from you, that's why.'

Grace smiled tenderly. 'Well, you didn't quite manage it. So you ain't as clever as all that, are you? Besides, the main thing is you know you've done wrong, and I know you won't do it again, will you, Jessie?'

She shook her head savagely. 'No. I'm sorry, I'm so sorry.'

'I know you are, pet, and your apology is accepted. Now you go up to bed and get some sleep, you've school in the morning.'

Jessie's mouth fell open. 'You ain't going to punish me then?'

Grace stared at her for a moment. 'No. Because if I did that then all the others would know you'd done something wrong and then want to know what it was. We'll keep this to ourselves, eh?'

Unexpectedly Jessie's thin arms flew around Grace's neck and hugged her tightly. Without another word, she hitched up her nightdress and raced upstairs.

Grace stared after her, deep in thought. Even if she had the money to buy material, there was none to be had unless it was coloured dark brown or black or made from parachute silk, and young girls could not be dressed in any of those things and be expected to feel special. No, somehow she would have to come up with an idea.

She rested her elbows on the table and pressed her fingertips to her temples, willing an answer to her problem because her girls were going to have a new dress for the party. She had nothing suitable in her wardrobe. If she had, she would gladly have used it, and the bit box was practically empty, the last remnants having been used to make the peg rug the children now sat on before the fire.

Asking Tom for help was out of the question at the moment. His mind was still centred on only one thing and that was his dead wife. When Grace knew he was home she took round anything left over from dinner, ensuring that at least he had a hot meal of some sort several times a week. All she received was a grateful look and a grunt of thanks before he shut the door. No, at the moment he could not be burdened further. And neither could Clara. She had done more than enough to help ease the situation. Grace's face clouded over in worry. Why had Clara hurried out like that? It was too late to call now, and herself dressed in her night-wear, but she would find out tomorrow after work. She hoped it was nothing serious.

A picture of Philip Janson suddenly came to mind and she rested her chin in her hand. Did she dare? Did she dare ask him if his wife had any old clothes she could unpick to reshape the material? She raised her head. Yes, she could. For the sake of those children she could, and she would do it tomorrow.

Philip Janson stared absently into the fire. He had been distracted since his four grandchildren had been shooed upstairs by Cecily for their nightly bath. He just could not get that woman out of his mind, the woman he had unexpectedly encountered at Grace Wilkins's door. He knew who she was. The more he thought about it, the more positive he became.

How could anyone forget an expression, a tone of voice, a once familiar gesture even of someone they had loved so deeply? Even if that love had been many years before and had ended abruptly with no reason given. A love that had gone so deep was never entirely forgotten, however many years lay in between.

He sighed so deeply that Katherine, who had been leafing through a magazine, raised her head sharply. 'What is it, darling?' she demanded. 'You've been acting strangely all night.'

'Have I? Oh! I'm sorry.'

'Well?'

Philip leaned back in his chair and tented his fingers. 'I'm positive I've seen someone today I never thought I'd clap eyes on again.'

She frowned quizzically. 'Who? Who did you think you saw?'

He looked at her for a moment hesitantly. 'Clara.'

Katherine froze. 'Clara?' she gasped, and stared at him stunned for several moments. 'Don't be silly, Philip,' she bristled.

He took a deep breath. 'I'm not being silly, Katherine. If I say I think I've seen Clara, then I have.'

The magazine she had been holding slipped out of her fingers and slid on to the carpet. 'Where? Where do you think you've seen her?'

'In a house on Mere Street.'

'On Mere Street? What were you doing there?'

'I'd gone to see an employee of mine. She lives at number ninety-one and Clara was there. I know it was her, Katherine.'

She stared at him in amazement and swallowed hard. 'You're mistaken, Philip. The last we heard from Clara was she was in Brighton and that was years and years ago. If she had moved back to Leicester, why to an area like that? And if she had ever moved back, don't you think we would have known?'

Philip stared at her thoughtfully. Maybe he had been mistaken after all. Maybe the woman in Grace Wilkins's house had just had a likeness to Clara that the darkness of the night had accentuated.

Katherine rose, walked over to a small table at the back of the room and poured herself a sweet sherry. Glass in hand, she turned and looked at her husband. 'What were you doing visiting an employee?' she asked, taking a sip of her drink.

'She wasn't well. I had sent her home. I was just checking on her welfare, that's all. Besides, Katherine, the company does own a block of those properties including the one Mrs Wilkins lives in, so I've every right to go there if I please.'

Katherine's mouth fell open. 'The company owns property in that street? I never knew that.'

'It's not something you would know. My father purchased

the houses when they came on the market . . . oh, many years ago now. We own a straight block of sixteen apart from one right in the middle. That was a single sale, the deal done before my father had a chance to do anything about it.' Philip looked hard at his wife standing rigidly across the room. 'Why all this interest in property, Katherine? I should have thought you'd have been more interested in the possibility of my having seen Clara.'

'I am. Of course I am. I'm sorry, darling. I would like nothing more than to hear news of her. But nearly forty years have passed since we last heard anything. Don't you think, if she had have been living so close, she'd have let us know?'

Philip nodded. 'I suppose you're right.'

'I am right.' She sat down again, put her glass on an occasional table to the side of her Regency wingback chair and pulled a handkerchief from her pocket to dab her eyes. 'Don't rake up the past on a whim, Philip. Please don't, I can't bear it.'

He looked across at her, concerned. 'I'm sorry, Katherine. You're right. It couldn't possibly have been Clara.' He rose and made for the door. 'I'll fetch us a hot drink.'

Holding the handkerchief to her nose, she thoughtfully watched her husband leave the room.

Chapter Twenty-Two

The hammering on the door was growing louder. It was very apparent that whoever was on the other side was not going to go away.

Clara was not expecting anyone but more importantly did not want to see anyone. It would be Grace. She had also called yesterday after work but Clara had declined to open up. How could she explain to her friend that the man she worked for, the one she thought so highly of, was the very same man who had ruined her life?

The hammering continued and she stared blindly across the room, twisting the bottom of her cardigan between her hands. The last thing she wanted to do was open the door, be civil to whoever was calling. It was beyond her at the moment. Since her encounter with Philip Janson all the good work Grace and Bessie had done to nurse her gently back into society had been cruelly undone.

The stabbing pain in her heart seared sharper as once again she relived those few moments on Grace's front doorstep the night before last. The man she had loved so deeply, whose baby she had lost and mourned all those years, the man who had caused the rift from her beloved family, hadn't even recognised her. Not a flicker had crossed his face, and unbelievably this fact hurt more than all the rest put together.

And why did this all have to happen now? This coming

Saturday would have been her daughter's thirty-ninth birthday. This fact made the pain of remembering all the harder to bear.

Tears of grief for her wasted life welled up and flooded down her lined face. Surely God could not make her suffer more than she had already over the last forty years? Surely she had served her time? But it appeared she hadn't. She was sentenced to go to her grave suffering for falling in love with the wrong man. Just when she thought the past had been buried and she was beginning to live her life again, it had reared its ugly head to remind her of what she had done.

The front door thumped again. The sound echoed around the house and Clara jerked rigid. Please, she wanted to scream. Please go away and leave me alone. But whoever was outside the door was obviously not going to. She would have to answer it before the whole street heard and descended, demanding to know what was wrong.

Her hand on the knob, she slowly inched the door open and frowned, confused, seeing the immaculately dressed young man standing on the pavement.

He doffed his hat.

'Miss Smith?' he asked. 'Miss Clara Smith?'

She frowned and nodded.

'My name is Clarence Hadley from Blackett and Hodges, solicitors.' He handed a printed card to her which she instinctively took and glanced at. 'May I come in?'

She raised wary eyes. 'Why?'

Clarence Hadley coughed discreetly as he glanced up and down the street. 'I really think I should come in, Miss Smith. Business is best not discussed on the doorstep.'

He smiled at the confused old lady as she stood aside, allowing him entry.

'Good night, Mr Janson.'

Philip raised his eyes from the papers he was reading and gestured with his hand, smiling as he did so. 'Good night, Grace. See you in the morning.'

He sighed wearily, leaned back in his chair and ran his hand through his thick thatch of greying hair. It would be a few hours before he saw his home tonight. He had to read through all this latest batch of Government legislation and digest it before he even thought of leaving for home. The Government were always changing the regulations because of the war, and the longer it continued and the more it deepened, the more paperwork arrived on his desk. But, regardless, Winston Churchill was a good leader, an excellent leader, the only one who could get them through this dreadful time, and if Mr Churchill and his cabinet continually changed the rules to foil the enemy, the least he could do was read, digest and abide by them. But he could have done without this latest load arriving on his desk today.

Philip silently scolded himself for his annoyance. It was people like himself who were faring best in this war, getting rich and fat at others' expense. Due to demand for munitions and heavy artillery, his business was thriving. His wife had money to burn on food and other commodities not found in normal shops. He never returned home after a hard day's graft to face bread and scrape or the 'luxury' of rabbit stew. He sometimes wished he did. It might make him feel better, akin to his own workforce. He was also continually being patted on the back for the part he was playing in helping to keep supplies rolling. So why didn't he feel good?

He knew the answer. He wasn't doing his bit by sitting behind a desk. If he had been a younger man he would willingly have volunteered to fight for his country. It sickened him to hear the daily bulletins from the battlefields. The carnage had raged for nearly three years and 1941 saw the war at its most desperate. The Germans had overrun Europe and controlled the majority of the Atlantic coastline. All the British Armed Forces, as well as the home-based units, were tasked to the limit, pooling all resources, using desperate measures to keep the enemy from penetrating the British coastline. How long, he thought, before the remainder of the world, including the mighty United States, was dragged into the fighting?

He felt this was bound to happen before it was finished. The Germans would not be completely crushed until Britain and her allies fought together to bring about their demise. The result would be more people killed; more damage to buildings; an acceleration in the horrors already facing millions in Europe. Philip shook his head in sadness at the futility of it all. Every other businessman rubbed his hands in glee at this chance to prosper, but not him, not in these circumstances.

He sighed again and suddenly noticed the large bag at the side of his desk. He groaned. In his busy state he had forgotten to give Grace the children's clothes Cecily had sorted out, the clothes that he knew Grace had had to swallow her pride to ask for. He had not minded her request in the least; he already admired her greatly for what she had undertaken and was glad to help in any some small way.

The clothes were all things his grandchildren had grown out of and he felt sure Grace would be able to put them to good use. Cecily had been going to give them to the Red Cross, but on hearing of Grace's plight, had been only too happy to hand them over. He had wanted also to ask Katherine if she had anything useful but she had arrived home quite late in the evening from attending some good cause or another and had seemed so preoccupied he hadn't wanted to bother her. He frowned. 'Preoccupied' wasn't quite the right word. Katherine had seemed distracted. He had had to address her several times before she had answered him.

His eyes settled once more on the pile of papers and he stared at them thoughtfully. It wouldn't hurt him to have a break from all this reading. He already had a long night ahead of him and an hour out was neither here or there. He would continue for a while, giving Grace a chance to get home and see to her adoptive family before taking the clothes around to her. The walk would do him good and it would save Grace herself from carrying the clothes home tomorrow. He also had an ulterior motive. He could maybe approach her and ask after the woman who had been in her house the night he had called. Then, once and for all, he could put that matter to rest.

Chapter Twenty-Three

A weary Grace had just turned the corner of the street, extremely cold, desperate for a cup of tea, promising herself that she would do exactly what Philip Janson had told her and put her feet up. Her much needed rest might only be for a few snatched minutes but the thought of even that was welcome. Just then a distraught Polly came flying up to her.

'Oh, Auntie Grace, Auntie Grace!' she cried breathlessly. 'I was just comin' ter get yer.'

'Get me? Why?' She put her bag down on the icy pavement and took hold of Polly's arms. She had no coat on and was freezing to the touch. 'What's wrong?'

'It's them.' She pointed a shaking hand towards her own house. 'They're waitin' for me dad.'

'Who is, Polly? Calm down and tell me properly.'

Wild-eyed, Polly took several breaths. 'It's me granny and grandad, and me Auntie Bertha. They're waitin' fer me dad to come 'ome. I let 'em in, Auntie Grace. I didn't know what to do.' She shuddered violently. 'They're gonna move in, Auntie Grace. They reckon me dad ain't fit to look after us.' She raised innocent eyes. 'Me granny called you a trollop.'

Grace gasped. 'She called me what?'

Polly started to cry. 'Don't let 'em move in, Auntie Grace. Me mam 'ated 'em. She wouldn't let 'em near us.'

Grace grabbed Polly and held her in her arms, her mind

racing frantically. Bessie, who had always talked at length on any matter she held her own particular views on, had only once opened her heart to Grace about her family and then her words had been short and sharp. They were trouble, jealous of Tom and her, and it wouldn't have bothered Bessie if she never clapped eyes on them again. Her savage tones had stopped Grace probing further. It was obvious how strongly Bessie felt about them, and if she was here now she would be creating merry hell.

'Where are your brothers and sister?'

Polly, head buried in Grace's coat, sniffed back tears. 'With Auntie Connie, 'elping to get the tea. I popped round to see if me dad was 'ome. I do that sometimes. I make him a cuppa and we kind of have a chat. I tell him what we're all doing.' She looked up at Grace. 'It weren't wrong of me to do that, was it, Auntie Grace?'

She smiled tenderly. She had suspected all along that Polly did this but hadn't mentioned her suspicions in case it spoiled any chance of a reconciliation between Tom and his children. Besides, it had been Polly's secret and Grace had respected that.

'Of course it wasn't wrong, Polly. In your way you're helping your father.' She patted the girl's head affectionately. 'You're his daughter and he loves you. His grieving for your mother hasn't stopped that.' As she spoke her mind whirled. She had no idea what time Tom would be home. He travelled the length and breadth of the country in his clapped out lorry, delivering parts to factories.

She knew that driving anywhere these days was hazardous. Road signs had been ripped down to foil the enemy; petrol, even if you carried a permit, was hard to locate; and driving at night was dangerous to say the least with the continual threat of air raids, and manoeuvring a bulky vehicle down unlit country roads with the small slit of light allowed to show through headlamps must be a nightmare. No journey could be timed, so if Tom was out then there was no telling when he would get back. It might not even be today, it could be tomorrow or even the day after. By then it could be too late. Whatever Bessie's family had in mind would already have happened without Tom there to stop it.

What on earth was she to do? Her instincts told her to intervene, but Tom might not take kindly to that.

It was Polly who made up her mind.

'Please, Auntie Grace. Please do summat!' she wailed beseechingly.

Grace grimaced. 'I'll do what I can.' She held Polly at arm's length. 'Now you get back home and tell Auntie Clara to come.' The more back up she had against these as yet unseen relatives, the better.

'I ain't seen Auntie Clara.'

'You haven't? She isn't at my house helping my mother?'

Polly shook her head and wiped her hand under her nose. 'Auntie Connie was saying earlier she was worried about her. She sent me round, but Auntie Clara never answered the door. And it were locked.'

Grace pressed her lips together. Her mother wasn't the only one worried about Clara. She just hoped to God her friend wasn't ill again. She had been around herself yesterday and got the same response as Polly but had thought Clara was just having an early night. This obviously wasn't the case. Her instinct told her all was not well and a stab of fear for her friend shot through her. Unfortunately Clara would have to wait a while. The immediate situation was more urgently needing to be dealt with.

'Do any of the others know about all this?'

Polly shook her head.

'Good, then don't mention it. I don't want the rest of them getting upset needlessly.' She picked up her bag and handed it to Polly. 'Take this with you, please.'

She took the bag. 'You will . . .'

'Polly, just go home, there's a love, and I'll do what I can.'

She smiled wanly. 'Okay.' She gave Grace a tight hug. 'I do love you, Auntie Grace, and so did my mam. She wouldn't want them movin' in, and nor will me dad. But I know you'll sort it.'

The look of complete trust and devotion on her pretty face brought a choking lump to Grace's throat and she watched for a moment as Polly turned from her and ran home.

Fired by this trust and by what Bessie had told her, but mostly by terrible thoughts of what the future would hold if these relatives got their way, Grace squared her shoulders and marched down the entry.

Without knocking, she opened the back door and walked through to the living room of the Rudneys' house.

Two women were cutting slices of bread and thick wedges of cheese at the table. Immediately Grace's hackles rose. The food was Tom's rations though they seemed to have little regard for this. A large fire burned in the grate. Grace stared at it, horrified. Did they not know how precious coal was?

She felt her arm being grabbed and jerked round to see a wizened, stubbly-chinned old man to the side of her. He was almost swamped by a threadbare army greatcoat as worn by soldiers in the first world war. He stank of something disgusting and Grace held her breath, trying hard not to wrinkle her nose in disgust.

'A' you the trollop?' he asked, a wicked grin spreading over his gnarled face, revealing toothless gums.

At his question, the younger of the women abruptly stopped what she was doing, straightened up and chomped noisily on a mouthful of food, eyeing Grace disdainfully. Her clothes, like those of her father and mother, who was at the side of her spreading marge thickly on slices of bread, were crumpled, the wraparound pinafore she wore under her shabby brown coat stained and greasy.

As Grace surveyed them all she quickly decided that they obviously had not seen sight of soap and water for months. Grace considered herself poor, her own clothes badly needing replacing, but at least she kept herself clean. In her mind there was no excuse for filth. Even with the terrible shortages of necessities, soap and water were still readily available. The thought of the children even associating with these people, let alone being cared for by them, filled her with horror.

'Who a' you?' Bertha asked.

'I'm Grace Wilkins.'

The words had hardly left her mouth before Bertha interrupted. 'Oh!' she sneered, ramming the last of the bread into her mouth. 'We wondered 'ow long it'd be before you came round ter poke yer nose in. Well, this is Rudney business so clear off!'

Bessie's mother's head jerked up. 'It's 'er, is it? So you're the one, eh?'

'The one what?' Grace asked, fighting to keep her voice even. Shaking her arm free from the old man's grip she advanced further into the room, her eyes fixed on the women.

'The one's what's turning our Tom's 'ead,' the old woman spat, roughly elbowing her daughter out of the way so as to get a better view of Grace.

She was small in stature but wide in breadth, and very ugly. Her numerous chins were covered in hairy warts, heavy jowls wobbled as she spoke. And, as with her husband, Grace could almost see the awful stench spiralling up from her. For a fleeting moment she wondered how on earth a woman such as Bessie could have come from such stock. Bessie's mother interrupted her thoughts.

'You ain't fit ter be watchin' our Bessie's kids,' she continued. 'Not someone like you.'

'Someone like me?' Grace frowned deeply. 'And what is that supposed to mean?'

'You know exactly what I mean! Don't play the bloody lady wi' me.'

'No, don't play the bloody lady. We know your type.'

Bertha received a sharp dig in the ribs from her mother. 'Shut yer gob when I'm speakin'.' She sniffed haughtily and returned her attention to Grace. 'Them kids want lookin' after proper and as we're their family, we're the ones ter do it. We're moving in.' She turned to her husband. 'I've seen enough 'ere to know what we've bin told's true. Go and get the bags.'

'Now just a minute. You ought to wait for Tom . . .'

'Tom! 'E don't know what time a' day it is, lerralone what's happening under 'is nose.' She glared across the room again at her husband standing idly by the door, fiddling with something hidden under his coat. 'Did I not tell yer ter go and get the bags?'

'Hang on,' Grace addressed him. 'You'll do nothing 'til Tom gets home. This is his house and he has a right to say who lives here.'

'This was my daughter's 'ouse and I'm 'er mother, and if I say I'm moving in ter care for the kids, then I am.' She spun on her heel. 'Will you go and get those bloody bags!' she yelled at her husband, her harsh voice reminiscent of grating metal.

'No,' Grace cried, holding up her hand in warning. 'I said, you'll do nothing until Tom gets home. Now I'll ask you to leave and come back when he returns.'

The old woman's nostrils flared, her face turning a deep red. 'Oh, yeah, so you can warn 'im and move in yerself. Well, we ain't 'aving it.' She thrust out her head, eyes bulging. 'We know all about you, madam.'

'Know? Know what?'

'That yer packed yer 'usband off ter war, even though 'e 'ad a key job, then got rid of yer own daughter just so yer could get yer 'ands on our Bessie's Tom and 'er 'ardly cold in her grave. Well, it ain't gonna 'appen, lady, 'cos we'll be 'ere ter make sure it don't.'

Grace gawped. 'I don't know what you're talking about.'

She sneered. 'Don't play the little innocent. It won't wash.'

'No, it won't,' echoed Bertha. 'We've bin told, see.'

'Told? Told what?'

'What's going on?' a deep voice asked.

They all turned to see Tom's broad frame filling the doorway. Walking towards the table, he pulled off his coat and laid it across the back of a chair. He eyed the mess on the table and looked across at his mother-in-law.

'I see you've helped yerselves.' He turned to Grace. 'Have you been introduced to my in-laws?'

'We don't need no introductions. We know who this trollop is,' the old woman spat.

Tom glared across at her, his face filling with anger. 'Trollop! Did you say trollop?'

'I did. And that's what she is,' sneered his mother-in-law knowingly, folding her flabby arms under her vast bosom.

Acutely embarrassed, Tom spun round to face Grace. 'Grace . . .'

She placed her hand on his arm. 'There's no need to apologise, Tom. They've already told me what they think of me. I would like to know, though, where they got these lies from.'

'Lies?' Bertha spat. 'I say it's not lies. We can see fer ourselves it's true.'

'True? What's true?' demanded Tom.

'That she's set 'er cap at yer, that's what,' Bessie's mother yelled. 'And you in mourning fer our Bessie! It's unseemly, so it is. Can't yer see that's she's gettin' at yer through the kids? "I'll look after 'em, Tom," ' she mimicked. ' "I'll warm yer bed, Tom . . ."'

His face turned ashen and he clenched his fists. 'How dare you?' he exploded. 'How dare you speak about Mrs Wilkins like that? And as for callin' her a trollop . . .'

Grace grabbed his arm. 'Tom, it's all right . . .'

'No, Grace, it's not,' he said, pulling free and moving around the table. 'I won't 'ave anyone speak of you like this.' He towered over the women. 'I don't care what you've 'eard, you can tek it from me that Mrs Wilkins 'as been nothin' but kindness. My Bessie thought the world of 'er and so do I, and if I hear you say another word against 'er, I'll knock yer both into next week!'

The old woman raised her fat hand, her face filled with mock pity. 'Now, Tom, yer grieved, yer 'urting. Can't yer see what this woman,' she looked scathingly over at Grace, then back to him, 'is tryin' ter do?'

'Stop it,' he demanded savagely. 'I may be grieving, but I ain't stupid.' He turned from them, walked towards the table, slapped his large hands flat on top and stared over at them. 'I know what your game is. You're not interested in my kids' welfare or my own. You just want to get your greedy hands on this house. You've always been envious of this house. You could have had one yerselves if yer'd all got off your lazy backsides and worked. But no. Yer all whine and moan how badly life's treated you with not a notion of how yer could better it yourselves. Well, my Bessie was in no doubt about you lot. Have you forgotten you tried this trick once before when we moved into Leamington Street? She was pregnant and you were going to come and 'elp whilst she had the baby. And you wouldn't have moved out again! You'd have taken over and turned it into the same sort of disgusting hovel you live in now.'

The women were staring at him, mouths gaping.

He pointed towards the door. 'Now get out, and don't come back. And if I 'ear any of these lies repeated, I shall personally come round and sort you out, so be warned.'

Welded together, Bertha and her mother began sidling towards the door.

'You'll be sorry,' the old woman warned. 'She was right. She was right to come to us.'

'She?' frowned Grace. 'Who's she?'

The old woman laughed harshly. 'Someone who don't like you, I can assure yer. But we ain't ones ter split on our friends.'

'No, we ain't,' spat Bertha. 'But she was right, weren't she, Mam?'

'Yeah, she wa', and I'm gonna get the authorities. Let's see what they have to say about all this.'

Tom laughed harshly. 'Authorities!' he bellowed. 'They'd take one look at you and laugh, and I know for a fact they'd condemn your house.' He laughed again, harshly. 'Authorities indeed. Just get out before I do summat I might live to regret.'

He turned his back on them, running his hand through his thick thatch of hair.

'Have they gone?' he asked Grace.

She went into the kitchen and scanned the yard. It was empty. She was just about to close the door when the old man appeared and thrust something at her which she instinctively took.

'I got 'em for the kids,' he whispered, then disappeared back through the gate.

She shut the door and stared blindly into space. 'She', they had said. 'She' had been to see them. All of a sudden the truth hit her. That 'she' had to be Ida. Who else would have done such a terrible thing, said such terrible lies, but Ida? There was no one else Grace knew who hated her so much. But how could she have done it? Grace shut her eyes tightly. What could she herself do about it? She had no proof. If she challenged Ida, she would flatly deny any charges. Oh, that woman! her mind screamed. Well, just thank God Ida's nasty plan to get the children from under her feet had not worked. If it had, the results could have been catastrophic for Tom and his family.

She realised she was still holding on to something and absently stared at it. It was a long broom handle, tied the length of which hung several pairs of black plimsolls. She frowned. Shoe shops displayed their wares in such a fashion. In fact Heard's on St Saviour's Road had poles of plimsolls just like these hanging outside the shop. She had seen them tonight on her way home. She shook her head in disbelief. The old man must have swiped the pole on his way past and hidden it under his coat. Shaking her head again, she propped the pole against the sink and headed back into the living room.

'They've gone,' she said, relieved.

Tom was now sitting in the armchair by the fireplace, holding his head in his hands. He did not look up as she entered.

'I'm so sorry, Grace. What they were sayin' about you was unforgivable.'

She moved towards him and laid her hand on his arm. 'It's all right, Tom. We know it's all lies and have nothing to reproach ourselves for.' She sighed deeply and looked at him, concerned. 'Are you all right?'

'I'm fine,' he said, raising his head. 'But I could have done without them.' He gazed around the room and his eyes filled with tears. 'They've defiled this house,' he muttered, and abruptly rose and paced the peg rug in front of the fire. 'This is all I have left of my Bessie and they've ruined it by coming 'ere.'

'No, they haven't, Tom,' she whispered. 'Bessie is still here with you. These are just four walls. You don't need to keep the house as a shrine to remember her.'

He stopped his pacing and eyed her sharply.

'Tom,' she spoke firmly, 'what happened was terrible. But Bessie would go mad if she knew how you were grieving. She loved you, Tom. She'd want you to go on living. I knew her well enough to know that. She certainly wouldn't want you to mourn her for the rest of your life.' She paused for a moment and her face softened. 'And your children need you.'

'Do they?'

'Yes, 'course they do. They need you more than ever now, just like you need them.'

He raised his hands and cradled his head. 'Oh, God, I miss her,' he groaned, agonised. 'It's so hard, Grace. I see her face everywhere. I picture what happened. If only I'd 'ave been 'ere . . .'

'Tom, stop it. Stop it now.'

His head jerked up and he stared at her. He bit his lip, ashamed. 'I'm sorry, Grace.'

'Don't be, Tom. You're angry . . .'

'Angry!' he erupted. 'I've gone past that, Grace. I've gone past the anger, the pain, the trying to understand why. I've cried enough to fill Groby Pool. But there's one thing I'll never understand and that's 'ow those . . . those vultures could come round 'ere for the pickings. Though thinking about it, I'm surprised they ain't bin before. I suppose they were just waiting.'

Grace grimaced. How could she tell him her suspicions about her mother-in-law? She smiled wanly. 'That's people for you, Tom. Still, maybe they've done you a favour.'

'Favour?'

'They've forced the issue. Their coming here has made you face facts.'

'Mmmm.' He sighed deeply and raised his head. 'Yes, you could be right.' He ran his hand over his chin. 'I'll always 'ave me memories. No one can take those away, can they?'

'No,' she said, shaking her head. 'Those are yours to treasure forever.'

He smiled at her. 'Yes, they are. And I'll always treasure them.' He sat down again in the armchair. 'What am I going to do about the kids, Grace?' He shrugged his shoulders despairingly. 'How am I going to care for 'em properly, working the long hours I do?'

'I could still help.'

He looked up at her. ''Aven't you 'ad enough?'

She shook her head. 'No. They've been a pleasure. To be truthful, they've filled a gap in my life. It's me that should be thanking you for entrusting them to me. And don't forget, Tom . . .' She lowered her head suddenly, feeling the old guilt rise for the part she felt she had played in Bessie's untimely death. With difficulty she pushed those thoughts away and took a breath. 'Don't forget,' she repeated emotionally, 'Bessie was my dearest friend. The least I can do for her is care for her children.'

He sighed deeply. 'I'll always be eternally grateful. She thought the world of you, did my Bessie. She was always singing your praises. One of the 'appiest days of 'er life was when you two became friends.' He raised his eyes to the ceiling. 'She was a good woman and I loved her.' He smiled. 'Bessie was a lot of woman to love, but she's gone and I have to get on with things. If it had been me that'd died, Bessie wouldn't have stopped living. She'd have squared her shoulders and got on with it. She was that kinda woman.'

'Yes, she was. And if she was here now, she'd have took the brush to that so-called family of hers and given them what for.'

Grace couldn't help herself, she started to laugh at the

vision of Bessie chasing those two awful women and her father round the table, the broom aloft, yelling blue murder.

Tom visualised the same picture and his laughter was music to Grace's ears. He laughed until tears spurted from his eyes. Finally his mirth subsided.

'I needed that, Grace, thank you.' He rose and stood with his back to the fireplace. 'Are you sure about still 'elping me out? Only I feel it's such a lot to ask. You've done so much already.'

She smiled in pleasure. 'I'd be honoured. Between us we'll work something out that suits us all. The children won't suffer in the slightest. Why not leave them with me until the weekend? That will give us time to put some sort of plan together.' She paused for a moment. 'Why not come and have tea with us tonight?'

His eyes lit up in pleasure. 'Could I? I'd like that.' He glanced at the table and what was left of his weekly rations. 'Will you 'ave enough?'

'We'll make it enough.' She laughed. 'This war had taught me lots of things, Tom, but the main one is how to stretch an ounce of whatever to go round like a pound.'

'Oh!' he exclaimed. 'I nearly forgot.'

'Forgot? Forgot what?' she asked, worried.

'I've eggs.'

'Eggs! Tom, you have eggs? Real eggs?'

He nodded, smiling. 'Only three, but they're real, Grace. I got 'em from a farm on my journey back today. I 'elped the farmer once tow his tractor out of a ditch. If I'm passing that way I pop in if I've time, and if they've anything going spare they give it to me. Nice people they are.'

Grace clasped her hands in excitement, her mind dwelling on what she could make for the children with three real eggs.

'They're in the lorry. I'll get 'em on the way out.'

'Oh, Tom. What a feast we'll have! Eggs. I can't believe it.'

She looked so excited and so grateful for the gift, and he knew her joy was in the fact that others not herself would benefit from such a simple thing as three eggs. Impulsively he moved towards her, grabbed her tightly and kissed her on the cheek. 'Thank you,' he whispered. 'Thank you so much for all you've done.'

For a moment he stared into her blue eyes and wondered how on earth he would ever have coped without this lovely woman's help, and not for the first time he thought her husband a fool.

In turn she stared back at him, startled by his display of emotion. Bessie had been a lucky woman, she thought. But then Bessie had always known that.

She took a deep breath. Unbeknown to Tom his impulsive display of gratitude had awoken in her long forgotten memories. The feeling of a pair of strong comforting arms around her, tender lips on her cheek. She suddenly felt a deep sadness for all the things she had been deprived of and for a fleeting moment felt envious of what Bessie had had.

Suddenly she pictured Clara and all the years she had shut herself away from the world. How different her life would have been, just like Grace's own, if she had had a man who really cared for her.

Clara . . . Her thoughts brought to mind her friend's absence.

'Oh, Tom, I need your help.'

'Anything, Grace.'

'It's Clara. We haven't seen her for two days and I'm worried about her. I think she may be ill again. Polly went round this afternoon after school and said the door was locked. We might need to break in.'

'And you want to borrow my muscles? Come on then.' He made to get his coat then stopped. 'I saw a man leaving her house.'

'A man? Leaving Clara's house? When?'

'Earlier on, when I came home. He was kinda posh. Not the usual type for round here.'

'A' you sure?'

'Yeah, I'm sure. I remember thinking it strange 'cos Clara really doesn't have visitors, does she?'

'No. No, she doesn't. Oh, Tom, I don't like this. I don't like this at all.'

Chapter Twenty-Four

Across the other side of town in a similar terrace off the Hinckley Road, Sybil Gamble looked with concern at her lodger curled up in the well-worn moquette armchair. Sybil had two such chairs and a settee but none of them matched. Unimportant matters such as that did not bother her. What was the point in having posh furniture just for the kids to ruin?

Her kids, Russell aged seven, Natalie five, and Janet four, were running around the room causing mayhem, the few toys they possessed scattered everywhere. Sybil did not mind them running riot after they had had their tea, the remains of which were still on the table by the window. She reckoned they slept better worn out.

She stretched her legs across the settee and yawned. 'Cool it, you kids,' she shouted. 'Yer making enough noise to wake the dead. You can start picking your toys up, it's time fer bed.'

'Ah, Mam,' wailed Natalie. 'We're playin'.'

'Call that noise playin'? Why can't yer be like other kids and play quietly? Auntie Charlie's trying ter read.'

Charlie shut the magazine she was leafing through and smiled wearily. 'It's all right, Sybil, the children don't bother me.' She beckoned Natalie over. 'Go and get one of your books and I'll read you a story.'

Natalie beamed in delight. 'Red Riding Hood?'

Charlie tried not to grimace. Red Riding Hood had been the chosen story for the last five nights and to be truthful she was sick of it. But she would not hurt the child's feelings. 'Red Riding Hood it is. I wonder if the wolf will get her this time?' she said, laughing, then pretended to growl menacingly.

Natalie ran from the room, shrieking in delight.

Charlie uncurled her legs and stretched herself. 'I don't know what's worse, Sybil. Nights, afternoons or mornings. I won't be sorry to see the back of these shifts. Though the way this war's going we'll be on them forever.'

'Yeah, twelve hours at a stretch is soul-destroying. Still, money's good even if we ain't got n'ote ter spend it on.'

'Ah, but think of all the things yer can buy when the war's over.'

'Yeah, I suppose. The first thing I'll get is a decent pair of stockings and a block of Pan Stick. But, to be truthful, we might earn more money, yet by the end of the week I still ain't got n'ote left. I don't know where it all goes to.'

Charlie smiled. By the time she paid her board to Sybil and put a few shillings in the bank, she didn't have much either. But at least her wage didn't have to feed and clothe three boisterous growing children with permanently empty bellies like Sybil's had. She needed every penny she earned from her long arduous shifts and Charlie strongly suspected her own lodging money came in handy too.

She realised Sybil was staring at her. 'What's wrong?'

Sybil shrugged. 'There's n'ote wrong wi' me, gel. But I can tell there is with you.'

'I'm fine, Sybil, just a bit tired that's all.'

'Tired! You shouldn't be tired at your age. You should be raring to go dancing. In fact, I rather fancy going out meself.' Her blue eyes twinkled. 'We could see what talent's lurking. It's at least two weeks since you had a date.'

'Yes, and he was like a wet weekend. No, not tonight, Syb, thanks all the same. I've to get up at five and so have you. And what do you mean "at my age"? I'm only a few years younger than you are.'

'Yeah, I know, but sometimes you act ten years older. Sometimes I wonder if it's you that's married and got the kids and me that's single.'

Charlie laughed. 'Yeah, I wonder that myself, with your conquests.'

Sybil rose and stretched herself, then bent down and gathered up several of the children's toys. 'Yeah, well, as I've said before: What the eyes don't see, the heart doesn't grieve over. I'd stake me life that my old man has dipped his wick at every possible opportunity. I bet that ship he's on is a den of iniquity when it's in foreign parts. Typical sailor he is. If he was here now he'd be all over you regardless of whether I was in the room or not. He's such a flirt. Loves the women he does. And this war is just perfect for him. I can hear him now. "What the heck? I could be dead tomorrow." '

'And you don't mind?'

'Not a bit. I know he loves me and I love him. I knew what he were like when I married him. Oh, I felt good, Charlie. Of all the gels he could have had, he chose me. There was a few broken hearts the day we married, I can tell yer,' she said proudly.

Charlie smiled, leaned back in her chair and raised her eyes to the ceiling. 'I wonder if I'll ever get married?'

'Course yer will, a good looker like you,' Sybil said with conviction. 'You are choosy though.'

Charlie lowered her head. 'Wanting somebody that's got more than looks isn't being choosy, Sybil. When I marry I want a man I can talk to as well as enjoy in bed.'

Sybil eyed her. 'And you know all about the bed business, do yer?'

Charlie blushed.

'I thought not. You save yerself, gel, 'til Mr Right comes along.'

'I intend to,' she said, willing herself not to redden in embarrassment.

All the women at work talked about was sex, and as broad-minded as Charlie felt she was, her lack of knowledge on the subject left her somewhat on the edge of the conversations. Regardless, though, she was proud that at twenty-two she was still a virgin. This war had lowered drastically the number of unmarried virgins. Couples in love, and many desperately wanting to think they were in love, knowing it was a possibility that death was just around the corner, readily gave in to their bodily needs when a couple of years previously they would have waited until signing on the dotted line. She wasn't going to be like that. If and when she met the right man, she wasn't going to give herself until she felt it right.

She curled her legs under her again, her eyes growing distant. A vision rose before her, a vision she desperately tried to push away. Of her mother. It was at times like this, when she was tired and feeling just a little bit lonely despite being constantly surrounded by people at work and at what was now her home, that she missed her mother the most.

She would remember all the happy times they had shared. She remembered all the special things her mother had done for her as a child. The notes from the tooth fairy; the little present especially for her from Santa Claus; the painstakingly painted boiled egg from the Easter Bunny. And as she had grown older, the note packed inside her snack at breaktime at school, just saying, 'I love you, Charlie.' But most of all, how each time they parted they would hug and kiss each other twice and whisper those magic words, 'And one for luck.'

All these things and more that she had forgotten had forged the deep bond that only they had shared. So how, she thought, bewildered, as she had so many times over the last four months, could her mother cut her off in such a way? It didn't make sense. It wasn't as though they had had a row; that she had done something awful. So why?

And then she remembered how her father had striven to spoil all those special things her mother had done by his caustic comments and looks of disapproval. He frowned on anything and anyone that brought a little joy into their lives, and by his conniving and manipulating ways soon put a stop to anyone or anything that did. And she remembered that even as a child she had known that he enjoyed the hurt he caused and could still see the look of pleasure in his eyes at the power he knew he had over them both.

She closed her eyes and leaned her head back against the chair. Her father she had not missed, would never miss, but her mother . . . How she longed to feel her comforting arms around her; to hear her voice. As she blinked back a tear she realised Sybil was speaking to her.

'It's yer mam, ain't it?' she said knowingly. 'Why the bloody hell don't you go round there and straighten things out?'

Charlie's eyes shot open. 'Because I can't, that's why. You know fine well I can't.' She manoeuvred her body upright. 'If my mother had wanted to patch things up, she would have replied to my letter.' She sighed deeply. 'I have to believe what my Granny Wilkins said, that my mother is better off without me. If my father and mother are getting on better, I can't jeopardise that. You don't know what things were like before. He treated her awful, Sybil.'

'Yeah, I know, you've told me.'

'Well then, you must understand why, much as it breaks my heart, I have to keep away for my mam's sake.'

Sybil cradled the toys to her chest thoughtfully. 'Would yer like me to go round and speak to her? See what I can do?'

'What! Oh, no. No, thank you, Sybil. You might just come

face to face with my father and I wouldn't wish that on anyone, let alone a good friend like you.'

Sybil exhaled sharply. 'Well, what about yer other granny and grandad?'

Charlie smiled wanly, her eyes misting over. 'Ah, you'd like them, Sybil. They're very special people and I love them very much.'

'In that case, why ain't yer kept in touch?'

Charlie sighed heavily. ''Cos they're old and I can't drag them into something that I don't even understand myself.' She ran her fingers through her hair. 'I have to face facts, Sybil. If my mam wants to contact me, she knows where I am.'

Natalie ran into the room brandishing her book. She clambered up on Charlie's knee. As she settled the child comfortably, she smiled across at her friend.

'Thanks for listening to me. I feel better now. And we could go out on Saturday night if you can get a babysitter.' Her eyes twinkled. 'See what talent's lurking.'

Sybil grinned. 'I'll get a babysitter, don't you worry.'

Charlie had just started to read the first line when the wail of the sirens started.

'Oh, bloody hell,' groaned Sybil. 'Come on, kids,' she shouted. 'Get yer stuff and let's get down the shelter before all the best places are took. You grab the flasks, Charlie, I'll get the bedding. Come on, kids, before we're blown sky high.'

Chapter Twenty-Five

The sirens started just as Grace and Tom arrived at Clara's back door.

She looked worriedly up at him. 'We'd better get back and get the kids and me mam and Ida down the shelter.'

He raised his head and studied the sky. It was cloudy. Now and again the moon broke through, but it was only a quarter moon and the light cast was hardly noticeable. The drone of enemy planes approached.

He listened for a moment then shook his head. 'We'll not get it tonight, Grace. Those planes are heading northwards. Manchester, maybe Liverpool or further. It's too cloudy here for a raid. The pilots can't see what they're aiming at.' He smiled and looked down at her in the darkness. 'For once I'm glad Leicester's in an "'olla", as my old auntie used to say. "Young Tom, it's damp and rainy, 'cos we live in an 'olla." '

''Olla?' she grimaced.

Tom laughed. 'A hollow, Grace,' he said, carefully pronouncing the 'H'. 'A few miles either way out of town there's hills to climb, and I should know. My old lorry struggles to get up 'em, especially when it's fully loaded. Sometimes I worry I'll have to get out and push, especially if I'm 'eading through the Vale of Belvoir.'

'Oh . . . I didn't know that,' she said, looking at him in awe.

They both studied Clara's house. It was in complete darkness, the blackout curtains fastened tightly before the windows. Outsiders would never be able to tell if a light was shining inside or not and that was how it should be, but regardless the house appeared abandoned, cold and empty, devoid of life.

Grace shuddered. 'I don't like it, Tom. It was just like this when I found her so ill in bed that time.'

He grimaced. 'Before we do 'ote rash, we'd better knock first though, just in case.'

He leaned forward and rapped his fist heavily several times against the wood. Grace prayed the door would open and Clara's smiling face would appear to welcome them in. But it didn't. Not a sound of movement was heard. He rapped again and got the same result.

'Clara!' he shouted. 'It's Grace and Tom. Open the door, me duck.'

They stood for several moments in silence.

'Force it open. Please, Tom,' Grace pleaded. 'I know she's in there. I just know it.'

'Okay, stand back then.'

He hesitated for a moment, then taking several paces backwards, charged, heaving his muscled body against the door. It shuddered. He repeated his actions. This time the lock yielded and the door burst open.

Grace did not hesitate. She barged past Tom and into the dark kitchen, through the living room, searching as she did so, and into the front.

They found Clara slumped in the armchair staring blankly into the fire. Grace knelt before her and gently took her hand. It felt cold to the touch. She turned her head worriedly to Tom who was standing hesitantly in the doorway.

'I think we should get the doctor, Tom.'

Clara slowly turned her head and stared at Grace, her

eyes for several moments unfocused then registering surprise. 'Hello, Grace, I didn't hear you come in, dear.'

Tom advanced into the room and awkwardly stood to the side of the chair. He gazed down at Clara worriedly.

The old lady looked dreadful. Her clothes were crumpled, her usual well-groomed white hair a mess. Her skin was reminiscent of yellowing parchment stretched across her face.

'Shall I get the doctor then, Grace, or what?'

Clara's head jerked up. 'The doctor! I hope not for me. I'm fine.' Her eyes glazed over and she stared through Grace distractedly.

'Er . . . shall I'll mash some tea then?' he offered, unsure whether his presence was still required; whether he was in the way.

Grace nodded up at him gratefully. 'Could you also pop next-door and tell my mother where I am? She'll be worried.'

He nodded and left the room.

She turned her full attentions back to Clara, deeply concerned. She couldn't for the life of her fathom what was wrong. And something was dreadfully wrong, of that she had no doubt.

'Clara,' she spoke softly, 'what is it? What's happened?'

She turned her head and stared at her blankly.

'Clara, please. I'm your friend. I'm worried about you. Please tell me what's wrong. Maybe I could help.'

'No one can help, Grace dear. It's too late.'

'Too late? Too late for what?'

Clara appeared not to hear Grace's question. She had turned her attention back to the fire. It had burned low and the noise of the clinkers settling was loud in the room. She struggled up.

'I'm quite forgetting myself. Please forgive me, dear. Take off your coat or you'll feel the cold when you leave. I'll put some more coal on the fire.'

Tom returned carrying two cups, looking hesitantly around for a place to put them down. Clara had such lovely furniture which he knew the hot china would mark.

Grace hurriedly rose. 'Clara usually uses the tray in the kitchen,' she whispered. 'It's no problem, Tom, I'll get it.'

'Oh!' he said, suddenly feeling inferior at his lack of etiquette. Not that Grace had made him feel embarrassed, but shame filled him all the same. In his haste to make the tea he had forgotten that Clara was a lady. A prim and proper lady, but very nice with it. Entirely the opposite of the lot he'd thrown out of his own house only minutes ago.

Grace returned with the tray, complete with cloth and saucers, and he put the cups on it, then approached Clara and took the copper coal scuttle from her. 'I'll do that. You sit down and drink yer tea.'

She smiled at him warmly. 'Thank you, Tom.' She looked at the two cups on the tray. 'Where's yours?'

Still holding the scuttle, he straightened up. 'Oh, I . . . er . . .'

'Oh, you must join us, Tom. Mustn't he, Grace?' she said, busying herself with the tray. 'The biscuits. I've a tin somewhere. Oh, no, silly me. We can't get proper biscuits now, can we? Not with this war. Oh, dear, never mind.' She raised her eyes to Tom. 'Come on, dear, sit down. I want to hear what you've been doing since I saw you last. It's a few weeks now, isn't it?' She looked at him expectantly. 'You must have plenty to tell, what with all your travelling up and down the country.'

Tom and Grace exchanged looks.

Without a word Tom finished the job in hand and Grace fetched him a cup of tea.

They sat down facing her, Tom feeling awkward in his hobnail boots and shabby working clothes.

Clara handed Grace her cup. 'Sugar, dear?' she said,

searching the tray for the basin. 'Oh it's not here,' she said, making to rise.

'I'll get it.' Tom jumped up and fetched it.

Grace took a sip of the tea, eyeing Clara worriedly from beneath her lashes. She felt they had humoured her long enough.

'Clara,' she said, putting down her cup. 'I want to know what's happened.'

'Happened, dear?' She sounded puzzled. 'I don't understand.'

'You do, Clara. Now come on. What is it?'

Clara's hand started to shake, her cup clattering loudly in its saucer. Tom stretched over and took it from her.

Her face suddenly crumpled in distress. 'Oh, Grace dear. I've had such a shock.' She lowered her head, clasping her hands tightly. 'It's this house . . . my house. I have to leave it. Friday morning, I have to go.'

'What? But I don't understand,' Grace said, bewildered. 'But why? Where a' you going?'

Clara forced a smile. 'It seems to the country. I've been found a cottage. I've been told I'll like it. It sounds very nice.' Her voice faltered. 'Maybe you'll be able to visit?' The smile vanished and two fat tears overspilled to fall down her face. 'Oh, Grace . . . Tom . . .' She raised her eyes beseechingly. 'I don't want to go! Many times I would have done anything to get out, leave all this behind and return to my former roots. But after all these years, I've finally found happiness and friends and the thought of leaving . . . Oh, dear, I don't think I can bear it.'

'Then why go?' Grace asked in alarm.

'Because I have to. I've no choice.'

Tom frowned, perplexed. 'Is this anything to do with that man?'

Clara looked at him mystified. 'Man?'

'The one I saw leaving earlier.'

'Oh, that man.' She wrung her hands. 'Yes, I'm afraid it is. He works for the firm that represents the beneficiaries of the gentleman who owned the house.'

'Beneficiaries?' queried Grace.

'Yes. He's died, you see, and they have sold it and of course that means I have to leave.'

Grace frowned confused. 'But, Clara, I remember you telling me that you owned this house.'

'And I thought I did, dear. But it appears I don't.'

Tom and Grace looked at each other then back at Clara.

'If you didn't own the house, Clara, you must have paid rent?'

'Rent? I've never paid rent, dear. If I'd had to pay rent the inheritance that I live off would never have lasted.'

'But you've lived here for forty years, Clara. In all that time you must have been paying somebody something?'

'But I haven't.' She looked at Grace as though she was stupid. 'I would know if I'd been paying rent, now wouldn't I?' She solemnly shook her head. 'That's why this is all so confusing.'

Grace looked at Tom. 'There's something wrong here. It doesn't make sense.'

'To me neither.' He leaned forward. 'Did this man give you anything? A letter or something?'

Clara fumbled in her cardigan pocket and pulled out the calling card he had given her. 'Only this.'

Tom took it from her and studied it; Grace looked over his shoulder.

'Seems genuine enough,' he said.

'Oh, he was a very nice young man and very sorry for what he came to tell me. It was he who found me the cottage in the country.'

'Who instructed him?'

'Instructed him what, Grace?'

'Instructed him to find you somewhere else to live?'

She raised her eyebrows. 'I don't know. I didn't ask.' She ran her hand across her forehead. 'I suppose I should have but I was so confused, you see. All this is such a shock for me.' She eyed them, deeply worried. 'What am I going to do?'

Tom ran his hand over the day's growth on his chin. Grace sighed deeply and sat back in her chair. Both for the moment lost for words; both deeply concerned for Clara's plight. Not only for the fact she was having to leave, but that the whole situation didn't somehow ring true. Something was wrong.

For Grace the thought of her friend being forced by events beyond her control to live in unfamiliar surroundings, amongst people she did not know, filled her with dread and her mind raced frantically, searching for something she could do about it.

'You're saying you knew nothing about any of this 'til this bloke came a-calling?' Tom asked Clara.

'No. Not a thing.'

He studied the card again, turning it over between his fingers. 'Would yer mind if I kept this?'

She shook her head.

'Have you something in mind?' Grace whispered to him.

'Well, only that I could pay these solicitors a call in the morning. My load won't be ready 'til ten.' He shrugged his shoulders. 'But I don't suppose they'll tell me any more than they 'ave Clara.'

'But it would be doing something, Tom. We can't just let her leave without trying.'

A thought suddenly struck Grace and she leaned forward. 'Clara, you told me that it was your sister who bought this house. I remember you saying she organised everything.'

'So she did.'

Tom frowned. 'It's what exactly she organised I'd like ter know.'

Grace nodded. 'Me too. Well, what about getting in touch with her and seeing what she has to say about it all?'

Clara smiled distantly. 'I'd like to see Katy again. I wonder what she looks like now? Whether she married?' Mentally she shook herself. 'I wouldn't know where to begin looking for her, dear. I don't even know if she still lives in Leicester. Forty years is such a long time,' she said, grabbing the end of her crumpled cardigan and wringing it between her hands.

Yes, a lifetime ago, thought Grace. She ran her hands exasperatedly down the side of her face. Clara was beginning to become agitated, that look of distress creeping back into her face. And sitting here talking about it was getting them nowhere. It was action that was needed. But apart from Tom's suggestion of tackling the solicitor, what course of action could they take? If the house was sold as Clara said, then it was all too late. But why had she not been given prior notice? And also, as a longstanding tenant, a chance to purchase the house?

Grace sighed heavily. In just a little over a day's time, this very dear lady would have to leave her home. Suddenly she felt so helpless.

'I can't let you do this, Clara,' Grace said suddenly. 'Look, it'll be a bit of a squash, but you're welcome to move in with me.'

For a fleeting moment Clara's face lit up, then her joy vanished.

'I couldn't, Grace. It would be asking too much of you. You have the children, and your mother and Ida. You haven't the room.' She smiled gratefully. 'But thank you for the kind offer. There's nothing for it, I'm afraid. Whether I want to or not, I have to leave.'

Grace's offer got Tom wondering. An idea began to form, one which would solve several immediate problems, but did he dare suggest it to such a lady as Clara? He cleared his throat, praying he wasn't about to offend her.

'I've . . . er . . . been thinking.'

Two pairs of eyes turned to him.

He shuffled forward to perch on the edge of the seat. 'It's just a thought, Clara, but hear me out.' He took a breath. 'I want the kids ter come home. Grace has had them long enough and it's about time I took up me responsibilities again. But,' he glanced quickly at Grace, hoping she understood what he was trying to do, 'I can't manage ter care for 'em properly with the 'ours I 'ave ter work. You know 'ow it is. Sometimes I don't get 'ome for several nights at a stretch. So I was thinking on gettin' some 'elp.'

'Help?' Clara queried.

'Yes, live-in help.' As he spoke his plan took shape. 'I was thinking I could turn the parlour into a bedroom for meself. Then the one . . .' He paused and swallowed hard. 'The one Bessie and I shared could be for the live-in person. All theirs to do what they wanted with. I've been thinking along those lines for some time now.' Again he eyed Grace, hoping she would back up his next lie. It wasn't a lie really, though, not in the context or for the reason it was being told. 'Me and Grace were only just discussing me plans tonight.'

A warm glow spread through Grace. What a wonderful person this big man was. Now she knew exactly why Bessie had been so happy with him. She glanced at Clara, listening intently and hoping with all her heart his plan worked.

'Yes, that's right,' she said, winking discreetly at him. 'We were only just discussing this earlier this evening.'

'Oh, I see.' Clara paused thoughtfully. 'This live-in help, Tom. What would they have to do?'

He looked at her blankly and then at Grace for guidance.

'Just looking after the children. That's right, isn't it, Tom?'

'What? Oh, yes, just looking after the kids really, and doing a bit of washing and cooking. I'll do the rest of it when I come 'ome. It'd only be light duties. I need someone ter see 'em off ter school and be there when they come 'ome. To be part of the family really. It'd 'ave ter be someone kindly, someone they liked.' He coughed, embarrassed. 'That's why I'm thinking of you, Clara. It'd suit you down to the ground. And the kids know yer.' He bent his head, eyes studying the carpet. 'No disrespect meant but it'd be like 'em 'aving a granny.' He raised his head, his face pink. 'I'd pay a' course. Though I couldn't go ter much,' he added worriedly.

Clara sat back in her chair, her lined face creasing further in thought. Tom's job offer sounded so appealing. She would have the family she had always longed for. She'd be a granny just as he had said. What a lovely thought. She could do all the things she'd thought would never be allowed her. And it wasn't as though she didn't know the children. Not as though she didn't know what she was in for. And she wouldn't be doing Grace down either. She would still have Jessie and Tony and would be on hand should Clara herself get into difficulties – which she envisaged she could. If she accepted this position Tom would be able to carry on his work without worrying for his family. And for her own part, she wouldn't have to leave the street and her friends, the likes of which she knew she would never find again.

She raised her head, eyes bright. She didn't need to think further. She didn't need to sleep on the idea before making her decision.

'Would you mind very much if I accepted, Tom dear? I like the sound of this job very much. But there would be one condition, and I'm afraid I would have to insist on your agreement first.'

His face fell. He swallowed hard. 'What condition?'

'That no payment changes hands. I would feel it an honour and a privilege to help with your children. And a welcome into your home is more payment than the job deserves.' His mouth opened and she raised her hand to silence him. 'I'll only accept on that condition.'

His face broke into a broad grin and he held out his hand to shake on the bargain. 'It's a deal, Miss Smith.'

Clara shook back. 'The pleasure's all mine, Mr Rudney.'

She rose. 'Now who would like another cup of tea?' she said delightedly. 'I know I would.'

They left Clara's house half an hour later. Before they turned down the entry, Grace took Tom's arm and pulled him to a halt.

'That was a wonderful thing you did, Tom, and no mistake.'

He studied his feet in embarrassment. 'No more than you've both done fer me.' He raised his head. 'And don't deny it, Grace. I do need her.'

'Yes, but all the same, it were grand of you, Tom. You've saved that old lady. She would surely have wilted away stuck in the middle of nowhere amongst people she didn't know.'

'Yes, well. It were the least I could do. And don't forget, I only offered after your suggestion of 'er movin' in with you.'

She smiled. 'Well, let's settle for it being a joint success.' She smiled as she resumed walking. 'I hate to think what she's been through these past two days. At least she'll sleep tonight.'

Tom smiled warmly. 'Yes, I think I will as well. It's been some day for me too.'

When the Rudney children realised their father had come to visit they fell on him, shrieking in delight. They shrieked even louder when Grace and he told of the plan for them to return home and Clara to come and live with them. Although sad to be leaving Grace, they all thought it a wonderful idea.

As the whoops of delight resounded, Connie pulled Grace aside. 'What's all this about Clara and 'er 'ouse?' she asked, puzzled.

'I'll tell you all about it later, Mam,' she whispered. 'When this lot are in bed and I can talk to you proper.'

Connie nodded. 'Oh, all right,' she said, intrigued. She nudged Grace in the ribs. 'Look at that old sour puss,' she said, eyeing Ida crossly. As usual, she was sitting bolt upright in her armchair, hogging the fire, eyeing the proceedings with a tight scowl of disapproval. 'She 'ates to see 'appiness, does that one. You'd think she'd be glad Tom's meking an effort for the sake of his kids.'

Grace did not look directly across at Ida. At that moment, the way she felt about her mother-in-law, she couldn't trust herself not to say something she might regret, and she also knew that Ida's face was portraying her own feelings about the fact that her little plan had failed. She just nodded in agreement with her mother. 'And he is, Mam, a big one. It'll be a good while yet 'til he's fully back to normal. If he ever is,' she added softly. She gazed at her mother fondly. Grace knew Connie too was making a big effort to come to terms with her own loss and fully understood what Tom had gone through. But never, Grace knew, would her mother understand what made Ida tick. No, two such opposite characters could never have lived under one roof. It took a lot of willpower on Connie's part to stay civil to Ida, but Grace knew she did it out of love and respect for her daughter.

She put her arm round her mother's slight shoulders and gave her a hug. 'I love you,' she whispered.

'Ah, ged off, yer daft 'app orth,' Connie grinned.

Grace's ears pricked as above the din the children were making, a knock sounded. 'I'm sure that was the front door.'

'Well, you'd better answer it then whilst I get this tea on the go. I held it back 'oping you'd not be too long. I know 'ow you like to sit with the kids and have a natter. And it's good Tom's here. You did well there, our Grace.' She glanced scathingly at Ida. 'She ain't getting none of those eggs he got. She can starve for all I care.'

Grace tried to keep her face straight. 'Mam, keep your voice down, she'll hear you.'

'I don't care. If she had a decent bone in her body she'd get off her backside and give me an 'and. She's sat in that chair all afternoon, lazy cow.' She turned towards the kitchen. 'Go on and answer that door before whoever it is freezes ter death.'

Grace smiled to herself as she made her way down the dark passage and pulled across the blackout curtain.

It took her a moment to adjust her eyes and recognise the man who stood on her doorstep. It was Philip Janson. He doffed his trilby and handed her a bag. It was large and heavy.

'Those clothes I promised you. Unfortunately I forgot to give them to you today, so I thought I'd drop them round to save you carrying them home tomorrow.'

'Oh, Mr Janson,' she exclaimed. 'This is most kind of you. I'm really grateful.'

'I know that, Grace, and Cecily was only too glad to know the clothes were going to a good home.'

The sound of childish laughter reached them. 'Er . . . would you like to come in and have a cup of tea and meet the children?'

Philip smiled appreciatively. There was nothing he would have liked more, but it was obvious Grace had her hands full and he felt he would be in the way. 'Thank you, my dear, but I must get back to the office. I'm still wading through those Government papers.'

The look of disappointment on her face did not escape him.

'All right. Maybe some other time then,' she said.

'Yes, some other time. I'll see you tomorrow then.' He put on his hat. 'Make sure you have a good night's sleep.'

'I will, thank you.'

He set off down the road and she shut the door. Suddenly a thought struck her and she yanked the door open and called after him. A moment later he returned.

'I'm sorry, Mr Janson, but I have a problem. Well, it's not me, it's a friend of mine. My neighbour to be exact. I wondered if you could help shed some light?'

'I will if I can,' he said, smiling kindly, stepping into the passage out of the icy wind.

'Well, I just wondered if you knew what the situation was regarding someone who has lived in a house for nearly forty years and has now been asked to leave with hardly any warning.'

'I take it that it's rented property.'

'Er . . . yes. Well, we thought it was owned but it appears it's rented, but we don't know who's been paying the rent.'

Philip looked at her, confused. 'Grace, I'm afraid you're not making much sense.'

'No, I'm not, am I?' She laughed. 'I'll start again.' Connie's voice, over the rest of the hullabaloo, could be heard gathering everyone to the table. 'I'm sorry about the din.'

'That's all right, Grace, please don't apologise. It sounds a very happy din. Anyway, you were saying?'

'Oh, yes. My friend next-door, Clara . . .'

'Clara?' he interrupted, his heart leaping.

'Clara Smith.'

For a second she was puzzled by the look of disappointment on his face.

'Oh, Clara Smith. I see.' So it wasn't his Clara after all.

Just someone who reminded him of her. 'Sorry. You were saying that this Clara Smith has lived next-door for forty years and . . .'

'Well, out of the blue she's been given notice to get out. Only two days' warning, which is not as strange as the fact that she's been found a new place to live out in the country. Clara's no idea who gave instructions for that. And that's not all . . .'

'Isn't it?'

'No. She was always under the impression that she owned the house. Her sister told her she'd bought it for her. And now it's transpired that she didn't. But no rent has ever been paid. Well, Clara's never paid any rent. So who has?'

Philip frowned. 'Yes, it does all appear odd. Very odd. I take it you would like me to see what I can find out?'

'Oh, Mr Janson, would you? I would appreciate it. Because it's all rather a mystery.'

'Yes, it is. I'll tell you what I'll do. I'll contact my solicitor and ask him to make a few enquiries. You'll have to give me something more to go on.'

'I've told you all I know.'

'It's not much, Grace.' He glanced at the number on her door. 'Your neighbour's will be, what, eighty-nine?'

'That's right.'

'And her name is Clara Smith. Anything else?'

She shrugged her shoulders. 'No, sorry. Oh, just a moment.' She turned and ran down the passage and came back several moments later with the card which she handed to him. 'This is the name of the firm that's handling the business. And they're also the ones who got Clara the new cottage in the country.'

He peered at the lettering on the card. 'Blackett and Hodges. They're a reputable firm all right.' He took a deep breath. 'Leave this with me.'

'Thank you, Mr Janson. I'm much obliged.'

'I'll leave you to get back to your family then. Good night, Grace.'

'Good night, Mr Janson.'

Chapter Twenty-Six

Katherine roused herself as Philip climbed into bed. She sleepily turned over.

'You're late tonight, Philip. What time is it?'

'Just after twelve.'

She frowned, raised herself and leaned across to look at the clock. 'It's nearer twelve-thirty. What've you been doing until this time of night?'

He slid under the sheets and settled the covers around him. 'I didn't leave the office until late. I did telephone. Didn't you get my message?'

'Yes, I did. But I didn't think you'd be this late.'

'Well, I never intended to be. But after I finished in the office, I dropped in to see old Stonnington.'

She eyed him keenly. 'Your father's old solicitor. I thought he was dead.'

'By rights he should be. He's well over ninety.' He flicked off the light and snuggled down.

'What made you go and see him?' she asked, yawning. Her eyes flew open, alarmed. 'Oh, Philip, you haven't invited him over for dinner, have you?'

'Well . . .'

'Oh, Philip, you haven't! This is really too bad.'

'I shouldn't worry, Katherine. Although his mind's still as sharp as a razor, he's practically bedridden. I doubt very much he'll take the invitation up.'

She sighed, relieved. 'Thank goodness for that. I wouldn't have a clue who to sit him next to. From what I remember of him he's an old grouch.' She plumped up her pillows and settled back. 'So what did you go and see him about?'

He folded his arms at the back of his head and studied the shadows across the ceiling. 'Just to pick his memory, that's all. I've been asked to help with a problem and I must admit it's rather intriguing.'

'Is it?' She turned her head and looked at him in interest. 'Well, tell me then.'

'At the moment there's not much too tell. Just a mystery about a woman who's been asked to vacate her home at short notice. It concerns a neighbour of Grace Wilkins, an employee of mine. This Clara Smith . . .'

Katherine heard no more. The name Clara Smith had been enough to freeze her rigid. She threw back the covers and dived from the bed, grabbing her dressing gown.

Philip looked across at her, confused. 'What's the matter, Katherine?'

'Nothing!' she said sharply. 'I've a headache. I need some aspirin.'

He drew back the covers and got out of bed, slipping on his slippers. 'I'll get them for you.'

'I'm quite capable. Just go back to bed, Philip.'

Her abrupt tone caused deep concern to rise within him. He couldn't for the life of him fathom what had caused this sudden change of mood or brought on the headache. She had been fine several moments ago. Deep in thought, he slipped off his slippers and climbed back into bed. She had been happy until he had started talking about Grace's mystery. But why should that have such an effect on Katherine? Maybe it was just a coincidence. She was prone to sudden headaches. He turned over, settled down and closed his eyes. He'd had a long day, another faced him tomorrow, and he needed to sleep.

Down in the spacious kitchen Katherine paced the wooden floor. One hand held a bottle of aspirin. With the other she scraped back her hair, which stood out wildly. Her head was throbbing, her heart beating painfully. Philip's words were still ringing in her ears.

Wrenching off the bottle top she shook out two white tablets, tilted back her head, opened her mouth and threw them in. They stuck to the back of her throat and she heaved. Rushing to the sink she poured a glass of water and drank it down, shuddering violently at the disgusting taste of the pills still lingering. The pain in her head sharpened. It stabbed like a pneumatic drill hammering relentlessly inside her skull.

She shook out two more tablets and swallowed them down. Still the pain, still the words screaming in her head. She fell back against the sink, clutching the bottle to her chest. Her worst nightmare had come true.

For years she had believed she was safe, the terrible secret she harboured firmly hidden away deep down in the darkest recesses of her mind, locked up and forgotten about. Now, through events not remotely envisaged, that hiding place had been unlocked and her secret forced out, in imminent danger of discovery. No, not just severe danger, there was no doubt it would be discovered. Once certain questions were asked, it was only a matter of time before the truth would out.

And she had thought she had been so clever, so thorough.

What could she do? What actions could she take to stop the avalanche she knew would quickly descend upon her so that all she had achieved was ruined? She saw her life disintegrating around her, caving in, blown apart, and felt powerless to stop it.

The pain grew in severity and two more pills disappeared down her throat. Again she prowled the floor, and the more she tried to think, the more the pain in her head intensified.

A stiff drink, that was what she needed. She had to clear her head. She needed to rid herself of pain, to think straight.

Slipping the bottle of aspirin into her pocket she rummaged wildly through the cupboards then round the pantry. Stashed behind a tin of Bird's Custard Powder and several tins of Baxter's soup she unearthed a bottle of Armagnac. The tipple for visitors was kept in the cabinet in the drawing room, but Philip's and her own favourite brand, which was now so hard to come by, was kept hidden away for special occasions.

Well, this was a special occasion. Her life was about to be ruined. What more special an occasion could there be than that? Her shaking hands had trouble unscrewing the top. With brute strength she finally managed and poured a generous measure into the glass and drank it down. She repeated her action, then again, then replenished her glass and cradled it between her hands.

The alcohol began to take effect and a hot flow of sensation flooded her veins. She raised the glass to her lips and drained the contents. That was better. Once the pain in her head lessened, she'd be able to fathom a plan of action.

Grabbing the bottle by its neck she made her way unsteadily towards the large pine kitchen table that dominated the centre of the kitchen, then groped for the back of a chair and pulled it out. Her bottom nearly missed the seat and she had to grab the table to stop herself from falling on the floor.

Once safely seated she refilled her glass. The pain in her head was so severe she thought it would burst. She thrust her hand in her pocket and pulled out the bottle of pills. Shaking out two, she stared at them. These damned pills are useless, she thought. They hadn't even begun to cure her headache. If anything, it was far worse. She emptied the bottle of its contents into her palm. Six more went into her mouth, washed down with a large gulp of brandy, then she drained the glass.

It slipped through her fingers and clattered on the table, rolling on its side to rest with a clink against the now half-empty bottle. She slumped back in her chair, her head rolled back and her eyes scanned the ceiling. The beams running across the ceiling rippled and swayed like stormy waves on the ocean. Her stomach churned and she quickly righted herself, desperately fighting to focus her eyes. She reached for the bottle again and refilled her glass, popping a few more pills absently into her mouth.

She sipped slowly and as she did so visions of her family floated before her. There was Philip, her beloved husband. Her eyes softened. What she wouldn't do for Philip. Her eyes narrowed. What she hadn't done for Philip. A smile touched her lips. And now here was Cecily. 'Hello, Cecily,' she slurred to the vision. 'And how's my daughter?' Her voice rose sharply. 'Eh, how are you, my daughter?'

She began to laugh, a harsh hysterical sound that shrilled loudly round the empty kitchen. The laughter subsided and her eyes grew distant. What would they both say if they knew? She reached for the bottle again and topped up her glass, a good measure spilling on to the table.

Upstairs in bed Philip turned over. The emptiness to the side of him caused him to waken. He frowned at the space where his wife should be sleeping and the memory of her getting out of bed with a headache came back. He flicked on the bedside lamp and glanced over at the clock. It said one-forty-three. He grimaced. She had been gone for over an hour. What on earth was she doing? Fearing something had befallen her, he hurriedly pulled back the bedclothes, slipped on his dressing gown and slippers and went in search of her.

The sight of her sprawled over the table in the kitchen,

clutching a glass of something resembling brandy, made him gawp. He rushed towards her. 'Katherine, what on earth's the matter?'

With difficulty she turned her head and stared at him. 'Philip. Darling Philip,' she cried huskily. 'My dear husband. How are you?' She saluted him with her glass, then drank greedily.

'You're drunk.'

She laughed. 'How clever of you.' She reached for the bottle. 'Yes, I'm drunk. But not as drunk as I intend to be.' She filled her glass right to the top then waved the bottle at him. 'Have a drink, Philip. Have a drink with me. Have a drink with your wife, the mother of your child, the grand-mother of your grandchildren.' She narrowed her bloodshot eyes and thrust her face towards him. 'You're going to need it. Oh, boy, are you going to need it!' She started to laugh hysterically. 'You'll need a case of it by the time it's all finished.'

He wrenched the bottle from her and put it on the table. 'Katherine, this is absurd. Put that glass down and come back to bed.'

'Bed! How can I sleep with all this on my mind?' She glared at him scathingly. 'Why couldn't you leave it, Philip?'

'Leave? Leave what? Look, you're not making any sense. I thought you had a headache . . .'

'A headache? Yes, I've got a headache. And you,' she cried, wagging her finger, 'gave it to me!'

'Me?' He squatted on his haunches and tried to take her hand which she pulled away. 'Katherine, tell me what's wrong. Please?' he begged.

A movement behind them startled him and he turned his head to see Cecily standing in the doorway. She advanced towards them, tightening the belt on her dressing gown whilst eyeing her mother in concern.

'I heard voices. What's going on, Pops?'

He stood and shrugged his shoulders. 'I don't know. Your mother came down to get some aspirin for a headache and I've found her like this.' He walked towards her, not wanting her to see her mother in such a state. 'Go back to bed, Cecily.'

She peered over his shoulder. 'I want to know what's wrong with Mother. Mother, what is it?' she called.

Katherine's head wobbled and she tried to focus upon Cecily. She began to giggle. 'Mother!' she cried. 'She called me Mother. Did you hear her, Philip? She called me Mother.' Her eyes widened in alarm and she clamped her mouth shut. Now why had she said that? She hadn't meant to say it. She really ought to be careful. The room began to swirl. Her head sagged and her eyes followed the swaying brown liquid in her glass.

'She's drunk,' Cecily snapped, looking accusingly at her father.

'I know. Now please, Cecily, go back to bed. Leave me to sort your mother out.'

'But what did she mean about me calling her Mother?'

'I don't know. It must be the drink talking.'

'But Mother doesn't drink. Well not to this extent.'

'Cecily,' he spoke firmly, 'please go back to bed.'

She sighed, annoyed. 'If you insist. But I wish you'd remember that I'm thirty-nine, Pops, not a child.' She turned on her heel and left the room.

'Philip. Where are you, Philip?' Katherine called. Her face crumpled and two large tears splashed into her brandy. 'They've left me,' she addressed the glass. 'They've gone. I knew they would. Oh, it's all been wasted.'

Philip knelt down next to her. 'I'm here, Katherine.'

Her head jerked up and her face was wreathed in delight. She threw her arms around his neck, nearly strangling him, the glass and its contents flying across the room to shatter. 'Oh, Philip, Philip. Please don't leave me, Philip. Please, Philip, please,' she wailed beseechingly. 'I love you. I've always loved you.' She pulled back and thrust her face into his, the strength of her brandied breath nearly knocking him backwards. 'I've made you happy. You have been happy. I know you've been happy.'

'I have, Katherine,' he said in bewilderment. 'I've been very happy. But what are you talking about?'

Her face clouded and she thrust him from her and struggled from the chair. 'What?' she spat. 'You ask me what?' She lurched across the room. 'Where's the Armagnac?' she shouted. 'Someone's stolen my drink.'

He leapt after her and grabbed her by the pine dresser just as her legs buckled beneath her. Her arm caught a china teapot and it fell to the floor with a crash. Katherine dropped down after it, scooping up the pieces and cradling them in her hands. 'My teapot,' she wailed. 'Oh, my teapot.'

Instinctively he grabbed her wrists and shook the sharp pieces of china from them. Her hands were cut and bleeding, the blood dripping down her perfectly manicured nails and on to the floor. He dragged her to the sink, pushed her hands forward and ran the tap. All the time his mind was racing, looking for a reason for her unusual behaviour. He kept coming back to the same thing. It had something to do with Grace's mystery. Katherine had been fine until he had spoken of that.

Her hands bound tightly by a towel to stem the blood from the tiny cuts, he steadied her against the sink and took hold of her arms.

'I want to know what's got into you, Katherine. It's got something to do with Grace Wilkins's mystery. Now you tell me,' he demanded, 'what's upsetting you so much?'

She started to laugh. 'Mishtry?' she snorted smugly. 'It's

no mishtry, Philip. It's quite simple really.' She lurched forward and headed for the table. Snatching the bottle she waved it before him. 'Have a drink.' Before he reached her, she had taken a large gulp.

He took the bottle from her. 'You've had enough.' He headed for the sink and emptied what was left then spun round on his heel. 'Now tell me, Katherine. I want to know.'

Her head swam alarmingly and a pain so severe it doubled her over stabbed through her stomach. She fell to the floor clutching her middle.

Suddenly the kitchen was illuminated in a blaze of white light and Katherine shielded her eyes. Through the light an eighteen-year-old Clara drifted towards her, arms outstretched, sad eyes pleading. 'My baby,' she was saying. 'What have you done with my baby?'

She stared at the apparition, at the grief-filled eyes, at the sorrowful face, and suddenly the dreadful deed she had done filled her with remorse and shame. Her own eyes filled with tears which gushed down her face.

'I had to, Clara,' she faltered. 'I had no choice. You were trying to steal Philip off me. I loved him. Don't you see, Clara, I couldn't live without him? He was mine. I had to take the baby. It was for the best.' Her voice rose beseechingly. 'You were just a child yourself. You would find someone else. But I couldn't live without Philip.'

'But it was mine, Katy. The baby was mine.'

'I know,' she sobbed. 'I know. Please forgive me.'

Katherine felt a hand grip her arm and looked up to see Philip beside her. His face, the face that she loved with all her being, was looking at her so coldly, filled with such shock. She had to make him understand, couldn't bear to see the hatred in his face. 'I had to, Philip. Please understand . . . Please!'

'The baby, Katherine. The baby you said was ours. Was it Clara's?'

She shrank before his gaze, filled with such horror as he waited for her answer.

'Oh, Philip,' she cried. 'Cecily should have been ours . . . ours!' The unbearable pain in her stomach now filled her body, she clawed at the air with her hands. 'Please understand, I did it because I love you. I couldn't lose you, Philip. Philip!' she screeched. 'PHILIP!'

But he was gone.

Chapter Twenty-Seven

Philip shuddered violently, but it wasn't from the frosty cold that seeped through his nightclothes. Ghosts from the past weren't just passing by, they had stopped and were jumping up and down, mocking him. He hunched over and tucked his numbed hands under his armpits. How long he had sat here he did not know. How he had got here he did not know. Where he actually was, he wasn't quite sure. But trivial matters such as these were of no significance.

People around him were beginning to stir, a new day was beginning, but to him this was of no consequence. All his mind's eye could see was a vision of Clara and she was holding a baby – their baby. A baby that had been denied her because of all the elaborate lies told by Katherine. Katherine – his own wife. Katherine – Clara's sister.

Why? his mind screamed. What had driven her, possessed her, to devise and carry out such lies? They had denied Clara – a sister she was supposed to have adored – the right to her own child. And that child had rightly belonged to himself and Clara, conceived, albeit mistakenly, out of deep love between two people who had planned to spend their lives together. Katherine's lies had kept them apart and caused untold distress.

The answer to the question he already knew. Katherine had told him why. It was all because of love – her selfish love.

Love. The word echoed in his head. He himself had loved Clara with a passion only experienced once in a lifetime. Oh, Clara. Even now after forty years her memory still had the power to quicken his heart and sear the pain of loss deep within his soul.

'Oh, Katherine, how could you?' he whispered, distraught.

He wrapped his arms around his body tightly and shuddered again. He had lived with her for forty years, had lain beside her and made love to her, sharing daily life like any normal couple whilst he had striven hard to forget the past and what it might have held with Clara.

Katherine had been an attentive wife, a loving wife, and they had had a good life together. But he hadn't known her, hadn't understood her well enough even to suspect she was capable of carrying out such a terrible deed and, far worse, able to live with her conscience afterwards. At this moment in time he wasn't sure how he felt about her, if he could ever look her in the eye again.

He raised his head and studied the still dark early-morning sky. To be honest, he could understand what had driven her. When faced with the horror of losing Clara to another man, as Katherine had told him, he had wanted to kill, had wanted to take a knife to the unseen lover who had stolen what Philip felt was rightfully his. But his honour had stopped him, and it had been this and a strong sense of morality that had led him to the altar to marry Katherine. And the baby. She had told him it had been conceived the very night she had tearfully told him of Clara's faithlessness. Their lovemaking had resulted entirely from his grief. He had hungrily accepted Katherine's advances, had selfishly turned to her, wanted her purely to comfort his own loss. A loss that over the passing years he had painfully learned to live with, but never quite recovered from.

And what of Clara herself? How had she coped all these

years, thinking her baby was dead? He suddenly saw the face of the woman who had answered Grace's door. The face was much older but the Clara he remembered, the vibrant, wonderful young woman he had fallen in love with, still remained. And now he understood her reactions. She had recognised him. After all these years, she had known him. Did her reaction mean she still cared? Had she suffered as much as he? Philip squeezed his eyes tightly shut. He doubted it. He doubted another human could have borne such pain. But how did he tell her all of this? How did he begin to explain? After all, she had a right to know.

He felt a desire to rush to her now. Beg her forgiveness for accepting Katherine's story. Try to explain how he had striven to cope, believing she had deserted him for another; how he had unforgivably accepted without question the baby had been Katherine's; of how the first he knew of the baby was after it was born, when Katherine had explained that she had hidden away during her pregnancy to avoid the shame.

And what of Cecily? Her image rose before him and he saw the stages of her life. She had been a beautiful baby and had grown and developed into a wonderful woman, now a mother herself. How would Cecily react if she knew that the mother she adored, the woman who had helped raise her, guide her, protect her, was not in fact her true mother? Like Clara, she had a right to know. But would it be right to tell her? The knowledge would surely break her heart.

He felt a hand touch his shoulder and slowly raised his head to stare into the kindly eyes peering down at him.

'Are you all right, sir?'

He scanned the face, his eyes wary. 'I'm fine,' he lied.

'You are Mr Janson? Mr Philip Janson?'

He nodded, confused.

'We've been looking for you, sir.'

'You have?'

The middle-aged policeman that the kindly but tired eyes belonged to had been just about to finish his long shift when he had been called upon to help in the search for the man sitting on the bench before him.

He hooked his arm through his and gently eased him to his feet. Philip Janson looked awful, his taut skin drained of colour, his slumped body shivering with cold. The man was in shock, obviously bewildered and confused. But, mused the policeman worriedly, could what had caused this shock be as great as the one he himself was about to deliver?

Katherine Janson was dead. Her body had lain on the kitchen floor for several hours before discovery by her daughter. And although an autopsy would have to take place, the examining coroner had already deduced that the bottle of aspirin and a vast quantity of Armagnac had been more than enough to do the deed. Had she known? he thought sadly. Had Katherine Janson known what she had been doing to herself as she had taken all those pills, washed down with alcohol on an empty stomach?

Well, these questions would have to be answered, but it seemed clear enough. She had not known what she was doing and neither had she been forced. Her death was by her own hand, brought on by events as yet unexplained. The time would come shortly to answer these questions but the immediate task was to get this man into the warmth before he himself became a victim of the Grim Reaper.

'Come along, sir,' the policeman said firmly. 'Let's get you home.'

Chapter Twenty-Eight

'The Yanks are coming!'

The cry went up and word spread throughout Leicester quicker than local gossip over the garden wall. It was 1942. The war had raged for three long years and their island had taken more than its fair share of bombardment. But the spirit of its people, despite the terrible damage and loss of lives, would still not be dampened.

Rationing was really beginning to bite. Coal, soap, and even sweets were now on the ever-growing list, and petrol for pleasure jaunts was totally banned.

All people of an age, especially women, had to work. It took a good excuse to be exempted. Even old ladies would sit in groups, knitting garments for the forces and sewing parachute silk, whilst mulling over local gossip. Labour was so short that conscientious objectors were given a choice by the MP Bevin. They either went down the mines, joined up or went to prison, the choice was theirs.

The German stranglehold on Europe was almost total, but this was about to change drastically. With the bombing of Pearl Harbour by the Japanese late in 1941, the might of America was joined to the conflict.

For the people of Great Britain emotions were mixed. Some breathed a sigh of relief, others voiced strong opinions against their involvement, but few doubted that America and its power would tip the balance.

For most of the man-starved young women in the British Isles, the arrival of the American soldiers meant only one thing. Once again they had a reason to doll up and visit the dance halls. American men were good-looking, better dressed than the British, had far more money to spend, and their fascinating drawl and polite manners were soon to bowl most of the women over, mothers and daughters alike. And what a way to break the monotony of the long drab days! The sight of a good-looking man belonging to a breed without the reserve inherited by their British counterparts was a real tonic. These men knew how to sweet-talk a woman, knew how to romance, knew how to enjoy themselves, and come hell or high water these men were going to have it all – just in case they didn't make it home.

The men of Britain were not so keen to welcome their new rivals. To them their American cousins, allies or not, were: 'Oversexed, overpaid, but far worse, over here'. And there was nothing they could do about it.

In and around Leicester several large purpose-built camps were hurriedly constructed to billet the US Forces whilst they readied themselves for the onslaught on Europe. Envious eyes watched wagonloads of provisions arriving to feed them. The American Government were making certain that their men were not going to march on empty stomachs. And neither were they going to be deprived of any creature comforts if young British womanhood got its way.

Charlie heard of their arrival via Sybil who was supposed to be on her way to the despatch department with her loaded trolley. The trolley was yanked to a halt and several cases of shells clattered noisily against the metal sides. Sybil grimaced. The shells held gunpowder.

'You'll blow us to smithereens one of these days,' Charlie

shouted over the drone of the machines and the tannoy blasting out *Workers' Playtime*.

'Never mind that,' Sybil erupted, flapping her hand excitedly. ''Ave you 'eard the news? Oh, God, I can't believe it,' she went on before Charlie could open her mouth. 'It's the best thing ter 'appen since this blasted war started. Their tanks are big, they're big, and their wallets are loaded.' She clapped her hands together in prayer and raised laughing eyes. 'Oh, Lord, let me at 'em.'

Charlie tucked a stray strand of hair back beneath her turbaned head, her eyes twinkling. 'Yes, I've heard. Who hasn't?' She inclined her head towards a fellow worker. 'Winnie's sister's gone to watch them marching through town.'

Sybil's face clouded over in envy. 'I wanna go, Charlie. I wanna see them Yanks for meself. Can't we bunk off?'

Charlie, who had not long been promoted to supervisor, put on her supervisor's face. 'No, we can't. We've work to do. I've no doubt you'll get plenty of opportunity to go Yank spotting. But it'll be after work.'

She tried to sound severe but secretly was just as desperate as her friend to see the new arrivals. Being a frequent visitor to the pictures she had often gazed longingly into the eyes of the likes of Gig Young, Cary Grant and Gary Cooper, and wanted to know if all American males were as good-looking and suave as portrayed in the films.

Sybil wasn't listening to her, her mind preoccupied. 'I've heard they've got nylons. Oh, what I'd give for a pair of stockin's!' She winked saucily. 'What I wouldn't give, eh!' She grabbed the handlebar on her trolley, heaved it into position and started to push. 'Friday!' she shouted over her shoulder. 'Me and you are goin' with the rest of the gels to the Hippodrome. There's talk it'll be packed wi' 'em, so we'd better get 'old of some beetroot to boil so we can stain our lips.' She pursed her lips and smacked a mock kiss at Charlie.

Charlie laughed as her friend manoeuvred the heavy trolley away. She'd get that beetroot herself if she had to go and raid her father's allotment. And gravy browning for her legs. If Sybil was going to force her to go dancing, then she wanted to look her best.

The children – minus Polly who, at the age of fourteen, had joined the ranks of the workers and had started her training as an overlocker at a clothing factory – were discussing the arrival of the Yanks on their way home from school.

Willy and Tony, dressed like twins in short grey trousers patched in the back, grubby grey socks wrinkled around their ankles, shirts hanging out, and woolly sleeveless green pullovers – Willy's unravelling at the bottom – knees grazed and legs bruised and scratched, drawstring sacking bags slung over their shoulders, were kicking stones along the path. They were listening to the girls' conversation with puzzled interest.

'What's a Yank?' asked Tony.

'It's when yer pull summat,' Willy answered knowingly. 'Me mam used ter say, "I'll yank yer ear off, our Willy, if yer don't stop earwiggin' at doors." ' For a moment a pain of loss filled him. He would do anything to have his mother back saying such things even if it meant a thick ear to go with it.

There was a loud guffaw from the girls at the back.

'No, it ain't,' sniggered Molly. 'A Yank is an American soldier.' She knew this because her friend at school had boasted to her.

Willy spun round. 'American soldiers! What about 'em?'

Jessie sniffed haughtily. 'They're arrivin' in Leicester, that's what. I fought everyone knew. That's why we've bin let out early, so the teachers can go and join the welcoming parade.'

Willy stared at her agog. He had somehow missed this

information. When his teacher had announced the unexpected half holiday, he had been too eager to get away to wonder why. And for someone who homed in on anything to do with soldiers, this was rather a blow to his pride. The parade? he thought. Oh, what was he missing?

'I godda go,' he whispered to Tony. 'I've just godda go ter see the soldiers. I bet they've got tanks. Oh, I godda see the tanks! I just godda.'

He was nearly wetting himself in anticipation. He had seen news-reel films at the pictures on a Saturday morning when either Auntie Grace or Granny Apple – as Clara was affectionately called – had spared them two jam jars and a penny each for the ticket, and pockets stuffed with anything to pelt the other kids with, they had run joyously to join the ever-growing queues of excited youngsters for a morning's revelry.

But how come he had missed this most important, most wonderful, most exciting news?

'A' yer goin' to see 'em?' asked Tony.

Willy glanced over his shoulder then back to Tony. 'I might.'

'Can I come too?' he whispered.

Willy sniffed. 'Yeah, I suppose, but don't let the gels know or they'll stop us. When we get home, we'll dump our stuff and say we're meetin' the gang on the reccy. Okay?'

'Okay,' Tony said excitedly.

Unbeknown to the boys, the girls were planning the very same excursion, only they were meeting their friends at the park.

Their excuses were successful and, silently jubilant, they all set off, the boys in one direction and the girls in another, neither realising their destination was the same.

On arriving at the Clock Tower, Willy and Tony had to push and shove their way through the crowds to get a front-line view.

Neither would ever forget the sight of the soldiers, some

marching, some in jeeps, some packed inside lorries covered by canvas, some inside the biggest tanks, gun barrels the length of a double-decker bus. The soldiers were grinning and waving at the crowd and handing out to lucky recipients bars of chocolate and sticks of gum. The boys both stood gawping in wonder. They were jostled and kicked by an excited cheering crowd waving patriotic Union Jacks, but this went unnoticed, so engrossed were they in the scene being played before them.

Willy cried out in shock from a sudden hard slap on the side of his head. Ear red and smarting, he spun round to face his sister Maureen who was standing glaring at him with hands on hips.

'Warra you two doin' 'ere?' she demanded.

Willy grimaced as he rubbed his ear. 'Warra you doin' 'ere?' he retaliated.

'I asked first.'

A breathless Jessie reached them, having struggled through the crowd. 'Wadda you doin' here?' she asked, scowling hard at Tony.

'Same as you, I expect,' Willy answered matter-of-factly. 'And if you tell, so will we.'

The girls looked at each other then turned back to them. 'Okay. We won't if you won't.'

The boys grinned triumphantly and returned to the parade.

A troop of black American soldiers marched by, proud and erect, broad grins stretched across their faces. Willy, never having seen a black man before, gawped. 'Why a' they painted black?' he asked no one in particular, grimacing hard.

'It's to fool the enemy, lad,' a tattered old man at the side of him chuckled. 'So they can't see 'em in the dark.'

'Stupid old bugger!' the middle-aged woman at the side of

him erupted. 'Them's our dark cousins whose ancestors come from Africa. They were took to America by force, poor old sods, and made to work as slaves.' She scowled at the old man who along with Willy was staring at her. 'Didn't you go to school?' Her eyes scanned him scornfully. 'No, probably not,' she deduced.

'What's slaves?' asked Willy.

'Ask yer teacher, me duck. Now I came ter watch the parade, not give an 'istory lesson.'

'Bloody knowall!' the old man hissed. He bent over and whispered in Willy's ear: 'You believe me, laddie, not that old trout. Them's white men blacked up ter fool the enemy.'

Willy decided to ask his teacher.

The crowd swelled further as more and more people arrived and soon excitement reached fever pitch. The crowd swayed and surged. Taken off balance, Willy was suddenly thrown into the path of an oncoming Jeep. It screeched to a halt, passenger and driver jumping out to race towards the boy lying prostrate on the ground, wheels just inches away.

Maureen, screaming in terror, rushed forward.

'Me brother! Oh, me brother!'

Jessie and Tony stood rigid in fear, anticipating the worst. The crowd immediately around held their breath; the rest were still too engrossed in the parade to notice what had happened.

Lieutenant Nathaniel Hefflefinger stared down horrified at the boy. He had always had a fondness of children, especially little boys, brought about by raising his own two sons. His little boys were now nineteen and twenty-two, both towering well over his own five foot eleven, and even though they no longer needed his protection in quite the same way, his fatherly instincts had never diminished. They overtook him now.

He knelt down and felt the boy's head, then his pulse, then

smiled gratefully. The lad was just dazed. 'You okay, son?' he asked.

Willy gingerly opened one eye, then the other. 'I think so.'

Nat sighed, relieved, and helped him to his feet, brushing him down.

'You sure now, son? Anything hurt?'

Willy shook his head. Out of the corner of his eye he spotted the vehicle. 'I like yer car, mister,' he said, gazing over at it in awe. He ran his hand lovingly over the bonnet, then raised star-struck eyes to the soldier. ''Ave you gorra gun? I've gorra gun, and a sword.'

'You haven't?' Nat said, amused.

'I 'ave, mister,' Willy said proudly. 'They're only wooden, mind.'

'I'm glad to hear it.'

Nat turned to Maureen. 'Your little brother's fine, young missy.'

But 'young missy' wasn't listening. She was gawping at Nat's driver, a strapping six-foot-three nineteen year old with the looks of a Greek god. Maureen was in love, so much so it had overtaken all concern for Willy. So was Jessie. Both girls had moved to stand beside him.

'This your car?' they asked the Greek god.

Maureen glared at Jessie. 'I saw him first,' she hissed.

'No, yer din't,' she replied.

'Tell you what,' Nat addressed his driver, his eyes twinkling, 'since we ran this young man over, I think the least we can do is make sure he and his buddies get home safe. Wadda you say, Jerome?'

Maureen and Jessie swooned. His name was Jerome. It was tattooed on their hearts.

'I think that's a good idea, Lieutenant,' he answered, adjusting his cap more comfortably on his head.

Willy's jaw dropped. 'Yer mean it, mister? You're gonna give us a ride in the car?'

'Yeah, yer mean it?' echoed Tony.

'It's called a Jeep, boys. And sure thing. Why don't you all pile in?'

Pile in they did, to sit squashed in the back like royalty, members of the crowd looking on with an envy which did not escape the children's notice.

'We won't 'alf be in trouble,' whispered Maureen.

'Who cares?' answered Jessie, her eyes boring into the back of Jerome's blond head.

Nat and Jerome climbed aboard.

Nat turned around and handed over several packets of gum and three bars of chocolate. 'Share those between you. Now where to?' he asked.

Grace heard about the arrival of the American soldiers for the umpteenth time via the young invoice clerk who sat at the desk next to her own. Her name was Susan Wiggins and she was an extremely plain girl of seventeen prone to hideous boils that would break out without warning in the crooks of her elbows and sometimes on her chin. These would be proudly displayed before she began the practised art of squeezing when she thought no one was looking. At the moment boils and such like were not of importance. Her mind was filled with other matters. She sat staring dreamily into space.

'They're all 'andsome, yer know, Mrs Wilkins,' she was saying. 'My auntie intergrated to America. She lives in I-de-ho, or summat like that. She married a Mormon. And 'e were 'andsome. Dead ringer for Ronald Coleman.'

'Was he?' Grace said absently, concentrating on completing the paperwork for the latest order received that would take at least two weeks to process through the factory and had to be out of the door yesterday.

'Yeah. She's got fourteen kids and they all live in one of them wooden 'ouses on wheels. Her 'usband left 'er and married another woman, and she had twelve.'

Grace raised her head and stared at her. 'Well then, young Susan, just you make sure you don't marry a Mormon.'

'Why?' she asked blankly.

Grace shook her head. 'Just take some advice, Susan, be careful who you marry.' It's a pity, she thought, that twenty-two years down the line she'd been unable to take her own advice.

'Me mam says I'll be lucky to marry anyone wi' a face like mine.'

Grace looked at her, astonished. 'Susan, there's nothing wrong with your face.'

'I'm ugly, Mrs Wilkins. I know that.'

She tried to hide pity. 'Beauty is in the eye of the beholder.'

Susan guffawed loudly. 'Well, I'll just 'ope I meet a blind man then eh? Or I could go round wi' a bag on me 'ead.'

Even Grace could not help but smile at her remarks. 'Come on, get back to work, we've orders to see to. If we don't then our men won't have anything to fight the enemy with. And if that happens your chances of meeting any man, blind or not, will be drastically reduced.'

'Oh, right yer are, Mrs Wilkins.' She snatched up her pen but before it touched the paper was back gazing into space, imagining her American soldier, the one she knew would never look at her because of all the pretty man-starved females ahead in the queue.

Grace shook her head, rose and made her way towards the Factory Manager's office. It was empty.

Betty, a skinny woman for forty-five, dressed in a brown boiler suit, head wrapped tightly in the uniform turban scarf, straightened up from her machine. ''E's popped out, Grace love.'

'Has he? That's unusual.'

'Ah, well, it ain't every day we gets the Americans landing, now is it? And them such an 'andsome lot. I'm off meself with the rest of the gels as soon as the shift's finished. 'Oping we might catch the tail end of the march. Are you comin' wi' us?'

Grace smiled gratefully. Like all the other women in the city she was also intrigued to see these handsome Americans, if only to check for herself that the rumours about them were true. Surely they couldn't all look like Clark Gable, have the height of John Wayne and be as smooth-talking as George Sanders? 'I can't, but thanks for the offer, Betty. I have to get home to the children.'

'Yer don't know what yer missing, Grace,' Betty said, shaking her head.

'No, maybe I don't, but you enjoy yerselves all the same.'

'We will, Grace, we will. And if I click,' she winked seductively, 'I'll mek sure he's a brother for you, eh?'

Grace laughed. 'You do that.'

As she skirted the factory floor she glanced down at the works order that needed authorising. With Reggie Love the Factory Manager gone walkabout she would have to go and see Mr Janson himself. This order could not wait.

She climbed the steel stairs towards the offices, wondering if Mr Janson would be free yet from his visitors from the MoD. They were a grim-looking lot, dressed in their dark navy suits, and had frowned a lot on their tour around the factory. Grace had bumped into the party as she had come out of the Ladies' toilet, feeling somewhat embarrassed.

Philip Janson had smiled at her and introduced her as his Production Assistant. She had felt proud to have her hand shaken by such dignitaries, but production assistant indeed! She was just a clerk.

As she reached the top of the stairs she thought of Philip Janson. How the man had changed over the past year. Well, she supposed, he had had an awful – no – terrible shock, one that had been bad enough to age anyone. Rumours had been rife around the factory as individuals surmised how his wife had come to be drinking such quantities of brandy – trust the toffs to have that when most men were struggling to buy a pint of beer – and taking all those pills. But when all was said and done the coroner's verdict had put it down to an accident due to diminished responsibility.

Philip Janson, during all that dreadful time, had been absent from the factory. In fact it had been three whole months before he had returned. But the man who had been running the business the day his wife died was not the same man who had come back.

All credit to them, during his absence his staff came up trumps. Not one order was late, not one order lost. Production output rose out of respect for him. And on his return he had recognised their loyalty and rewarded them with a bonus. It hadn't been much, but the little it was had been gratefully received. Even Freddy and Mabel, the cleaners, got a share. This gesture only reinforced their good opinion of the man and confirmed how glad they all were to be working for him.

But all had noticed the change in him. It was inescapable.

Gladys, his secretary, had gone for her dinner when Grace entered her office. Probably, like the others, she'd gone to catch a glimpse of the parade. Grace walked over and tapped on Mr Janson's door.

He was sitting at his desk which was piled high with paperwork.

On seeing her standing in the doorway he smiled. Or rather his mouth smiled; his eyes told a different tale. They were pained and filled with grief.

'Come in, Grace.'

She longed to rush towards this kind man, gather him in her arms and comfort him. He cried out for a comforting hug, did Philip Janson. But that was something she could not do. She was only his employee.

'I'm sorry to bother you, Mr Janson,' she said, advancing. 'But could you please sign this works order? Mr Love has gone out for his dinner and I need to start getting it processed if we're to have a hope of meeting the deadline.'

'Certainly, my dear. Take a seat.' He scrutinised her as she handed over the forms. 'You look tired, Grace.'

No more than you, she thought. 'Yes, I am a bit. Sleep's something we've learned to do without thanks to these air raids.'

Philip nodded in agreement. Although air raids or not, nothing made a difference to the fact that he had not slept properly since the night of Katherine's death.

He studied the papers, queried several points and, satisfied, signed his authority. He handed the forms back to her.

'Another good job, Grace. Well done. I honestly wonder sometimes how you manage to schedule these orders through the factory without proper training. You seem to have an inbuilt knack.'

She smiled in pleasure at his compliment.

He glanced at his pocket watch. 'I expect you'll be going down to catch the parade, Grace? That's where Gladys has gone.' He laughed. 'I bet that's where most of the staff have gone. Mind you, I won't be docking any wages for lateness back, it's a proud day for us. We need our American cousins and those who scoff are foolish. Now, you'd better hurry if you're going.'

'Well, actually, I wasn't going to bother. Not that I don't want to see the troops arriving. I think it's really exciting. But I wanted to get this order dealt with so the factory can get cracking on it, and I usually pop home at dinnertime to check on things at home.'

He leaned back in his chair. 'How are the children, Grace? Jessie, is it, and Tony?'

'They're fine, thank you.'

'No sign yet of a relative coming forward?'

She lowered her eyes. 'No. It's selfish, I know, but I keep my fingers crossed no one ever will.'

'That's understandable. You've grown quite attached to them. Any news from your husband?'

She shook her head. 'Not a word.'

'Mmm.' He looked at her thoughtfully. It was par for the course, Bernard Wilkins had always been a selfish bastard. He was probably laughing up his sleeve at the thought that his wife was suffering agonies over his absence. Little did he know Grace was thriving. Philip suddenly worried for her, wondered what would happen to her if and when Wilkins returned. Might be better all round if he didn't come back. Not that he wished him ill, but Philip was of the strong opinion that the likes of Bernard could be managed without and not only by his wife. He didn't quite know his own situation regarding re-employment of former employees but knew of one man he did not want back.

Meanwhile Grace stood waiting. Every time she was alone with Mr Janson he asked the same questions. How was she? How were the kids? The next one would be concerning Clara. He always asked after Clara, and Grace was never quite sure why. She presumed it was a genuine feeling of guilt because she herself had asked his help on a matter concerning Clara and due to his wife's untimely death, he could not put it into action.

'And how's that lady who moved in with your other neighbour to look after his children? You know, the one who had to leave her house. Clara, isn't it? Clara Smith?'

'Yes, that's right, Mr Janson.' She gave her usual response. 'She loves those children like they're her own.' Grace laughed. 'They call her Granny Apple.'

Philip's eyes widened in interest. This was a new piece of information. 'Why?'

'Granny Smith.'

'Oh, I see. Granny Apple. Yes, that's rather clever. And she doesn't mind?'

'She loves it. It makes her feel special.'

Philip smiled wanly. Clara didn't have to be made to feel special. She already was special. As usual he fought the compulsion to interrogate Grace further. He hungered for more news, but these snippets of information confirming nothing more than the fact that Clara was well and seemed happy, had to suffice. He knew Grace already wondered why he asked them, he could see it in her eyes. She was a bright woman. He was lucky to have her on his staff. He hoped she put his questions down to nothing more than general interest in a member of his staff. It wouldn't do for her to think otherwise, being so close to Clara.

He watched her turn to leave, then pause and look back.

'Oh, actually, Mr Janson, I wonder if I could ask you something?'

'Anything, Grace.'

She walked back towards him. 'Well, it's about Clara. Miss Smith. She has a sister that she lost touch with over forty years ago and would like to find her. We were discussing it last night. How would she go about that, do you know?'

Philip's face drained of colour. He fell back in his chair, gasping for breath. Grace stared at him in horror. He was having a heart attack. What did she do? She rushed around the desk and instinctively tried to loosen his tie.

'Keep still, Mr Janson, I'll get a doctor.'

He caught hold of her wrist. 'No. No doctor. I'll be fine in a minute.'

'But . . .'

'Grace . . . please . . . no doctor.' He tried to calm his breathing. 'Water, please. A glass of water.'

Her eyes darted round the office. On a cabinet by the far

wall was a tray holding several glasses and a cut glass decanter filled with clear liquid. As she poured she hoped it was water and not something like gin. Not being a drinker, she felt she wouldn't know.

He drank it down and she poured him another glass.

She stared at him worriedly. His face was the colour of parchment.

'A' yer sure you don't want a doctor, Mr Janson?'

He nodded. 'Quite . . . quite sure, thank you, Grace.'

He raised his eyes to her. His worst fear had come true. If Clara started making enquiries, it would only be a matter of time before certain facts emerged and these would lead to the full, shameful truth, which, since learning it well over a year ago, he could not bring himself to divulge to anyone. The longer he had deliberated, the harder it had got.

The story he had to tell would surely disrupt Clara's life, bring to her untold pain and misery as she relived the past. Would it be fair for Clara to have to face all this at her time of life?

And Cecily? His daughter had been devastated, her recovery slow from the death of the person she had known as her mother. Only now was she able to speak of Katherine without her eyes filling with tears. And then there were her children, his grandchildren. Could such a story be told to them?

Was it fair to any of them to share this great burden when he himself was still having difficulty coping with it?

But his hand was being forced. He had no choice. Unfairly or not, he had to unburden himself on Grace and make her stop Clara searching for her sister. Try to stem this avalanche before it buried them all.

He ran his hand nervously over his chin and took a breath.

'Grace, please lock the door and sit down. I have something to tell you which, believe me, I don't want to do. I don't want to drag you into it, but I have no choice.'

The look in his eyes and the tone of his voice chilled Grace's bones. Without a word she did as he asked and sat down in the chair facing him.

'This has something to do with Clara, hasn't it, Mr Janson?'

For a moment he stared at her. 'Not something. No. All, Grace. All.'

It took an hour. He started where it had all begun. The very first time his eyes had locked on his destiny. Three times during the tale he broke down in tears, twice Grace cried with him. Finally, wringing his hands in despair, he raised his eyes to her.

'You see why Clara has to be stopped? You must understand, Grace. You must. It would cause so much more pain should this all come out.'

She took a deep breath as a terrible weight settled upon her. In unburdening himself Philip Janson had not realised what a position he had put her in. He could not know that she herself knew the other side of this sordid story. Clara's story. And although she understood his own reasoning, appreciated how and why he had reached his decision, when all was said and done he was asking her now to deceive her very dear friend.

This whole situation had arisen from deceit and it wasn't fair that it should carry on. The person who had caused it all was now gone, could do no more harm. By the truth coming out, surely, something might be salvaged from the whole dreadful mess, if only peace of mind for the two people it had all begun with?

She hoped Clara would understand and forgive her for what she was about to do.

'Mr Janson, what about the hurt that's already been caused? What about the pain that Clara's lived with all these years? Her not knowing, not understanding. She thinks you abandoned her for another woman. She's grieved for you and the baby she thinks died, for over forty years. D'yer think it's fair that she does that for the rest of her life?' She clasped her hands and leaned forward, herself filled with Clara's agony. 'I witnessed her pain, Mr Janson. I saw the room she left as a shrine. I saw a woman who had no will to live. She has a right to know, Mr Janson. She has a right to know that her baby didn't die, that the man she loved did not throw her aside, and that the sister she idolised lied to her. And also that it was that sister who sold her house from over her to get her out of the way. You have to go to Clara, Mr Janson. You have to tell her all this. And then it's for her to decide what she wants to do. Cecily is, after all, *her* daughter.'

He stared at her blankly as her words hit home. His face filled with remorse and he groaned despairingly. 'I can't, Grace. I can't.'

'But you owe it to her! You owe it to yourself.'

He buried his face in his hands. 'Dear God, what do I do?'

She leaned over and placed her hand on his. 'Her sister took everything from her. You could give something back.'

He raised his head. 'You're right, Grace. I have to do this, don't I?'

She nodded her head. 'Yes, I'm afraid you do.'

His office door rattled. She rose, made her way over and unlocked it.

She was greeted by Gladys's astonished stare.

Grace's mind raced frantically. Gladys would want to know why she was inside the boss's inner sanctum with the door locked. 'Would you bring Mr Janson a cup of tea, please, Gladys?' she asked.

Gladys strained to look over her shoulder. 'What's goin' . . .'

She ushered Gladys back into the outer office. 'I have a problem, Gladys, that Mr Janson is helping me with. It's personal.'

'Oh.' She eyed Grace, intrigued. 'Oh, I see. If I can 'elp at all . . .'

'Thank you, Gladys.' She smiled sweetly as she shut the door, relocked it and sat down. The last thing Philip needed was Gladys asking questions.

'Would you be there when I speak to Clara?' he asked.

She shook her head. 'You have to do this on your own, Mr Janson. You need to meet Clara on neutral ground.'

'Yes, I do, don't I?' He smiled at her gratefully. 'Thank you, Grace. I feel better for our talk. I feel a burden has been lifted.' He sighed heavily. 'But worse in a manner of speaking now I know what Clara has suffered. I had always believed, you see, until Katherine's death, that she was happily married.' His bottom lip quivered and his eyes filled with tears. 'If I had known . . . known . . .'

'Oh, Mr Janson,' Grace said, choked. 'You see what I mean when I say you have to put this all right? If only for your own and Clara's sake. Your wife has gone. She left a terrible legacy behind. You must at least try to do right.'

He shook his head and rubbed his eyes. 'I doubt any of this could ever be put right. But, yes, I have to try. And I will.'

There was a knock. Grace rose again, unlocked the door and retrieved the tray from Gladys. She had made a pot of tea and put out two cups. Grace smiled in grateful appreciation.

It was another half an hour before she finally left the office and it was a thoughtful Grace who made her way home that night. She wanted to rush straight to Clara, try to prepare her friend for what she was about to hear. But she couldn't. It all had to come from Philip Janson. It had begun between the two of them and it had to finish that way, without any more outside interference.

She was greeted by the children shrieking in excitement,

babbling their news. Taking off her coat, she tried to calm them down so she could understand properly just what they were trying to tell her. It was Connie who finally had to do the deed.

'Oh, they were two lovely men, Grace. Ever so good wi' the kids. And polite. Oh, they called me "Ma'am". Me, Connie Taylor. I felt like royalty, I did really.'

'And they give us chocolate, Auntie Grace. Look, we saved you a piece.' Tony erupted, producing a square of the precious brown substance from his pocket.

'Yeah, and some gum stuff,' grinned Jessie. 'Tony swallowed his and Mrs Wilkins,' she narrowed her eyes and shot a scowl at Ida sitting over in her chair, 'said it'd tangle round his lungs and suffocate him.'

'It won't, will it, Auntie Grace?' Tony asked worriedly.

Grace accepted the chocolate, smiling. 'I doubt it, my dears. But I don't think you're supposed to swallow it, just chew. Anyway,' she said, gathering the children to her and kissing them both on the forehead, 'if you've had all this chocolate, I can't see you wanting any tea.'

'Ahhh!' they both wailed.

'Talking of tea,' Connie spoke guiltily, 'I invited 'em on Sunday. Well, it were the least I could do, young Willy causing 'em so much bother. Fancy managin' ter get himself run over like that.'

'They'd no business bein' down the town in the first place,' Ida erupted. 'I 'ope you're goin' to punish 'em, Grace?'

Connie turned on her, for once unable to hold her tongue. 'No one asked your opinion, Mrs Wilkins. The kids weren't doin' any 'arm. They only wanted to see the soldiers. I don't suppose you did anythin' like that when you were a kid. Too busy reading yer bible, I expect.'

Ida's face turned stony. 'Them kids might be better behaved if they read more of the good book. They might learn summat about manners too.'

'There ain't n'ote wrong wi' their manners.'

'Stop it!' Grace cried. She looked hard at Ida. 'It's for me to decide if the children need punishing. And you, mother.' Her eyes softened. 'I could do with a cup of tea.'

The look of hatred on Ida's face did not escape her. She followed her mother into the kitchen and ran her hand exasperatedly through her hair. 'Oh, Mam, what am I going to give those soldiers to eat? And I've hardly any coal to make a decent fire. If I had the money to buy an extra bag, the coalman couldn't give me it. He's struggling to cope securing rations as it is.' She realised Jessie and Tony were standing in the doorway. 'Oh!' She tried to sound severe. 'What am I going to do with you two?'

'It weren't us, it were Willy and Maureen's idea,' fibbed Jessie. Well, it was half true, she thought.

'Huh,' Grace said, unconvinced. 'Go and set the table while I decide what's to be done.'

'But they can come for tea?' Jessie cried. The thought of not seeing Jerome again was unbearable. She had been beside herself with joy when Auntie Connie had made the suggestion, and intended to make damned sure Maureen was not invited. Then she would have Jerome all to herself.

There was a tap on the back door and Tom strode in. Grace smiled a welcome as his large frame filled the tiny kitchen. Over the last year they had grown closer, brought together by concern for all the children. They were regular visitors to each other's houses and, unaware, Grace found herself looking forward more and more to his visits, especially when they would drink tea together, or just sit by the fire discussing the children's daily behaviour. Tom would sometimes talk about his work, and she hers, and before they both knew it, many pleasant hours had passed.

As time sped by, helped along also by the presence of

Clara and the peace of mind her help was giving him, the old Tom that Grace had first encountered was beginning to emerge.

''Ave you heard the latest?' he asked.

'Just this minute.' She pulled him aside, aware that Jessie and Tony were nearby. 'When the car – sorry, Jeep, rolled up nearly the whole street came out.' She bit her lip in mirth. 'Can you imagine what the gossip's gonna be like?'

Tom giggled. 'I can. Bessie would 'ave loved this one.'

Grace nodded. 'Yes, she would. And those who didn't come out, she would have gone and knocked on their doors. Anyway I don't think we need punish the children, do you? Just give them a stern talking to about going off without telling an adult first.'

'My sentiments exactly, Grace,' he said, relieved. 'There's bin no 'arm done. And the kids enjoyed themselves. My two are full of it.' He grinned mischievously. 'I'm sure I did worse when I was a kid.'

Grace laughed too. 'I expect you did,' she said, eyeing him knowingly. 'The only harm that's been done this time has been caused by my mother.'

Connie turned from her tea making and looked worriedly at her daughter. 'Me. What 'ave I done?'

'Invited these Americans for tea, that's what. What on earth am I going to give 'em?'

Tom scratched his head. 'I'll have a look in our pantry, and I could see if I can get some eggs. I have to go out that way tomorrow.'

'Oh, could you?'

'I'll try, and maybe I might scrounge a little butter. Though I can't promise.'

'Butter! Oh, goodness, Tom, that would be marvellous.'

'Well, I'll see what I can do.'

Grace turned to her mother, a twinkle in her eye. 'And

you, Mam, can make a cake. I don't know how, but being's this is all your doing, you can have that honour.' She tried to hide a smile at the look of horror on her mother's face at being given such an impossible task. She could see Connie's mind working overtime on how she was going to produce any sort of cake out of thin air. Ingredients were nigh on impossible to come by. She turned back to Tom. 'You will come, and bring Clara and the children? I'm quite getting used to the idea of this tea party. And we must do these soldiers proud. After all, they're strangers to this country and will be missing their own families.'

'Yeah, we'd all love to come. That's if yer sure?'

'I'm sure, Tom. It wouldn't be the same if you weren't there.' She blushed at her own comment, turned away from him and waved her hands at the children still standing in the doorway. 'Didn't I ask you to set the table?'

The children scuttled away.

Connie handed Grace a cup of tea. 'Got time for one, Tom?' she asked.

He looked at the inviting cup, at Grace, then back to Connie. There was nothing he would have liked more than to stay and have a natter with Grace. Even before she and Bessie had become friends he had admired her as an attractive woman, as well as pitying her for her choice of husband. Through tragedy they had been drawn together and now he felt something was developing between them. The more he saw of her, the more his feelings grew, and he knew, if he allowed it, those feelings would turn to much more, on his part at least.

But he felt guilty too. Towards Bessie, whom he still missed dreadfully, and towards Grace. He should not have these growing feelings for her. She hadn't done anything except extend the hand of friendship towards him and his family when he had needed it most. And this friendship, he knew, was continuing because of her own caring nature and the love she had for his children.

He glanced at her now as she put the cup on the kitchen table and donned her pinafore, tying the strings around her slim waist. She was so unlike Bessie in every way. Her neatly rolled dark auburn hair was slightly greying at the temples, giving her a mature, near aristocratic air. Several age lines were appearing on her face, but instead of detracting from they enhanced her good looks. Her skin appeared soft. He longed to reach out and gently touch it. Instinctively he stuffed his large hands down into his pockets just in case they took on a life of their own and did as he longed to do.

Grace Wilkins was a married woman, a friend of the family, and if he stepped out of line that friendship could – no, would – be severely jeopardised. He could not and would not risk that for anything. He was a fool even to think that if she wasn't tied to her cretin of a husband, the likes of Grace Wilkins would ever look at a great hulk of a man such as himself. One who could not offer her anything other than the life of hardship she already had.

Shuffling uncomfortably on his feet, Tom let his head droop and his eyes scan his own grubby working clothes. He had just come back from delivering a load of steel tubes to a factory in Birmingham. He was tired and hungry. The journey had been fraught with hazards due to the conditions of the country roads and the fact that his lorry kept playing up. It needed a new gearbox but parts were hard to come by and his boss would not invest good money whilst there was still mileage left in it. His poor faithful lorry would have to lie down and die before Harry Hamblin put his hand in his pocket. And there was the constant worry of running out of petrol.

Tom raised his head and planted a smile on his face. 'Thanks fer the offer, Connie, but I must get back. I ain't had a wash yet. Clara's boiling some water for me and she's just about ter put the tea on the table.'

Grace tried to hide her disappointment. 'Another time then, Tom.' Her face suddenly clouded over. 'How is Clara?' she asked casually. 'I haven't seen her today.'

'Clara? When I left her she was cryin' . . .'

'Crying!' She clasped her hand to her mouth. 'Tom, why was she crying?'

He stared at her, bemused. 'I was just goin' ter say, she was cryin' wi' laughter over this business with the kids.'

'Oh, that's all right then,' Grace said, relieved.

'Is it? Why?'

'Oh, nothing, Tom, nothing.' She turned from him, suddenly feeling a strong desire to confide in him what Clara was about to face. But she couldn't. It wasn't her place or business to divulge a friend's secret to anyone else. All Tom and Connie knew was that Clara had had a terrible tragedy in her youth which had caused her practically to lock herself away, and that was the way it would remain unless Clara chose otherwise. 'Well, I'd best get on.'

'Yes, me too.'

He turned and departed.

Connie leaned her back against the sink and stared at the closed door thoughtfully, then at Grace. 'I wonder what was on his mind?'

Grace was taking a loaf of bread out of the stone bread jar. 'What d'yer mean, Mam?'

Connie sighed. 'Only that 'e seemed a bit preoccupied, that's all.'

'Oh, he's just tired, you heard him say so.'

'Mmm, I wonder.' She looked hard at her daughter. And *you* must be blind, thought Connie.

Chapter Twenty-Nine

Two days later, Clara sat facing Philip over a tray of coffee in a secluded corner of the lounge of the Grand Hotel. He had offered her something stronger, but she had declined. Now she wished she had accepted. What he was hesitantly relaying to her, she was finding a struggle to believe.

His letter had arrived most unexpectedly. And yet, she wondered, had contact really been unexpected after their chance encounter, even though she had been convinced he hadn't recognised her? Since the night she had opened the door to him, she had been filled with expectancy – another chance meeting perhaps – but hadn't envisaged a request to meet.

She had nearly not come. Forty years was a long gap before facing again a person you had once loved; thought had abandoned you; someone who had caused you untold pain. But as she had sat and deliberated, wondered whether to confide in Grace and ask her opinion, she had reached the conclusion that she was stronger now, and this she must face. This was what Grace and Bessie had striven for when they had taken her under their wing, and she must repay that faith by facing Philip. And maybe somehow he could finally lay her ghosts by explaining to her why he had left her, why he hadn't answered the letter, why he had lied about his love for her.

She was trying hard to concentrate and comprehend just what he was telling her. She couldn't help but be moved by his pain-filled eyes, tortured eyes, eyes that had once been filled with so much love when fixed upon her own. Was it really all those years ago? It seemed like yesterday they had lain in each other's arms, exhausted but happy after making love. They both knew they shouldn't have done it, but passion had overtaken them and neither had regretted it.

'Clara.'

His concerned voice broke into her thoughts.

'Have you listened to what I've been saying?'

She slowly nodded. 'I was remembering, Philip, that's all. I was just remembering.'

He closed his eyes tightly and slumped back in his chair.

She reached over and touched his arm. 'Please don't distress yourself, Philip. Please don't. I heard what you told me. It was Katherine. She did it all. Oh, Katherine,' she whispered forlornly, and withdrew her hand. 'What made her do such terrible things?' Her eyes softened as she raised them to him. 'She must have loved you so very much.'

'But I didn't love her, Clara. Not like I loved you. And she took your daughter.'

'I know, and out of all this mess that's what I find hardest to bear. But we must find it in our hearts to forgive her. She's gone, Philip. Nothing can bring back and put right the past.'

He stroked his chin. Clara was right, but he wished he could muster such forgiveness. She was indeed a very special person, but he had known that when he had first fallen in love with her. 'I'll try, Clara. I'll try very hard.'

She took a deep breath and swallowed hard. 'Does she know? Does . . . Cecily know any of this?'

He shook his head. 'I couldn't bring myself to tell her.'

'And you mustn't. She must never find out.' She lowered

her head. 'Oh, Philip. I long to rush to her now. Long to tell her I'm her true mother. But I can't, we can't, it wouldn't be fair. What Katherine did was wrong. So dreadfully wrong. But it's all got to die with her. We must be the only ones who know about this.'

He slowly nodded his head. 'If that's what you want.'

'Oh, it's not, Philip, it's not what I want. But this knowledge would strip Cecily of her identity. Strip her of everything she's ever believed in and held dear. I couldn't do it to her. I do love her, you see. Even though I thought she was dead, I never stopped loving her. Or you,' she added softly. 'Even with all I thought you had done to me, I never stopped loving you, Philip dear.'

His face crumpled. 'Oh, Clara. Me neither, me neither.'

He awkwardly rose from his chair and she stood and they hugged each other tightly, as if afraid to let go.

'Would you like to come and meet Cecily and her children?'

'Oh, Phips, could I? As their long-lost auntie?'

'If you're really sure that's what you want?'

She smiled. 'It's what has to be, and maybe we could all get to know each other . . . again.'

'Oh, Clara, that's what I would like more than anything. And who knows what the future might bring?' He held her at arm's length. 'You called me Phips. You remembered.'

'I never forgot.'

He hugged her again. 'Come on,' he said, taking her hand.

Chapter Thirty

It was Saturday evening and all the children, with the exception of young Bobbie who was being read a story by Clara before being put to bed, were sitting on a low factory wall not far from home. Jessie and Maureen were discussing the forthcoming tea party, Willy and Tony war tactics and the fact that now 'their' American soldiers were involved, 'Itler, if he had any sense, would do a runner. This they had deduced from listening to the adults.

Jessie was getting fed up with Maureen's insistence that as she had seen Jerome first, then it should be she who sat next to him. Jessie had been just about to point out scathingly that the likes of Jerome were not going to look at ten-year-old Maureen whether she sat next to him or not. Then she remembered her age was roughly the same.

She jumped off the wall and bent down to pull up her socks.

'I'm bored,' she announced. 'Whose comin' for a walk?'

'Where to?' asked Maureen.

'I dunno. You suggest.'

Maureen shrugged her shoulders as she jumped off the wall to join her. 'We can't go far,' she said, remembering the severe telling off regarding their escapade into town to see the parade. She wanted nothing to impede her attendance at the tea party. She wouldn't mind that happening to Jessie, but definitely not herself. 'You know we've bin warned.'

Jessie scowled. 'I know, but I'm still fed up and it's too early to go in.'

'What about the park?'

'I'm fed up with the park.'

'Well, you suggest then.'

Willy was bored also. He and Tony had spent a pleasant afternoon up the bomb site. He fingered the rip in the back of his short trousers. That still had to be spotted by adult eyes and he did not relish the ticking off he was bound to get for his carelessness. His pockets were bulging with useless bits and pieces which to him were precious and might come in useful. He should have added them to the rest of the collection he kept under his bed when they had gone in for tea but he had forgotten and hoped none was lost falling out of his pocket now.

He was about to suggest to Tony another game of soldiers but instead turned to the girls. 'What about up the 'skin?'

They spun round to face him. 'The 'skin?'

He sidled up to them, Tony close behind. 'Yeah, the old derelict sheepskin factory.' His face crinkled mischievously. 'We could play 'ide and seek.'

'Oh, could we?' asked Tony, excited.

'Yeah. It's a great place for that. It's got these old tanks sunk in the ground and they've still got smelly green stuff in the bottom.'

Maureen scowled at him hard. 'Since when 'ave you known about this place?'

Willy shuffled on his feet. 'Micky O'Malley showed it me. It used ter be 'is gang's headquarters, 'til 'e fell in a tank and 'is mam scalped his arse. 'Parently 'e didn't 'alf stink. You cold smell 'im right down the street and 'e had to stay in for a day while 'is mam washed and dried 'is clothes.'

At that they all laughed. Micky O'Malley was a bully and

anything horrible happening to him was a joy to hear.

'And you went up there wi' 'im?' demanded his sister.

''E made me, sis,' he said defensively. ''E said if I didn't go and help 'im find the bag of shrapnel 'e'd lost when 'e fell in the tank, 'e'd beat me up.'

Well Maureen could see the logic in Willy's going. Micky O'Malley's beatings were legendary. He was as tough as they came, and if he demanded you did something, you did it or else.

'You won't tell Dad, will yer?' he asked, worried, wishing he'd never opened his mouth about the 'skin.

Suddenly this unseen old sheepskin factory took on an aura of adventure. Jessie and Maureen looked at each other. At least it was better than sitting on a factory wall arguing over the forthcoming tea party.

'Not if yer tek us and show us this place, we won't, will we, Jessie?' said Maureen.

'No, not if you show us we won't.'

Willy sniffed, he had no choice. 'Okay. But yer promise if Micky O'Malley and 'is gang are there, we scarper?'

'Yeah, yeah,' they all promised simultaneously.

Just then Polly, her arm linked through her friend Janey Greenwood's, walked up to them. The children gazed at her in awe. How she had changed since starting work. The old Polly with her lank straight hair, socks round her ankles, and a hem that was forever coming down, had disappeared. Polly had matured. She now had a chest. Well, the beginnings of one at any rate, and the bit she had was more than Jessie and Maureen possessed. They were both envious. She and her friend looked identical, dressed in navy blue skirts and white blouses, their hair rolled up at the sides, the rest left to flow down their backs.

Willy sniggered. 'What's that on yer lips, our Polly?' He pointed. 'And look at 'er legs. You've missed a bit, our Polly.'

Polly blushed. She had painstakingly rubbed away at an old red leather bound book and transferred the dye to her lips. It hadn't tasted very nice. Her legs were covered in a coating of gravy browning, not very successfully according to her little brother. She hoped any lads they encountered did not have such an eagle eye.

'Shuddup,' she hissed, and glanced at them all suspiciously. 'What a' you lot up to?'

'N'ote,' they all responded.

'Well, make sure you ain't. Come on, Janey,' she said, tugging her friend's arm. 'Let's leave the "children" ter play.'

'Goin' lookin' fer lads?' shouted Maureen after them.

The children all giggled.

Willy guided them down several streets and through several alleyways. Maureen started to get the jitters. None of them had bothered to enquire how far this place was: besides it was beginning to grow dark and the adventure was beginning to lose its appeal. She wanted to start her ablutions in readiness for looking her best tomorrow. She was going to rag her hair, scrub her face and tweeze her eyebrows with the tweezers she had nicked off Polly, who she hoped wouldn't notice before she managed to put them back.

'A' we nearly there yet?' she grumbled as they climbed over a low wall.

Willy pointed his finger. 'There,' he said proudly.

The old factory, surrounded by rows of terraced houses, was dilapidated to say the least. And it was near the canal. They could see water glistening with rays from the sun as it was slowly disappearing behind the buildings.

They all rushed towards it then slowed their pace, listening out for other presences.

Luckily there was none.

A happy hour was spent skipping between the old sunken tanks, the bottoms of which were still filled with the green slime Willy had described. They all laughed again, visualising Micky O'Malley falling inside and climbing out looking like the monster from hell. There was a huge pile of debris to hide behind, piles of bricks and fallen timbers. This was better than the bomb site.

Finally it was decided to play one more game before they had to get home and their absence was discovered.

Tony, hiding behind a large plank of wood, could hear Willy approaching. He grimaced. He didn't want to be the first caught. He wanted, just once, to win. Crouching down, he moved backwards, skirting many abandoned objects until he came to a stop against the factory wall. Stooping down, he flattened himself behind an old metal truck. They would never find him here. And they could call until they begged him. He wasn't going to come out.

Five minutes passed and Tony sighed. He was getting fed up now, waiting to be discovered. In the distance, he could hear Jessie's, Maureen's and Will's aggravated voices as they upturned objects, looking under and behind in their search for him. Crouching, he was beginning to stiffen. He straightened up and looked around. The old red-brick walls were crumbling and looked ready to fall down. Already most of the roof had disappeared. He liked this place, it was full of mystery. Suddenly in the gloom his gaze alighted on a window, the frame of which had rotted though the glass pane was intact. He went over to investigate.

Jessie spotted him first. He was standing on tiptoe peering through a window. With no thought as to why, she crept up and grabbed his shoulder. 'Gotcha!' she yelled. ''E's 'ere,' she yelled again to the others.

Tony jumped in shock and nearly lost his balance.

Jessie stared at him. 'What's up?'

Gawping, he pointed to the window.

Jessie, eyebrows raised, went over and looked through it.

She was gawping too when Willy and Maureen reached them.

'Look through the window,' she said. 'Go on, look,' she demanded.

They did as they were told.

'It's a miracle,' Jessie said, clasping her hands in delight. 'It's a true miracle.' She raised her eyes upwards as though expecting the Angel Gabriel to appear, trumpets and a chorus of 'Hallelujah' to sound.

Bunched together, they all stared through the window. Piled higher than they could see were precious black lumps they knew to be coal.

'It is a miracle, it is,' Maureen whispered in agreement.

They all turned from the wall and huddled together.

'Who's is it, d'yer reckon?' Willy asked.

The rest shrugged their shoulders. 'Dunno.'

'What d'yer reckon we should do?' Maureen asked.

They all stood silent for a moment, all thinking the same. They all knew that the procuring of coal was a constant worry and this miraculous happening across a lifetime's supply was a gift sent from God.

Little did they realise that in actual fact this gift from God was the Government allocation for the clothing factory further down, which kept its boilers stoked to run the machinery that made clothing for the forces.

Their thoughts didn't reach that far. All their minds could visualise was the happiness it would bring to countless families, including their own, should this discovery be shared.

'We can't tell no one,' Maureen said, worried. 'We shouldn't be 'ere for a start and it might belong to someone.'

'Of course it belongs to someone,' Jessie hissed, annoyed. 'But how are they gonna use all that lot themselves? It ain't fair when Auntie Grace and your dad ain't got none hardly.'

'No, it ain't,' the rest agreed.

424

They all stood silent again.

Jessie pursed her lips, her mind working overtime. They should just grab whatever they could find and take as much as they could carry, she suggested.

'It's stealing,' Maureen frowned.

'No, it ain't,' Jessie said firmly. 'We're always being told ter share what we've got. Well, whoever the coal belongs to should share wi' us. He's got far more than 'e can use anyway and he won't miss it unless 'e's counted all the lumps.'

They went back to the window and stared through it. Jessie was right. If anyone had anything extra in the neighbourhood it was shared with whoever was the most desperate, and at this time there were no people more desperate for this life-giving substance than their own families. Auntie Grace herself was worried witless as to how she was going to burn a decent fire in honour of their visitors. The answer to her problem was staring them in the face. Jessie was right. This was not stealing, not in the normal sense at any rate.

A plan was quickly formulated; the rotting window pushed through; vessels gathered, including an old rusty tin bath which Maureen and Jessie heaved between them, constantly worried their arms would drop off; some smelly old sacking found to cover their hoard.

How they managed to struggle through the now dark streets without being questioned was another miracle, especially considering the state they were all in. But they did so by keeping as much as possible in the shadows and following a slightly longer route down alleyways running past the backs of terraced houses. And the coal, more than a month's supply, was divided between two coal sheds as giggles of mirth were stifled, legs crossed for fear of wetting themselves, and the fuel stacked as quietly as they could, constantly worried of alerting the adults.

The task complete, they stood in Grace's entry, looking in

dismay at the state of their clothes. Until now they hadn't given a thought to that.

Again Jessie had the answer. They would go back and jump in the tanks. The green slime would do the trick. They were going to get in trouble for being late anyway. They could say they happened upon the factory by accident and Tony fell in and they all jumped in after to pull him out.

It would have to do. No other explanation they managed to come up with was as infallible as that.

It was not a pleasant thought, but the only one that would guarantee hiding the truth.

The very next morning Grace opened the door to the coal shed and her mouth fell open in shock. She called her mother and they both stood gawping. They questioned the children, but of course no one had any idea how the coal got there. Two doors down at the Rudneys' the very same happened.

The truth never did come out. The business of the mystery coal benefactor remained a mystery.

They did however, several weeks later, venture back again, but the window had been sealed. Ah, well, the pleasure the coal had brought had been more than worth the trouble they had all got into for 'falling' in the tanks. But then, after all, they had saved Tony.

The tea party was a great success. Maureen and Jessie, dressed in their best, hair brushed and wavy from rags, faces scrubbed, eyebrows tweezed, both got to sit next to Jerome.

'Their' American soldiers both turned up promptly at three, bearing gifts of a tin of whole turkey, several bars of chocolate and another tin filled with bacon. Having not seen such luxuries, let alone been able to afford them for many a long year, eyes widened in appreciation.

'Well, we know you Brits have had a hard time,' Nat had said, smiling. 'It's the least we could do.'

They left with a firm promise to return. Jerome, somewhat embarrassed by the attention he had received from the girls, was sceptical, but Nat was more than happy to oblige. Grace, Willy and Tony reminded him so much of his family back home. This family's friendship, he knew, would help to lessen the gnawing ache of longing he constantly felt for them.

He began to visit whenever possible, always bearing gifts, knowing whatever he brought helped to ease their constant misery over the meagre rations allotted. And it gave him so much pleasure to see Grace's eyes light up.

Little did he realise that for one person at least his growing attachment to the Wilkins family was causing resentment. Tom, although he had taken to Nat, try as he might could not help noticing the twinkle this tall good-looking American lieutenant bought to Grace's blue eyes, and could not stop a jealous lump sticking in his own throat.

Chapter Thirty-One

By the time 1943 arrived little had changed. Life for the inhabitants of the war-ravaged island of Britain continued the same. Constantly worried for loved ones abroad; constantly struggling to warm, feed and clothe themselves; constantly worried what Hitler and his allies would throw at them next. They had witnessed so much, heard so much, what else was left? The end to it all seemed as far away as ever.

Charlie stepped out of the dance hall, her face flushed, legs tired from Jitterbugging for the past several hours. Sybil caught hold of her arm and huddled into her friend's side for warmth.

She was giggling from the alcohol the Americans never seemed short of. 'What happened to that bloke you were with?' she asked Charlie. 'I thought he wa' a cracker. Did he ask for a date?'

She smiled as she turned up her collar. 'Yes, he did ask for a date, but I'm not going.'

'Yer not? Why?'

'He had hands like an octopus.'

'Did he? Oh? Yer should have passed him ter me!'

Both girls giggled as they hurried down the dark street. Charlie's back was beginning to ache from constantly being thrown under legs and over shoulders whilst doing the Jitterbug. These Americans sure knew how to dance and enjoy themselves, and throughout the whole evening they had been surrounded by men insistent that it was their turn for a dance. Charlie had enjoyed herself, as had the rest of the gang from the factory. The talk tomorrow would consist completely of latest conquests or lack of them.

Over the last few months Charlie herself had had several dates with very nice men, but no one she had wanted to become attached to. Sybil was often chiding her for being too choosy, but she could live with the jibes.

At this moment all she wanted to do was get home and climb into bed. They had to be up at five-thirty and it was now well past midnight and they had a good way to walk.

On rounding a corner all hell seemed to break loose. They had walked slap bang into a fight. It was too dark to tell what group was fighting which. Was it white Americans against black Americans, British against the others? It was impossible to tell, landing as they had done right in the thick of it.

Before they had a chance to turn and run in the opposite direction, the girls became separated and Charlie had to dodge this way and that to avoid flailing arms, falling bodies, and a good thump herself.

She suddenly felt her arm being grabbed and before she had a chance to do anything found herself being dragged down the street. She was thrust into a doorway and a hand clamped over her mouth.

'Shush!' a voice demanded.

She froze, eyes darting above the large hand clamped over her mouth, ears alert.

Finally the hand was released and she breathed freely.

'You're safe now,' a deep male voice said.

She turned and her eyes travelled upwards, resting on his face. 'Oh!' she exclaimed in alarm.

He raised his hand, stepping backward, his tall frame coming to rest against the wall of the doorway. 'Please don't be afraid,' the American drawl begged. 'I didn't mean to frighten you . . .'

'It's all right, really it is,' Charlie interrupted. 'I just got a shock.'

'Yes, I must be.'

'No, you're not, really. And thank you for what you did.'

'It was my pleasure, Miss . . . er . . .?'

She held out her hand. 'Charlotte Wilkins. But I'm called Charlie by my friends.'

Grinning broadly, he accepted her hand and shook firmly, his white teeth sparkling in the pitch darkness. 'Jethro Bartholomew White.' He laughed at her expression. 'My mother is to blame for the Jethro, she's a God fearing woman. My grandfather for the Bartholomew, and my great-grandfather for the White. I'm known as Kit.'

'Kit?'

'Yeah. My buddies at base call me that 'cos I used to have trouble handling my kit. Just couldn't seem to get it all inside my kitbag.'

She laughed at this. 'Hello, Kit. I'm pleased to meet you. Very relieved in fact.'

She released her hand from his firm grip and turned from him. Inching towards the edge of the doorway, she peeked out. 'Do you think it's safe now?'

He joined her. 'Yeah. The MPs will have rounded them all up and bundled them off.'

She bit her bottom lip anxiously. 'My friend? I wonder what's happened to her?'

'She ran off in the other direction. I saw her. I think she thought you were following.'

'Oh,' said Charlie worriedly. 'I hope she's all right.'

'She looked like a woman who could take care of herself.'

Charlie looked up at him, conscious of large brown eyes fringed with near black lashes gazing back at her. Her heart lurched. Kit was a very handsome man. She abruptly turned away to gaze once again down the empty street. 'Sybil can hold her own,' she said, swallowing hard.

She took a deep breath and turned once more to him, holding out her hand again. 'Well, thanks, Kit.'

He took her hand. 'I'll walk you home.'

The thought appealed to her. 'It's a long way,' she said, hoping the fact didn't put him off.

'Well, in that case I certainly will, ma'am. You shouldn't be walking the streets alone at this time of night. What would happen if you got stuck in the middle of another fight?' He grinned. 'And me not there to save you.'

Charlie's heartbeat soared.

She closed the door and leaned back against the passage wall. Sybil was home, she could hear her snoring upstairs. She closed her eyes, sighing dreamily. It was nearly time to get up and dress for work, but she did not care. She was in love. She, Charlie Wilkins, was well and truly smitten.

During the walk home Kit had protectively held her hand and she felt it belonged there. Her hand had been waiting all this time just for his. They had talked with a closeness usually achieved during a long association, not one of several minutes. He had told her of his family, poor farming folk, eking out a living from a tiny farmstead surrounded by the majestic backdrop of the State of Montana. Contrary to belief, not all Americans were rich. Of his hope to become a lawyer; of his struggle to pay his way through college by working long hours in drug stores and gas stations. The intervention of the war and America's involvement had temporarily put a stop to his plans.

Charlie had listened, her respect for this man growing.

She then told him of her own family and of their painful estrangement. Of how she missed her mother and hoped one day to be reunited. He said he understood, and she knew he did. During his life, he had seen and witnessed many awful things. His philosophy was that life was filled with trials of many different kinds. It was how you turned those trials into triumphs and benefited as a result, that counted.

She had never met a man like him before. He was everything she had ever hoped for and more. She felt so drawn to him. He had a depth to him, a sincerity, but also a sense of humour. How they had laughed. No man had ever made her laugh like that before.

She hadn't hesitated when he had asked to see her again. In fact, if he hadn't been bold enough to ask her, she would have asked him.

Charlie sighed again. She couldn't wait.

Chapter Thirty-Two

The knock on the door resounded loudly.

'Sit where you are and finish your tea,' Grace ordered the children as she rose, wiping her mouth on a napkin.

'I'll go,' offered Connie.

Ida said nothing, just continued shovelling down the food she had turned her nose up at when it had been placed before her moments earlier.

'Finish your tea, Mam, before it gets cold. I'll soon get rid of whoever it is.'

She opened the door to a blast of cold air. October 1943 was windy and wet, and tonight it was foggy. A thick fog, damp and clinging.

The woman at the door was wet and tired, desperate to curl up in a comfortable chair before a roaring fire. She blew her nose on her handkerchief whilst looking at Grace apologetically.

'Mrs Wilkins?'

Grace nodded.

She stuffed the handkerchief into her pocket and held out her hand. 'Mrs Warner. I'm from the council. I'm sorry to be calling so late but I wanted to be sure to catch you. You're out at work all day, I understand?'

Grace frowned. 'Yes, that's right.' Council, she thought rapidly. What on earth was a woman from the council doing

435

calling at this time of the evening? Then it suddenly occurred to her. 'Oh, I gave up the allotment a couple of years ago. When my husband went off to war. That's not a problem is it?'

Mrs Warner stared at her. 'Allotment? I haven't come about any allotment. No, it's the children.'

Grace clutched her hand to her chest. 'Children! You mean Jessie and Tony?'

Mrs Warner consulted some notes. 'Yes, that's right. Evacuees. Their mother was . . . well, she's no longer with us,' she said matter-of-factly. 'And you've been taking care of them in the interim.'

Interim? What did she mean, interim?

'Can I come in?'

'Er . . . yes, yes, please do,' Grace mumbled, standing aside.

'It's been very good of you,' Mrs Warner was saying as she walked down the passage. 'The Council are very obliged for the way you got stuck in.' She turned and patted Grace's arm. 'It was very good of you. Mind you, in these desperate times we all have to muck in, don't we?'

'Good of me? Stuck in? What do you mean?'

'About the children. How you took them in. Are they in here? Ah, yes. Hello, children. My name's Mrs Warner and I've some good news for you.' She spoke as though addressing two four year olds.

The children, mouths full of bread scraped with marge and sprinkled with a little sugar, stared at her blankly, then looked across at Grace who was standing bewildered behind her, as though to say: 'What's she going on about?'

Grace's hand suddenly shot to her mouth as the reason for the visit dawned.

'You've found a relative?' she asked hesitantly.

Connie's face fell.

Mrs Warner swung round. 'Yes, that's right, dear. An uncle.' She turned back to the children. 'Uncle Ernie.'

Jessie and Tony looked at each other then back at Mrs Warner. 'Uncle Ernie?'

'Yes, your mother's elder brother.'

'But he's . . .' began Jessie.

'Yes, that's right, dear,' she interrupted. 'He's been invalided out of the war and as soon as he found out about his poor sister, he got in touch with us. He's got a nice little flat and can't wait for you both to go and live with him.'

Ida's face lit up in delight. 'Now ain't that nice, kids? Going 'ome where yer belong.'

Connie glared at her; Grace was too distraught to hear what she said.

'We don't wanna go,' said Jessie flatly.

'Oh, don't be silly, child,' Mrs Warner replied disapprovingly. 'Of course you want to go. Mrs Wilkins can't look after you forever.'

'Well, we ain't going,' Jessie announced, her face set firmly.

'No, we ain't,' echoed Tony.

Mrs Warner smiled sweetly at them and turned to face Grace.

'Due to the circumstances Mr Moss, that's the uncle's name, has got a special permit to travel and is coming tomorrow. Have the children ready, please. We'll pick them up around two. That suit you? Good.'

'But just a minute, Mrs Warner. Have you checked this man out? Will he treat the children all right?'

'Oh, for goodness' sake. Of course we've checked him out! Well, as much as we can do, records being what they are at the moment. And he is their uncle. Of course he's going to treat them all right.' She looked at Grace as though she was an idiot. 'Well, I must be going. More things to do, you know, before I get home tonight. Goodbye, children. I hope

437

you've enjoyed your stay in Leicester. Don't worry, I'll see myself out.'

Grace sank down in her chair at the table. She pushed away her half-finished plate of food.

'We ain't going, Auntie Grace. We don't really have to, do we?' Jessie asked.

'Course you do,' Ida interrupted. 'You 'eard what that woman from the Council said. Yer uncle's comin' ter get yer. You don't mess wi' people from the Council.'

'Oh, shut up, you interfering old woman!' hissed Connie. 'Mother!'

'Don't Mother me. This woman 'as never liked the children. She's irritated the life out of 'em since the day they arrived.' Connie pushed her face into Ida's. 'Can't you see the kids are upset? They love my Grace like a mother. How d'yer think they feel, being told they're goin' ter live with an uncle they ain't seen fer years?'

Ida's face turned thunderous. 'Well, it's better they go now than be thrown out when my Bernard gets back. 'E won't tolerate strangers in 'is 'ouse.' She smirked at Connie. 'I'm not even sure 'e'll put up wi' you.'

Connie gawped. 'Why, you . . .'

'That's enough,' Grace cried. 'Just stop, stop it!'

Connie stared at her remorsefully. 'I'm sorry, me duck.'

'I know, Mam, I know.'

'Well, I ain't,' Ida spat, rising stiffly. 'The sooner they go the better, as far as I'm concerned.'

She shuffled from the room and her bedroom door slammed shut.

'I'll swing fer 'er, Grace. So I will.'

'No, you won't, Mam. She ain't worth it.' Grace stared hopelessly at the children. 'I'm sorry, kids, there's nothing I can do. I'm not even a relative, you see.'

Tony started to cry. 'But what about Willy and Maureen?

I'll miss 'em, I will. And Mr Tom. And Granny Apple. And soldier Nat.' He scraped back his chair, ran round the table and threw his arms around Grace's neck, hugging her tightly as he sobbed into her shoulder. 'I'll miss you most of all. I love you, Auntie Grace.'

A lump the size of a walnut formed in her throat. 'I love you too,' she whispered.

Sybil stared at Charlie, astounded. 'You ain't, Charlie?'

'I am. The doctor confirmed it this morning.'

Sybil sighed deeply. 'What does Kit say about it?'

'I told him last night and he's as delighted as me. He's asked me to marry him.'

Sybil sighed again in deep relief. 'Oh, that's all right then.' Her eyes filled with concern. It was all right Charlie announcing proudly that she was having a baby, but had she thought of all the consequences? For a start the baby's father was a foreigner. 'But have you thought about the fact that he's . . . well, he's . . .'

'In the US Army,' Charlie cut in. 'And could be killed? We've talked about that and we still want to get married.'

'But, Charlie, he's . . .'

'Yes, I know, Sybil. I'm fully aware of what people will say. He's marrying me because I'm having a baby. But that's not true. We love each other. I love that man more than anything. Baby or not, we'd still have got married. When the war's over, he's coming to Britain to live. Well, he can, can't he? He'll be married to a British citizen and he'll finish his degree. He's going to be a lawyer,' she said proudly. 'And I'll support him all the way.'

'Well, as long as yer happy, Charlie.' Sybil grinned broadly. 'I must admit, I fancy him myself. You make a great couple.'

'Thank you. You're happy for me then?'

Sybil nodded. 'Yes, I'm happy for you, gel. Just hope it

don't turn out like my little angels, eh?'

Charlie patted her stomach. 'I'll be more than happy if it does. You have great kids.'

'Ta. I think so too.'

Sybil paused thoughtfully. 'What about yer mam? You ought to tell her.'

Charlie lowered her head. 'Yes, I should. But I can't. I still don't understand why she didn't contact me, especially after that letter I wrote, the one I gave to my Granny Wilkins.'

'Ah, well, see how you feel later. You might change your mind. I'll always come with yer. Somebody's got to break the ice and she's a right to know she's about to be a granny.'

Yes, thought Charlie. In normal circumstances her mother would have been delighted at the knowledge she was about to become a grandmother. But there was nothing normal about any of this.

'Thanks, Sybil,' she said sincerely. 'I'll remember that.'

'A' yer seeing Kit tonight?'

Charlie's face fell forlornly. 'No. We had arranged to but he sent word to the factory. His Commander has stepped up training and he has to stay at base. He'll come round as soon as he can.'

'Oh, right. Looks like a good book then fer the pair of us, don't it? And you'd better put yer feet up. Remember, you've two to think of now.'

Charlie laughed. 'Yes I have, haven't I?'

Chapter Thirty-Three

Grace was sitting by the fireside. She laid the book she was reading down on her lap and stared into the fire. The children had been gone nearly three months and no word of their welfare had she received. She was desperate for news. Just a few words would do, to put her mind at rest.

Christmas had passed, the worst she had ever spent. It would have been bleak anyway, not being able to spare much for presents. But without the children it had been dreadful. Connie had done her best to cheer up the proceedings, as had Tom and Clara who had invited them all, even Ida, to join them on Christmas Day. Grace had gone, sharing what food they had, trying to make things special, but her heart hadn't been in it and neither had the others'. They all missed Jessie and Tony. Except Ida. She continually wore a smug look of satisfaction across her spiteful face.

Grace smiled as she thought of Clara. It was as if a miracle had happened. After all the pain and suffering those two dear people had gone through, against all the odds they were back together, just as they should have been over forty years ago. Clara, though, was insisting on taking things easy. She didn't want to rush matters, she had confided in Grace.

'I want to be courted. I want to have just a little of what I missed in my youth. Is that selfish, Grace dear?'

'No,' she had replied. 'It's romantic.'

Besides, Clara felt strongly about her commitment to Tom. She had said she would care for his children and would see that through, for a while still at least. Grace admired her and hoped Clara and Philip had many years of happiness before them.

Her head jerked as she realised someone had entered the room.

'Oh, Tom,' she sighed, relieved.

'I did knock,' he said apologetically.

'Tom, since when have you had to do that? You're like one of the family. Come and sit down.'

He looked around. 'Where's everybody?'

'Mam's in bed. She's tired. She's been tired since the kids left. I think it's affected her more than she'll admit. Looking after them helped to ease the pain of losing my dad. Ida's down the pub, no doubt, gossiping to her cronies.' She looked at him as he sat in the armchair opposite. 'You seem excited about something.'

'I am, Grace. I've had a letter from me boys.'

'Barry and Dennis?' Her face lit up. 'I am glad for you, Tom. How are they?'

'Seem well enough. Took the news of their mam badly, but that's ter be expected.'

'Any sign of them coming home on leave?'

'Not by the sound of it. This letter,' he held out an envelope, 'took two months to get 'ere. The one I sent months back explaining about Bessie took longer than that. It chased 'em all over the place.' He grimaced. 'Reading between the lines, I've a feeling they're in Italy.'

'Italy!' Her face fell. 'Oh, God, Tom, it's bad over there.'

'I know. But there's worse places, Grace. They could be in one of them concentration camps. We've all seen what the Nazis do ter prisoners.' With an effort he planted a smile on his face. 'Anyway, they couldn't say much, not wi' censorship, but they're both fine. At the time of this letter at any rate.'

'Good, Tom, good. Let's hope they'll be home soon, eh?'

'I can't wait, Grace.' He suddenly stared at her, alarmed. 'You've been crying.'

'No, I haven't,' she denied quickly. 'Got something in my eye.'

'Pull the other one, gel. It's those kids, ain't it?'

She sniffed. 'Yes, Tom, it is. I miss them so dreadfully. If only I knew they were all right.'

'What makes yer think they ain't?'

She shrugged her shoulders. 'No reason. Mr Moss seemed a nice enough man and very fond of the children. Only . . .'

'Only what?'

'Well, I've said this to you before and you think I'm being . . . well, just like a woman, as you men put it. It was the children's attitude. They wouldn't take his hand.'

'Well, like I've said before, what's strange about that?'

'Well, children do. If they feel safe and secure they take your hand. They didn't. They didn't even rush to welcome him when he arrived.'

'There's n'ote strange in that either. They hadn't seen him for at least three years.'

'I know, I know. But they seemed frightened.'

'Rubbish, Grace, you're making it up. You want to think they were frightened.'

She stared at him, shocked. 'Do I? Is that what you think?'

'I don't know what ter think, Grace. But the authorities wouldn't 'ave handed them over if they weren't 'appy.' He leaned over and patted her knee. 'Let them go, Grace, and get on with yer own life.'

She nodded and sighed. 'I know you're right, Tom. I'll try.'

He stared at her thoughtfully. This uncle was called Ernest

Moss and lived somewhere in Brixton. That was as much as Grace herself knew. His eyes travelled over the top of her head to fix blankly on the wall opposite. He had to take a trip down that way next week, according to his schedule. What if he paid a call? Couldn't be too many Mosses living in that area. Someone was bound to know where they lived.

It suddenly struck him. The woman from the Council was sure to have an address. He would go round and ask. But then, he thought, she might try and stop him, say it could upset the children. No, he'd do it all himself. For the sake of Grace's peace of mind, he'd go. Damn the extra time and petrol. Somehow he'd make an excuse to cover his tracks to his boss. Besides, it would be nice to see the kids again. He'd missed them himself, little rascals. Life around here had quietened down considerably since his own children had lost their partners in crime.

He smiled to himself. It certainly wasn't the same without them. The escapades they had all got up to had given them all a good laugh, after the children were out of the way of course. He felt it best not to tell Grace of his plan. Just in case something unforeseen stopped him from going.

His thoughts moved on to other matters and he shifted uncomfortably in his seat. 'Er . . . Grace?'

'Mmmm?' she said thoughtfully.

He took a deep breath. He wanted to ask her to go to the pub with him on Saturday night. They had a sing-song around the piano and he thought she needed to get out, take her mind off things for a couple of hours. And having her to escort would give him so much pleasure.

'Yes, Tom?' she prompted.

Her lovely blue eyes settled on him, her inviting mouth smiled – and his nerve left him completely.

'Oh . . . er . . . nothing. It were nothing.' He rose. 'Well, I must be off.'

She stared at him. 'You don't have to go. Stay and have a cuppa.'

'No, I'd better be off. Clara's meeting Mr Janson tonight. They're having supper together. Won't be long afore those two are wed, you mark my words.'

'And I'll be so happy for them.'

'Yeah, me too, although when that 'appens we'll all miss Clara. She's bin a Godsend, there's no doubt of that. I suppose I should start lookin' for someone else.' He walked to the door. 'See yer soon, Grace.'

'Yes, 'bye, Tom,' she said thoughtfully.

'A' you blind or what, our Grace?'

She swung her body round to see her mother standing in the other doorway. 'Pardon?'

Connie advanced, tightening the belt on her dressing gown. 'I said, a' you blind. That man's in love with you, our Grace,' she said, sitting down to rest her aching feet on the hearth.

'Mam, really!'

'I'm telling yer. You listen to yer mother. And if I'm not mistaken, you rather like 'im.'

'Mam, stop it, I'm a married woman. Tom and I are just friendly neighbours.'

'Yeah,' said Connie, unconvinced. She reached down and rubbed her legs. 'Got any of that liniment, Grace love? Me legs are killing me.'

Chapter Thirty-Four

Charlie was crying. Her shoulders shook and her body heaved in total despair. Sybil, who had just walked into the Ladies' to snatch a crafty cigarette, heard the sobs and after listening for a moment recognised them as her friend's. She thumped on the door.

'Charlie, is that you? What on earth's wrong, gel?'

'Nothin'. Go away, Sybil.'

'I'm not goin' anywhere 'til yer tell me what's the matter. Is someone dead?'

'No.'

'It's not the baby, is it?'

'No.'

'Well, what then?' she demanded.

'Leave me alone, please,' begged Charlie between sobs.

'I'm warnin' yer. Either open this bloody door or I'll crawl underneath.' Sybil glanced down at the none too wide space. 'And you know what'll 'appen. I'll get stuck, then I'll have ter scream me head off fer someone to rescue us. So if yer don't want all the factory knowing, yer'd better open the door.'

There was a pause and she heard the bolt slide across.

She pushed it open and squashed herself inside, locking the door behind her.

Charlie was sitting on the toilet, doubled over, hands covering her face; boiler suit and knickers round her ankles. But she didn't care what predicament Sybil found her in, she was too distressed to be bothered.

Sybil squatted down and placed her hand on her bare knee. 'What is it, Charlie?' she spoke worriedly.

Another wave of heart-wrenching sobs overtook her. 'Oh, Syb. It's Kit. He's gone.'

'I bloody knew it, the bastard!' she erupted. 'These Yanks are all the same. Get what they want then they scarper. I tried ter warn yer. He's probably married already, with a dozen kids back home.'

Charlie's head jerked up, her blotchy face and puffy eyes filled with anger. 'No, he ain't. How dare you speak about my Kit like that? It's his unit. They've gone abroad to fight. It's top secret so I've no idea where he's gone or when he'll be back. All I got was a scribbled note left with the guard on the gates.'

'Oh! Oh, I see. I'm sorry, Charlie. I didn't mean . . .'

She shuddered and her face softened. 'It's all right, Syb. I can't blame you for thinking that.' She sniffed forlornly, her eyes again filling with tears. 'What am I going to do? Oh, Sybil, I miss him already.'

Sybil sighed helplessly and tried to rise so she could put her arms around Charlie for comfort but the confined space caused her to stumble and she grabbed hold of the first thing she could lay hands on to steady herself. It just happened to be the toilet chain. The ancient tank rumbled loudly before it dispensed its water.

Charlie stared up at her. 'Now me bum's all wet,' she wailed.

Sybil clutched her hand to her mouth, in severe danger of collapsing with laughter. As she tried to control herself she scanned Charlie's face. 'Well, by the looks on yer, gel, there's only yer middle now left that's dry. Maybe I should get a bucket of water and finish the job?'

Charlie stared at her blankly, then dissolved into tears again. 'Oh, Syb,' she cried. 'How could you?'

'Ah, come on, Charlie. You're just feeling sorry fer yerself. You ain't the only one this is 'appening to. I ain't seen my old man fer nearly four years. How the bloody 'ell d'yer think I feel, eh?'

'Sybil, I'm so sorry. But it don't make this any easier.'

'Nor does crying yerself silly. Now come on, pull yerself together. And for God's sake pull yer drawers up, people might think we're funny.'

Charlie sniffed loudly as she struggled to rise and adjusted her clothes.

Sybil placed her arm around her. 'Come on, cheer up. You've the baby to think of.'

'I know. But I can't think how I'm going to cope on my own.'

'On yer own?' Sybil said, hurt. 'You ain't on yer own. I'll be 'ere for yer. We'll see it through together.'

Charlie raised her eyes in gratitude. 'Will you, Sybil?'

'Yeah, 'course. I'm yer friend, ain't I? And by the time Kit gets back, 'e'll 'ave a bonny baby ter bounce on 'is knee.'

Charlie smiled wanly. 'If he does come back.'

'Eh, that's enough. Now come on and swill yer face with cold water and let's get back before they send out the search party. Eh, and put a smile on that face a'yourn. You look like you're off to a funeral.'

Nat took Grace's hands. 'I'll miss you.'

She tried to smile. 'And we'll miss you too. Thanks for all the stuff you brought us. It didn't half come in handy. In fact, I don't know what I'd have done without it.'

'It was my pleasure.' He smiled over at Connie sitting in the armchair. 'My welcome into your family has made my stay here so much easier. I had something to look forward to, coming here. It's all right for the youngsters, brawling down the pub and chasing the broads, but me, give me a fireside any day and two lovely ladies to chat to.'

'Ged away with yer,' Connie grinned, flapping her hand. 'You be sure to give that wife of yours our regards. We've heard so much about her and your sons, we feel we know 'em, don't we, Grace?'

'We do. And when this war's over, you must all come and visit. We can't offer you much but you're welcome any time,' she said sincerely.

'And you to us. You'd love the States, Grace, and you, Connie. Everything is so big compared to here.'

'Yes,' Grace laughed. 'You've told us often enough. Your shoe boxes are bigger than our houses.'

He grinned. 'Well, not quite,' he said sheepishly.

Grace stared at him searchingly. 'So, Nat, do you know where you're off to? Oh, sorry, I shouldn't ask.'

'No, you shouldn't.' He eyed them both. 'But I know I can trust you. I've a feeling it's Italy, but that's all I can say.'

'Oh, that's where Tom thinks his lads are. Maybe you'll all meet up, eh? Wouldn't that be nice.' Her eyes softened. 'Nat, please take care.'

'Yeah,' Connie echoed. 'You watch yer back. And yer secret's safe with us,' she sniffed haughtily. 'Being's Ida's not here at any rate.'

'Oh, talking of Ida, say my goodbyes for me, please.' He smiled warmly at Grace. 'She's to be pitied, that woman, Grace. She's lonely.'

'Lonely?' interjected Connie. 'Wouldn't surprise me if she'd never had a friend in her life the way she carries on.'

'Mam!'

'Don't Mam me, it's true.'

Nat laughed. 'Well, I'd better run. I shouldn't have come

at all. We're leaving in a couple of hours. But I couldn't go without saying goodbye. Oh, and I mustn't forget Tom and the kids.' He laughed. 'How could anyone forget those kids?'

She smiled. The Rudney children would miss him too. 'I'll say goodbye for you.'

Grace walked him to his Jeep parked at the front.

Before he climbed in he took her in his arms and kissed her lightly on the cheek. 'Well, you take care of yourselves, and I hope that husband of yours comes home safely.'

'Yes, so do I,' she said, wishing she felt more sincere. She reached up and kissed him back.

He turned from her, climbed inside his vehicle, started it up and waved as he sped down the road.

She waved back until he had disappeared around the corner, then pulling up the corner of her pinafore, wiped a tear from her eyes and slowly made her way indoors.

Engrossed in their goodbyes neither Grace nor Nat saw Tom emerge from his front door.

He froze on spotting them in the embrace, his heart sinking rapidly as he watched Grace kiss the American. He was filled with despair on witnessing her tears as Nat drove away.

Tom climbed forlornly into his lorry and stared through the windscreen. That would teach him, he thought sadly. That would teach him a severe lesson for ever thinking there could ever be anything more between himself and Grace than just friends and neighbours.

Many hours later, his load dropped off and having managed to wangle some extra petrol from a garage owner he had grown friendly with over his years as a lorry driver – more than likely the garage owner had been swayed by the half dozen eggs he had also managed to procure on his journey down – he set off for unknown territory: Brixton.

His mood had lightened considerably by the time he

reached the outskirts of the borough. After passing through miles of destruction, knowing that as he ventured further he would witness far worse, he began to feel lucky to be alive, lucky he still had his house and his children to fuss over. Lucky that he still had Grace as a friend. 'You'd call me a stupid fool, Bessie,' he whispered to himself, then took a deep breath. 'Now let's find those kids.'

Parking the lorry in a cul-de-sac and locking it securely, he set off, not quite sure where he was headed, amazed at the similarity of these rows of houses to the ones back home. The only difference was that these houses were grey-brick and grimy as opposed to red-brick and grimy.

Shabby children played in the streets, the very same games – hopscotch, football, cricket – that the shabby children back home played. Women with turbaned heads pulled washing from lines strung across the streets and gossiped in doorways, even though it was cold. Every so often vast areas of bomb-damaged houses and buildings appeared, and it bought a lump to Tom's throat to see bewildered citizens still picking over and digging through the rubble of what was left of their homes.

He had asked at least a dozen passers-by, called in quite a few shops and popped inside several public houses before he got his first lead.

'Ernest Moss?' The old timer scratched his head. 'Looking for him, are you? What for?'

'N'ote sinister, I can assure yer. He's a mate,' Tom lied. 'Only yer know what with the war and that, I've lost his address.'

'You don't need to remind us Londoners about the war. Had the war up to here, cocker,' he said, flattening his gnarled hand under his chin. 'You lot up north have had it mild to us. A picnic, eh?'

Tom didn't want to get into a heated debate, his own

thoughts being that all of them north, south, east and west, had suffered equally as bad in one way or another. 'Yes, summat like that. Now d'yer know this man's whereabouts or not?'

'Never heard on him, but Hilda might have. 'Ere, Hilda,' he shouted across the bar. 'Heard of an Ernest Moss?'

'Eh?' the old woman shouted back, spilling some of her milk stout as she strained over the bar top to hear what was being said.

'I said, have you heard of an Ernest Moss?'

'Ernie Moss? Fanny's lad?' She scrutinised Tom then her face saddened. 'Fanny's dead now, 'course. Died of consumption.' She gazed into her glass, then raised her head and looked Tom straight in the eyes. 'Depends who wants to know?'

'This geezer here,' replied the old timer, irritated.

The old woman frowned. 'Does he owe you money?'

'Er . . . no, he's a friend.'

She snorted loudly. 'First friend I've heard of Ernie Moss having. He and his missus have just moved into number twelve further down. They had two rooms before that in Bank Street. Moved up in the world since they got those kids. His sister's they are. Madge was murdered, poor devil. But she must have left some money 'cos he's fair prospered. Anyway you can't miss it. It's the one with the new nets. New nets!' she scoffed. 'We can't even get a decent loaf and he's got new nets.'

Tom smiled gratefully. 'Thank you.' He slapped a florin on the counter though he could ill afford it. 'Buy yerselves a drink.'

The)old timer's face lit up as did Hilda's. 'Ta, mate.'

He pulled up the collar on his jacket as he left the pub. It was a quarter past five and beginning to grow dark and the already cold day had grown decidedly chillier. The darkening sky was already lit up with searchlight beams and Tom prayed that tonight there'd be no air raids. London had been bombarded from almost day one, suffering more than its fair share of destruction and grief. He had always thought that nothing the Luftwaffe did could beat the appalling destruction of Coventry which he had witnessed first hand, but even the small area of the capital he had seen today equalled that.

He found the house easily and scanned his eyes across the front before he knocked loudly on the door. It looked presentable enough and the roof was still intact which was something. And just as old Hilda had said, the nets certainly did look new.

The door was answered by a middle-aged woman. She was plump and homely-looking. She wiped her hands on her stained apron and eyed him sharply. 'Yes?'

'I've been told Ernest Moss lives 'ere?'

She looked at him warily. 'And who's enquiring?'

'My name's Rudney. Thomas Rudney.'

The woman looked blankly at him, the name meant nothing to her.

'A neighbour of Grace Wilkins who looked after the kids in Leicester. I was in the area meking a delivery and couldn't pass an opportunity to visit and see 'ow they're doin'.'

'Oh, so you're Mr Tom?'

He beamed. 'Yes, that's right.'

'Ah, the kids are always talking about yourself and Auntie Grace and all the others. We are grateful, you know, how you all took care of them after . . . after . . .' She wiped a tear from her eye with the corner of her apron. 'After Madge's terrible end. She was Ernie's sister. They were ever so close. Ernie came up as soon as we got word what'd happened. It were awful, just awful. We still can't believe it.'

Tom shuffled uncomfortably on his feet. 'Yes, it was.'

'Well, the kids will be sorry they've missed you.'

'They're not 'ere then?' His face fell in disappointment. 'When will they be back?'

She inhaled sharply. 'Not for a good while yet. Ernie's . . . er . . . taken 'em round to his mother's. They love going to their granny's. She spoils 'em .rotten. They've all gone for tea, only I couldn't go 'cos I had things to do.'

Tom ran his hand through his hair. 'Oh, I see.'

He looked at her thoughtfully, wondering why she did not ask him in to wait considering the distance he had travelled. 'Well, maybe I could pay a call there? I wouldn't like to go all the way 'ome not 'aving seen 'em. I don't know when I'll be back this way again.'

She looked at him anxiously. 'Well . . . er . . . I suppose that'd be all right. Only it's quite a walk.'

'I don't mind.'

'Oh, right.' She poked her head out of the door and looked up and down the street. Tom wondered what she was looking for. She righted herself and proceeded to give him lengthy directions. 'Think you'll find it okay?'

'Er . . . yes, yes. I think so. Twenty-four Green Street.' He smiled. 'My years as a lorry driver stand me in good stead when it comes to findin' addresses.'

She didn't look impressed.

'Right, thanks, Mrs Moss.'

'My pleasure.'

She shut the door.

Tom stared at it for several seconds before shaking his head. His past experience of Londoners had instilled in him a belief that they were a friendly generous people. This woman had dented that belief. Still, he thought ruefully, this war had changed lots of things. She was probably being cautious. Warning posters were plastered everywhere telling people to be careful and watchful of strangers. He grinned to himself. He might be big and careworn but a national threat, never!

The chilly evening air had grown even colder and Tom had already realised that he would have to spend the night in his lorry. The journey back home was bad enough in daylight, let alone at night during the blackout and especially after an already long day. He hoped his boss would be lenient when he explained the delay.

Following her directions to the letter, he traipsed down street after street, skirting several bomb sites and burned out workplaces. Finally he stopped and scratched his head. None of the streets in this area was titled green or even blue come to that.

He stopped a passer-by. 'No Green Street round here, mate,' the man said before hurrying on.

That was strange, he thought, and scratched his head again. According to her instructions Green Street had to be around here somewhere despite what that man had told him.

He turned and began to retrace his steps. Somehow he had obviously taken a right when he should have taken a left or even maybe carried straight on. On and on he walked, the streets now all looking the same. Several times he tried to stop and make enquiries. After the third rebuff he began to wonder if his Leicester accent was like a German's, so taken aback had people looked before they had hurried away.

His pace began to slow. He was cold, hungry and tired, having been up since four that morning. He judged the time to be nearing six-thirty at least. What if he found somewhere to have a cuppa and something to eat, then made his way back to Ernest Moss's? With a bit of luck, by that time, he would have returned with the children. He had made up his mind that regardless he was not going to return home to Leicester without seeing the children.

Still, though, he was happy on one front. From what he

had been allowed to see, they seemed to live in a nice home and Mrs Moss had appeared the motherly type. He suddenly frowned. Didn't she say that Ernest Moss had taken the kids to see his mother? He could have sworn old Hilda in the pub had said she was dead. Strange that. Someone had got their wires crossed.

The narrow lane he was walking down suddenly opened out on to a busy shop-lined street, albeit not with all the shops intact. Some had lost their glass, others disappeared completely. People were scurrying about on their way home. He paused at the corner, wondering which direction to take.

He decided the right and began to walk again, eyes peeled for somewhere that served beverages and anything edible. He didn't care what, he was ravenous.

More and more searchlights were beaming up, the sky now a criss-cross pattern, and by the looks on people's faces as they hurried by, they were expecting something. Tom sincerely hoped not. Maybe, he thought, they always looked like that, having been through so much, always on the look out for what could happen next.

The crowds ahead seemed to be disappearing underground and for a moment he wondered just where they were going. Then he realised they were going down the entrance to a tube station. He had never been on a tube train and quite fancied the idea. Or maybe they were all going down for shelter, to get a good place in case of a raid? He looked skywards. Did these people know something he didn't?

As he approached the entrance, his heart sank. Two shivering, raggedly dressed waifs were sitting cross-legged on the cold pavement, a crudely written sign around their necks: BOMB VICTIMS. They were both holding out bowls to passersby. The odd person was stopping, shaking their head sadly and slipping a few coins into the bowl. Grubby faces smiled up gratefully.

He put his hand into his pocket and searched around for any odd pennies. He hadn't much himself, having given that florin to the old timer and Hilda in thanks for their help.

He pulled out his hand and inspected the contents. It held a sixpence, two shillings, three pennies and two halfpennys. The sixpence and two shillings he put back in his pocket. He would need that if he was to get home. The little that he had to offer was surely better than nothing.

He drew up to them, smiled and put the change in the bowl.

'Ta, mister,'

Tom smiled, instinctively bending down and ruffling the child's hair. He straightened up and made to walk away, stopped and abruptly turned back. He stared at the children, then gasped.

'Jessie? Jessie, is that you?' Beneath the muck on her face it was hard to tell. But he had recognised the voice.

The grubby face stared at him, then broke into a delighted smile. 'Mr Tom!' she cried, and vigorously nudged the child at the side of her. 'Tony, it's Mr Tom.'

His head jerked up. 'Mr Tom!' he exclaimed.

Both children jumped up and threw their arms around him. 'Mr Tom! Oh, Mr Tom!'

He was speechless, trying to fathom what on earth was going on. Suddenly he felt a vice-like grip on his arm.

'What the hell's up with you, mate?'

The children dropped their arms and backed away, their faces filled with fear.

Tom swung round and came face to face with Ernest Moss.

'Clear off before I call a copper, bloody pervert!' Moss spat. 'Go on, piss off, yer dirty begger, propositioning little kids. Shame on you!'

'What!' Tom hissed disgustedly. He narrowed his eyes, then pushed his face into his accuser's. 'You don't recognise me, do you?'

Ernest's face clouded over.

'Yes, that's right. I'm Tom Rudney. I helped tek care of these kids in Leicester. Yours is a face I'd never forget. Nice Uncle Ernest. Some uncle you've turned out ter be!'

Ernest stepped backwards, aware of a crowd beginning to gather. 'It ain't what it looks like, mate.'

'Ain't it? What am I, blind or summat?' cried Tom, lunging after him. 'Yer using these kids as beggars.' He grabbed hold of the lapels on Ernest's thick winter coat and ran him up against a wall. 'I'm gonna have you for this.'

Ernest shook. 'I've told you, it ain't what it looks like. I didn't know what they were doing,' he babbled. 'You know Jessie. She's always been a little thief. I was out looking for 'em.'

'Liar!' Tom spat. He raised his hand and clenched his fist. 'See this? I'll knock you into next Tuesday if you don't stop yer lies. No wonder you had new nets at yer windows. What else has the kids' begging paid for, eh? Come on, what else?' He fought the urge to throttle the man.

'Knock him senseless,' a voice from the crowd shouted.

'Yeah, I'll help you.'

Tom swung round. 'Haven't you 'omes ter go to?'

'Suit yourself,' someone said.

'Jessie,' Tom called to the quivering girl clinging to her brother, 'go and find a copper.'

'No, no,' Ernest shouted, wild-eyed. 'Please don't. I've not long got out of prison. They'll lock me away again. Please,' he begged, tears gushing from his eyes. 'Please don't.'

Tom dropped his hands and stared at him in disgust. 'Hold it, Jessie,' he called. He stared at Ernest, his mind working rapidly. 'There's conditions.'

'Anything, anything,' he wailed, falling on his knees.

'One, that we go and collect the kids' stuff. Two, they come back with me to Leicester. And three, you sign a piece of paper relinquishing all rights. I'd sooner see these kids go in a 'ome than 'ave to stay a moment longer wi' you.'

Ernest nodded vigorously in agreement.

Tom turned, took off his jacket in which to wrap the frozen children and held out his arms. 'Come on.' He smiled reassuringly. 'I'm tekin' you home.'

Neither needed to be told twice.

It was nearly twenty-four hours before the lorry ground to a juddering halt outside Tom's house. He switched off the engine and as he did so a loud grating noise split the air and a dull thud followed.

Tom turned to Jessie and Tony, huddled together on the long seat at the side of him. 'That's the gearbox fell out. Ah, well, at least we're home.' He patted the steering wheel affectionately. 'Thanks, old gel.'

The adoring look on both children's faces was all the thanks he would ever need.

Grace almost fell on him when he walked into her living room.

'Tom!' she cried. 'Where on earth have you been? We've all been worried to death. Does Clara know you're home? Sit down,' she demanded, pulling out a chair. 'For God's sake, Tom, what happened to take you so long?'

Connie struggled from her chair, hurried to the table and poured him a mug of tea which she thrust at him. 'It's a bit stewed but it's warm. Well, come on, Tom, we're waitin'. Grace 'ardly slept a wink last night in worry. Me neither,' she added.

'Mam,' Grace scolded.

'Well, it's true. Ida slept. She don't worry about anyone but 'erself that one.'

'Mam,' scolded Grace again. 'Let Tom speak.'

'It's a long story.'

'We're all ears,' said Connie.

'Oh, Tom,' Grace said, pulling a letter from her apron pocket. 'Before I forget, your boss, Mr Hamblin, told me to give you this. As soon as you got back, he said. I bumped into him this afternoon just as he was about to knock on your door. I meant to pass it on to Clara but I forgot. Sorry.'

Tom took the letter and ripped it open. 'He's sacked me,' he said, aghast.

'What? But he can't do that, surely?'

'Well, 'e 'as, and no by your leave.' His face turned thunderous. 'This is just the kind of trick he would pull. I've been pushing for a rise, yer see. Ain't had one for the last three years. I can't say as I'm surprised about this. Anyway, it's about time me and 'im parted company. I've worked me guts out for that bloke and no thanks 'as 'e ever given me.'

'But what will you do?'

Tom held out his hands. 'Grace, there's one thing we ain't short of at the moment and that's work. I'll sweep streets. I ain't bothered as long as I'm paid. Anyway, enough of this.' His eyes lit up excitedly. 'I've brought someone to see you. Well, two people actually.'

Grace's mouth fell open. 'Oh, Tom, who?' she whispered alarmed, her hand going instinctively to her hair. 'I'm a mess. The table's a mess.' She began to gather the dishes.

He laughed. 'I don't think they'll be bothered a jot about what state you or the table's in.' He turned towards the door. 'Come in, kids.'

With whoops of delight, Jessie and Tony bounded through the door throwing themselves at Grace and Connie.

Hugging the children tightly, they both raised questioning eyes to Tom.

'As I said, it's a long story. But they're 'ere for good if you want 'em.'

Grace looked down at the children in bewildered delight, two pairs of hopeful eyes looking into hers. She had yet to learn the reason for their return, but knowing Tom as she did it would be a valid one. And it must be something dreadful for them to be here now. For a moment she worried just what it was. She kissed the tops of their heads then her gaze travelled to Tom standing by the table, watching the proceedings with obvious delight.

A warm glow rushed through her. He had done this for her. He had extended his journey to check on the children all because he knew she was worried about them. And he had known without asking that she would take them back. And if for some reason that was not possible, she knew also he would have taken them himself.

As a result of his selfless act he had lost his job. Her heart went out to him. She felt the desire to rush to him, hug him as tightly as she was now hugging the children, thank him profusely for what he had done. But she knew she didn't have to. He already knew how deep her gratitude went.

It was then that she knew that she loved him. Tom, the gentle giant of a man. Tom, a man as opposite to Bernard as she could imagine. As she gazed at him his eyes caught hers and he gave her an affectionate wink, and blushed. It was then she knew also that her mother was right. The feelings she had for him were returned.

But these feelings they shared would remain unspoken. There could never be anything more than friendship between them, a deep regard, a mutual respect between two people drawn together by tragedy and its aftermath. And why? Because she was married to Bernard. A man who had never done anything selfless in his life. A man who had no respect or regard for anyone other than himself. Regardless, a man she was tied to.

She took a deep breath. 'Oh, Tom,' was all she could manage to say.

Three days later Philip Janson called personally on Tom. He

caught the man, sleeves rolled up, about to ascend a rickety ladder to clear out a blocked gutter.

'Have you got a minute, Tom?'

He stared in astonishment for a second before responding, 'Er . . . yes, certainly, Mr Janson.' He moved away from the ladder, rolling down his shirtsleeves and buttoning them up. 'If it's Clara yer wantin', I think she's just popped ter the town.'

'No, it's yourself, Tom. I'd just like a word.'

'Oh, right,' he said, a little worried. 'Please come inside.'

Taking off his trilby Philip followed him through. Tom suddenly felt somewhat embarrassed by the shabbiness of his home and the clutter created by the children. Clara did a wonderful job, there was no denying it, but even she had her limits.

'Is it about Clara?' he asked. 'She's wantin' ter leave, is that it, and daren't tell me?'

Philip shook his head. 'If she wanted to leave, Tom, I wouldn't be having such a hard job convincing her to marry me.' His eyes twinkled. 'Be assured, Clara is more than happy. I'm sorry to say!' He pulled out a chair at the table. 'Look, why don't you sit down?'

'Oh, right, thank you.'

Tom accepted the invitation to sit at his own table. Philip followed suit in a chair opposite.

He cleared his throat. 'I have to be honest, Tom. Clara has told me about your losing your job and the reason behind it. You're to be commended. It was a good thing you did.'

'Thanks,' he said, embarrassed.

'Have you anything else yet?'

'Anythin' else? Oh, you mean a job. Well, yes actually, thank goodness. I start at Bradshaw's on Monday.'

'Doing what?'

'In the cloth store.'

'And do you think you'll be happy there?'

''Appy?' He shrugged his shoulders. 'It's a job, Mr Janson. 'Appiness doesn't come into it.'

'But you enjoyed your job driving. Won't you miss it?'

Tom stared at Philip Janson, wondering where this conversation was leading. 'Yes, I will. If I 'adn't 'ave enjoyed what I did, I wouldn't 'ave stuck with 'Arry 'Amblin so long. He was a crook, Mr Janson, I don't mind tellin' yer.'

'I know that.'

'You do?'

'Yes. But then so are many people these days. See an opportunity to make a extra shilling and they'll take it. I stuck with him because he wasn't quite as greedy as some of the others and I knew exactly how much he overcharged me and how he did it. Anyway, I've decided that my operation is now big enough to stand its own delivery fleet.' Philip smiled. 'When I say delivery fleet, I mean a couple of lorries, three at the most to start.' He paused for breath. 'I want you to handle it for me, Tom.'

'Me? You want me?'

'Yes, I do. You're just the man for the job.'

'But I ain't 'ad any experience . . .'

'Tom, what you don't know about this job I'm offering, you can learn. You've had more than enough experience on the road and I'll stake my life you know more than you give yourself credit for. A man like you doesn't go round with his eyes shut. Now, are you interested?'

Tom eyed him keenly. 'Yes, I am.'

'Good. Come to my office tomorrow and we'll discuss terms.' He smiled. 'The wage I'm prepared to offer will be a sight more than I suspect you'll be getting at Bradshaw's and what you got with Harry Hamblin. Do a good job for me, Tom, and I'll see you right.'

Grace could not believe how quickly the children settled,

considering the hell they had gone through. It quickly transpired that Ernest Moss's sole purpose in securing them was to put them to work for him. No sooner had they arrived in London than they had been put on the streets begging, taking money off unsuspecting people, watched over all the time by their evil uncle.

Grace, if asked, would never have been able to express her full horror. And never, she vowed, never ever would she allow anyone to take them again.

How Bernard would accept this state of affairs on his return, she decided not to speculate. A time would come when she would have to face that prospect. But maybe, as it had for others, the war would have changed him and he would show compassion and welcome them as she herself had done. She could always hope, because part with the children she could not.

Christmas 1943 was a sight different to the previous one. The table was spartan, presents small, but with happy faces they sat down to eat – all but one that was, but Ida's scowls of disapproval they were all used to and put up with as a matter of course. Ida was keeping most of her thoughts to herself. They would all keep quite happily until her son's return, then the others would all suffer for what they had put her through, especially Grace.

Tom's job was progressing well. Philip was pleased with him. Adapting to being a boss, giving orders when used to receiving them, had given Tom a few sleepless nights but after a couple of bad mistakes and wrong judgements which he readily admitted to, he was proving his worth, beginning to feel glad he had accepted the position and starting to repay the faith Philip had shown in him.

He and his children joined Grace for Christmas dinner, as did Clara who had been expected to join Philip and his family. But she wouldn't miss Christmas dinner with her friends for anything. As Grace sat down and glanced around at the happy faces, her heart momentarily sank. One face she would have done anything to see smiling back at her was Charlie's.

More than ever her daughter's absence concerned her and the pain she felt, especially at this time of family togetherness, was almost unbearable. Even the return of Jessie and Tony could not take away the ache inside for the child she had given birth to, raised and cared for, loved above all else. All she could hope was that Charlie was safe, well and happy, and that one day Grace would open the door and find her standing there. And what a joyous day that would be!

Chapter Thirty-Five

Charlie screamed out in pain and grabbed Sybil's hand, gripping it tightly, her nails digging in. 'It's cutting me in half, Sybil! I can't stand it, really I can't.'

Wincing in pain, Sybil prised her hand from Charlie's and grabbed up a wet flannel to bathe her sweating brow. 'Now, now, gel. It ain't as bad as all that. Why, I'd sooner give birth a dozen times than break me leg. Now that *was* bad.'

'I'm not lying, Sybil. This baby's too big. Ahhh!' She screamed, as another contraction hit her. 'I want my mam.'

Sybil bit her lip anxiously. At times like these all daughters wanted their mothers, no one else would do. In normal circumstances her mother would be here now. It should be her bathing her daughter's forehead instead of Sybil, just as her own mother had done when she had given birth to her three.

Charlie had been in labour for the last twenty-four-hours and was exhausted. Sybil looked at her worriedly as she continued spongeing. Charlie was groaning softly, waiting for the next contraction, face ashen, her hair matted and soaking wet with sweat. Sybil threw the flannel into the bowl sitting on the table at the side of the labour bed and went in search of a nurse.

She found one scurrying down the corridor, carrying a bedpan covered by a cloth.

'My friend needs you.'

Nurse Thompson paused hesitantly. Twenty other patients needed her also. Nurses were in short supply, most having been pulled off to take care of the war wounded who had poured into the city, with more arriving daily. She had been on her shift for the last ten hours and was exhausted herself. 'The doctor will be here in a minute,' she said, making to hurry off.

'You've been saying that for the last three hours!'

A fraught Nurse Thompson turned on her. 'Don't you know there's a war on?'

'Sod the war,' Sybil erupted. 'My friend's in there 'aving a baby.' She grabbed her arm. 'You'll come with me now.'

Just then, through the rubber swing doors, a doctor appeared. Like the nurse he looked in dire need of a good night's rest, two would have been even better. Sybil flew at him. 'My friend needs yer, doctor. Come quick. I think there's summat wrong with the baby.' This was a lie but she felt it was the only way to get some attention.

The doctor hurriedly followed her. While he examined Charlie, Sybil paced up and down the corridor. The doctor finally appeared.

'Well?' she asked anxiously.

'Your friend's doing fine. Her labour is progressing normally.'

'Oh, thank God fer that! How much longer d'yer think, doctor?

He smiled. 'If I knew that, my dear, I'd make a fortune. It'll come when it's ready.' He patted her arm. 'There's a canteen down the corridor. Why don't you go and get a cup of tea? Your friend is sleeping at the moment.'

Sybil smiled, relieved. 'I think I will. Ta, doc.'

The baby did take its time. Sybil had another six hours of anxiously pacing up and down, spongeing brows and having her hands bruised from Charlie's painful grip before the baby finally put in its appearance.

'She's beautiful, Charlie!' cried Sybil. 'Oh, I could just eat 'er.'

Charlie gazed down at the bundle in her arms. 'Yes, she is, isn't she?'

Sybil turned to the nurse clearing up after the birth. 'Ain't she just the sweetest thing?'

The nurse eyed the unmarried trollop in the bed disapprovingly and then the baby. 'Mmmm,' she mouthed before turning away.

Sybil scowled at her before she turned back to Charlie. Her friend was exhausted but blooming with happiness. 'Kit will love 'er.'

'Yes, he will.' Charlie's eyes filled with tears. 'Oh, but I do miss him.'

'Yeah, well, yer won't 'ave time, not with little madam 'ere meking her demands.'

Charlie looked at her daughter again, her heart filling with love. 'She can demand all she likes.' The tears she'd managed to quell a moment ago when she had thought of Kit somewhere abroad, unaware he had just become a father, overflowed to spill down her face. 'Oh, Sybil,' she sobbed, 'I want my mother. She should be here.'

'D'yer want me to fetch 'er? I will.'

Charlie eyed her worriedly, then shook her head and gazed back down at the baby. 'I don't know what to do, Sybil. I desperately want her to see her granddaughter.' She raised her eyes. 'But how would she react? I saw the way the nurse looked at me just then. And the doctor when she was born.'

Sybil sighed softly and gently took her hand. 'You knew what to expect, Charlie. You knew it wouldn't be no picnic.' She gazed across at the baby contentedly asleep in her mother's arms. This child, albeit born out of love, would not find life easy. But regardless it had had a better start than some. It had a mother that loved it and a doting father, judging by the letters received, who couldn't wait to get home and marry the woman he loved. 'Your mother has a right to know. Let me fetch her, Charlie. At least afford her the opportunity to mek up 'er own mind 'ow she feels about this. She deserves that, surely?'

Charlie shook her head. 'I can't, Sybil. I love her too much to put her through it. Besides, can you imagine my father's reaction? When he finds out, he'll hit the roof. And even if my mother did want to visit, he'd make her life unbearable again if she defied him. No, I can't, Sybil. I can't jeopardise her happiness for the sake of my own.'

Sybil patted her hand. 'Suit yerself, gel. Maybe you'll feel differently later on. When Kit comes home, eh?'

Charlie smiled wearily. 'Yeah, when Kit comes home I'll think about it. I'll have him to support me.'

Grace was to find out about the baby via Ida's wicked tongue. She had learned it from one of her cronies down the pub who had a niece working at the hospital as an auxiliary.

Grace had come home from a trying day at work. Everything had seemed to go wrong at once and it had taken all her efforts to sort things out. Now she was tired and wanted nothing more than to curl up in front of the fire. But she could not while there were still things around the house that needed attention.

She was sitting at the table snatching a few minutes with a cup of tea. Tony and Jessie were around at the Rudneys', her mother sitting in a chair opposite darning some socks. Ida as usual was reclining in her armchair, legs stretched out on the hearth. Despite the atmosphere that always hung over the house when Ida was about, Grace was enjoying a few moments' peace.

Ida sniffed haughtily, glancing scathingly at the two people she most hated. She had sat patiently whilst waiting for the perfect moment to impart the news which had set her squirming in deep pleasure when it had been told to her. Now was the time.

'So.' The word sharply split the silence and a corner of Ida's mouth twitched at the sight of Grace and Connie paying attention to her. She stared straight into Grace's eyes. 'How d'yer feel about becoming a granny, eh?'

Grace frowned. 'Pardon?' she said, bemused.

'Oh, deaf now, a' yer? I said, 'ow d'yer feel about becoming a granny? Must be a shock, eh?'

Connie looked at Grace and raised her eyebrows. The woman had finally flipped her lid, she thought.

Grace put down her cup. 'Mrs Wilkins, just what are you going on about?'

Ida grinned as she eased her bony body more comfortably into the armchair. 'Fire needs more coal. It's burnin' low and I'm gettin' cold.'

'Well, it'll have to burn low, Mrs Wilkins. What we have has to be eked out 'til we get our next ration next week. Now you know that as well as I do. You'll have to do like we do and put on another cardi or summat. What was that you said? Something about a granny, wasn't it?'

'That's right, I did. And it's you,' she said, wagging her gnarled bony finger. 'You're the granny.'

'Me?'

Ida cackled harshly. Oh, she was going to enjoy this. 'That's what I said. It's all over the street. They all know about that little trollop of a daughter of yourn just giving birth. But what do they say? The nearest and dearest is always the last to find out.' Her mouth tightened disapprovingly and she folded her arms. 'I always knew what that little madam was about. My Bernard'll disown her . . .'

Grace shot up from her chair. 'Where is she? Where's my Charlie?' she demanded.

Ida's head jerked back. 'In the Royal . . .'

Her mind racing frantically, Grace shot to the kitchen and grabbed her coat from the hook.

'Eh up,' Ida shouted after her. 'I ain't finished yet. I ain't told yer the best bit.'

Connie appeared in the doorway, her face wreathed in worry. 'Oh, Grace . . .' Words failed her. She watched helplessly for a moment as her daughter struggled to pull on her coat. 'Look, I'll go with yer,' she offered.

'No, Mam, you stay here.'

'But, Grace, yer can't go and face summat like this on yer own . . .'

She was gone.

Connie turned back to face Ida. 'You wicked woman!'

Ida sniffed haughtily. 'Well, someone 'ad ter tell 'er,' she said defensively. Dismissing Connie, she turned her head towards the fire. Yes, she had enjoyed that, but a sudden anger crept over her at the thought that Grace's abrupt departure had denied her the right to impart the information she was keeping until last. And she was only sorry that she couldn't be there to witness what she saw as Grace's final downfall. But one thing she had no doubts on and that was that after today her daughter-in-law would never be able to hold her head up in these streets again. And serve her right. Grinning smugly, she turned back to Connie.

'I could do wi' a cuppa. Although ter me, *you* look like you could do wi' a gin!'

Grace arrived at the Royal Infirmary breathless, having ran practically all of the way. The only thing on her mind was the thought of seeing Charlie, her precious daughter. After all this time desperate for news, continually fighting the gnawing ache in the pit of her stomach, at long last her prayers had been answered.

The baby, for the moment, did not enter into it. She hadn't seen it, had not held it in her arms, hadn't felt the tug at her heart. Nothing mattered, not the whys, not the wherefores – time for questions and hopefully answers would come later. All that mattered to her, all that was important, was seeing her daughter.

But what would Charlie's reaction be? Would she herself be welcome? These thoughts she pushed to the back of her mind as she raced down the streets.

After numerous enquiries trying to find out where Charlie was, she paused before the door to gather her wits. She took several deep breaths and, with heart thumping painfully, her hand trembling, she knocked and pushed the door open.

Charlie was lying in bed dozing. As the door opened she opened her eyes and, on seeing her mother, put her hand to her mouth in shock.

'Charlie,' Grace whispered hesitantly.

'Mam,' she gasped. 'Mam, is it really you?' She struggled to ease herself up on the pillows, then her face crumpled and her arms flew out in welcome. 'Oh, Mam, Mam!'

Grace rushed towards her and gathered Charlie in her arms, hugging her tightly and sobbing softly into her shoulder. 'Oh, Charlie, Charlie,' she choked over and over.

Charlie cried also, clinging to her mother, afraid to let her go, afraid she was dreaming. 'Oh, Mam,' she wailed. How many times she had yearned for this moment, dreamed of it, prayed for it, and it was finally here. She was holding her mother.

Finally Grace pulled back and searched Charlie's face. 'Why, Charlie? Why?'

She wiped her eyes and stared at Grace, bewildered. 'But you know why, Mam.'

'No, I don't, Charlie. I just came home from Clara's to find you had gone.'

Charlie frowned quizzically. 'But didn't Granny Wilkins explain? I told her where I was going, gave her my address, and asked her to ask you to visit me so I could explain fully why I was leaving. She said she would.'

Grace shut her eyes tightly and shook her head.

'But what about the letter?'

'What letter, Charlie?'

'The one I gave . . . Oh, Mam, she never told you or gave you the letter?'

'No, Charlie, she didn't.'

'Oh, Mam! How could she do this? And I thought all this time you didn't care. She told me you didn't. Told me you didn't want to see me again.'

Grace gripped Charlie's hands. 'What? She said what? When? When did you see her? When did she tell you these lies?'

Charlie explained what had happened the night she had left home, and also about her visit and Ida's reaction. Grace buried her face in her hands in despair, groaning. All this time she had mourned Charlie's leaving, felt responsible, carried a dreadful burden. And all the time Ida had known exactly where her daughter was, and known also that her daughter was suffering in the same way.

'Oh, Mam, she's wicked! My own grandmother's wicked. I don't want to see her ever again,' said Charlie ferociously.

Grace took a deep breath. The time had come to deal with Ida. But at this precise moment Grace and Charlie were back together, something she had begun to believe would never come about. Ida was not going to spoil this. She had done enough damage.

'Charlie, let's forget about your grandmother for the time being. Me and you have a lot to catch up on. Don't let's waste another moment.'

Just then the door opened and a nurse came bustling through, carrying a bundle. 'Time to feed the baby, Mrs . . . er, Miss . . . er . . .' She looked at Grace enquiringly.

'I'm her mother,' she said, rising. 'And I presume this is my granddaughter. Can I see her, please?' she said, walking towards the nurse, a broad smile of anticipation on her face. She noticed a look of pity mixed with something else she couldn't quite fathom cross the nurse's face and turned hurriedly to Charlie. 'Is the baby all right?'

Charlie swallowed hard, glanced quickly at the nurse, then back to her mother. 'She's fine, Mam.'

'Oh, that's all right then. For a moment I thought there was something wrong.' She took the bundle gently from the nurse and gazed downwards at the sleeping infant.

She froze for a moment, her mind not quite registering what her eyes were seeing – what she had expected to see. Mixed emotions raced through her. So this was what Ida had been desperate to tell her. As she stared down in bewilderment, her granddaughter stirred and opened her eyes. Big brown eyes, fringed round with long black lashes. The baby seemed to smile up at her grandmother and Grace's heart melted. It was instant love. The same kind she had experienced when holding her own daughter for the very first time. 'Oh, Charlie, she's beautiful.' She turned to her daughter sitting anxiously in the bed. 'She is, Charlie. She's beautiful.'

'You mean it, Mam?' she asked worriedly.

'Charlie, I've never meant anything so much. Her father must be such a handsome man to have fathered such a child.'

'Oh, Mam, he is,' she cried, relieved. 'You'll like him – no, love him when you meet him. He's a wonderful man.'

Grace smiled warmly. 'I'm sure he is. If you love him, Charlie, and I've no doubt you do, then I will also.'

She looked down again at the smooth dark coffee-coloured skin, at the black curly hair springing proudly, at the contented smile which at this moment she felt was meant just for her, and her heart filled with joy. What did it matter who had produced such a child? If her daughter had chosen him, fallen in love with him, planned to spend the rest of her life with him and him her, that was all that mattered.

Skin colour was not an issue. What other people said or how they reacted was of no consequence. Life was not going to be easy for Charlie and her child thanks to other people's misguided prejudices. But Grace had always been proud of her daughter and nothing had changed. She would stand by her, no matter what, as she would now stand by and help protect the baby in her arms.

She turned to the nurse hovering close by. 'She's beautiful, my granddaughter, isn't she?'

Taken aback, the nurse nodded. 'Yes, she is,' she said begrudgingly and pursed her lips. Women who went with black men were the lowest of the low in her book. This baby wasn't the first half-caste child to be born since the black American soldiers had arrived, and neither would she be the last. Although she counted the woman in the bed to be amongst the luckier ones. Most of the men did a runner as soon as they found out they were about to become fathers. But that was a factor in many pregnancies during this war, regardless of race or colour. Still the grandmother seemed to have accepted it, which was something, she supposed. The nurse took a haughty breath. 'Do you need any help feeding the baby?' she asked curtly.

'No, thank you, nurse. I've my mother here now.'

Grace turned and smiled at her daughter, eyes filled with love. 'Yes, that's right, you have. And I'll always be here for you, Charlie. Nothing will ever part us again.'

It was several hours before Grace returned home. The long walk back had afforded her an opportunity to gather her thoughts. She knew exactly how she was going to tackle Ida.

Discarding her coat, she made her way towards the living room and sat down at the table, pulled off her shoes and rubbed her aching legs.

Sitting in her chair, Connie stared at her worriedly. 'Grace?'

She smiled, sighing happily. 'I have the most beautiful granddaughter, Mother. And you're a great-granny, isn't that wonderful? Charlie's asked me to take you in tomorrow and you can see her for yourself, but I know you'll love her. She's just the prettiest thing. The image of Charlie.' She turned to face Ida. 'Would you like to come, Mrs Wilkins? She's your great-granddaughter too.'

Ida's jaw dropped in shock. She had sat for the last few hours filled with glee, anticipating Grace's shock and its aftermath. This she had not expected in the least.

'Me? You expect *me* ter visit?' She shook her head vigorously. 'Oh, not on your nelly. I'll not associate wi' any nigger lover, and nor will my Bernard. She's no granddaughter of mine,' she spat.

Grace shot a warning glance at Connie.

Her face hardened. 'I'll ask you not to use words like that in this house, Mrs Wilkins. Charlie's intended is a human being, a wonderful one from what she's told me. His skin colour is of no importance.'

'It is in my book.'

'Well then, that's your problem because there's not many people you do like, is there, Mrs Wilkins, regardless of race or colour? And as for Charlie not being a granddaughter of yours, that's of no importance either, because she never was, was she? You've never treated my Charlie like a grandmother should. That's always been your loss, Mrs Wilkins. My mother will vouch that Charlie is a wonderful granddaughter.'

'Yes, I can. The best,' Connie said with conviction.

'And as for Bernard,' Grace continued, 'I don't think it's

your place to anticipate his feelings regarding all this, son or not.' She smiled over at her mother. 'Any tea going, Mam?'

'Yes, 'course me duck. You must be desperate. Come and sit by the fire while I mash a fresh pot.' Connie rose and hurried to the kitchen. There were many questions she wanted to ask Grace, but not now. When Ida was out of the way.

'Just you wait 'til my Bernard comes back. 'E'll disown 'er!'

'That may be so, Mrs Wilkins, and I'll deal with that when the time comes. In the meantime, Charlie will need all the love and support she can get caring for the baby, and I would ask you to help as much as you can when she comes home.'

Ida gawped. 'Home? What? Yer mean 'ere?'

'Yes, I do.' She watched Ida's face fill with horror at the thought.

'If she comes, I go.'

'That's your choice, Mrs Wilkins. Nobody's asking you to leave. But if that's what you want, I'll not stop you.'

'Oh, chuck an old lady out, would yer?'

'I'm doing nothing of the sort. But I'm not your keeper.'

Ida's mouth clamped shut. She wished wholeheartedly she hadn't threatened to leave. She'd nowhere to go and Grace knew that. But to back down now, well, she couldn't.

'You'll be sorry,' she spat, struggling up from her chair. 'You'll see, you'll be sorry.'

Grace shook her head sadly as Ida scuttled from the room.

Connie returned with the tea. 'Has she gone? Good. Now yer can tell me all.' She handed Grace her cup and sat down in the chair opposite. 'I can't wait to 'ear about this lovely little addition to our family, our Grace, and I can't wait ter see 'er!'

Chapter Thirty-Six

Clara smiled affectionately down at Kitty as she tidied the covers more comfortably around the dozing infant in the pram. She returned to the bench and sat down.

'She's nearly asleep, bless her.'

Grace raised her face and felt the hot rays warming her skin. It was a lovely sunny June day in 1944 and if she shut her eyes it would have been like any other idyllic summer before the war had started. As it was, they were all waiting anxiously for news of the D-Day landings.

In the distance she could hear Tony and Jessie, Maureen, Willy and young Bobbie as they chased each other round the trees in Spinney Hill Park along with several other children. For a moment she longed for Bessie to be here to see how her children had grown. She would have been proud. Proud too of the way her husband had coped. Grace suddenly missed her friend dreadfully and tried to quash the guilt she felt at the feelings she harboured for Bessie's husband.

Oh, Tom! Just the thought of that lovely big man sent her heart galloping. She sighed forlornly. It was inevitable that such a man would find another woman at some stage in the not too distant future and Grace would have to prepare herself to face it when the time came.

'You should have gone with Connie and Charlie up the town,' Clara was saying. 'I could have handled this lot.'

She smiled across at the children.

Grace lowered her head. 'I'm quite happy, thank you, Clara. It's good for Charlie and her grandmother to spend time together.' She glanced protectively across at the perambulator. 'Besides, I like nothing better than taking Kitty for a walk.'

'Yes, any excuse. And I can't blame you, Grace. She's a lovely child.'

'Yes, she is. Did you notice, she turns her head when you call her name? She is bright, she's going to go places that one, and I'll do all I can to make sure she does. Without interfering of course,' she added.

'The doting grandmother, eh, Grace?'

She smiled. 'Something like that. All we need now is for Kit to come back safe. I know Charlie's more worried than she says. But at least his letters are regular.'

Clara nodded. There was nothing she could say to comfort Grace. News of the fighting abroad was patchy to say the least. Tom was also worried for the safety of his boys, but there was nothing anyone could do but wait – and hope.

Grace shouted across to the children to mind themselves then turned around to face Clara. 'Are you ever going to tell me or not?'

She looked at Grace in surprise. 'I'm sorry, my dear?'

'Clara, stop it. You've something on your mind. Something you're dying to tell me. So come on, out with it.'

Clara smiled cagily. 'Oh, all right.' She took a deep breath. 'Philip and I are getting married.'

'Oh, Clara!' Grace gasped, delightedly throwing her arms around the older woman's shoulders and hugging her tightly. 'I'm so glad. And it's not before time. When?'

'Oh, shortly.' She bit her lip anxiously.

'It's Tom and the children, isn't it?' Grace pressed.

Clara nodded. 'Yes, it is. I can't find it in my heart to tell him, Grace. He's been so good to me and I love those children like my own. But, well, I do love Philip and I was afraid he'd stop asking me so I agreed.'

Grace's face softened affectionately. 'Clara, you must do what your heart tells you. Besides, I know Tom has been waiting for this. He'll be fine now, Clara. You've done a grand job but you must go to Philip. And anyway, it's not as though you're going to the end of the earth, is it? You can always visit.'

'Yes, I can, can't I, dear? But I will miss them so much.'

'Yes, and they you. But if I'm not mistaken those children will never be off your doorstep, so missing them is not an issue.' She clasped her hands excitedly. 'Oh, but you're going to be so happy, Clara. Philip is a wonderful man.'

The conversation settled into talk of weddings and everything associated with the forthcoming big day.

'I'm going to tell Tom as soon as we get back. It's not fair to stall, not now I've made up my mind.'

'You're right, Clara. It'll give him plenty of warning to make other arrangements. If he wants to, that is. He might feel able to go it alone. After all, the children are a bit older now.'

Clara suddenly looked at her searchingly. 'Grace dear, about Tom . . .'

'What about him?' she asked anxiously. 'He's not sick or anything, is he?'

'No, no, nothing like that . . . it's just . . . well. Look, Grace, I hate to see you both suffering so much. I know you love him and he you. I've seen the way you both look at each other . . .'

Grace held up her hand to stop Clara's flow. She couldn't bear it; couldn't bear to hear spoken what was in her heart. Nobody would ever know how she lay in her bed at night, tossing and turning as she wrestled with her conscience, feeling remorse and guilt for her feelings towards this man. Nothing could ever come of it so any talk was pointless. All it did was deepen her wounds and strengthen her longing. 'Don't, Clara. Please, don't.'

She abruptly rose and stretched herself. 'Well, we must be getting back,' she said lightly, taking hold of the pram handle-bar. 'This little one will be wanting her feed soon.' She called across to the children: 'Come on, you lot. Time to go home.'

Clara caught her arm. 'I'm sorry if I upset you, Grace.'

'It's all right, Clara. I know you'd never upset me intention-ally. But please don't think any more about me and Tom. Believe me when I say there's nothing between us and never will be.'

Both walked down the path. The children galloped up behind them.

'Are we still comin' for tea, Granny Apple?' asked Tony.

Clara ruffled the boy's hair. 'Yes, of course. I've made a jelly especially.'

'A jelly!' Grace exclaimed. 'How on earth have you done that?'

'Secret recipe, dear,' she said, winking. She leaned over and whispered in Grace's ear, 'I've yet to see if it's set, but we can hope.'

They parted company at the Rudneys' front door. 'You sure you won't join us?' Clara asked Grace.

'I might pop in later for a cup of tea after I've seen to Kitty. Anyway, you've enough to feed.' She turned to the children. 'Behave yourselves.'

'We will,' they all shouted, disappearing down the entry.

Grace parked the pram at the back door. Little Kitty was still sleeping and she decided to leave her out in the warm air until she woke. Clara's mention of Tom had unsettled her and she felt the need to busy herself, get her mind on other matters.

Distractedly she put on the kettle and lit the gas. Gathering several items to put on the table in readiness for when Charlie and her mother returned, she walked into the living room. Suddenly she froze as she caught sight of the large figure standing by the fireplace.

On hearing her enter he slowly turned to stare over at her. 'Bernard!' she gasped.

A sickening anticipation settled in her stomach. She advanced into the room and put the items down on the table, aware that his eyes were watching her every move. She raised her own to his. 'Er . . . when did you arrive?' she asked lightly.

'About 'alf hour ago. And where were you? Why weren't you here?'

'I would have been if I'd known you were coming. I've . . . er . . . just been for a walk.'

'Huh,' he grunted.

She suddenly noticed he was leaning heavily on a walking stick. 'What's happened to you?' she asked, alarmed.

'I nearly lost me leg, that's what. And you'd've known if you cared a jot!'

She gawped at him. 'Known? How could I have known? I haven't had a word from you in all the time you've been gone.'

'That's no excuse. I was fighting, Grace. Out there facing God knows what. How d'yer expect me to write?'

Well, others do, she wanted to say, but wrung her hands, ashamed. 'I didn't know where to write to, Bernard. I would have otherwise.' She turned to the table and laid the plates she had brought in earlier. 'Look, sit down, Bernard. I'll make some tea.'

'Sod the tea! And I ain't a visitor, Grace. I live here, remember?' He glanced over at her scathingly and watched her squirm. 'Oh,' he smirked knowingly, 'I can see that I've not come back a moment too soon. I bet you've lived the life of Riley while I've bin gone. Well, I'm back now, Grace. So all those little habits you've picked up in my absence, you can forget.'

She gulped and wrung her hands. 'You're back for good?' she asked tentatively. 'You're not just here on leave?'

'Ah, that's what you were 'oping, wasn't it, my dear? Well, do I look fit enough to go back, you stupid woman? Look at me, I'm practically a cripple.' He glared at her. He was never going back. Never.

His thoughts travelled back to the day he was injured. Artillery fire had been blasting around him, bullets flying everywhere. Scared out of his wits and with no thought for anything other than his own precious neck, he had crawled off, making sure he was unobserved, to hide in a barn. He had left them all to it. No way was he going to be killed.

Suddenly out of nowhere several Germans had entered the barn, rifles aimed. He had felt fear then, fear like he'd never known. He had dropped his gun, his hands shooting up in surrender.

'Don't kill me, please,' he had begged. 'I surrender, I surrender!'

The German soldiers had frozen then started to advance towards him when suddenly a shell exploded right behind them. Bodies had scattered everywhere. The blast blew Bernard out of the barn and when he awoke he was in a hospital somewhere in France, about to have a large piece of shrapnel removed from his leg.

As he came round he spied an officer conversing with the doctor and another fear swept over him. Of course. He would have to explain his presence in the barn when all his other colleagues had been at the other side of the farmyard and scattered across the adjoining fields. His mind had raced frantically. In his rush to save his neck, he hadn't had time to think of a plausible excuse.

He had shut his eyes and revisited the scene. He could always say that in the mayhem, the confusion, he had somehow got split up from the rest of his unit and taken shelter in the barn, but he knew that would not wash. They were clever, these officers, they would soon realise the truth. Officers he did not like. He had not one ounce of regard for any army personnel, thought them all stupid to have joined in the first place. At least he had had a valid excuse. Escaping the noose seemed more than valid to him.

From the very first day of arrival at camp, his life had taken a turn for the worse. No longer was he in control. No longer was his life his own. He was forced to obey commands, tackle tasks he thought beneath him, and he had not liked it one little bit.

He saw this opportunity as probably his only chance of getting out. For a man who was a master at lying and conniving this should be easy. And so it had proved, because that's when his 'amnesia' had hit.

For months he had cleverly fobbed them off in this way, and his 'injured leg' – which in fact had fully healed weeks ago – still gave him such terrible pain, he maintained, he could hardly walk. Just recently he had claimed his memory had begun to return, but the breathing space had given him plenty of time to perfect his excuse.

He had spotted the small band of German soldiers entering the barn, and with his colleagues all otherwise occupied had heroically taken it upon himself to go after them. That's why he had been in the barn. Bernard himself had known that nobody could be sure of the facts as at the time there had been too much going on. And as no one had witnessed his entry, they had to take his word for it.

His excuse seemed to satisfy his superiors and he had been left in peace to string out his injury. Well, so far as he was concerned it would not heal enough for him to return. It would not heal properly till well after this blasted war was over.

His reason for joining in the first place was no longer a threat. He had learned long ago after flicking through some old back copies of newspapers kept at the nursing home he had been transported to in Essex, that Madge Cotting's killer had been caught. Anger as the words had leapt out at him had boiled over. He needn't have joined up in the first place!

That anger still filled him as he flared his nostrils and filled his lungs. 'I shall need constant care, so if yer still working, you'll have ter give up yer job.'

Grace's heart sank rapidly, a feeling of doom settling upon her. All hope of a change in her husband evaporated. She could see, she could tell, her life was going to be worse than before. Suddenly she saw the last two years flash before her. Such a lot had happened, but through it all she had been happier without him there. And now, without warning, with no time to prepare herself, he was back and Grace would be back to square one – back to a life of misery.

She watched him play out a dramatic wince of pain as he sat down in the armchair, resting the walking stick at the side. He looked at the empty chair opposite.

'Where's my mother?' he demanded.

Grace took a deep breath. 'She no longer lives here, Bernard.'

His head jerked. 'What? What d'yer mean, she no longer lives here? Why?'

'Because she chose to go, that's why.'

'Chose!' He narrowed his eyes. 'You got rid of her, you mean?'

'No, I did not. She left because she felt she couldn't live here any longer.'

Suddenly Kitty started to cry.

'What's that?' he growled, turning his head towards the kitchen. 'Babysitting for the neighbours, I presume? Well, tek it back, I want some peace.'

Her hand flew to her mouth. She had to tell him about Kitty.

She made for the door, stopped and turned. 'That's our granddaughter, Bernard.'

He swung himself round and stared at her blankly. 'Granddaughter!' he spat. 'Granddaughter? Yer mean, Charlotte got married without asking my permission?'

Grace paused by the door. 'She doesn't need your permission, Bernard. She's over twenty-one.' She just couldn't bring herself at this moment to tell him Charlie was not married. A bigger issue had yet to be faced.

She gathered Kitty up in her arms. 'Well, here goes, my darling,' she said, kissing her affectionately on the cheek. 'Come and meet your grandfather.'

Holding her breath, she stood before him, holding Kitty close to her. Kitty suddenly shrieked with baby laughter and held out her tiny hand towards Bernard.

His eyes bulged as he scanned the baby. 'What's that?' he hissed. 'Is this some kind of joke?'

'This is no joke, Bernard,' said Grace lightly. 'This is Kitty. Say hello to Grandad, Kitty.'

He rose, his damaged leg suddenly forgotten. 'Get it out, now! Get that thing out of my house! And you can tell its mother if she ever darkens my door again, I'll personally stick my boot up her arse and kick her out. And the same goes for the black bastard she's married to!'

'Bernard!' exclaimed Grace, horrified. Kitty started to cry. 'Shush,' she soothed. 'Bernard, you don't mean that?'

'Do it now. I mean every word. And another thing. Go and fetch my mother. You bring her back – *now*.' He glared at her in disgust. 'Oh, I see it all now. No wonder she left.

487

Couldn't stand the shame. And you're just as bad. Harbouring a nigger lover. Well, she's no daughter of mine, and neither is that anything to do with us either. Is that understood? Now get it out.'

Grace backed away, horrified. 'Bernard, please, think about this . . .'

'There's nothing ter think about. Now are you going to obey me or do I have ter do it meself?'

'No, Bernard,' she whispered. 'I'll do it.'

'Well, hurry up about it.'

Slowly she turned, going outside and laying the crying Kitty in the pram. 'Shush,' she soothed. 'Don't cry, pet. It'll be all right. Grandma's not going to let anything happen to you or your mother.'

She raised her head and stared blindly down the yard. She might have known Bernard's reaction would be as bad as this. She knew further conversation, even pleading, would be of no use. His mind was made up, and when that happened you did as you were told or faced the consequences.

She suddenly pictured Tom and how he had reacted to Kitty. Instantly, on being presented to her, he had gathered the baby into his arms and nursed her proudly. An onlooker would have thought the child was his own flesh and blood, the way he had taken to her. What a shame Bernard couldn't do likewise. Didn't he realise just what he was missing?

Again her thoughts flew over the last two years. Two whole years in which for the first time since her marriage she had been happy. And the reason for her peace of mind was the fact that the person who caused most of her grief had been absent.

It suddenly hit her what a fool she had been. A fool and an idiot to have stuck with him for twenty-five years, when deep down she knew he could not possibly ever have loved her. If he had done, there was no way he could have treated her so. She didn't want to live with him any more, didn't want to cook for him, clean for him, care for him, and the thought of lying down beside him in the marital bed filled her with dread. The thought of his hand touching her made her shudder.

Anger suddenly filled her at his demand that she should have nothing more to do with her own daughter and grandchild. Just who did he think he was to order such a thing? She had already missed two precious years of her daughter's life through the malicious spiteful actions of his mother. Not for anybody was she going to miss another minute.

Grace turned and gazed tenderly down at Kitty, and knew what she had to do. Something she should have done a long time ago. She just prayed she wasn't too late.

Ida stared at her smugly. 'So, eatin' humble pie now, are we, Grace Wilkins? I knew my Bernard'd demand I come 'ome.'

She turned and grinned at the old woman hovering behind her. 'See, I told yer, Ada, didn't I? I told yer my stopping wouldn't be for long.'

Ida, in her gloating, missed the look of relief on Ada's face.

'Wait 'ere,' she addressed Grace sharply. 'I'll go and get me things.'

As soon as she was out of earshot Ada shuffled up to Grace. 'Sooner you than me, love. That woman's drove me daft. I never realised before what you'd to put up wi'. When she asked me ter take her in, I felt sorry for 'er. What a mug I was! A' you sure yer want 'er back?'

Grace just smiled.

On arriving home Ida hurriedly hobbled ahead, leaving Grace to carry all her bags. She hugged her son tightly. 'Ah, yer back, son, yer back! Thank God. Praise the Lord. Oh, what on earth yer done ter yer leg?'

''Ello, Mam. Come and sit down. Me and you 'ave a lot

ter catch up on.' He looked at Grace blankly as she entered the room heaving Ida's suitcase.

'Put the kettle on, Grace. Mam could do with a cuppa tea. Couldn't you, Mother? You can put her clothes away later.'

'You'll have to make your own tea, Bernard. I've got things to sort out.'

'Yes, you have, haven't you? Well, hurry up about it. You can make the tea when you get back.' He turned to Ida. 'Now, Mother, tell me all that's been going on. And I want to know everything . . .'

Grace paused for a moment in the doorway of the Rudney living room to survey the happy scene before her. They were all, Tom, Clara and the children, sitting around the table laughing over something one of the kids had done.

On spotting her, Tom's face lit up, his delight at her presence immediately obvious. He scraped back his chair and stood up. 'Grace, you've come! Move up, kids. Willy, go and find another chair.'

'No, don't do that, please.' She took a deep breath and looked him straight in the eye. 'Could I have a word, please, Tom?'

He frowned at her quizzically, suddenly worried by the look on her face. 'What's wrong, Grace?'

'Please could I have a word in private?'

'Yes, sure.'

They all looked at her.

'Please,' she said, 'finish your tea. Clara, I've left Kitty outside . . .'

'Leave her to me, Grace dear.' Clara knew something was afoot by the look on Grace's face, but knew also that now was not the time for questions.

'I'll fetch her,' volunteered Polly.

'No, I'll do it,' cried Maureen, jumping up and racing outside.

'If you want somewhere private, use my bedroom,' offered Clara.

'Thank you,' Grace replied.

Tom led the way. Once inside, he shut the door and turned to her.

'What is it, Grace?'

Wringing her hands, she stared up at him. Well, it was now or never.

'Tom, do you love me?' As the words left her mouth she prayed that her instincts were correct, that Clara's and her mother's were too.

His jaw dropped and he just stared at her, bewildered. He hadn't known what to expect when Grace had asked to talk to him, all sorts had raced through his mind, but never once this.

'Tom, please. I asked if you love me. The least you can do is give me an answer.'

'Oh, Grace,' he said huskily. He turned from her and ran his hand through his hair, then turned back. 'You know I do. But why are you asking?'

'Tom, please answer me properly. If you love me, say it. I need to hear you say it.'

He gulped. 'Grace, I love you. I've loved you for a long time now. But . . .'

'Enough to marry me, Tom?' she cut in.

His face filled with emotion, he rushed towards her and gathered her in his arms. 'Yes, I do. More than enough.'

She raised eyes filled with love. 'I come with a lot of baggage, Tom, you know that, don't you? There's my mother, Charlie and the kids.'

'Grace, I'd take the whole street if it meant I had you.' He raised his eyes heavenwards and shook his head. 'I don't believe I'm hearing this. I can't take it in.'

'Believe it, Tom,' she whispered. 'Now, for goodness' sake, give me a kiss.'

He needed no more telling.

Grace had never been kissed with such passion, such longing, and the feel of his lips on hers, his big arms wrapped around her, was so right. She and Tom belonged together, of that she had no doubt. A flood of emotion filled her being. It was a wonderful experience to feel wanted, something she had never felt before. Now she never wanted that happiness to depart.

Finally they pulled away from each other.

'I'm not dreaming this, am I, Grace?'

'No,' she said, smiling. 'You're not dreaming, Tom. Like you, I've wanted this for such a long time, but I couldn't because of Bernard. Well, he's come back, Tom, and I've realised that I could never live with him again. Not just because of the way he is, but because of my feelings for you. I also knew that if I didn't say anything, you never would.'

'That's only because I respect you, Grace, and didn't want to lose your friendship, not because I didn't want to.'

'I know that, Tom.' She rested her head on his chest and his arms encircled her protectively. 'I hate to tell you this, but we're all coming tonight. Do you think you can find the room?'

He glanced down and laughed, a big bellow of joy. 'I'll find the room, even if I have to sleep on the roof.'

All the arrangements settled, Grace departed. Maureen was standing on the pavement outside her door, waiting to catch Charlie and Connie on their way home from the town. Grace smiled. What a surprise they would both get when they heard the news! But she knew both would be happy for her and more than willing to put up with the new arrangements till things could be sorted out properly.

She found Bernard and his mother still huddled together in the fireside chairs.

He glared up at her. 'Took yer time, didn't yer?' He struggled to rise, his 'injury' suddenly returning, and stood with his back to the fireplace. 'My mother's told me everything, and I'm not happy. But before I give you a piece of my mind, I want me tea and so does Mother.'

Ida folded her arms, face filled with a broad smirk of satisfaction. 'Yes, I'm famished, and I want none of them slops you usually dish up. Not fit for human consumption.' She looked at her son pitifully. 'But I had to eat it, Bernard, she'd 'ave starved me otherwise.'

'Yes, all right, Mother,' he snapped. Already she was beginning to get on his nerves. 'Well, get to it,' he ordered Grace.

'You'll have to make your own tea, I'm afraid.'

They both stared at her.

'What did you say?' asked Bernard, surprised.

'I said, you'll have to make your own tea. I won't be here.'

'What d'yer mean, yer won't be 'ere? Listen 'ere, madam, you might have run riot in my absence but I'm back and it stops now, got that?'

'She's gone loopy. See, I told yer, Bernard, din't I? She's a law unto 'erself now is that one. You'll 'ave ter sort 'er out.'

'Shut up, Mother.' He turned on her angrily, then back to Grace. 'A' you going ter get that tea or what?'

'I've told you I'm not. Aren't you listening to me, Bernard? Well, I'll say this next bit only once because I'm in a hurry, you see.' She took a deep breath. 'I've finally found someone who really cares for me. Someone who truly loves me, Bernard. And whose love I return.'

'What!' he bellowed, gawping in alarm.

'Yes, I'm leaving you, Bernard. I'm doing something I should have done years ago. I'm going to live with Tom Rudney.'

His jaw nearly hit his chest. 'Over my dead body!' He snorted in mirth. 'You're seriously expecting me ter believe you're leaving me for a low life like him? Don't make me laugh!'

'I wasn't trying to be funny, Bernard. In fact, I'm deadly serious. Besides, I don't know why you're making such a fuss. You've only ever treated me as a housekeeper, never as a wife. In any case, you have your mother to care for you.' She smiled at Ida. 'You've got what you wanted, Mrs Wilkins. You've got your son back. And as far as I'm concerned, you're welcome to each other! Now, if you'll both excuse me, I have some packing to do.'

Before she could move Bernard made a lunge for her and grabbed her arm, gripping it tightly. 'You ain't going anywhere,' he snarled. 'You're my wife, do you hear? If you think you're going to make a laughing stock of me, then you've another think coming.' He pushed his face into hers. 'You leave this house and you'll live ter regret it. I'll hound you, I will. I'll make yer life a misery. And I'll never divorce yer.' His eyes were ablaze, jaw set. 'Rudney, indeed!' he hissed. 'Don't make me laugh.'

He gripped her arm tighter and shook her. He shook her so hard her head wobbled and she cried out in pain.

'Leave her be!' a voice shouted. 'Leave my Auntie Grace alone!'

Jessie hurtled forward and threw herself at Bernard, fists beating at him.

'You hurt my Auntie Grace! You're a bad man! Bad man!' she screamed.

Bernard released Grace and thrust Jessie forcibly away.

'What's she doing here?' he bellowed, rubbing his shins.

Grace caught hold of Jessie and protectively pulled her close, backing away.

'She lives here.'

'Lives here!' His face contorted in anger. 'You're looking after the kids of a common prostitute. Well, I've seen it all now.'

'My muvver wasn't one of them,' Jessie cried. 'You're a liar!' She raised her head to Grace, eyes beseeching. 'She wasn't, Auntie Grace, she wasn't.'

Grace looked at her with compassion. 'No, she wasn't, love.' When Madge Cotting's story had properly unfolded, Grace had decided not to tell the children of their mother's employment as a fortune teller nor of her association with a criminal who had eventually turned out to be her killer. Living with the fact that she had been murdered was, she felt, enough for them to cope with. Her troubled eyes darted towards Bernard. 'Please,' she begged, 'she's just a child. Leave her out of this.'

'Child? She's n'ote but a little thief and I'll not have her in my house.'

Outraged Jessie flew at her accuser. 'It's you that's the thief. You, you!' she cried, thumping him with her fists and kicking him with her feet.

Bernard wrenched her away and she fell against the table, banging her head. Like lightning she gathered her wits and ran to Grace. 'He's a thief! He is, Auntie Grace. I saw him, I did. I saw him!'

Bewildered, Grace's eyes darted to Bernard then down to Jessie. 'You saw him what, Jessie?'

'I saw him wearing a soldier's uniform. Only he wasn't a soldier, not then. And he pretended he'd hurt his leg.'

'How dare you?' Ida erupted. 'How dare you lie about my son like that? Why, you little minx!'

Jessie grimaced angrily at her. 'Liar, am I? Well, he stole your walking stick.'

Ida gawped. 'Is this true, Bernard?' she demanded.

A look of fright flashed across his face, which then con-. torted in anger. 'Of course it ain't,' he spat.

'It is, and I ain't a liar.' Jessie wagged her finger at him. 'I saw you go with that woman. I followed you, see. I followed you.'

Grace stared at him, mortified.

'Woman?' she addressed Jessie. 'What woman?'

'The woman he met in the pub when he was wearing the uniform. If you want proof, I could take you and show you where they went, if you want?'

Bernard's face was ashen. He wanted to grab hold of the child and wring her scrawny neck. He thought he'd escaped all this. He gulped. That little thief had followed him, and from what she was saying, had watched his every move. They were all staring at him accusingly. Even his own mother. His own mother, his ally, was staring at him, horrified.

Ida narrowed her eyes at Jessie, then her son, and suddenly knew the child was telling the truth. 'She ain't lying, is she, Bernard? She's tellin' the truth.' She grabbed up her walking stick, raised it and brought it down hard against the back of his legs. 'Me own son,' she wailed disbelievingly. 'Me own son. How could yer?'

The look written across Bernard's face was all Grace needed. She took Jessie's hand and stared blankly at him.

'Goodbye, Bernard,' she said.

Chapter Thirty-Seven

After five long years of misery, at last the war was finally over. Across the length and breadth of the British Isles church bells rang, ships' hooters sounded, and the cheers of the jubilant population filled the air. At long last life could begin to return to normal, and there wasn't a person alive more than ready for that.

Mere Street was buzzing with activity. All sorts of tables were lined down the middle, complete with dozens of chairs. The tables were filled with food, rationing forgotten for the moment. Across the street, home-made banners and flags fluttered in the breeze. Happy smiling people were coming and going, carrying all manner of things that they thought would make the party go with a swing. Children were darting everywhere, those causing a nuisance receiving a sharp slap round the ear. At the bottom of the row of tables stood a piano being tuned ready for the sing-song.

Grace joined Tom on the doorstep. She was holding the year-old Kitty in her arms. Tom turned and tickled Kitty under her chin and the child shrieked in laughter at the man she knew as Grandfather.

'What time did Charlie say she'd be back?' he asked.

Grace smiled up at him as he slid his arm round her and pulled her close. 'Any time now. I hope the party doesn't start before she does, though. I don't want her to miss anything.'

'Grace, this party'll go on most of the night. We'll be lucky if any of us gets any sleep. Be assured, our Charlie won't miss anything.'

Just then she appeared before them, a mite breathless. 'Oh, I ran all the way.' She thrust a bag of shopping at Tom, which he took, and grabbed her daughter from Grace's arms. She kissed Kitty lovingly on the cheek. 'Has she been all right?'

'Good as gold,' replied Tom.

'How would you know?' scolded Grace. 'You've been moving tables around all morning.'

He grinned at her sheepishly. 'She's always as good as gold. Why should she be any different today?'

Grace shook her head at him, laughing. 'You old softy! Was the town packed?' she asked Charlie.

'Couldn't move Mam. The queues were terrible. Everyone's trying to get stuff for their parties. What I managed to get is in the bags. I didn't do too badly though.'

'I don't know why you two are fussing, there's enough on those tables to feed all of the street for a week.'

'Men,' chided Grace. 'Oh, Charlie, there's five letters arrived from Kit today.'

'Five?' she shrieked. 'Five! Did you hear that, Kitty, we've five letters from your daddy today.'

Without further ado she shot inside to open her precious mail.

Tom grinned. 'I can't wait to meet this young man of hers.

'No, me neither. It'll be a red letter day when he comes home, there's no doubt of that. And for Barry and Dennis,' she added. 'The same treatment goes for them too.'

Tom gazed at her tenderly. 'I do love you, Grace,' he whispered.

'I know. And I love you too.'

He quickly glanced around. 'Look, while we're on our own for a minute, I need ter speak ter yer, Grace.'

'Can't it wait 'til later?'

'It could. But you tell me when we get five minutes on our own? Not that I'm complaining, mind.'

'I know you're not,' she laughed. 'Oh, look.' She pointed across the road. 'Tony, Willy and Bobbie are hiding under that table. And – Oh, they've got a plateful of food. Why, the little monkeys!'

'Leave 'em be, Grace. Let them have some fun.'

'You really are a big softy, I knew you'd say that. You're right though. Besides, Mrs Riddle's got her eyes peeled. She'll spot them in a minute and then they'll soon scarper.' She turned her attention fully to him. 'Now, what did you want to say? Oh, here's Clara and Philip!' She threw her arms affectionately around her friend as Tom shook Philip's hand.

'How was the honeymoon, Clara?' asked Grace.

'It was wonderful,' she said, looking at Philip.

'You both look well, I must say, and we're so glad you could make it today.'

'Oh, I wouldn't miss this for the world.'

Grace smiled. 'Go through. I'll be with you in a minute. Tom just wants a word.'

Clara and Philip disappeared inside.

'Now, Tom, what was it you wanted to say?'

'Mind yer backs!' Connie ordered as she shoved her way past, her hands full with a tray of piping hot sausage rolls. The sausage was more bread than meat, but they would do. People would be too happy enjoying themselves to notice just what they were eating – or so she hoped at any rate.

'Just look at your mother,' laughed Tom. 'You wouldn't think she was getting on for seventy-five.'

'Ah, you will when she starts flagging in a little while. You'll see. Just after this party starts, she'll be falling asleep across the table.'

'She a good 'un though, Grace.'

'The best,' she replied.

She suddenly spotted a neighbour making their way over and grabbed Tom's hand. She marched him down the street and around the corner where she sat him on a low factory wall. 'Now, what was it you wanted to say?'

He looked up at her, standing over him, and his eyes twinkled. He grabbed her around the waist and pulled her close. 'Just that I think it's time we were married, don't you?'

'Yes,' she said softly. 'I do. I'll go and see about getting a divorce.'

'Thank you, Grace. I want that more than anything in the world. And I also think it's time that we moved. It's getting a bit ridiculous livin' just doors up from Bernard and 'is mother, and I know you feel uncomfortable although you've never said as much. Anyway, with my job doing far better than I dared even 'ope, and Philip paying me very generously, we can more than afford it.'

'Yes, you're right. But not too far, eh, Tom? I need to be able to get to work and also get home quick, in case the kids need me.'

'You don't have ter work, yer know.'

'I know that, Tom, but I want to. Do you mind?'

'Mind? I don't mind at all as long as you're 'appy.'

'I am happy, Tom.'

'Then that's all that matters.'

She sighed softly. 'Do you think Bessie would mind?'

'What, about us? No, Grace. You can put any thoughts like that out of yer mind. Bessie would be wishing us all the best, that much I do know.'

'I'm glad, Tom. I just want to feel she'd approve.'

'More than approve. She'd be shoving us up the aisle. Now stop worrying, Grace.'

'Well, I suppose we'd better get back. The others will

be wondering where we've got to.'

'Ah, do we 'ave ter?' he wailed playfully. 'Can't we just stay 'ere, the two of us?'

'No, we can't. As much as I'd like to. We've family and guests to see to.'

'Spoilsport.' He grinned wickedly.

She laughed too then bent her head and kissed him on the lips. She smiled tenderly down at him then kissed him again.

'And one for luck,' she whispered joyfully.

JOSIE

Lynda Page

Josie Rawlings is a saint!

Well, she *must* be to care for her cantankerous old grandmother and tolerate her conceited cousin Marilyn, who attracts all the boys, having fun when she should be helping Josie run their vegetable stall in Leicester's market square. And when Marilyn's ex-sweetheart Stephen – whom Josie has secretly worshipped since childhood – drunkenly finds comfort in Josie's arms, it seems that her goodwill has been stretched to the limit. Surely, one day her virtues will be rewarded?

Things don't look too bright, though, when Josie's inheritance is stolen and her grandmother's death brings eviction from the only home she has ever known. Determined to rise above these bitter blows, Josie struggles to support herself, and, desperate for affection, stumbles into an ill-fated love affair.

But there are those who *do* recognise Josie's worth; genuine friends who rally round and see her on the road to success. And, although she is unaware of it, one man, in particular, is keeping a close eye on her progress . . .

FICTION / SAGA 0 7472 4511 8

PEGGIE

ONE WOMAN'S STRUGGLE TO
FULFIL HER DREAMS

Lynda Page

An unexpected windfall gives Peggie Cartwright the
lucky break she deserves. At last she can save her
family from financial ruin. Ever since Cyrus Crabbe
stole her father Septimus's brake and claimed it as his
own vehicle, Sep has dreamed of the day when he
would run a bus service for the villagers of
Leicestershire to put the Crabbes out of business once
and for all. It now looks as if that day is in sight.

But Cyrus Crabbe is a dangerous man, determined to
stop the Cartwrights from succeeding. A wicked
remark from his acid tongue forces Septimus to
abandon his beloved brood, and as Sep's absence
stretches from weeks to months, Peggie watches her
mother sink into a deep decline. Peggie's brothers and
sisters are used to heartache but when Billy is beaten
black and blue and Cyrus's son Reginald turns his
attentions to young Letty it seems that none of the
family is to be spared . . .

Peggie knows it is up to her to keep the business afloat
and spirits raised. For no matter what obstacles are
thrown her way she is determined to fulfil her father's
dream.

FICTION / SAGA 0 7472 4798 6